WELCOME TO THE TIME OF LEGENDS

The Warhammer world is a land of brave heroes, and the rise and fall of powerful enemies. Now for the first time the tales of these mythical events have been brought to life in a new range of books. Divided into a series of trilogies, each brings you hitherto untold details of the lives and times of the most legendary of all Warhammer heroes and villains. Combined together, they will reveal some of the hidden connections that underpin the history of the Warhammer world.

THE BLACK PLAGUE

The tale of an Empire divided, its heroic defenders and the enemies who endeavour to destroy it with the deadliest plague ever loosed upon the world of man. This series begins with *Dead Winter* and continues in *Blighted Empire*.

THE WAR OF VENGEANCE

The ancient races of elf and dwarf clash in a devastating war that will decide not only their fates, but that of the entire Old World. The first novel in this series is *The Great Betrayal*, and is followed by *Master of Dragons*.

BLOOD OF NAGASH

The first vampires, tainted children of Nagash, spread across the world and plot to gain power over the kingdoms of men. This series starts in *Neferata*, and carries on with *Master of Death*.

Keep up to date with the latest information from the **Time of Legends** at *www.blacklibrary.com*

TIME OF LEGENDS

· THE LEGEND OF SIGMAR ·
Graham McNeill

Available as an omnibus edition, containing the novels
Heldenhammer, Empire and *God King*

· THE SUNDERING ·
Gav Thorpe

Available as an omnibus edition, containing the novels *Malekith,
Shadow King* and *Caledor* and the novella *The Bloody Handed*

· THE RISE OF NAGASH ·
Mike Lee

Available as an omnibus edition, containing the novels *Nagash
the Sorcerer, Nagash the Unbroken* and *Nagash Immortal*

· THE BLACK PLAGUE ·
C L Werner

Book 1 – DEAD WINTER
Book 2 – BLIGHTED EMPIRE
Book 3 – WOLF OF SIGMAR (2014)

· THE WAR OF VENGEANCE ·
Nick Kyme and Chris Wraight

Book 1 – THE GREAT BETRAYAL
Book 2 – MASTER OF DRAGONS
Book 3 – ELFDOOM (2014)

· BLOOD OF NAGASH ·
Josh Reynolds

Book 1 – NEFERATA
Book 2 – MASTER OF DEATH (December 2013)
Book 3 – BLOOD DRAGON (2014)

AGE OF LEGEND
Edited by Christian Dunn
A Time of Legends short story anthology

Book Two of the War of Vengeance

MASTER OF DRAGONS

Chris Wraight

BLACK LIBRARY

With many thanks to Nick 'Son of Grungni' Kyme, even if he is a dwarf-sympathiser.

A BLACK LIBRARY PUBLICATION

First published in Great Britain in 2013 by
Black Library,
Games Workshop Ltd.,
Willow Road, Nottingham,
NG7 2WS, UK

10 9 8 7 6 5 4 3 2 1

Cover illustration by Fares Maese.
Map by Nuala Kinrade.

© Games Workshop Limited 2013. All rights reserved.

Black Library, the Black Library logo, Warhammer, the Warhammer logo, Time of Legends, the Time of Legends logo, Games Workshop, the Games Workshop logo and all associated brands, names, characters, illustrations and images from the Warhammer universe are either ®, ™ and/or © Games Workshop Ltd 2000-2013, variably registered in the UK and other countries around the world. All rights reserved.

A CIP record for this book is available from the British Library.

UK ISBN: 978 1 84970 502 8
US ISBN: 978 1 84970 503 5

No part of this publication may be reproduced, stored in a retrieval system, or transmitted in any form or by any means, electronic, mechanical, photocopying, recording or otherwise, without the prior permission of the publishers.

This is a work of fiction. All the characters and events portrayed in this book are fictional, and any resemblance to real people or incidents is purely coincidental.

See Black Library on the internet at
www.blacklibrary.com

Find out more about Games Workshop
and the world of Warhammer at

www.games-workshop.com

Printed and bound by CPI Group (UK) Ltd, Croydon, CR0 4YY

It is an age of legend.

In the elder ages when the world was young, elves and dwarfs lived in peace and prosperity. Dwarfs are great craftsmen, lords of the under deeps, artificers beyond compare. Elves are peerless mages, masters of the dragons, creatures of the sky and air. During the time of High King Snorri Whitebeard and Prince Malekith, these two great races were at the pinnacle of their strength. But such power and dominion could not last. Fell forces now gather against elves and dwarfs. Malekith, embittered by his maiming in the Flame of Asuryan, seeks to destroy them both but still darker powers are also at work. Already strained, disharmony sours relations between them until only enmity remains. Treachery is inevitable, a terrible act that can only result in one outcome... War.

The dwarf High King Gotrek Starbreaker marshals his throngs of warriors from all the holds of the Karaz Ankor, whilst the elves, under the vainglorious and arrogant Caledor II, gather their glittering hosts and fill the skies with dragons.

Mastery of the Old World is at stake, a grudge in the making that will last for millennia. Neither side will give up until the other is destroyed utterly. For in the War of Vengeance, victory will be measured only in blood.

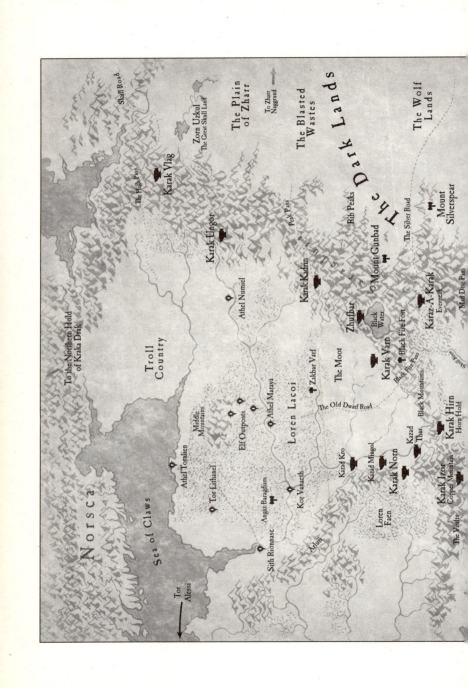

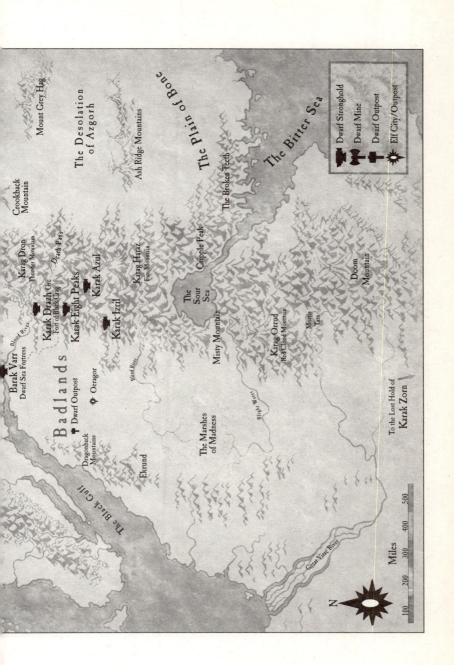

I
DRAGONSONG

CHAPTER ONE

Arian saw the three black, wedge-shaped sails on the eastern horizon and his heart went cold. They emerged out of nowhere, taut triangles of sable in the dawn sun-glare, moving fast against a running swell.

'Full sail!' he shouted.

The crew were already complying. Sailors hauled to unfurl the buffeting mass of white sailcloth. The fabric filled out, catching the brisk easterly, making the ship jerk forwards in the water and cutting a line of foam through the waves.

The *Ithaniel* was not a warship; she was a light cutter, a dispatch-runner, a jack-of-all-trades employed by Lord Riannon to pass missives and personnel between the hawkships of the main fleet. She was fast, but not the fastest. She carried two quarrel repeaters – one fore, one aft – and a complement of thirty spearmen amidships.

None of that would make much of a difference, for Arian had seen the look of the sails coming after him. He knew the manner of ships they belonged to, and why they ran fast through the contested northern ocean.

'How long have we got?' asked Caelon, the master's wind-bitten face screwed up against the glare.

'We can beat west,' said Arian, 'hard as Khaine's blades. Might stumble into one of Riannon's patrols.'

Caelon didn't look convinced. 'Anything else?'

'Move the bow-fixed repeater aft. We'll loose a few as they close. Might even take one out.'

'It will be done.'

'They'll come up fast,' warned Arian. 'I've seen this before. We'll need to jig around like a hare or they'll eat the wind from our sails before noon.'

Caelon ran a nervous hand through his long brown hair. He was from Chrace, a veteran of many battles and didn't quail easily, but the odds did not favour them and he knew it. 'And the cargo?'

Arian smiled coldly. 'The cargo. Perhaps we'd better let him know. If he's awake, that is.'

Caradryel of the House of Reveniol was a light sleeper, easily disturbed by the sway and creak of a sea-going vessel. He habitually used the morning hours to recover his equilibrium; unconsciousness, as he was fond of remarking to himself and others, was his natural and optimal state. Involuntary assignment to Riannon's war-staff had not succeeded in altering the habits of a short lifetime, something he was perfectly aware did not endear him to the duty-minded crew.

For all that, by the time the captain had made his way down to his cramped cabin, Caradryel was awake to receive him. The prince pushed himself upright, smoothing silk sheets over his knees. His pale blond hair fell about his shoulders, stiff from salt and sun and badly in need of beeswax and lustre-oils.

The barbarism of war, he reflected sadly.

Arian had to duck as he entered.

'Bad news, lord,' he said, glancing sidelong at the crumpled sheets with poorly hidden disapproval.

'I heard the commotion,' said Caradryel. 'The cause?'

'Three druchii raiders, closing fast. We're no match for them, I'm afraid, and they have the weather on us.'

'Regrettable. How long have we got?'

'A few hours. We're bearing hard west, but unless Mathlann conjures something they'll overhaul us before sunset.'

Caradryel drew in a long breath. He would have to put in an appearance on deck, which was an irritant. 'Thank you for informing me,' he said. 'Given the circumstances, I think the best we can do is put up a creditable fight. Do you think we'll take one down with us?'

'I've mounted the repeaters aft,' said Arian. 'If they fail to spot them we might get a scalp.'

'Very good. I'd have done the same. And I assume we're now bearing full sail?'

Caradryel enjoyed seeing the look of exasperation on Arian's face when he enquired about nautical matters. Both of them knew that his experience of commanding a ship of any kind was somewhere less than negligible, though the game of pretending otherwise amused Caradryel almost as much as it annoyed Arian.

'Of course,' said Arian stiffly. 'We have archers in the high-top and spearmen arming in the prows. If you have any further recommendations, though, do be sure to pass them on.'

Caradryel bowed. 'I certainly will. Now, if you will give me just a few moments I will join you on deck. It may take me a while to choose a robe.'

Arian stayed where he was. 'You realise, lord, how serious this is?'

Caradryel gave him a steady look. 'I do indeed.'

'I cannot see a way out of this. The druchii are not merciful captors. You may wish to make... preparations.'

Caradryel smiled. 'Captain, you deserve better than ferrying princelings between the fleets. Calm yourself – I have no intention of dying under traitors' blades.'

Arian looked unsure how to reply. Caradryel maintained the smile – the polished, courtly smile that had carried him smoothly through a hundred encounters and came as easily to him as sleeping.

'For they are such grotesque blades, are they not?' Caradryel added. 'No taste, our fallen kin. No taste at all.'

The hours did not pass quickly. The three dark-sailed hunters steadily hauled the gap closed, sailing with reckless skill through a wind-chopped sea. Arian drove the *Ithaniel* as hard as he had promised to, straining the rigging and almost losing the mainsail twice. The crew worked as hard as he did, for they all knew the odds; only at the very end would they take up bow, blade or spear, ready to fight to the last, knowing that captivity would be far worse than a clean death in combat.

Arian leaned over the railing of the ship's sloping quarterdeck, watching the foam-edged wake zigzag away towards the enemy. On either side of him stood two big repeater crossbows, each one wound tight with iron-tipped bolts. The shafts were huge – as thick as his thigh and longer than he was tall.

By then he could make out the detail on the lead druchii corsair: a rune of Khaine on a satin-black ground, elaborate and gauche. It looked like a spatter of blood on dark glass, glistening wetly in the strong sun.

Like most of those now serving in the Phoenix King's navy, Arian was not old enough to remember the time before the Sundering. Horror and grief had thinned the ranks of those who had been there at the time, eight hundred years ago during the dark days when his race had cracked itself apart. Arian could, though, remember the subsequent years of horrific bloodshed. He could remember believing, long ago, that a reconciliation would somehow be found.

Now he entertained no such dreams. He knew, as all on Ulthuan surely knew, that war would now be with them for as long as any could foresee. Most of the druchii who crewed the corsair ships would not have been born in Ulthuan and would have only a sketchy knowledge of their ancient home. Most of the crew he commanded had never known a world in which the druchii were not mortal enemies from a frozen land across the oceans. The two sundered kinfolks now looked at one another and saw nothing more than an enemy, as alien now as the greenskin had always been.

How far the sons of Aenarion had fallen.

'They sail like maniacs,' observed Caradryel.

Arian hadn't heard him approach. He remained poised on the railing, eyes fixed out to sea. 'They know what they're doing.'

'If you say so. Why not explain it to me?'

Arian pointed out the lead vessel. It was still too far out for a bolt-shot, but every buck of its prow brought it closer. 'That's the one they want to close first. Caelon's spied grapples in the bow and it's stuffed with troops. I'd guess fifty, maybe more.'

'And the two others?'

'They'll eat our wind,' said Arian grimly. 'They'll swing out as they get closer, cutting our sails flat. When we're hooked by the lead corsair they'll close back for the kill.'

'I see. Anything you can do about that?'

Arian had to hand it to the prince: his tone was one of amiable curiosity, unmarked by the slightest tremor of fear. He might have been discussing the merits of the wine from his father's vineyards. 'Caelon knows this ship better than his own wife,' said Arian. 'We'll slip the trap for as long as we can, praying the wind drops or we spy ships of the fleet.'

'And what, do you suppose, are the chances of that?'

'I would not lay money on it.'

'Then we are hoping for the miraculous.'

'You could say that.'

Caradryel laughed. It was a light, unaffected sound, and it made several of the deck-hands turn from their labours. 'I should not fret, captain,' he said. 'The miraculous has a way of following me. Always has. Should you wish to, you might give thanks to the gods for having me amongst your crew this day. In any event, try not to look so worried – it is not, as they say in Lothern, *good form.*'

Caradryel could only watch as the corsairs did exactly what Arian had predicted. They ran fast, dipping through the pitch of the waves before crashing up again with spiked prows. More details became visible – curved hulls glossy as lacquer, black pennants fluttering around bone-like mastheads, ranks of warriors in ebon armour, crowding at the railings, eager for the boarding to come.

Caradryel withdrew from the quarterdeck and walked unsteadily towards the prow. As he did so he scoured the western horizon. The sky was clear, the wind remained strong, the seas were empty.

Dying here will annoy my father, he thought to himself as he drew his sword from its scabbard. *That, at least, is something.*

His blade had not been well cared for and showed signs of rust along the edges. Caradryel had never been a warrior. He had never been much of anything, though that had never shaken his inner confidence. He had always assumed that his time would come and his path would open up before him like the petals of a flower.

'Bolts!' came a cry from the high-top, and spearmen on either side of him crouched down low. Caradryel followed suit, pressing himself to the deck. A second later the air whistled with crossbow quarrels, some of them thudding hard into the wood, some sailing clear.

Before Caradryel could react, the *Ithaniel* opened up with

its own bolt throwers and the recoil shuddered down the spine of the ship. Spray crashed up over the prow, salty and death-cold. He pushed his head up from the deck and saw two black sails standing off, eating up the wind just as Arian had predicted. The other one had tacked in close, bursting through the heavy swell like a pick hammered through ice.

Another volley of bolts screamed across the deck at stomach-height, barely clearing the rails. Caradryel saw a spearman take a quarrel in the midriff, another catch one in the thigh. Several shots scythed through the sailcloth, slashing it open and cutting the ship's speed. Archers mounted in the masts let fly in return. Caradryel couldn't see the results of their shots, but he guessed they would be meagre.

He kept to his hands and knees and crawled towards the high prow. He heard the aft repeaters loose again, followed by the *crack* of wood splintering. For a moment he thought Arian had scored a hit, but then the *Ithaniel* bucked like an unbroken stallion and slewed round hard.

Caradryel was thrown over to the nearside railing, still ten paces short of the prow. He stared back down the length of the ship. Spearmen were running towards the quarterdeck. The lead corsair was now right on the *Ithaniel*'s stern and loosing grappling hooks.

Caradryel gripped his sword two-handed and wished he'd paid more attention to the expensive lessons he'd been given back in Faer-Lyen. For all that, fear still eluded him. He'd never found it easy to be afraid. The overriding emotion he felt was irritation, a nagging sense that something was *wrong* – that dying in the middle of the ocean on a nondescript errand-runner was not how he was meant to leave the world.

'Repel boarders!' came Arian's powerful voice from the quarterdeck, followed by a commendable roar of determination from the spearmen around him. Caradryel watched them form a knot of resistance, their speartips glinting in the sunlight. 'For Asuryan! For the Sacred Flame!'

Then, as the *Ithaniel* fell away and the corsair warship rose up on a rolling wave-front, he saw the foe revealed – ranks of druchii swordsmen, four-thick along the pitching railing of the enemy decking, poised to leap as the grapple-hooks pulled tight. Caradryel saw them jostling to get to the forefront – they outnumbered the asur by at least two to one, and that was before the other two ships drew alongside.

Caradryel started to stagger back the way he'd come, teetering along the tilting deck with sword in hand, certain he'd be no use but belatedly determined not to cower in the prow while fighting broke out at the other end of the ship.

Such a waste, he thought, gripping the blade inexpertly and thinking of the fine silks of his robe, the ancient towers of Faer-Lyen in the mountains, the future he'd planned out in the courts of Lothern, Caledor and Saphery. *Such a stupid, terrible waste.*

He made it less than ten paces before falling flat on his face, slammed down against the deck by sudden wind and movement. He tasted blood on his lips and heard an echoing rush in his ears. He cursed himself, angry that he'd already tripped over his own feet.

But then he lifted his head and saw the reason he'd fallen.

He had not tripped. Amid the sudden screams he had just enough wit to realise that his role in the combat had suddenly become entirely irrelevant, and that no one else – druchii or asur spearman – had any further part to play in what now unfolded. The battle had been snatched away from them, swatted aside contemptuously by power of such splendour that it made the world itself around him seem diminished into nothingness.

Caradryel hardly heard the sword fall from his fingers. He barely noticed that his jaw hung open stupidly and his eyes stared like a child's.

It had all changed. In the face of that, and for the first time in his short, privileged life, Caradryel at last learned the heady rush of true, undiluted fear.

Arian didn't see it coming. Caelon didn't see it either, nor did the sharp-eyed archers in the masts. Very little escaped the eyes of the asur, so it must have moved fast – astonishingly fast, faster than thought.

The druchii were slow to react, but even when they did it was painfully inadequate. Whoops of relish changed into screams of terror just before it hit them, snapping the grapple lines and whipping the rigging into tatters. Arian saw some of them leap into the water rather than face it. He'd fought druchii before and knew they were no cowards, but he understood the panic. What could they do? What could they possibly do?

He barely held on to his wits himself. Part of him wanted to bury his head in his hands, cowering against the decking until it shot clear again.

'Fall back!' he shouted, somehow dragging the words out of his throat. 'Man the sails and pull clear! Pull us clear!'

He didn't know if anyone heeded him. He didn't even turn to look. All he could do was watch, gazing out at it as if newborn to the world and ignorant of all its wonders.

As long-lived and mighty as the children of Ulthuan were, some powers in the world still had the heft and lineage to overawe them.

'Dragon,' he whispered, the word spilling reverently from his cracked lips. It might have been the name of a god. 'Holy flame. A *dragon.*'

Caradryel pressed himself up against the railings, trembling and useless.

The wind itself had changed – it was as if the elements of air and fire had suddenly burst into violent union. The ships rocked crazily, thrown around like corks by the downdrafts from splayed wings.

The noise was the most terrifying thing. The *Ithaniel*'s spars shivered and the water drummed as if under a deluge. The sound was unforgettable – the mingled screams and battle-cries of a thousand mortal voices, locked together and blended into a pure animal bellow of rampant excess.

After the noise came the stink, a charred-metal stench like a blacksmith's forge, hot, pungent and saturated with the wild edge of ancient magic.

And then, finally, how it looked.

Its body was taut like a hunting hound, ribbed with steely plates, vivid, glistening, a shard of a jewel hurled into the heavens. It twisted in the air, flashing a long sapphire-blue hide. Its wings shot out like speartips, splayed with membranous skeins of bone-white flesh. Its tail was prehensile, snapping and flicking; its jaws gaped, blurry from heatwash and snarls of smoke, lined with teeth the length of a mortal's arm, crowned with drawn-back horns and tapers of ridged armour.

It was immense. Its shadow compassed the druchii corsairship, and its wingspan alone dwarfed the slack sails, turning what had been a daunting hunter into a drifting hulk.

Caradryel dragged himself upright, heart beating hard. As he did so the dragon came around for another pass. Flames thundered from its gaping jaws and hit the centre of the druchii vessel, punching clear through, shattering and carving, before exploding in a ball of steam as seawater gushed through the breach. The dragon swooped past and its tail lashed out, striking the reeling corsair amidships and breaking its spine. The warship wallowed in a flaming whirlpool for a moment before sinking fast, pulled down below as if grasped by greedy hands.

The dragon surged away after the remaining two ships. They had both turned hard into the wind and were beating a furious retreat, but it was hopeless. Caradryel steadied himself against the *Ithaniel*'s railing. The dragon reached the first corsair with a single wing-thrust, shooting across the water faster than a thrown spear. It vomited another burst of flame then pounced on the remains, seizing a mast-top in its maw and savaging it. The ship broke apart in a flaming tumble of splinters and shards.

Then the second. A score of heavy wing beats, a diving attack, a lash of the long sinuous tail, and it was over. All that remained of the corsair squadron was a miserable collection of bobbing flotsam. Those druchii not killed by the flames went under quickly, dragged down by their armour. A few deck-slaves clung to the wreckage, shivering from the shock, the cold, the awe.

Caradryel was unable to do much more than observe. The sight both scared and thrilled him – the exhibition of such power went far beyond anything he had seen before. The dragon's movements were almost lazy in their effectiveness, as if the creature were barely summoning up more than a token effort. As he gazed up at the wheeling wingtips Caradryel found himself lost in the arrogance of it. It was primordial. It was astonishing.

He knew then why it made him afraid: he couldn't control it, couldn't *hope* to control it. It was as pure and mindless as the storms that raced down from the Annulii. Caradryel had never encountered anything that he truly believed he couldn't control, whether through manipulation or flattery or the careful use of well-placed bribes. A dragon, though… Only a fool or a demigod would try to master that.

The creature came to a halt before the *Ithaniel*'s prow, maintaining its position in mid-air with a heavy sequence of downbeats. Its long, lean head rose high above the mast-top and its tail slashed through the waves below. Hot, metallic air washed across the decks, making the sails fill and flap.

Arian was the first to recover. He stood up in the prow, looking tiny under the shadow of the beast.

'My lord!' he cried, saluting. 'Our thanks!'

It was then that Caradryel saw the figure mounted on the dragon's shoulders. He wore silver armour chased with black runes and a tall helm crested with drake-wings. A heavy crimson cloak hung around him, pooling in the muscle-hollows of the dragon's hide. One silver gauntlet rested on the dragon's neck, the other held a naked blade.

He looked like a figure out of ancient legend – an avatar of Aenarion brought back to life.

'Where are you headed?' the dragon rider called. His voice rang clearly across the waves – a calm, authoritative voice, coloured with the aristocratic accent of Caledor.

'Lothern, lord, on business for the Lord Riannon.'

'Then make your way. More druchii will taint these waters before the sun sinks and I do not have the leisure to slay them all.'

Arian bowed. 'We had not been warned of corsairs, nor did I dream to see a dragon rider aloft. Is something amiss?'

The dragon rider laughed wryly. 'Amiss? That depends on your point of view. The Phoenix King returns to his throne, hence the seas are alive with intrigue and dragons are on the wing. Our meeting here was by chance – on another day you would have been alone with your assassins.'

'Caledor returns!' cried Arian. 'You bring great tidings, lord.'

The dragon rider didn't reply. His steed beat its wings fiercely, bearing them both higher and away from the ship. Caradryel found himself wishing they would linger. The spectacle of it all – the dazzling, bejewelled creature of the high airs, the aura of raw magic bleeding from its armoured flanks – it was a heady, intoxicating presence.

A few powerful downbeats, though, and the dragon was spiralling away from them. Mere moments later it was little more than a speck of glittering blue against an empty sky.

The *Ithaniel* drifted on the open sea, alone again, surrounded by the blackened evidence of the dragon's power.

Arian stirred himself. 'Lower the boats,' he ordered, moving down from the quarterdeck. 'Take aboard survivors. Slaves will be freed; druchii taken to Lothern. With haste! We must be under sail again soon.'

Spearmen and deck-hands shook themselves and stumbled back to work. The ship was quickly thick with activity as repairs were made and wounds bound up. Tales of the dragon could wait until they were safely in port.

Amid it all, Caradryel remained motionless, staring up at the heavens, his hands still clutching the rails.

That is true power, he thought. *That is greatness. The one who controls such power controls the world.*

He didn't notice Arian coming up to him, a wide grin on his face. The captain stooped to pick up Caradryel's discarded sword and handed it to him, blade-first.

'Dreaming?' he asked. Many lines of anxiety had fallen away from his face.

Caradryel took the sword and sheathed it self-consciously. 'A dragon rider,' he said, trying to affect disinterest. 'How unexpected.'

Arian laughed. 'We were honoured. Did you not see the livery? You were in the presence of the king's brother.'

'Imladrik?'

'And you missed your chance for advancement.'

'The Master of Dragons,' Caradryel remarked. 'What great fortune.'

Arian turned away, a smile playing on his lips. 'I thought you didn't believe in fortune,' he said, heading back up to the prow to oversee the retrieval of the boats.

'I don't,' murmured Caradryel, too soft for hearing, his mind working hard.

CHAPTER TWO

Imladrik sat loosely in the saddle, no longer giving directions to his mount but letting him find his way amid the paths of the skies. Draukhain headed south-west, gliding languidly. The destruction of the druchii squadron had been a trivial task for one of his breeding and his enormous lungs worked as rhythmically as ever, untroubled by the diversion, drawing in the chill wind and transmuting it into fiery exhalations.

The work may have been easy but the orders had been an insult. Dragons were rare and perilous creatures; to turn them into celebratory attendants of Caledor's homecoming was an ignorant misuse of power.

You are angry.

Draukhain's mind-song echoed in Imladrik's head like one of his own thoughts.

Not angry, Imladrik returned. *Weary.*

Weary? I have borne you aloft a hundred leagues. Draukhain snorted, sending flecks of smouldering ash cascading over his immense shoulders. *I am weary; you are angry. You rage against your brother who commands you.*

Ah. You read my thoughts now.

I do not need to. This anger is a waste – it serves no purpose.

Imladrik shifted in the saddle. After hours of flight his limbs were tight and his muscles raw. The ocean glittered below him, a shallow curve extending in all directions, glossy with reflected sunlight. Soon the sun would begin to dip, descending in golds and reds towards the western horizon, but for the moment the world looked pristine, awash with light, just as it must have done in the dawn following creation.

My brother shows disrespect, mind-sang Imladrik. *To you, great one. He does not understand you.*

How many are left who truly understand, kalamn-talaen? Do not judge him for that.

Kalamn-talaen: the little lord. A whimsical title, one the dragons used to distinguish between Imladrik and the great-grandsire of his bloodline, Caledor Dragontamer, whom they called *kalamn-kavannaen*, the great lord. Imladrik had heard their minds burst into joyous celebration at the very mention of the Dragontamer – perhaps he had been the only mortal other than Aenarion to command their total respect. The rest of the asur, Imladrik included, were merely indulged, as if in homage to that one undying example of greatness.

It is not like you, Imladrik returned, *to be so magnanimous.*

No, it is not. Draukhain snorted again, producing a gout of glutinous smoke that rolled across his sapphire-scaled skin. *But I am in a good temper this night.*

For the ending of so many druchii?

Maybe so. Or maybe the golden sun on the sea, or maybe your company. Who can tell?

That brought a smile to Imladrik's stern face. *I am glad one of us is, whatever the cause.*

They flew further west. The first cliffs of Ulthuan became visible as a blurred line of dark grey against the horizon.

Master of Dragons

The rock-ramparts grew in size, steadily accumulating detail and definition. Soon the eastern curve of the Annulii could be made out, vast and gold-glittered and crowned with ice.

Where shall I bear you, then? sang Draukhain, dipping his head and sweeping closer towards the scudding wave-tops.

Do you have to ask? returned Imladrik. His mind-voice, unguarded for a moment, was a mix of yearning and resignation. He didn't mind giving that away – Draukhain was hard to deceive, even for one with his command of dragonsong.

A deep, grinding sound rumbled up from Draukhain's belly. Imladrik knew how to interpret the sound, for he understood the great dragon's soul nearly as well Draukhain knew his own: the creature approved, was reassured, understood his reasons and wished him well for much earned repose and restoration. All these things could be divined from a single harmonic. Dragons were creatures of music and instinct, more eloquent in gestures than they were in words.

Draukhain banked over to the left, pulling fractionally to the south, aiming towards the high peaks, to the realm of Cothique.

We shall be there before the sun sets, sang Draukhain.

Do not hurry, returned Imladrik, watching the last of the light on the water as it flickered beneath him. *Enjoy the remains of this day. You have earned it, even if none but I will ever know it.*

She was not waiting for him. She never lingered on the balcony, staring up into the skies for his return, pining like a maiden for her lover in the poetic romances of Avelorn. Her work was too important, too all-consuming for that.

When he found her at last, after slipping through the gates of Tor Vael and up the echoing stairways, she was doing what she always did, so absorbed in it that the rest of the world might have been a fiction spun in the minds of others.

Imladrik paused at the entrance to her chamber. She was bathed in the light of dusk from the open window, framed against a darkening vista of high mountain-slopes. She was seated, her shoulders stooped over an angled caelwood writing table.

Imladrik leaned against the doorframe, his movements silent, his breath shallow. He watched her trace the shape of runes against parchment, working the quill deftly. He saw her grey eyes latched on to her work: twin vices of concentration. He saw her hands moving. He saw her slender frame crouching over the desk, and regretted the tight curve of her spine. He had warned her about it often, offering to have a new chair made, pleading with her not to work for so long without rest.

His lips twitched into a smile. She never listened. She had always been stubborn – not angry, never irritable or shrewish, just stubborn – like the hard, dark rock of his homeland.

'My lady,' he said softly.

Yethanial's head jerked up. She glared at him, startled as if roused from a deep sleep.

Then she leapt up, her grey robe rustling around her. Her pale face brightened and the grip of exertion fell away from her features.

'My lord!' she cried, her voice ringing with joy.

Imladrik laughed, pushing himself away from the door to meet her. They embraced, clasping one another tight.

As he pressed against her, Imladrik drew in her familiar aromas of homecoming: coarse woollen fabric, inks that stained her fingers, crushed petals of the seaflower he had placed in her hair before he'd left. He guessed that he would smell of sweat, brine and dragon. Yethanial professed never to mind that; he doubted whether he believed her.

'I was not expecting you,' she said, nestling her face into his shoulder.

'I told you I would return before nightfall.'

Master of Dragons

'Then I did not listen.'

'You never do.'

He pushed her away, holding her at arm's length to get a better look at her.

He thought then, not for the first time, how different they were. Imladrik knew well enough how he looked: tall, broad-shouldered, his body tempered into hardness by the demands of riding the great drakes. He knew how severe his features were, hewn roughly, so he'd been told, like the white cliffs of Tiranoc. He knew his long hair, a dull bronze like his mother's, hung heavily around his shoulders, pressed flat by the dragon-helms he wore in battle.

Yethanial, by contrast, was like a dusk-shadow: slight, her limbs as lean as mages' wands, her glance quick and her smile quicker. In every movement she made, the sharpness of her scholar's mind spilled out. In her eyes it was most unavoidable – those steady grey eyes that seemed to look within him and prise out his innermost thoughts.

It was her eyes that had snared Imladrik long ago. He had gazed into them on the windswept cliffs of Cothique during their long formal courtship and revelled in their elusive, darting intelligence. Now, after so many years together, they still had the power to captivate.

'The flower I gave you,' he said.

Yethanial's hands flew to her head, searching for what remained of it. 'It was lovely. I cherished it. But, somehow–'

'Somehow, during the day, you forgot it was there,' smiled Imladrik, taking her hands back and pressing them gently into his own. 'Your work consumed you. What are you doing? May I see it?'

Yethanial looked apologetic. 'Not finished, of course.'

She led him to the desk. A battered leather-bound book rested, clamped open, on the left-hand edge. Next to it was a pinned leaf of heavy vellum, fresh-scraped and as white as bone. She had been working on it, transcribing text from the flaking pages of the book. Only a part of one page had been completed, but Imladrik could see the emerging pattern of it. She had traced out runes carefully, leaving spaces where gold leaf and coloured inks would be applied. The text had been painstakingly drawn in black ink, and several discarded quills littered the floor around the writing desk.

'These books were not well-made,' she said, glancing at the open volume. 'But their contents are precious. When I am done I will take this to Hoeth to be bound. They can create books that will last for as long as the world endures.'

Imladrik looked at the script. It wasn't in Eltharin, even though the characters were familiar. 'I cannot read it,' he said.

'Few can. It was written before the time of Aenarion – we only have copies of copies. The speech is called *Filuan*. These are poems. I find them beautiful.'

Imladrik tried to decipher something of them, but made no progress. He was not a gifted loremaster – only the language of swords and of dragons had ever come easily to him. 'What do they speak of?' he asked.

'The same things our poets speak of,' she said, running a finger lightly down the edge of the vellum. 'Love, fear, the shape of the world. They must have been very like us. I would hate their words to be lost forever.'

Imladrik considered asking her to translate some for him, but decided against it. He would pretend to appreciate it, she would see through him, and a small cloud of irritation would come between them. He had long ago resigned himself to their fundamental differences.

'I wish I could understand it as you do,' he said softly, pulling her close again. 'I feel like a barbarian out of the colonies.'

'You are a barbarian out of the colonies.'

'I miss you, when alone up there.'

'Then stay,' said Yethanial. 'We can dwell wherever you wish

Master of Dragons 31

– Kor Evril, Tor Caled, an empty barn in the mountains.'

'Anywhere but Elthin Arvan.'

'What is there in Elthin Arvan?'

Imladrik almost replied. He could have said: freedom, open lands as wild as at the dawn of creation, dark woods that stretched from horizon to horizon, untouched by the hand of civilisation and rich in both peril and majesty. Then there was Oeragor, the city he had founded but not seen for over twenty years, a half-finished sanctuary he had hoped to turn into a desert jewel for the two of them to grow old in together.

But he said nothing. They had covered this ground before and he knew when to retreat from a hopeless cause.

'I am back now,' was all he said. 'My duties are here.'

Yethanial rested her head in the crook of his shoulder. It was an almost childlike movement; one of trust, of contentment.

'That gladdens me,' she said.

Dawn brought rain, hard and slanted from the east. It drummed against Tor Vael's lead roofs and gurgled down its granite walls.

Imladrik awoke before Yethanial. He slipped soundlessly from the sheets and opened the shutters of her bedchamber. The view from the window was dove-grey and rain-blurred. In the east he could make out the smudge of the ocean. Nowhere in Cothique was far from the sea.

He breathed deeply, inhaling the salt-tang. He felt rested. He stretched, feeling long-clenched sinews in his back and shoulders unfurl.

'My lord,' said Yethanial, sleepily.

Imladrik smiled, turning. 'My lady.'

She sat amid a pile of linen, looking flushed with slumber. He went over to her, embraced her, kissed her, smoothed her grey-blonde hair from her brow.

'Hungry?' he asked.

'As if starved for a year.'

Imladrik sent for food. In the time it took the servants to prepare it, the two of them rose and dressed. They broke their fast in an east-facing chamber of the old tower. The rain lashed against the glass of the windows and the wind sighed around the walls as they ate, making the fire in the grate gutter and spit.

Imladrik leaned back in his chair. The kitchens at Tor Vael cooked food the way he liked it: plain. He swallowed the last of a round oatcake and reached for a goblet of watered-down wine.

Yethanial had been as good as her word; she ate ravenously, like a scrawny mountain wolf at the end of winter.

'It troubles me,' said Imladrik.

'What troubles you?'

'That you do not look after yourself when I am away.'

Yethanial shrugged. 'Too much to do.'

'You have servants here.'

'Yes, and I have been cooped up with them for too long. Tell me of the real world.'

Imladrik took a cautious sip of wine. 'What do you wish to know?'

'Everything.' Yethanial crossed her arms, waiting.

'Well, then. My brother heads back to Ulthuan and Lothern runs with rumour. They tell me he has won his war in the colonies, that the stunted folk are defeated, and that we can at last turn our attentions to ridding the world of druchii.'

'The stunted folk are defeated? Should I believe that?'

Imladrik leaned forward, his elbows on the table. 'Have you ever met a dwarf?'

'I have read accounts.'

'Scrolls do not tell the truth of it.' Imladrik felt his mind roving back over the past, the years he had spent in the wilds. 'Imagine, somehow, if rock were to come to life, growing limbs and a heart. Imagine that every virtue of rock – durability, endurance, hardness – were somehow condensed into a living thing.'

Yethanial smiled affectionately. 'Language is not your gift, my lord.'

'It is not. But think of it: a race of stone, as resolute as granite, as unyielding as bedrock. That is the dawi.'

'Dawi?'

'What they call themselves.' Imladrik shook his head. 'And they are not defeated. Menlaeth has killed one of their princes, but dozens more remain under the mountains. I have seen those places. I have seen halls of stone larger than our greatest palaces. I have seen their warriors gathered around the light of ritual fires, each one wearing a mask of iron and carrying an axe of steel.'

Imladrik looked down at his hands. Speaking of such things took him back. 'They can never be defeated,' he said. 'Not there, not in their own realm. I tried to tell my brother that.'

Yethanial listened carefully. 'I am sure he took account of that.'

Imladrik's lip twitched in a wry smile. 'I met the dwarf prince he is said to have killed. Halfhand, they called him. A brave warrior, though headstrong. The dawi will hold a thousand grudges against us now, and they will never stop.'

'But they will have to relent soon, no? They cannot fight us forever.'

Imladrik's smile remained on his lips. 'Relent? No, I do not think they have a word for that.' He took another swig of wine. 'I read the tidings from Elthin Arvan. They tell me that Tor Alessi will soon be attacked again. There are dozens of dawi thanes, all with their own armies. Athel Maraya is exposed too. It is only arrogance that makes us believe these places are invulnerable.'

'But here we are told–'

'Here you are told that the war will be over in a year, the colonies will expand and the dawi will soon be suing for peace on their knees.' Imladrik looked into his goblet sourly. 'It is lunacy. At Athel Numiel even the infants were butchered, so they say. Menlaeth has set the fire running; I hope he understands the inferno that will come of it.'

Imladrik put the goblet down. 'I love my brother,' he said, his jaw tight. 'Or I try to. He is the mightiest of all of us, the crown is his by right, but...'

Yethanial rose from her chair and hastened to his side. She knelt beside him, catching his hands in hers and pulling them to her lap. 'You do not have to pretend, not with me.'

'I never pretend.' Imladrik shot her a bitter smile. 'The dragons see through it, so I lost the knack. Believe me, I do not envy him. He has our glorious father to live up to, and I would not wish that on anyone.'

'You both have that to bear.'

'My name will not be in the annals. When I remember to, I pity him. I wish to help him, but he takes no counsel.'

Yethanial's mouth twitched into a smile. 'Remind you of anyone?'

Imladrik gave a hollow laugh. 'I am surrounded by the stubborn. Why is that? Do I attract them?'

'Some of them.' Yethanial stroked his hands. The touch was soothing. 'I have made you melancholy. I did not mean to.'

Imladrik slipped his hands free and reached for her, pulling her towards him. 'No, it is me – I have let the past intrude. I was over there for a long time.'

Yethanial nodded, looking up at him with sad knowledge written in her features. 'It has been over twenty years. How much longer will you need before you let it go?'

Imladrik didn't reply. He knew that his face would give away his answer if he spoke.

I will never let it go.

Yethanial reached up to press her hand against his heart. 'I am not a fool, my lord. I know enough, but it is over now. You came back, and the gods know we have enemies enough in Ulthuan to keep you busy.'

Imladrik nodded. They were the words he needed to hear.

'Whatever you left behind,' she said, 'whatever part of you that remains there, think of it no more. Think of me. Think of the realm you are charged with defending, for you are loved here on Ulthuan. Your troops would march beyond the gates of madness if you led them there. Remember that.'

Imladrik lowered his forehead against hers. 'And you are loved more than life itself,' he said. 'You remember that.'

'Always.'

They remained like that for many heartbeats, their limbs entwined. They said nothing as the rain ran down the glass and the gusts shook the stonework. For all the world outside cared, they might have been an image of Isha and Kurnous, frozen outside time.

But they remained mortal. Time passed, and the clatter of servants coming to retrieve the silverware broke their communion. Yethanial extricated herself before they entered, smiling bashfully, kissing Imladrik on the cheek and taking her place at the table.

Imladrik retrieved his wine, swilling it in the goblet before taking a draught. He felt unsettled. Duties would call for him soon – orders relayed from Lothern and Tor Caled, demands on his time, requests for aid. Part of him wearied of the burden of it, but part of him wished for nothing more. His duty would take him away from Tor Vael, away from Yethanial, but also from the emotions that preyed on him whenever he was forced to confront them.

Whatever you left behind, he told himself, looking up at her and wishing his smile could be more carefree, *whatever part of you that remains there, think of it no more.*

CHAPTER THREE

Liandra stood, shivering, in the hills above Kor Vanaeth. Her robes were heavy from rainwater and hung like dead weights.

She ran a grimy hand through her copper hair.

Mud, she thought grimly, gazing across her domain. *Filth. Every year it gets dirtier. What in the name of Isha am I still doing here?*

As the years had passed, it had become harder to answer that question. The colonies were a hard place to live in for one of her breeding. The landscape was heavy with sludge, an endless grind of snarled, twisted, muck-thick forest. Everything was washed-out, mouldering, greying at the edges.

Stubbornness, she concluded, glowering at a rain-washed sky. *I cannot bear to see them win.*

She looked down at Kor Vanaeth's walls, half a mile away. Some sections hadn't been completely rebuilt, though years had passed since the dawi had razed it. It had been hard to attract artisans back, and harder still to secure the materials they needed. The stonewrights of Tor Alessi were busy with the city's own immense defences and were loath to spare any of their fellowship for outlying fortresses.

Liandra began to walk, retracing her steps down the rain-slushed path into the valley. Her robe-hem dragged behind her, sodden.

When her father had founded Kor Vanaeth it had housed over thirty thousand souls. The streets had burst with life, spilling beyond the boundaries of the walls and into the forest.

Hard to remember that now. Fewer than five thousand had returned. Most had done so out of loyalty to Liandra's father, though a few saw opportunities to advance themselves amid the rubble. Some dark-eyed souls had just suffered too much and wanted to take something back.

Twenty-five years. So much work, and so little to show for it. They were vulnerable still. If another army swept down the valley, even one half the size of the one that had destroyed them before, not a single stone would be left standing.

Liandra felt her fists clench. The movement was almost involuntary; she had caught herself doing it more and more often.

I am changing. This war is changing me.

Sometimes she awoke angry, fresh from vivid dreams of slaughter. Sometimes she awoke in tears with images of the slain crowding in her mind. And sometimes, more often than she liked, she awoke after dreaming of him.

The years had not dulled the loss. It was for the best that he had gone back to Ulthuan. He belonged amid its refined spires of ivory, just as she belonged in the wilds of the east, doused by the rain and up to her ankles in blood-rich filth.

'My lady.'

Alviar's voice made her start. She hadn't seen him approach, trudging just as she had done up the steep hill-path from the valley. That was sloppy; her lack of sleep was beginning to take its toll.

Master of Dragons

'What is it?' she demanded, more sharply than she'd intended.

Her steward bowed in apology. 'You asked me to tell you when we had word from Tor Alessi.'

'And?'

'Messengers are here. They bring greetings and news from the Lady Aelis. Do you wish me to summarise?'

'If you please.'

'Aelis agrees with you: now that Caledor has gone, the dawi will be quick to rally. She has tidings of new armies gathering in the mountains. She asks you to join her. She says she cannot promise to protect Kor Vanaeth when fighting resumes.'

Alviar was so dutiful. He spoke like a scribe reeling off trade accounts. Liandra had preferred Fendaril, but he, of course, was dead.

'What of Salendor?' she asked.

'Lord Salendor is already at Tor Alessi, along with the Lords Caerwal and Gelthar. In the absence of the King, a war council has been formed. They call themselves the Council of Five.'

'Those are four names, Alviar.'

'They hope for yours to be added.'

'Do they, now?'

'Salendor in particular, they tell me,' said Alviar.

'Salendor is a brute,' said Liandra. 'He understands the dawi, though. He knows how to fight them. If he wants me to be there then I should perhaps consider it an honour.' She pressed her lips together ruminatively. 'Do you remember, Alviar, when Caledor left us?'

'Clearly.'

'He thought he'd won the war for us. I heard him say it. *Now finish the task*, he told us. I felt like laughing. No one would tell him the truth. He left for Ulthuan with no idea of what we face.'

'I should say not.'

Liandra clasped her hands before her, pressing her chilled flesh against the rain-wet fabric of her robe. 'We accomplished so much here. I cannot leave now. I was not here when the dawi came the first time, and that weighs on my heart.'

'Shall I tell them that?'

Liandra shook her head slowly. 'No. No, I will give it more thought. You offered them lodgings?'

'Of course. As much comfort as we could make for them.'

Liandra breathed in deeply, looking around her, sucking in air that tasted of damp and rot. 'So what would you do, Alviar?'

'I would not presume to have an opinion.'

Liandra smiled. 'None?'

'You are a mage of the House of Athinol. You require the counsel of princes, not stewards.'

'Princes may be fools, stewards may be wise. But you speak truth – I've been starved of equals ever since...'

She trailed off. It was still hard to say his name.

'Enough,' she said. 'Return. Tell them they will have their answer soon.'

Alviar bowed and withdrew, retracing his steps down the shallow slope towards the city.

Liandra watched him go. When he was gone she resumed her vigil, alone at the summit, watching over the city of her father as the cold wind whipped at her robes.

Now finish the task, she mused.

Sevekai ghosted through the deep dark. His movements were silent. Years in the wilds of Elthin Arvan had only honed his already taut physique; his reactions had always been sharp, now they verged on the preternatural.

The others were still on his heels, just as they had been on every fruitless trail since leaving Naggaroth: Verigoth with his pallid skin and dewy eyes; Hreth and Latharek, the brutal twins, their glossy hair as slick as nightshade. The two sorceresses, Drutheira and Ashniel, prowled ahead, lighting the way with purple witch-light. Malchior, their counterpart, brought up the rear.

A whole party of assassins, gaunt from the wild, buried deep in the twisting heart of the Arluii. They were lean from hunger, their skin drawn tight over sharp bones. Elthin Arvan had not been kind to them. Why should it have been? After what they had done to it, a measure of hatred was richly deserved.

Only Kaitar looked untouched. Kaitar the enigma, Kaitar the cursed. Sevekai loathed him. There was something deeply wrong with Kaitar. His eyes were dull, his manner disquieting. None of the others liked Kaitar; he himself seemed to care little either way.

Sevekai avoided Kaitar's gaze, just as he had done for all the years they had suffered one another's company. It had been surprisingly easy to work with someone and barely exchange words. Their routine tasks – slitting throats, administering poisons, squeezing tender flesh – lent themselves to a cold, mute kind of pragmatism.

Now, though, after so long without word from the Witch King, Drutheira had taken matters in hand. It could not continue as it had been. They had done what was required of them and had now been forgotten. So she had taken them south, then up into the peaks, then down again, deep down, burrowing through cold, lost shafts of feldspar and granite. Sevekai could only guess how far they were underground now. He liked the chill of it, though. It cooled his limbs and made him feel languidly murderous.

'Be still,' whispered Drutheira from ahead.

The druchii froze. Her witch-light died away, plunging them into darkness.

Sevekai switched to a state of high awareness. Twin blades

slipped soundlessly into his hands. He tensed, feeling the muscles of his arms tighten and the hairs on the back of his neck rise.

For a few moments, nothing changed. Then, from far away, from far down, he heard it – a long, low rumble, as if the mountain itself stirred. Then silence.

'What is this, witch?' whispered Kaitar. His voice gave away his uncertainty. That in itself was unusual; Sevekai had never heard him sound uncertain before.

'I told you,' replied Drutheira. 'The weapon.'

'The *weapon*,' he repeated. 'I asked you before what it was.'

Drutheira's voice remained perfectly calm, perfectly poised. Sevekai had to hand it to her: she knew her craft. 'Do you doubt me, Kaitar?'

Sevekai smiled wolfishly. He could just make out the ivory glow of her bleached-white hair. She was savagely beautiful, as cruel and fine as an ice-goad.

'No more than you doubt me,' said Kaitar. 'Tell me what you know, or I go no further.'

'Just what have you sensed down here, Kaitar?' asked Drutheira, her voice intrigued. As she spoke, a soft blush of colour spun into the void, lighting up her alabaster cheek. 'What worries you?'

'You do not wish to provoke me.'

'Nor you, me,' she said, before relenting. 'It is a relic, one that will cause the asur more pain than we have ever caused them. If that does not stir your curiosity then maybe you are in the wrong company.'

Sevekai saw Kaitar's face flicker between doubts.

'Maybe I am,' Kaitar said, 'but you could retrieve it yourself. There is no reason for me to be here.'

'Why do we wait?' hissed Malchior from the rear of the party, unable to hear what was being said. 'We need to move.'

'Yes we do, so do not be foolish!' snapped Drutheira to Kaitar. 'Without me to guide you, you'd stumble down here for days. I'd happily watch you starve but I need every blade for what's to come. If you had doubts you should have voiced them on the surface.'

Kaitar hesitated. Still, the uncertainty; Sevekai enjoyed that.

'So be it,' Kaitar muttered at last, drawing a curved knife. 'Take us down. But this blade will be at your back.'

'And this one at yours,' said Sevekai, shifting his weight just enough to prod the tip of a throwing dagger into Kaitar's tunic.

Kaitar turned to glare at him. Sevekai shot him a frigid smile.

'Watch your step,' Sevekai warned. 'The stone's slippery.'

Slowly, deliberately, Kaitar sheathed his blade again.

'Very good,' said Drutheira mockingly. 'Now, if we may?' As she turned back down the tunnel Sevekai caught the look of capricious enjoyment she gifted him.

They crept onwards, going near-silently, treading with feline assuredness in the black. The tunnel wound ever deeper, switching back and plunging steeply. It became narrow, barely wide enough to take two abreast, clogged with stalagmites and glossy tapers of dripping rock.

A second rumble ground away in the depths, then faded. Sevekai's heartbeat picked up. He knew something of what they sought, but not everything – Drutheira was miserly with information even with her allies. Kaitar said nothing further, but Sevekai could sense the tension in him. He kept his daggers to hand, poised for use. Slipping one between Kaitar's shoulders would be no hardship – he just needed the faintest of excuses.

The air began to heat up. Sweat ran down Sevekai's temples. He felt minuscule trembles in the rock as he walked, as if the entire underworld shivered in anticipation.

'It lies in the chamber beyond,' said Drutheira. 'Go silently. Follow my lead.'

Then she set off, creeping through the pitch darkness.

The tunnel floor sloped downward steeply, then levelled out. Sevekai could sense the roof opening up. The floor became flatter, as if made level by mortal hands.

'Go no further,' said Drutheira, halting them. 'This is the place. I think we may risk a little magic – the sight is worth it.'

Her staff flared, throwing out a curtain of purple-blushed illumination. Sevekai shaded his eyes against the glare, then peered cautiously through his fingers.

They were on the lip of a vast, perfectly circular chasm. It must have been a hundred feet across, as dark and clotted as the maw of Mirai. A narrow ledge ran around the perimeter, barred by cracks and heaps of rubble. Other tunnel entrances were visible at intervals, leading off to Khaine-knew-where. The cavern roof soared away above them, lost in shadow.

One by one the druchii crept out onto the ledge, going warily. Latharek hung back, hugging the near wall, looking sickened by the precipitous drop.

'Behold its chamber!' cried Drutheira, sweeping her staff-tip around her and throwing light up the walls.

Huge pilasters loomed up over them, each one carved with immense runes of containment. Sevekai could sense the magic bleeding from them like a physical smell, sulphurous and metallic.

As soon as he saw the runes, Kaitar turned on Drutheira. 'Dhar,' he snarled, reaching for his blade.

Drutheira smiled wickedly. 'What did you expect?'

Kaitar sniffed. It was an odd gesture – like a dog hunting the scent of its prey. His eyes suddenly widened. 'No. Do not do this.'

Drutheira shrugged. 'A little late, I fear.'

Her staff exploded with power, sending crackling lines of energy lashing out against the pilasters. The aethyr-force slammed into the runes, shattering them. A rumble like thunder welled up from the chasm depths, sending loose rubble clattering down the sides of the shaft.

Sevekai staggered, nearly losing his footing. Kaitar's head snapped around. He looked terrified.

'What do you fear, Kaitar?' asked Drutheira, her violet eyes glittering with mirth. 'No druchii fears Dhar.'

Kaitar's face changed into something bestial. 'Fool!' he slurred. 'You cannot control it!'

'You have no idea what I can control,' said Drutheira imperiously.

Kaitar went for her, lunging out with his blade. Latharek was closest. He tried to block Kaitar, ducking low to shoulder him off the ledge. Kaitar lashed around, grabbing Latharek and hurling him away. Off-balance, Latharek tumbled clear over the chasm edge, screaming as he plummeted.

Drutheira fled along the ledge, hurrying around to the far side of the chasm, her staff still blazing. More runes shattered, sending fragments spilling into the vault. The stone walls trembled again, rocked by something huge and muffled from far below.

'You cannot stop this!' cried Drutheira.

Kaitar went after her. Malchior attempted to seize him but Kaitar twisted away from his grip. Hreth darted at him next, blade in hand. For a moment Sevekai thought Hreth got a dagger to stick, but Kaitar somehow angled away at the last moment. They grappled on the edge of the ledge, blows flying furiously, before Kaitar punched his dagger into Hreth's stomach and wrenched it free with a flourish.

Something terrible had happened to Kaitar – his eyes gleamed with unnatural light, his limbs moved with ferocious speed. He was demented, raving, slavering with fear and fury. Whatever Drutheira was doing had made him crazy.

Sevekai went for him, dagger in each hand. Kaitar parried with his blade, desperate to get past and go after Drutheira.

In the flurry of jabs Sevekai managed to wound him, stabbing a dagger-point deep into his arm before pulling sharply away.

It should have stopped him. It should have severed tendons, sliced muscle. Kaitar merely grunted and rushed at him faster. Sevekai got his blade to block just as Verigoth came at Kaitar from behind, dropping a throttle-cord over his neck and yanking it tight.

Kaitar's eyes bulged and his cheeks went purple. Verigoth dragged him back from the brink and for a moment Sevekai thought he'd pinned him. Then Kaitar's hands flew over his shoulders and grabbed Verigoth by his armour. With a ferocious lurch, Kaitar doubled over and hurled Verigoth headfirst into the chasm.

That was impossible. That was *madness*. Verigoth was strong – the strongest of them all – and he'd been thrown overhead like a child.

By then Drutheira had reached the far side and begun destroying more runes. Kaitar's gaze switched back and forth: Ashniel and Malchior blocked him from the left, Sevekai and the wounded Hreth from the right. He looked like a trapped animal.

Sevekai twirled his daggers in his hands and advanced again. Kaitar let slip a strangled growl and crouched down against the stone.

Then he leapt.

If any doubt remained that Kaitar was more than mortal, the leap quashed it. Sevekai could only watch as Kaitar flew high into the air, his limbs cartwheeling, propelled by some unnatural strength far out over the drop. He flew straight at Drutheira, his eyes blazing with anger, his arms outstretched to grasp her. She watched him come with a playful smile on her pale lips.

'Impressive,' she murmured.

But just as Kaitar reached midway, a column of fire thundered up from the depths, spearing out of the gloom and engulfing him in a gale of flame. He screamed – a horrific, otherworldly sound that rang round the chamber.

Sevekai dropped to his knees. The heat was incredible, pressing against his face like a vice. After the long trek in the dark, the sudden brilliance made his eyes sting.

Drutheira revelled in it. Her robes flapped about her.

'*This* is the weapon!' she crowed. '*This* is the weapon!'

Sevekai had no idea what she was talking about. He shrank back from the heat and the noise, just as all the others did.

An instant later the fires gusted out and something vast and dark surged up out of the chasm, rising on a tide of ruin, wreathed in oily smoke. With a twist and snap of immense jaws it ended Kaitar's wretched screaming. A hard bang echoed around the vault, like a steel hammer falling on an anvil. Cracks shot across the walls and rubble rained down from above.

The creature kept rising, buoyed by an updraft as hot as a forge. Vast wings stretched out, bat-skin black and pierced with chains. Ophidian flesh snaked and coiled on itself in the flickering gloom.

'You *know* me, creature!' cried Drutheira. 'You know what I am. Listen to me! The druchii have returned. Listen! We have come to reclaim what is ours.'

Sevekai looked on, unable to do anything but cower. A solid mass of curled, distorted black flesh loomed high up over them, hovering across the face of the chasm. Its hide glistened in the witch-light, reflecting from a thousand tight-woven scales. Ragged wings brushed against the shaft's wall. He saw spines, curved teeth crowded along a jagged jawline and talons the length of an elf's body. Gold chains, some broken, hung from an armoured torso, and iron runes had been branded and hammered into its flesh.

A dragon. A black dragon. One of Malekith's own creations, as warped and ruined as anything to emerge from his embittered mind.

'Your will is broken!' shouted Drutheira, speaking in the tone of command she used when spellcasting. 'Your mind is enslaved. You are *ours*, creature.'

The beast hissed at her, and flickers of blood-red flame danced across the void.

'Do not resist!' warned the sorceress. 'You belong to the druchii. We never forget. We never release.'

That brought a sudden gush of flame and a roar that made the whole shaft shiver. Flames kept coming after that, guttering and snorting, breaking the murky darkness with a dull glow of crimson.

'Serve me!' commanded Drutheira, raising her staff fearlessly. 'Serve *me!*'

The beast screamed back, but it did not attack. If it had chosen to it could have wiped her out just as it had consumed Kaitar. Its jaws opened and closed, revealing a long, lolling tongue the colour of burned iron. Its eyes – slits of silver – flashed furiously.

Sevekai saw the truth then: the powerful magicks that had cracked and twisted the creature's mind still held. It would not attack. It writhed, snorted and flailed, but its fires stayed subdued.

Drutheira smiled savagely. 'You know who your masters are. You sense us. You *smell* us.'

It screamed at her again, and echoes rang around the vault. Drutheira pointed the staff directly at it. 'The wards are broken. When I call, you answer.'

The dragon's wings thrashed, sending acrid air washing over the ledge. Its tail scythed, swishing in dumb frustration. Sevekai could only marvel at the imbalance: such a monster, held in check by a fragile, white-haired sorceress. Whatever magic had been used to crack the creature's mind must have been of astounding strength.

'Go!' cried Drutheira, raising her arms. 'Break out! Your will is mine! Your power is mine!'

The dragon coiled in on itself, writhing in a paroxysm of rage. Its eyes rolled, its jaws clamped shut.

Then it obeyed. With a clap of ebony wings it surged upwards, climbing fast. Sevekai saw then that the cavern had no roof – it was a shaft soaring upwards, carving through the heart of the mountain like an artery. The dragon ascended rapidly, lighting up the walls in a corona of red. The wind whistled in its wake, howling up out of the depths before falling, eventually, back into echoing silence.

Sevekai crept to the edge and risked a look down. He could barely make anything out, though the shaft stank of death. Hreth, lying next to him, gurgled weakly. His innards were visible between blood-drenched tatters of clothing.

Drutheira was breathing heavily and her pale cheeks were unusually flushed.

'So what did you think?' she asked, calling out to them over the gulf. 'Magnificent, eh?'

Malchior scowled back, his expression dark. 'You let it go.'

'It'll come when called. Unlike some, it is *utterly* faithful.'

Sevekai smiled wryly and got to his feet. Ashniel picked her way around the ledge toward Drutheira. 'What now?' she asked.

'To the surface,' the sorceress replied. 'It will be waiting.' As she spoke, the cavern shook again. The cracks that had opened after Kaitar's death widened. 'And we should hurry – this place is perilous now.'

Ashniel and Malchior hastened to follow her. Sevekai, following suit, felt the stone tremble under his feet.

'Wait!' called Hreth, dragging himself along the ledge. 'Some help, brother?'

Sevekai glanced at him scornfully. Shameful enough to be defeated; bleating about it compounded the crime.

'Sorry, brother,' he replied coldly. 'I think you would slow me down.'

More rumbles broke out, echoing dully from the depths.

Sevekai broke into a jog, gliding surely across the uneven ledge surface. When he got to the tunnel entrance Malchior and Ashniel had already gone through, but Drutheira was waiting.

'You planned it all?' he asked her. 'For Kaitar?'

Drutheira placed a finger on his lips. 'Later, I promise. For now, trust me.'

Sevekai grinned. 'Not an inch.'

More cracks opened up, snaking up the height of the chamber. A low growl welled up from the deeps, prising what remained of the pilasters from the rock walls.

'We need to move,' said Sevekai.

'So we do.'

Drutheira slipped into the tunnel and hurried up the incline.

Sevekai took one last look at the chamber. Chunks of rock were beginning to fall freely, splitting from the mountain and tumbling into the shaft. Whether as a result of Drutheira's magic or Kaitar's violent death, the whole shaft was falling in on itself. Hreth still struggled on, stuck on his hands and knees as debris rained around him.

Sevekai couldn't resist a wintry smile. It was always pleasant to witness the demise of a rival.

Then he turned on his heels and raced into the tunnel, following Drutheira back into the dark.

CHAPTER FOUR

Lothern was not the oldest of the dwellings of the asur, nor the wisest, nor the most steeped in the thrum and harmony of magic, but it was the most magnificent, the most imposing, the most martial, the most sprawlingly and gloriously worldly.

Clusters of bone-white spires soared into the air, each reflected in the deep green of the lagoon that lapped before them. Immense statues of the gods stared out across the waters, their golden faces cast in expressions of austere superiority. Crystal coronets shimmered under the glare of strong sunlight and the sky blazed a clear blue, washed clean by the rain squalls and now as pure as a mage's spyglass. A thousand aromas rose from cargo heaped high on quaysides, and every crate, barrel and sackcloth was branded with the esoteric mark of far-off realms and colonies.

The royal fleet lay at anchor in the glassy lagoon. Each warship had been decked out in red and gold, their sails furled and their pennants rippling in the breeze. Mail-clad troops lined every thoroughfare, and their chainmail sparkled.

The waterfront rang with boisterous celebration. Crowds thronged along the long quayside, pushing past one another to gain position. All eyes looked up at the greatest spire of them all – the truly colossal Phoenix Tower, rearing up sheer above the water's edge, its flanks as pure as ivory and its crystal windows flashing in the sun.

Caledor II stood on the Tower's ceremonial balcony, a clear hundred feet from ground level, and drank the vista in. The acclamation of his people made his heart swell. Adulation was good for him. It vindicated everything he had done since setting sail from the same quayside six years ago.

They worship me, he thought, gripping the marble railing with silver-edged gauntlets. *Just as they worshipped my father, they worship me.*

Seldom had so many of the fleet's eagleships been concentrated in one place. The fortified cliffs that surrounded them, all bristling with turrets and banners, added to the sense of excess, of overflowing command, of invulnerability.

Nothing in the colonies would ever compare to Ulthuan, not even if the asur laboured there for a thousand years. Nothing would ever shine so vividly, or be filled with as much vivacity, or give harbour to so many of the Phoenix King's dread vessels of war.

Lothern was the heart of the fleet; thus, Lothern was the heart of power.

'Good to be back, my liege?' asked Hulviar, standing beside Caledor on the balcony. The seneschal wore his ceremonial armour, piped with gold filigree and lines of inlaid jewels.

'I can breathe this air without gagging,' replied Caledor, waving at the crowds below. Every movement he made seemed to elicit fresh cheers. 'My boots are free of mud. Best of all...' He smiled contently. 'No dwarfs.'

'Indeed,' agreed Hulviar with feeling. 'So will you address them now? They have been waiting a long time.'

Caledor gazed out indulgently. He felt reluctant to do

anything to break the spell of massed veneration. Kingship was in large a matter of theatre, of display, and moments such as these were priceless.

Still, though. They wouldn't wait forever. 'Sound the clarion.'

Hulviar motioned to an attendant in the shadows. A moment later a fanfare rang out, cutting across the water and stilling the crowd to an expectant hush.

'I will be heard by them all?' whispered Caledor.

'The mages are prepared,' said Hulviar. 'Speak as comes naturally, my liege; the deafest of them will hear as if they were alone with you.'

Caledor placed both hands on the railing and pushed his shoulders back. He knew full well how resplendent he looked – artisan-fashioned armour of ithilmar and silver, a heavy cloak of sky-blue, long blond hair pulled back from his brow by the winged crown of the Phoenix Kings.

'My people!' he cried, and they cheered again. Soldiers along the terraces clashed their blades against their shields, sending an echoing wave of noise rolling across the lagoon.

Caledor couldn't prevent a fresh smile. The occasion called for dignity, but he was enjoying himself too much.

'My *people*,' he said again, waiting for the hubbub to die down. 'I return to you at the start of a new dawn for Ulthuan. Not since Aenarion's time have we known such victory. The druchii fall back under our relentless onslaught. The Witch King cowers in his frozen land, knowing his fate draws ever closer.'

That brought heartfelt cheers. Every soul gathered below would have lost someone to druchii raids; hatred for Malekith never needed to be stoked.

'But I need not tell you this – you know the truth of it. I come here this day to tell of victory in the east, for we have triumphed! We have triumphed over the mountain-folk. The stunted creatures of Elthin Arvan are defeated, and I myself,

Caledor the Second, slew the son of their High King in single combat.'

Hulviar reached into a pouch at his belt and withdrew a shrivelled, stinking hunk of dried flesh. He handed it to the King, who lifted it up for all to see.

'They called him "Halfhand",' said Caledor, swinging the trophy from side to side as if it were a piece of meat brought back from the hunt. 'No longer – I call him "No-hand"!'

Snorri Halfhand's severed hand, cut from his arm at the wrist before the remnant had been thrown away, dangled from Caledor's grasp. The grey flesh was a mess of black, dried blood, the fingers little more than maimed stumps. At the sight of it the crowd burst into contemptuous laughter.

'They came to this realm and I cut off their beards,' Caledor went on, revelling in the reception. 'They did not take that lesson well, so I went to their realm and cut off their hands. When *will* they learn? Will we have to slice off every extremity, one by one?'

More laughter.

'So much for this *War of the Beards!*' Caledor said, flinging the severed hand back at Hulviar. 'The stunted ones dared to challenge their betters, and thus have been bloodied. They will think twice before assaulting our colonies again. Should they now sue for peace and come before me on their knees, we shall be magnanimous. But if they dare, if they *dare*, to rise up against us again, we shall visit vengeance on them *a thousandfold*.'

Laughter was replaced by roars of approval.

'We shall root them out of their holes and drag them into the sunlight,' Caledor promised, warming to his theme. 'We shall burn their mines and flood their holds. We shall seize their goods and make prisoners of their wives – though what use one might have for such creatures, I have little idea.'

More laughter, crude this time.

'So I tell you: rejoice! Rejoice in the valour of our legions,

Master of Dragons

in the strength of our fleets, in the matchless spellcraft of our mages. No force of the world can stand against us. First will the dawi fall, then the druchii, just as any power must fall that sets itself against the chosen ones, the children of Aenarion!'

The cheering was thunderous.

'From henceforth, this day shall be known as the Day of the Severing. It shall mark our crushing of the dawi in their own domains. Until the sun sets, do no work. Drink wine, feast well, revel in your leisure: you have laboured hard in the years since my father's death, now take your ease and bask in the glory of his son's accomplishments.'

He leaned forward, stretching out his fists.

'I told you that a new dawn has broken over Ulthuan,' he cried. 'It shines on the reign of *Caledor the Second*.'

That brought the loudest cheers of all. Soldiers resumed their shield-clanging salute; whole bunches of flowers were hurled up at the tower's stonework. Caledor basked in it all, smiling benignly, waving regally, before finally, just as the prepared casks of strong wine were opened along the water-front, withdrawing from the balcony's edge.

He passed into a gilt-and-mirror chamber to the rear, followed by Hulviar. The cheers from the quayside went on and on, persisting even after glass-paned doors were closed against the noise.

'That went well,' said Caledor, taking the crown from his brow and handing it to a waiting attendant.

Hulviar drew the strings tight on the bag containing Snorri's hand and dangled it with distaste. 'What do you wish me to do with this, my liege?'

Caledor pulled his gauntlets free and discarded them. 'Whatever you will. Feed it to your swine, throw it into the sea, I care not.'

Hulviar gave him an uncertain look. 'You know, of course, that his father still lives? And his cousin? They're sure to seek vengeance.'

'Of course. They shall meet the same fate.'

'Our lords in Elthin Arvan are not so sure. They make requests for more arms. They are worried.'

'What would they have me do? Go back again? Nursemaid them?'

Hulviar leaned closer. Aside from a couple of attendants who knew how to keep their eyes and ears to themselves, the chamber was empty; even so, he kept his voice low. 'Far from it. You have already been away six years, and that is a long time for the throne to be empty. You know how these things work, my liege: the court grows restive without a strong hand to guide it.'

'Is this a lecture coming?' asked Caledor, irritably. The address had been a triumph; he had no desire to be dragged back into intrigue, something of which there seemed to be an infinite supply in Lothern. 'If so, make it short.'

'Your homecoming has been a success, my liege,' said Hulviar. 'Your position is strengthened, but you are not the only popular name in Ulthuan. Before you returned there was another on the lips of the rabble.'

'Imladrik.'

'Your brother has won renown against the druchii – they have no answer to his dragons. Some whisper that he would wear the crown well, too.'

'Who whispers this?'

'No names, my liege, just rumours. But they persist.'

Caledor shot Hulviar a flinty look. 'My brother has no ambition for the throne. Anyone who knows him would tell you that.'

'Just so, but that – if you will forgive my saying so – is neither here nor there. Others can use Imladrik whether he wishes them to or no.' Hulviar's face was almost apologetic. 'Your brother is the greatest dragon rider of our age, but no statesman. He can be made into a figurehead.'

The beginnings of a scowl formed on Caledor's smooth

brow. The joy of his homecoming felt soured, and that darkened his mood. Even now, just at the moment of triumph, the tangled skeins of his family history were ripe to pollute it all. 'Then he must be sent away again,' he muttered. 'He professed to love the colonies; he can mire himself in war there.'

Hulviar nodded, looking satisfied. 'A judicious course, but he will not go willingly. He has taken up residence in Tor Vael.'

'Tor Vael,' said Caledor, scornfully. 'His dreary wife's tower. So *unalike*, those two.'

Hulviar shrugged, as if to say, *what can one do?* 'He seems to find it amenable.'

'He has had the run of it for too long. I shall send messages there. He will not refuse an order.'

'Indeed he will not, but I understand he is not there: he goes to commune with the drakes. Perhaps it would be best to meet him in person, in Kor Evril.'

Caledor shook his head with irritation. 'I love my brother, Hulviar, but the age of the dragons was drawing to a close even before our great-grandsire walked the mountains. He would do better to devote himself to his own kind.'

Hulviar smiled. 'As you have done, my liege.'

'Quite,' agreed Caledor, already preoccupied by the arrangements he would have to make to secure his position. 'See that all this is put in motion, Hulviar. Your advice spoils my mood, but I see the sense of it.'

'It shall be done,' said Hulviar, bowing smoothly.

Sevekai loped along, keeping his head low. Drutheira, Malchior and Ashniel went ahead, guided by their flickering staffs. The tunnels wound their way tortuously up through the mountain's core, worming like maggot-trails in rotten meat. It was hot, dust-choked and treacherous underfoot, but the druchii went as surely as night-ghouls, never pausing, never missing a footing.

So Drutheira had known Kaitar was tainted. She'd kept the knowledge to herself, as close and devious as ever. Sevekai admired that. He admired her perfect calmness in the cause of deception, the effortless way she discarded those who blocked her path back to Naggaroth. He wondered whether the day would come when she tried to dispatch him, too. That would be an interesting challenge, a potentially enjoyable test. Drutheira was powerful, for sure, but he had tricks of his own, some of which he'd kept secret even from her.

He noticed light growing around him. The purple flickers of witch-fire died out, replaced by a thin grey film on the stone. They were jogging up steeply now, angled hard against the heavy press of heart-rock.

'Stay close,' warned Drutheira. 'The dragon flies.'

The tunnel opened up around them. Sevekai caught sight of its entrance – a jagged-toothed mouth, opening out on to a screen of grey.

They ran for it, emerging into the pale light of an overcast day.

They were on another ledge, high on the shoulder of a narrow gorge. Vast, blunt peaks crowded around them with their heads lost in mist. The Arluii mountains were always bleak and rain-shrouded.

Sevekai leaned against the cliff at his back, catching his breath. The ledge was not wide – a few yards at its broadest. To his left it wound higher up, clinging to the gorge-wall like throttle-wire. To his right it snaked down steeply and headed into the gloom of the gorge. Straight ahead was a plunge into nothing. Fronds of mist coiled over the lip of the brink, gusting softly in the chill wind.

'So where is it?' demanded Malchior, turning on Drutheira with a face like murder.

Drutheira looked at him irritably. 'Give it time.'

'We had it in our power,' Malchior insisted. 'Down there. Why did you–'

Before he could finish, a thin cry of anguish rang out over the gorge. They all looked up.

Far up, part-masked by cloud, the black dragon was on the wing. It flew awkwardly, as if flexing muscles that had been cramped for too long.

Sevekai let slip a low whistle. 'Ugly wretch,' he said.

Drutheira laughed. 'Ugly as the night. But it's ours.'

The dragon circled high above them, unwilling to come closer, unable to draw further away. Its screeches were hard to listen to.

Ashniel gazed up at it with the rest of them. 'So what now?'

'This road leads east,' said Drutheira. 'It will take time to break the beast. But when we do–'

She didn't hear the wheezing until too late. None of them did, not even Sevekai whose ears were as sharp as a Cold One's.

He burst out of the tunnel mouth, limping and bleeding with a blade in hand. Sevekai whirled around first, seeing him go for Drutheira. For a moment he thought it was Kaitar, then he saw Hreth's familiar expression of loathing. Left for dead, somehow he'd clawed his way back up to the surface.

Hreth leapt at Drutheira, who was standing on the lip of the ledge. Sevekai pounced instinctively, catching him in mid-leap. The two of them tumbled across the rock. Sevekai felt blood splash over him from Hreth's open wounds.

'Kill it!' cried Drutheira, but he couldn't twist free to see what she was doing. Hreth's fingers gouged at him, scrabbling for his eyes. Sevekai arched his spine, shifting Hreth's weight, ready to push him away.

He caught a brief glimpse of Hreth's face rammed up close to his own. It was just like Kaitar's had been – dull-eyed, hollow, staring. Sevekai suddenly felt a horrific pain in his chest, as if something were sucking his soul from his body.

A wave of purple fire smashed across him, hot as coals.

Hreth flew away from him, shrieking just as Kaitar had done. He crashed into the cliff face, burning with witch-light, before springing back at Sevekai.

Sevekai dropped down and darted to one side, but Hreth grabbed his tunic and dragged him to the brink. Another bolt of witch-light slammed into Hreth, propelling him over. With a terrible lurch, Sevekai realised he was going over too.

He tried to jerk back, to shake Hreth off him, to reach for something to grab on to, but it was no good – a final aethyr-bolt blasted Hreth clear, dragging Sevekai along in his wake.

For a moment he felt himself suspended over nothing. He saw Hreth's maddened grimace, felt the spittle flying into his eyes.

'Sevekai!' he heard someone cry – it might have been Drutheira.

Then everything fell away. He tumbled through the void, breaking clear of Hreth and plummeting alone. He had a brief, awful impression of rock racing by him in a blur of speed, the wind snatching at his tunic and a howling in his ears.

Something hit him on the side of the head, rocking it and sending blood-whirls shooting across his eyes. After that he knew no more.

The highlands above Kor Evril had the look of a land cursed. Cairns of ebony littered the steep mountainsides. Little grew. The winds, as hard and biting as any of the Annulii, moaned across an empty stonescape, stirring up ash-like soil and sending it skirling across stone.

Only those of the bloodline of Caledor had learned to appreciate the Dragonspine's stark rawness. Fissures opened up along the flanks of the high places, sending noxious fumes spewing into an unspoiled sky. Foul aromas pooled in the shadows, gathering in mist-shrouded crevasses and lurking over filmy watercourses. The air could be hot against the skin or as frigid as death, depending on which way the capricious wind blew. It was a land of extremes, a battle-ground of elemental earth, harsh air and raging ocean.

Imladrik stood before the cavern's wide mouth, breathing heavily. His cheeks were flushed from the climb into the Dragonspine, his body lined with sweat. A stench of burning metal rose up from the charred soil. Kor Evril was far below, miles away, down in the fertile lands to the south-east. It had taken two days to reach the cavern, a long, painful slog on foot.

Now at his destination, his eyes shone. He felt invigorated. The sensations, the smells, the incessant low rumble of steam and wind – they were the things he had been born to. Something in his blood responded to it – he had always felt the same way, ever since his father had taken him into the peaks as a child.

'This is the forge of our House,' the great Imrik had told him. 'This is where we were tempered. As the sea is to Eataine and the forests are to Avelorn, the fire-mountains are to Caledor. Forget this truth, and we lose ourselves.'

Imladrik had taken the words to heart, returning to the Dragonspine whenever he could. Even during times of warfare he had made the pilgrimage, renewing himself, reciting afresh the arcane vows he had made so long ago.

A dragon rider was a restless soul, condemned to rove the passages of the air for as long as the bond existed between steed and rider; if he had a home on earth, a true home, then it was the Dragonspine.

'Such a thing has not been seen for many years,' Imladrik said. 'We are honoured, Thoriol.'

Imladrik's travelling companion stood close by. Thoriol tended to his mother in looks, with pale colouring and slender frame. Only his eyes were the same as his father's – emerald, like summer grass.

Thoriol said nothing. He looked doubtful, standing dutifully beside his father, the collar of his robe turned up against the heat rolling down from the cavern entrance.

'I remember my first summoning,' said Imladrik, lost in the memory. 'We tell ourselves that we choose them, but of course they choose us. We are like swifts to them, our lives flitting across the path of theirs.' He smiled broadly. 'But who can tell? Who really understands them? That is the majesty of them: they are an enigma, an impossibility.'

Thoriol drew in a deep breath, wincing against the foul air. He looked paler than normal. 'You are sure this is the place?' he asked.

Imladrik put a reassuring hand on his shoulder. 'I have been watching this peak for ten years. When I saw the first signs, I thought of you. Others have been studying for longer, but – forgive my pride – I wanted you to have the honour. New blood is so rare.'

'And if...' Thoriol broke off. He looked nauseous. 'And if it does not choose me?'

'*She*,' corrected Imladrik. 'Can you not tell from the way the smoke rises? She is a queen of fire.'

Thoriol tried to calm himself. 'I sense nothing. Nothing but this foul air.'

'I taught you,' said Imladrik proudly. 'The songs will come. You have my blood in your veins, son. Take heart.'

Imladrik drew himself to his full height. He was clad in the silver armour he wore when riding Draukhain, embellished with a drake-winged helm and crimson cloak. The runes inlaid into the metal seemed to smoulder, as if aware they were close to the foundries where they had been made. Thoriol, wearing only brown acolyte's robes, looked insubstantial.

Both of them carried swords. Imladrik bore Ifulvin, Thoriol an unnamed blade from the armoury. Once he became a rider it would be rune-engraved and named.

Imladrik raised his blade before him in a gesture of salute.

'Soul of ancient earth!' he cried. 'Wake from sleep! Let your spirit rise, let your heart beat, let your eyes open.'

Thoriol mimicked his father's movements. He shut his eyes, mouthing the words he had been taught in Kor Evril. A thin line of sweat broke out on his brow.

Imladrik felt the familiar thrill of power shudder through him. The cavern mouth gusted with fresh smoke, swirling and tumbling over the dark rocks.

You know my voice, he mind-sang. *You sensed my presence in your long slumber. Come now, answer the call. I have been calling you since you first stirred. Listen. Awaken. Stir.*

The gusts of smoke grew stronger. The air before the cavern entrance seemed to shimmer from sudden heat, and a low hiss emerged.

Thoriol held his ground. Imladrik heard him begin his own dragonsong, haltingly at first, then more assuredly. He had a clear voice; a little tremulous, perhaps, but greater command would come in time.

My will is before you, mind-sang Thoriol. *Bind your will to mine. Our minds shall be joined, our powers merged. We shall become one mind, one power.*

Imladrik felt his heart burn with pride. He remembered singing the same words, many years ago, just as nervous and uncertain as Thoriol was now. It was a momentous thing, to summon and bind a dragon. Once forged the link could never be broken; the names of a dragon rider and his steed ran down together in history: Aenarion and Indraugnir, Caledor Dragontamer and Kalamemnon, Imrik and Maedrethnir.

'She approaches,' Imladrik warned, maintaining the summoning charm but letting Thoriol's voice take over the harmony of the song. 'Do not waver now, I can feel her mind reaching out to yours – seize this moment.'

Thoriol kept singing. His words were clearly enunciated,

echoing through the aethyr with perfect clarity. *Our minds shall be joined. Our powers merged. One mind, one power.*

The shadows at the cavern entrance shuddered, shook and were broken. A golden shape, sinuous and dully reflective, slid slowly into the shrouded sunlight. It uncurled itself, stretching out lazily, extending a curved neck atop which rested a sleek, horned head. A pair of golden wings unfurled, splayed out to expose rust-red membranes blotched with black streaks. Two filmy eyes opened, each slitted like a cat's.

The dragon's back arched. Like all her kind, she was massive – many times the height of the figures that stood before her. Her shadow fell across them, throwing down an acrid pall of hot air and embers.

Imladrik gazed up at her. She was magnificent. Though only half the size of the great Draukhain, she still bled that mix of raw potency and feral energy that was the truest mark of the dragon-breed. Her hide glistened as if new-forged metal. Her enormous heart, still sluggish from her long slumber, began to pulse more firmly.

Thoriol took a step closer, his blade raised. Imladrik could sense his trepidation. Every fibre of his being longed to help him, to ease the passage between them, but this was something Thoriol had to do for himself.

The stirring of a hot-blood, a Sun Dragon, was a rare thing, and such spirits were hard to tame. Though they couldn't match the sheer power of the Star Dragons or the cool splendour of the Moon Dragons, they brought a wildness and vivacity that thrilled the heart of any true Caledorian. This one was young, perhaps no more than a few centuries. Imladrik could sense her fearlessness, her savagery.

At that instant, he knew her name: Terakhallia. The word burned on to his mind as if branded there.

Our powers merged. One mind, one power.

Thoriol's mind-song continued. His voice became more

powerful. Imladrik listened with pride. Terakhallia drew closer, taking cautious steps down the slope towards the young acolyte. Her great head lowered, bringing her jawline almost down to the level of Thoriol's sword. For a moment the two of them stayed like that, locked in the mystical dragon-song, bound by a symphony as old as the winds of magic.

One mind, one power.

Then, without warning, Terakhallia belched a gout of ink-black smoke, coiled her tail, and pounced into the air. The downdraft was tremendous, knocking Thoriol to his knees and nearly sending Imladrik reeling.

Thoriol cried aloud. The bond was cut.

'Father!' he gasped, instinctively, his blade clattering across the stones.

Imladrik recovered himself and watched, grimly, as the serpentine form rippled up into the heavens. Terakhallia's golden body flashed in the sunlight. Her blood-red wings flexed, propelling her upwards like an arrow leaving the bowstring. It was over so quickly. Once aloft, a dragon moved as fast as a stormfront, thrusting powerfully on wings the size of a hawkship's sails.

Imladrik felt his heart sink. For a moment longer he watched the Sun Dragon gain height. He had the power to call her back. If he chose, he could command her; alone of all the asur living, he could have summoned her back to earth.

But that would have been unforgivable. He would not do it, not even for his son.

Imladrik glanced at Thoriol. As he did so, catching the boy's anguish, he felt a pang of remorse.

'Why?' asked Thoriol, standing up again with difficulty. 'What did I do wrong?'

Imladrik shook his head. 'Nothing, lad. They are wild spirits. Some answer, some do not. It has always been that way.'

Thoriol's face creased with misery. The exertion of the

dragonsong was considerable; he looked suddenly drained, his shoulders slumped, his blade discarded. 'I knew it,' he muttered. 'It was too soon.'

Imladrik went over to him. He knew the pain of a severed link, of a bond that was not completed. 'There will be others, son. Do not...'

'You *knew!*' cried Thoriol, his eyes wide with anger. 'You knew. Why did you even bring me?'

Imladrik halted. 'Nothing is certain. Dragons are not tame.'

'Neither am I.'

Thoriol pushed past Imladrik, ignoring his lost sword and limping down the slope, away from the cavern entrance.

'There are others!' Imladrik called after him.

Thoriol kept on walking. Imladrik watched him go.

Was he too young? he asked himself. *Did I push him too fast?*

He went over to the sword and picked it up. The steel at its tip was scorched from Terakhallia's fiery breath. The Sun Dragon was long gone, free on the mountain air. She would not return for many days, and when she did her soul would be even wilder, even harder to bond with.

Imladrik felt failure press on him. Perhaps their spirits had been misaligned. Perhaps the boy needed more time. Perhaps he himself was to blame.

He tried not to let himself consider the alternative, the possibility that burned away in his mind like a torturer's blade: that Thoriol did not have the gift, that unless the fates granted Imladrik and Yethanial another child, mastery of dragons would die with him and the House of Tor Caled would never produce a rider again.

I could not live with that.

Moving slowly, his heart heavy, Imladrik began to walk. He would have to hurry to catch Thoriol; when the boy's temper cooled, they would talk, discuss what had happened, learn from it.

Even as he thought it, though, he knew that the failure

would change everything. Something new was needed, and he had no idea what it would be.

Imladrik shook his head, pushing against the ashen wind and picking up his pace. His mood of exhilaration had been doused; the descent to Kor Evril would be harder than the climb.

CHAPTER FIVE

Drutheira stared out at the sun setting over the Arluii. Neither of the others had spoken to her since the grim trek down from the gorge, not even Ashniel. Occasionally she had caught them looking sidelong at her, but the accusatory gazes had quickly fallen away. They were still scared of her. Sullen, but scared.

Now, crouched around a meagre fire and with the wind snatching at their robes, the questions came haltingly.

'You're sure you finished it?' asked Malchior.

'Of course I'm sure,' snapped Drutheira.

'But Hreth–' started Ashniel.

'It wasn't Hreth. Khaine's blood, even you could see that.'

'Kaitar,' said Malchior.

'Yes. Or whatever was inside Kaitar. And we banished them both.'

Drutheira found it hard to concentrate. Her mind kept going back to the final glimpse of Sevekai as he sailed over the edge. The Hreth-thing had been little more than a grasping bundle of ashes by then, but Sevekai had been alive.

She shouldn't have cared, and didn't know why she did. They had shared a bed together, of course, but Drutheira had shared the beds of many druchii and not mourned their deaths a jot. Their relationship had been neither close nor deep; they had been thrown together by their orders, both refugees in the grime of Elthin Arvan seeking a way home, so she should have cared as little for Sevekai's death as she had for all the other many deaths she had either caused or witnessed.

Perhaps it was the fatigue. She felt like she had been crawling across the wastelands forever, hunted by both dawi and asur, forced to creep into mountain hollows and make temporary homes in the trackless forest like any common bandit. Even the simple task of getting back to Naggaroth had proven beyond her. For the first time in centuries, she felt vulnerable.

Are we still capable of loyalty? she mused, watching the sun sink lazily towards the western horizon. *Do we even remember what it is? Could we go back?*

She knew the answer to that even as she asked the question. They had all made their choices a long time ago; she certainly had. Sevekai had been so young – he'd had no knowledge of the Ulthuan that had been, the one that she had fought alongside Malekith for mastery of. He could never have known how deep the wounds ran; he had not lived long enough to learn to hate purely, not like she had.

For a long time hatred had been enough to drive her onwards: hatred of the asur, hatred and contempt for the dawi, hatred of those in Naggaroth who had plotted and connived to see her exiled to the wretched east in pursuit of a mission of thankless drudgery. Now, perhaps, the energy of that hatred had dissipated a little.

I am exhausted, she admitted to herself at last. *Unless I find a way to leave this place, to recover my spirit and find fresh purpose, I will die here.*

'So what of Kaitar, then?' came Ashniel's voice again, breaking Drutheira's moody thoughts. 'Still you tell us nothing.'

Drutheira glared at her. The three of them sat on blunt stones in a rocky clearing. The fire burned fitfully in the centre of the circle, guttering as the mountain wind pulled at it. Mountain peaks, darkening in the dusk, stretched away in every direction. The Arluii range was big, and they were still a long way from reaching its margins.

'What do *you* think he was?' asked Drutheira.

'Daemon-kind,' said Malchior firmly.

'How astute,' said Drutheira acidly.

'But why?' asked Ashniel. 'Kaitar was with Sevekai for years. He followed orders, he killed when told to. Can you be sure?'

'You saw it leap. It was a shell. As was Hreth.' She poked at the fire with her boot. 'Banished, not killed. You never truly kill them.'

Malchior kept looking at her, a steady glare. 'How long did you know?'

'A while. Sevekai guessed it too.' Drutheira suppressed a glower. Malchior was a thug, not half as clever as he supposed, and explaining herself to the two of them was tiresome. 'But none of my arts would divine it. For as long as the orders from Malekith were in force I couldn't move against him, but it has been over a year now since I was able to commune. Time to test Kaitar's mettle, I thought.'

Ashniel snorted. '*Test* it?'

'If he had been druchii the dragon would not have harmed him. Up until then, believe me, I was not certain.'

'So it was all for him,' said Malchior. 'The dragon in the dark.'

'I've been hunting that dragon for thirty years. An opportunity presented itself: skin two slaves with one knife.'

The dragon still shadowed them. She had not yet attempted to ride it – it was too soon. Its spirit was wild and frenzied, damaged like a cur beaten too often by its owner. The only thing stopping it from killing them all was the bond of magic placed on it hundreds of years ago.

Urislakh, it had once been called; the Bloodfang. The black dragon still answered to that name, though only grudgingly, as if unwilling to remember what it had been in earlier ages.

She didn't know where it was at that moment. Possibly aloft and out of sight, possibly curled up in some dank crevasse hissing out its misery. The beast would come back when Drutheira summoned it – her leash was long, but it was still a leash.

Ashniel still looked pensive. 'So what does it mean?' Her frail, almost fey features were lit red by the firelight, exposing the hollowness of her cheeks. The rose-cheeked bloom she had once worn when in the carefree courts of ancient Nagarythe had long since left her. 'Was Kaitar one of Malekith's creatures?'

Drutheira shook her head. 'Daemons serve their own kind. We have been duped.'

She let the words sink in. It was a shameful admission. No greater crime existed in Naggaroth than to be made a fool of, to be deceived by a lesser race; and of course, to the druchii, *every* race was a lesser race.

'But for what?' asked Malchior, speaking slowly as his mind worked. 'What was its purpose?'

'Who knows?' said Drutheira impatiently. 'Maybe it was watching us. Maybe it was whispering everything we did to its dark masters. Maybe it was bored by an eternity of madness. You should have asked it before we killed it. Perhaps it would have told you.'

Malchior flushed. 'Don't jest.'

Drutheira sneered at him. 'I wouldn't dream of it. We have already been made fools enough.'

'So you care not.'

'Of course I care!' she shouted. The firelight flickered as her sudden movement guttered the flames. She collected herself. 'It still lives, somewhere. We have lost four of our number. The asur and the dawi will kill us when they find us. That is it. That is the situation. Of course I care.'

Neither Ashniel nor Malchior replied to that. Ashniel chewed her lower lip, thinking hard; Malchior stared moodily into the fire. Drutheira watched them scornfully. Their minds worked so sluggishly.

'Then what do we do?' asked Ashniel eventually.

Drutheira sighed. The sun had nearly set. Shadows had spread across the clearing and the air had become chill. She felt weary to her bones. 'What we have been trying to do: get back to Naggaroth. I cannot commune, so we must get to the coast. Malekith must be told that he has daemons amongst his servants.'

Malchior looked up at her, his eyes bright with a sudden idea. 'We have a steed.'

'It will not bear us all,' Drutheira said. She watched the last sliver of sunlight drain away in the west. In advance of the moons rising, the world looked empty and drenched in gloom. 'In any case, I did not raise the beast merely to test my suspicions of Kaitar. We have more than one enemy in Elthin Arvan.'

Her eyes narrowed as she remembered her humiliation, years ago, at the hands of the asur mage on the scarlet dragon. The pain of it had never diminished. The long privation since then had only honed the sharp edge of her desire for vengeance.

'We cannot leave yet,' she said, her voice low. 'Not until I find the bitch who wounded me.'

She smiled in the dark. She could sense Bloodfang's presence, out in the night, curled up in its own endless misery.

'And we have a dragon of our own now,' she breathed.

* * *

Liandra heard the voice before she awoke. It echoed briefly in the space between waking and sleep – the blurred landscape where dreams played.

Feleth-amina.

She stirred, her mind sluggish, her body still locked in slumber. Then her eyes snapped open and her mind rushed into awareness. She had been dreaming of Ulthuan, of fields of wildflowers in the lee of the eastern Annulii, rustling in sunlit wind.

Feleth-amina.

Fire-child: that was what the dragons called her. The dragons always gave their riders new names. They found Eltharin, she was told, childish.

Liandra pushed the sheets back. It was cold. Nights of Kor Vanaeth were always cold, even in the height of summer. Shivering, she reached for her robes and pulled them over her head. Then, barefoot, she shuffled across the stone floor of her chamber to the shuttered window.

Feleth-amina.

It was Vranesh's mind-voice. Those playful, savage tones had been a part of Liandra's life almost as long as she could remember. The two of them had been bonded for so long that she struggled to recall a time when the link had not been present.

Where are you? she returned, fumbling with the shutter clasp.

You know. Come now.

Liandra opened the heavy wooden shutters, revealing a stone balcony beyond. Starlight threw a silver glaze across the squat, unfinished rooftops of Kor Vanaeth. Her tower was the tallest of those that still stood, though that was hardly saying much.

Vranesh was perched on the edge of the railing, waiting for her. The sight was incongruous – Liandra half-expected the balustrade to collapse under the weight at any moment.

I was asleep, she sang, still blurry.

You were dreaming. I could see the images. Your dreams are like my dreams.

Liandra rubbed her eyes and reached up to Vranesh's shoulder. Familiar aromas of smoke and embers filled her nostrils.

Do you dream? she sang.

I have known sleep to last for centuries. I have had dreams longer than mortal lifetimes.

Sleep to last for centuries, sang Liandra ruefully, settling into position and readying herself for Vranesh's leap aloft. *That would be nice.*

The dragon pounced. A sudden rush of cold wind banished the last of Liandra's sluggishness. She drew in a long breath, then shivered. It would have been prudent to have worn a cloak.

'So what is this?' she said out loud, crouching low as Vranesh's wing beats powered the two of them higher. 'Could it not have waited?'

Below them, Kor Vanaeth began to slip away.

It could have waited, but the mood was on me. You have not summoned me for an age, and I grow bored.

Liandra winced. That was true enough. She had been over-occupied with the rebuilding for too long and, in the few quiet moments she had had to herself in the past few months, she had known it.

Forgive me, she said, her mind-voice chastened.

Vranesh belched a mushroom of flame from her nostrils and bucked in mid-air. The gesture was violent; it was what passed for a laugh. *Forgive you? I do not forgive.*

Imladrik had told her that. Liandra remembered him explaining it to her, back when she had asked why the dragons suffered riders to take them into wars they had no part in.

'They do not suffer us,' he had said. 'They have no masters, no obligations, no code of laws. They do what they do, and that is all that can be said of them. These things: blame, regret, servitude – they have no meaning to a dragon.'

'What does have meaning to them?' she had asked.

She could still see his emerald eyes glittering as he answered. 'Risk. Splendour. Extravagance. If you had lived for a thousand ages of the world, that is all you would care about, too.'

I cannot remain here all night, she sang to Vranesh. *I will freeze, even with your breath to warm me.*

Vranesh kept going higher, pulling into the thinner airs. *You will be fine. I wish to show you something.*

The stars around them grew sharper. Wisps of cloud, little more than dark-blue gauzes, swept below. The landscape of Elthin Arvan stretched away towards all horizons, ink-black and brooding. Faint silver light picked out the mottled outlines of the forest – Loren Lacoi, the Great Wood. The trees seemed to extend across an infinite distance, throttling all else, choking anything that threatened their dominance.

You are changing my vision, sang Liandra.

Not my doing.

Liandra smiled sceptically. Vranesh had only a semi-respectful relationship with the truth.

Let us call it coincidence, Liandra sang.

Something had definitely changed. She could see far further than usual and the detail was tighter. She almost fancied she could see all the way to the Arluii range, or perhaps the Saraeluii, impossibly far to the east.

Tell me what you can see, sang Vranesh.

Liandra narrowed her eyes as the dragon swung around, giving her a sweeping view of all that lay beneath them. Stark sensations crowded into her mind. The intensity was almost painful.

'I see lights in the dark,' she said softly, speaking aloud again. 'Just pinpricks. Are they watchfires?'

They are the lights of cities, sang Vranesh.

'Ah, yes. That is Tor Alessi, along the river to the coast. And Athel Maraya, deep in the forest. How is this possible? And that must be Athel Toralien. They are like scattered jewels.'

What else do you see?

'I see the forest in between them,' said Liandra. 'I see the whole of Elthin Arvan resisting us. We are invaders here. The forest is old. It hates us.'

Vranesh wheeled back round, pulling to the east. Her body rippled through the air like an eel in water, as sinuous as coiled rope. *It does not hate. It just is.*

Like the dragons, Liandra sang.

There are many things we hate. What else do you see?

Vranesh flew eastwards. The dragon's speed and strength in the air were formidable. Liandra doubted any were faster on the wing, save of course the mighty Draukhain. Ahead of them, blurred by distance and the vagaries of magical sight, reared the Saraeluii. Liandra had visited them many times, always in the company of Imladrik. Those mountains were truly vast, far larger than the Arluii, greater in extent even than the Annulii of home.

They daunted her. The dark peaks glowered in the night, their flanks sheer and their shadows deep. She had never enjoyed spending time in those mountains – that was the dawi's realm, and even before war had come it had felt hostile and strange. She looked hard, peering into the gloom. She began to see things stirring.

I see armies, she sang, slowly. As Vranesh swept across the heavens in broad, gliding arcs, she saw more and more. *Huge armies. I see forges lit red, like wounds in the world. I see smoke, and fire, and the beating of iron hammers.*

It was as if the entire range were alive, crawling like a hill of angry insects. Pillars of smog polluted the skies. The earth in the lightless valleys shook under the massed tread of ironshod boots.

Endless, Liandra sang, inflecting the harmonic with wonder. *So many.*

Vranesh swung around again. *Now you see what your scouts have seen. You see why you are needed. The storm is coming. It will roll down from those mountains soon and it will tear towards the sea.*

Liandra sighed. She understood why the dragon had shown her such things. *Kor Vanaeth cannot stand*, she sang.

I did not say that. But you should think on where your powers are best employed. You should see what choices await you.

Liandra's mind-voice fell silent. She had always known that hard decisions would come again. Like water returning to the boil, she felt her ever-present anger rising to the surface.

They killed thousands at Kor Vanaeth, she sang bitterly.

They did. We both saw it.

Liandra clenched her fists, just as she always did. The gesture had become habitual. *I wish for nothing but to see them burn.*

The druchii first, sang Vranesh. *Now the dawi. Can you really kill them all?*

The night seemed to gather itself around her as the dragon soared. It toughened her resolve, helped her to see things clearly. Salendor was already preparing to march, to bring the war back to the stunted ones before they could seize the initiative. Perhaps he was right to.

I cannot, she sang savagely, feeling the lava-hot energy of the beast beneath her. *But you can.*

Sevekai awoke.

For a long period he didn't try to move. The spirals of pain were too acute, too complete. More than one bone was broken, and he saw nothing from his left eye. A vague, numb gap existed where sensations from his limbs should have been.

Master of Dragons

At first he thought he might have been blinded. Then, much later, the sun rose and he saw that he had awoken during the night. Little enough of the sun's warmth penetrated down to the gorge floor, though – the difference between night and day was no more than a dull, creeping shade of grey.

When he finally summoned up the effort to shift position, the agony nearly made him pass out. He tried three times to pull himself to his knees. He failed three times. Only on the fourth attempt, dizzy with the effort, did he drag himself into something like a huddled crouch.

He was terribly, horribly cold. The shade seemed eternal. The rocks around him were covered with thin sheens of globular moss. Moisture glistened in the underhangs, dripping quietly. When he shivered from the chill, fresh pricks of pain rushed up his spine.

Awareness came back to him in a series of mismatched recollections. He remembered a long trek into the mountains with the others. He remembered Drutheira's black-lined eyes staring into his, the raids on trading caravans deep in the shadow of the woods and then the dull-faced visage of Kaitar.

Kaitar.

That name brought a shudder; he couldn't quite remember why. Something had been wrong with Kaitar. Had he died? Had something terrible happened to all of them?

Sevekai's forehead slumped, exhausted, back against the rock. He felt his lips press up against moss. Moisture ran into his mouth, pressed from thick green spores. It dribbled down his chin, and he sucked it up.

It was then that he realised just how thirsty he was. He pushed himself down further, ignoring flaring aches in his back and sides, hunting for more water.

Only when he had trawled through shallow puddles under low-hanging lichen and licked the dribbling channels from the tops of stones did he feel something of a sense of self-possession begin to return. He lay on his back, breathing shallowly.

He had fallen a long way. He could see that now, twisting his head and gazing up at the sheer sides of the gorge. A hundred feet? Two hundred? He should be dead. The rubble that had come down with him alone should have finished him off.

Sevekai smiled, though it cracked his lips and made them bleed. It was all so ludicrous.

Perhaps this is death, he thought. *Perhaps I shall haunt this place for a thousand years.*

He looked up again. As his senses became sharper, as his mind put itself back together again, his thoughts became less fanciful.

For fifty feet or so below the ruined ledge he'd fallen from, the rock ran straight down, a cliff of granite without break or handhold. Then, as it curved inwards towards the gorge's floor, it began to choke up with a tangled mess of briars, scrub and hunched trees. Down in the primordial gloom, a mournful swathe of vegetation had taken hold, clinging on grimly in the perpetual twilight. It was dense and damp, overlapping and strangling itself in a blind attempt to claw upwards to the light.

For all its gnarly ugliness, that creeping canopy was what had saved him. As Sevekai gazed upward he could see the path he had taken down – crashing through the branches of a wizened, black-barked shrub before rolling down across a clump of thornweed and into the moss-covered jumble of rocks where he now found himself.

It was still unlikely. He should still have died.

He let his head fall back again. He could feel the heavy burden of unconsciousness creeping up on those parts of him that still gave him any sensation at all. Night would come again soon, and with it the piercing cold. He was alone, forgotten by those he had trekked up into the mountains with. He knew enough of the wilds to know that strange creatures would be quick to sniff out wounded prey in their midst. He was broken, he was frail, he was isolated.

A crooked smile broke out again, marring the severe lines of his thin face. He felt no fear. Part of him wondered whether the plummet had purged fear from him; if so, that would be some liberation.

I will not die in this place, he mouthed silently. He did not say the words to encourage himself; it was just a statement of belief. He knew it, as clearly as he knew that his body would recover and his strength would return. The scions of Naggaroth were made of hard stuff: forged in the ice, sleet and terror of the dark realm. It took a lot to kill one – you had to twist the dagger in deep, turning it tight until the blood ran black.

He had killed so many times, had ended so many lives, and yet Morai-Heg still failed to summon him to her underworld throne for reckoning.

Even as the light overhead died, sending Sevekai back into a dim-lit world of frost and pain, the smile did not leave his face.

I will not die in this place.

CHAPTER SIX

Yethanial looked up from her work, irritated. She had slipped with her last stroke, jabbing the tip of the quill across the vellum. The servant was well aware of his crime, and waited nervously.

'I told you I was not to be disturbed,' said Yethanial.

'Yes, my lady, but he would not accept my word. He is highborn, and refuses to leave.'

Yethanial looked down at her work again. At times she wondered why she cared so much. No one other than her would ever read it.

'Tell him to wait in the great hall,' she said. 'I will see him there.'

The servant bowed, and made to leave Yethanial's chamber.

'Wait,' she said, lifting her head. 'What did you say his name was?'

'Caradryel, of the House of Reveniol.'

'I have never heard of it.'

'From Yvresse, I believe.'

Yethanial shook her head. 'There are more noble houses in

Ulthuan than there are trees in Avelorn. What does that tell us?'

The servant looked uncertain. 'I do not know, my lady.'

Yethanial shot him a scornful glance. 'Deliver the message. I will come down when I am ready.'

He was waiting for her in Tor Vael's great hall. 'Great' was somewhat optimistic; the space was modest, capable of holding no more than several dozen guests, bare-walled and with only a few drab hangings to lighten the stonework. The fireplace was empty and had not been used for years. Yethanial did not often entertain guests; as she had often complained to Imladrik, she found their conversation tiresome and their manners swinish.

The present occupant lounged casually in one of the two great chairs set before the granite mantelpiece. His long blond hair was artfully arranged, swept back from a sleek face in what Yethanial supposed was the latest fashion in the cities. He wore a long robe of damask silk, a burgundy red with gold detail. It looked fabulously expensive.

Yethanial walked up to him. He did not rise to greet her.

'My servants tell me you will not leave,' she said.

Caradryel raised a thin eyebrow. 'That is not much of a greeting.'

'I have important work. State your business.'

He settled into the chair more comfortably. 'Ah, yes. The scholar-lady. You are spoken well of in Hoeth.'

Yethanial paused. 'Hoeth? You bring word from the loremasters?'

Caradryel laughed; an easy, untroubled sound. 'Loremasters? Not my profession, I'm afraid. I only use parchment to light fires.'

Yethanial folded her arms. She knew that she must look impossibly drab next to him in her grey shift and barely-combed hair, and cared nothing for it. 'Then you are running out of time here.'

'Something I am sure you must be short of, so I will come to the meat of it.' He pushed himself up higher in his seat. 'I was serving in the fleets, sent there by a father who despairs of my ever performing gainful service to the Crown. He is wrong about that, as it turns out, but that is not something you or he need worry about. My time aboard ship turned out to be instructive, though not in the way he hoped for.'

'I am just burning to know how.'

Caradryel flashed her another smile – the effortless, artful smile of one who has spent his life flitting through the privileged circles of courtly classes. 'I saw a strange thing. We were attacked by corsairs. I have never been one to scare easily, being of the view that my destiny is almost certainly a great one and thus the gods have a clear incentive to keep me alive, but I admit that I did not like the way the situation looked. I had made my preparations to meet death in a suitable manner when, quite unexpectedly, salvation came out of an empty sky.'

Yethanial struggled to control her impatience. Caradryel clearly enjoyed the sound of his own voice and fancied himself a storyteller. She could see the steady confidence radiating from his languid frame and wondered what, if anything, justified it.

'A *dragon rider*, my lady,' Caradryel went on. 'Rare enough even on the fields of war. Vanishingly rare in the open seas. When the shock of it had faded, I reflected on that. I could not help but feel that my earlier judgement had been vindicated: I am being preserved for something special. That is a comfort to me, as you might imagine.'

'Or a delusion.'

'Quite; time will tell which. But here is the thing: the rider was your husband, the King's brother. When this became known, the crew of the ship fell into the kind of fawning adulation that is embarrassing unless directed at oneself. And that prompted me to think further on it.'

'Any brevity you can muster would be welcome,' sighed Yethanial.

'Our beloved ruler, Caledor the Second, has returned to Ulthuan. His victory in the east has bolstered his strength at court, but he is not without enemies, who think him vain and unwise. Factions exist that wish for an end to the fighting in Elthin Arvan. They would not move against him openly, but there are other things they can do to undermine a king. I know how the courts work, my lady, and so does he. The crown does not suffer rivals. Caledor will act; he may have already done so. Your husband, you should know, will not be suffered to remain in Ulthuan.'

Yethanial smiled thinly. 'And you understand all of this from one chance encounter at sea.'

Caradryel shrugged. 'That was the start of it. I have friends in all sorts of interesting places, and they tell me the same thing. A story is being whispered all across Ulthuan, passed from shadow to shadow.' He gave her a sad, almost sincere, smile. 'Lord Imladrik will be sent back to the colonies, my lady. Nothing can prevent it.'

Yethanial felt her face grow pale. 'Is this why you came?' she demanded. 'To pass on tittle-tattle and gossip?'

'Not at all. I can do that far more productively in Lothern.' Caradryel rose from his chair and bowed floridly. 'I came to offer my services.'

For a moment, Yethanial was lost for words. As she struggled, Caradryel kept talking.

'They say your husband is the greatest dragon rider since the days of the Dragontamer. Having seen his prowess at first hand, I have no doubt they are right. When it comes to the arts of state, though, he is a neophyte. My guess is that he thinks statecraft beneath him, as do you. You despise the likes of me; you think us gaudy parasites on the real business of life. Of course you are right: we are parasites. But necessary ones.'

Master of Dragons

Caradryel fixed her with a serious look, the first he had given her.

'I can help him,' he said. 'I can guide him. When he is alone in Elthin Arvan, beset by enemies on both sides of the walls, I can give him counsel. Believe me, he will need it.'

Yethanial's surprise ebbed, giving way to anger. Caradryel must have been half her age, and yet felt free to lecture her as if speaking to a child. She drew closer to him, noticing for the first time that she was taller.

'Save your counsel,' she said coldly. 'It, and your presence here, are not welcome. I do not know to whom you have been speaking, nor do I care to. My husband's business is here in Tor Vael and it is no one's concern but his and mine. You clearly have little regard for the sensibilities of this house, so let me enlighten you: three dozen guards stand ready on the far side of this door. Should I order it, they will rip those robes from your back and drive you all the way back to Yvresse for the sport of your long-suffering subjects. I am close to giving that order. If you disbelieve me, feel free to provoke me further.'

Caradryel met her gaze for a little while. His blue eyes flickered back and forth, as if testing her resolve, or perhaps his own. Eventually they dropped, and the smile melted from his face. 'So be it,' he said, adopting a breezy, resigned tone without much conviction. 'I made the offer. That is all I can do.'

Yethanial said nothing. For some reason, her heart was beating hard.

Caradryel bowed. 'I was told you were a shy soul, my lady, much taken up with books. I see that you have been under-sold.' He started to walk away. 'Should you change your mind–'

'I will not change my mind.'

'Just in case, I can be found at Faer-Lyen. You will not have to look hard; I have many friends who know me well.'

'How fortunate for them.'

Caradryel smiled again ruefully, reached the doors, and took the handle. He almost said something else, but seemed to change his mind. He bowed, turned on his heel and slipped through them. As he departed, his damask robes gave a final flourish.

Yethanial watched him go. Only once the doors had closed did she look down at her hands. They trembled slightly.

She had spoken as firmly as she was able, something she disliked doing. Perhaps it had fooled him. She had not fooled herself, though. His prediction had shaken her; his assertiveness had shaken her.

She stirred herself, ready to climb the stairs to her chamber and start the process of writing again. As she prepared her mind for the labour, though, she knew it would not come easily this time. The moment had gone. Other thoughts would preoccupy her now, ones that she had believed consigned to the past over thirty years ago.

Lord Imladrik will be sent back to the colonies, my lady. Nothing can prevent it.

That was not true. It could not be true – those days were done with, over.

Yethanial moved away from the fireplace, forcing a measure of calm onto her speculating mind. She pushed Caradryel's infuriating smugness from her thoughts, returning to the labour of scholarship that had occupied her before his interruption.

I will not permit it. I have my dignity.

She reached the stairs and started to climb, her grey robes whispering across the stone.

Nothing can prevent it.

Imladrik had never loved Kor Evril. Its walls were dark, hewn from the volcanic rock that riddled Caledor and gave the kingdom its untamed aspect. They were as old as the bones of

Master of Dragons

Ulthuan, having been raised in the days when Aenarion still walked the earth and daemons sang unchecked in the aethyr.

He preferred the open sky. Walls made him restless; towers made him feel confined. Perhaps it was the dragons that had done it to him; once one had ridden on the high paths, circling under the sun with the whole world laid out like a crumpled sheaf of parchment, the confinement of mortal chambers became hard to bear.

Imrik, his father, the one known to Ulthuan as Caledor I, had warned him of it. 'They say steed and rider become alike,' he had said. 'They get into your mind, the dragons. Beware of that: they are creatures of another world. Never believe you control them. They only come to you if they see themselves already inside you – the dragon becomes you, you become the dragon.'

Imladrik knew the truth of that. He had started to speak like Draukhain, even to think like him. When they were apart, which was most of the time, he would sometimes catch himself pondering strange images of far-off mountains or shorelines. He knew then that Draukhain was on the wing, perhaps thousands of leagues distant, and that the great creature's mind was reaching out to him.

Did he share such an understanding with any of his own kind. With Thoriol? With Yethanial? He wanted to say that he did.

But he had never shared their minds as he had shared Draukhain's. He had never become one with them, lost in the joy of flight, of killing, in the perfect freedom that had existed since before the coming of the ancients and the ordering of the earth into its mortal realms and jealousies.

At times he felt like one of the poor fools who sipped the nectar of the poppy, forgetting themselves, gradually slipping from the real world. They, too, lost themselves in dreams. How different was he to them? If he wanted to, could he break free of it?

Possibly. But the question was moot; he would never want to.

He approached Kor Evril's gates on foot. A clarion sounded and the heavy wooden doors swung inwards. Guards raced out to greet him, bowing the knee and lowering iron spear tips in homage. They bore the colours of his House – crimson, bone-white, black.

Imladrik strode past them, barely checking his stride. 'Where is my son?'

'He has not been seen, my lord,' replied one of the guards, hurrying to follow him. 'I thought he was with–'

'He was,' said Imladrik grimly. 'He chose to descend alone.' He walked briskly through the narrow streets, ignoring the startled looks of his people. They stared at him from narrow windows. They were not used to seeing their lord travel without an escort, with the black dust of the mountain caking his robes and with two swords in his hands. 'He was not seen on the road?'

'He was not,' said the guard. 'I will send out patrols.'

'No need. I know where he has gone. I will go after him myself.'

The guard bowed, struggling to keep pace as Imladrik pushed up towards the citadel's main tower. 'My lord, there is something else.'

'Make it brief,' snapped Imladrik, maintaining his pace. His failure with Thoriol still rankled. The ceaseless war with the druchii would call him away again soon, so he needed to make his peace before then. The two of them needed to speak, like a father and son should. His duties had always taken him away. That was the cause of the rift – it could be healed, given time, given patience.

'The King is here, lord,' said the guard, looking up at Imladrik's stern face with some trepidation. 'He arrived last night.'

By then Imladrik was approaching the central tower, his own keep, and he could see it for himself. Two banners hung over the gateway: one the gold and white of the Phoenix Kings, the other the pale blue of Caledor II.

He felt his heart sink. He gazed up at the high window, knowing that Menlaeth would have installed himself in there with his entourage, waiting for his subject to come to him.

It was a petty indignity. Imladrik paused, toying with the idea of turning on his heels. He was the inheritor of the title once carried by his illustrious ancestor, and need bow to no living monarch.

'My lord?' asked the guard, hovering uncertainly. 'Shall I send word that you are coming?'

Imladrik briefly glanced up at the sky – a wistful look. He half expected to see Draukhain up there somewhere, spiralling in the emptiness, his long sapphire body twisting in perfect freedom.

The dragon becomes you, you become the dragon.

'Do no such thing,' he said dryly, pushing the doors open and walking inside. 'I shall announce myself. It is always nice to give my brother a surprise.'

Imladrik's audience chamber was a long, many-pillared space, lit by tall arched windows that sent clear bars of sunlight across the stone floor. At the far end stood a low dais, upon which sat a throne of obsidian. Imrik's old battlestandard hung behind the throne, scorched at the edges. The dragon's-head device had faded over the years.

Caledor filled the throne out pretty well. His fur-lined robes spilled over the arms. His longsword, Lathrain, rested against the obsidian, still sheathed in its ancient woundmetal scabbard. Hulviar, the king's seneschal, crouched on the steps to one side, wearing a high-collared jerkin of worsted wool and a thick cloak.

Imladrik smiled to himself. Hulviar had always felt the cold.

'Brother,' said Caledor warmly, rising from the throne and coming to greet him.

Imladrik met the embrace, kissing his brother on both cheeks.

'You look terrible,' Caledor said. 'You *smell* terrible. Have you been rolling in charcoal?'

'I have been in the mountains,' replied Imladrik, thinking much the same about his brother's primped and perfumed attire. 'It takes its toll.'

'Your people told me you were up there,' said Caledor, returning to the throne and brushing his robes down. 'I asked when you would return and I was told that no one knew. It could be tomorrow, it could be in a month, they said.'

Imladrik stood upright before the dais. He could feel his muscles ache from the long hike down but did not send for a chair. 'What do you want, Menlaeth? I am tired, I have much to do. If you'd wanted me I could have come to Lothern.'

'I know, brother, but are you not grateful? *I* have come to see *you*. Not every King would have made such an effort. Can you imagine our father doing it?' Caledor's face clouded. 'Can you imagine him ever pulling himself away from his wars long enough to speak to either of us?'

'No, I cannot.'

'Now I am back from wars of my own, and it has been too long since we spoke. So I am here, and I am glad to see you, though I am not sure I would have waited a month for the privilege.'

Imladrik glanced at Hulviar, who studiously ignored his gaze. 'I heard your reception in Lothern was worth seeing.'

Caledor inclined his head modestly. 'It was. And our passage across the seas was equally splendid, thanks to the escorts you arranged. I am grateful.'

Imladrik paused. Was he being sarcastic? He couldn't read his brother's expressions any more. For that matter, he couldn't read anyone's expressions any more. 'Please, Menlaeth,' he said. 'Tell me why you are here.'

'Very well,' said Caledor. 'I am sending you back to Elthin Arvan.'

Imladrik stood stock still. The words hit him hard. For a moment, he thought he might have misheard. Then he thought that Caledor might have misspoken. Then he realised that no error had been committed – that was what he was being told.

'This is an honour for you,' Caledor went on. 'The dawi are easy prey: we will have victory after victory. I have seen for myself the glory it brings. You too will earn a reception in Lothern, and they will greet you as they did me – like a god.'

'Madness.' The words seemed to spill out of their own accord. 'You were barely there a year. You have seen only a tithe of their strength.'

Caledor shot him an indulgent look. 'No doubt! No doubt there are thousands more, and you can root them out, one after the next. You can take the dragons, too, as many of them as will cross the ocean. Imagine when the dwarfs see *them*. I don't think they truly realise what a weapon they are.'

'They are not weapons,' said Imladrik, his voice low.

'Of course, no, they are not: they are ancient and wonderful beings. I forget that sometimes, so it is good to have you here to remind me.'

Imladrik struggled to keep his anger down, mindful of where he was and whom he spoke with. 'I cannot go back,' he said. 'Not now. We are taking the war to the druchii. A thousand plans are in motion. My troops–'

'–will serve just as ably under another commander,' said Caledor coolly. 'And what is this "I cannot"? Is that how you were schooled to talk to Kings?'

'I am used to Kings making wiser choices,' said Imladrik.

Hulviar pursed his lips. Caledor's face went a shade paler. 'This is not a request, brother,' he said, his tone frostier. 'I am still the regent of Asuryan in this realm. Unless, that is, you can think of a better candidate.'

Imladrik laughed, suddenly understanding. 'Is *that* what this is about? You should find yourself abler counsellors.' He took a stride towards Caledor, and his metal-shod boots clinked on the stone. 'I have no desire to sit on your throne, nor to wear your crown. By the gods, I have no desire to lead armies at all – if duty did not demand it I would happily spend my days in the Dragonspine. Forget those who whisper in your ear; we are winning the war against the druchii, and I will not leave it.'

Caledor's face flashed briefly with anger. '*Will not?* Let me remind you, brother, of how things stand. I have the mandate of the Flame. I built the fleets that spread our power over the world. I broke the grip of the corsairs. I slew the prince of the stunted folk and sent his armies reeling.'

Imladrik listened to the litany wearily. Perhaps it sounded impressive to his brother; to his own ears, it sounded painfully insecure. Both of them knew that their father had been gifted the title 'Conqueror' by the people. Caledor II was desperate to make a similar mark in the annals and so threw himself into one battle after the other, neglecting all else but war. That might fool the rabbles of Lothern and Tor Alessi, though it fooled no one who had actually known Imrik.

'And *you*,' said Caledor, almost scornfully. 'The Master of Dragons. What *is* that, even? An old title from a dusty lineage. They are *dying*, Imladrik. They have been dying for centuries and nothing will halt it. You have wasted your life with them, trying to coax out a little more ore from a mined-out shaft.'

Imladrik met his gaze evenly. 'You know nothing of them.'

'So you have always told me, but by Khaine, brother, your piety riles me! You speak of mystical nonsense and then expect me to take you seriously, and in the meantime there are real wars to be fought. My gold buys the making of a thousand warships. Every day we ferry more soldiers to Elthin Arvan – you think it happens by itself? And all the while you commune with your... creatures in the hills.'

'I will not go.'

Caledor rose from the throne. Imladrik saw the brittleness there: the raised veins in his neck, the tight line of his jaw. So it had ever been with him, always just one step away from battle-rage.

'Then I order it,' said Caledor through gritted teeth. 'I order you to Elthin Arvan. You will wage the war against the dawi. You will not return until their forces are broken and the colonies are secure.'

'We *do not need* to fight them!' Imladrik shouted, struggling to curb his exasperation. 'You *provoked* them, time and again. They are proud, they do not suffer slights, and you shamed them. You shamed them in the worst possible way, and you do not even know it.'

By then they stood only inches apart. Imladrik was the taller, the leaner, but Caledor was the stronger. Thus it had always been with them – the older brother staring up at the younger.

'And what of you, brother?' Caledor spat, his eyes flat. 'You will speak up for anyone but your own kind. They killed thousands at Kor Vanaeth, thousands more at Tor Alessi. At Athel Numiel they butchered infants for sport. What would you have me do – roll over for them? Beg for mercy?'

Imladrik shook his head in disgust. 'The war is a sham. It always has been. Our father would never–'

'Do *not* mention him!' Caledor's voice rose in fury, skirting hysteria. 'This is not his time! It is *my* time! It is *my* time!'

Imladrik pulled back as if burned. The frenzy in Caledor's voice was disconcerting. 'Gods, listen to yourself. What has happened to you?' He forced himself to relax, his fists to unclench. 'Just *think*. We can take the war to the druchii, just as we were always meant to: my dragons, your ships. There need be no jealousy between us. I have always been content to follow you. Come, you know this.'

Caledor hesitated then. His face remained taut, locked in outrage, but something else flickered across it: embarrassment, perhaps. Imladrik hardly dared to breathe.

Then Hulviar's silky voice broke the silence.

'This is false policy,' interjected the seneschal. 'We will lose the colonies. My liege, recall the determinations made–'

Imladrik whirled on him. 'Silence!'

Hulviar recoiled, raising his hands in self-defence. By then, though, the damage had been done; Caledor's resolve returned.

'You will go to the east,' Caledor ordered, his voice firm again. 'Either you will go by your own will or you will be sent there under the custody of more dependable subjects. You are mighty, brother, but even you cannot defy the will of the Crown. If you try, it will break you.' His voice lowered, just a little. 'I do not wish to break you.'

Imladrik's heart beat hard, the blood thudding in his ears. The twin swords in his hands felt heavy. He felt the potential in them, and for an instant imagined the storm he could unleash if he chose to.

Caledor did not waver. Imladrik stared down at him, his mind a torment of emotions, his face a mask. Then he looked away.

'You are the Phoenix King,' he said, softly.

'And your brother,' added Caledor, relenting a little with a half-smile.

Imladrik turned away, ready to stride back down the length of the hall. He shot a withering glance at Hulviar, then started to walk.

'For what's it's worth,' he said.

CHAPTER SEVEN

Thoriol lay back against the cushions, feeling his muscles relax. Soft lute music filled the background, calming him, easing the tensions that had filled his mind during the long descent from the mountains.

He didn't like to think back over the journey. He had taken a steed from one of the hardscrabble settlements just outside Kor Evril and ridden along stony tracks down to Lothern, weathering incessant salt-thick wind until Eataine's gentler land had taken hold.

The country of Caledor had always left him cold, and he had never understood what his father saw in it. To his eyes, it was all black rock and smouldering craters, scoured by the elements and beset by legends of past glory. In comparison to Cothique, his mother's land, where grass-crowned cliffs stood proudly against the ocean and the air was sweet from the woodlands of Avelorn, it seemed a meagre, desolate place.

As a child Thoriol had been proud of his father's lineage. He had boasted to his playmates about it, enjoying it when they had stared back at him, mouths open, as he had told them stories about the great dragons. Some of them had even been true.

Thoriol smiled as he remembered. It was hard not to smile. After nearly half a decanter of *heliath* the whole world seemed essentially benign.

He looked around him. The house of pleasure was much like most of the others he had spent time in, though, this being Lothern, more richly appointed. Long drapes of diaphanous silk hung from high ceilings, wafting from the gentle movement of bodies. The tinkle of a fountain sounded from somewhere close by, part-masked by the hum of conversation. He saw lissom figures drifting in and out of the various private chambers, both male and female, all with the flushed cheeks and sparkling eyes that spoke of exotic consumptions. The light was subdued; a dim cloud of reds and purples, thick with curls of smoke.

Thoriol shifted on his couch, enjoying the give of it against his skin. After so long in the saddle it felt good to be somewhere more civilised. You had to be discreet – such places were secretive by nature – but if you knew the right palms to press it was always possible to find what you were after.

The failure with the Sun Dragon barely troubled him now. It had troubled him, badly, just after it had happened. For a time he had allowed himself to be tortured by familiar feelings of inadequacy, the same feelings that had dogged him ever since he had been old enough to understand that his boastful tales of dragons and battles would need to be replaced one day with deeds of his own. After a while even his old playmates had stopped thinking of his heritage as a blessing – none of them had had such achievements to live up to as they reached gingerly towards adulthood.

Thoriol had his mother's temper in so many things. He had loved the books she had shown him as a child, poring over them, tracing the runes on the parchment, committing the sacred words to memory. He had imagined he would end up as a loremaster like her, locked in some isolated tower studying the mysteries of the aethyr or the poetry of the sages.

Master of Dragons

But his mother had never pushed him to follow that path, and when his father had begun to school him in the lore of the dragon riders, she had supported him.

'This is important,' she had told Thoriol, smiling reassuringly. 'Think of it: you are the heir. One day you will ride the great ones into war. Part of me envies you, for I will never understand them, but do this for him. Do this for both of us.'

He had wanted to tell her then, but somehow the words never came. As the months passed it had become harder to change course. His tomes of lore had been left in Tor Vael, slowly mouldering – after that he had worked to grow used to the cold and the hardness of life at Kor Evril. He had studied diligently, memorising the rites of summoning, learning the mental disciplines, spending hours in caverns in an attempt to decipher the tremors and hisses that gave away the rousing of a dragon below.

On some days he had truly believed he could master it. There had been times – not many, but they had existed – when he had looked up into Caledor's bleak skies and seen the raw beauty in them that so excited his father.

But he had never truly fooled himself. He had always known the truth, and had festered away in resentment of it. There had been times when he had wanted to shout it out aloud, to rage at his father who had worked so patiently with him.

'Can you not see it?' he had wanted to yell. 'I have no talent for this! You know every nuance of these creatures – are you no judge of my own?'

Throughout it all Imladrik had never been cruel, never domineering; it was just that he had never understood, not even for a moment, why one of his bloodline would not leap at the chance of becoming a dragon rider. Imladrik was doing what a father should – passing on the keys to greatness, schooling him, nurturing the talent that surely lay somewhere buried deep within.

Thoriol took another long draught of *heliath*.

At least the deceptions were over. That, along with much else, was a comfort.

'You are new here,' came a lilting voice close to his ear.

Thoriol turned to see a hostess curled up on the couch next to him. She had dark hair, as straight as falling water, and almond-shaped eyes. The scent of cloves rose from her high-collared dress.

'True,' he replied, propping himself up on an elbow to get a better look at her.

'Is everything to your satisfaction?' she asked.

'Quite, thank you.'

'I can fetch more *heliath*. Or a dream-philtre.'

'Dream-philtre?'

She smiled conspiratorially. 'The poppy.'

'Ah. I thought that was… prohibited.'

'You have a trustworthy face. I believe you can keep a secret.'

Thoriol laughed. 'I keep many secrets.'

'Tell some to me?' the hostess asked. 'I am as discreet as the night.'

'I'm sure.' Thoriol held his goblet up to the diffuse light. The cloudy blooms from the lanterns reflected in the cut crystal. 'I did not come here to talk. I came here to forget.'

'We can help you with that. We can help you with anything.'

Thoriol saw his reflection in the glass. He gazed at it wearily. 'Can you help me to escape?'

'That is a speciality.'

'You do not know whom I am escaping from. He is powerful. Very powerful.'

'Many powerful figures come through these doors,' said the hostess.

Thoriol found himself looking at her lips as she spoke. They were such soft lips.

'They are all much the same as one another,' she added, 'once you get under the robes.'

Thoriol laughed again. For some reason, he found himself wanting to laugh at almost everything she said. 'I like you.'

'I am glad. Tell me more about where you wish to go.'

'As far as possible,' said Thoriol wistfully. 'I would go where nobody knows me. I would spend my days with no expectations. I would take time, I would think. Perhaps I would reconsider some choices I have made. Perhaps I would change a great deal.'

The hostess nodded. Her hair shimmered strangely as her head moved, as if it were a single sheet of silk.

'Do you see that one, over there?' she asked, pointing directly ahead of her.

Thoriol followed her manicured fingernail. In a booth opposite lounged a tall elf in a white gown. He was drinking from a goblet, watching the people move around him absently. He had a blunt face for one of his race, by the look of it bitten by a life in the open air. A scar ran down his right cheek, pale and raised.

'What of him?' asked Thoriol.

'I think you might get along,' replied the hostess.

'Maybe we would.'

'Perhaps I might introduce you.'

'Maybe you should.'

The hostess smiled at him. It was a comforting gesture; almost maternal. 'Your glass is empty. More *heliath*?'

Thoriol looked at his goblet. He hadn't noticed that he'd drained it. 'What was the other thing?'

'A dream-philtre. I can get that for you. Just ask.'

Thoriol lay back on the couch, stretching his arms lazily. A languor spread throughout his body, warming him pleasantly. 'That would be nice.'

The hostess placed her hand on his arm lightly. 'Whatever you wish,' she said. 'You are amongst friends here.'

* * *

Draukhain plunged through the night sky. He let slip a grating roar, like metal being dragged across an anvil. He was in a savage mood.

Imladrik gave him his head. He too was in a savage mood.

Together they wheeled and dived above a seething mass of cloud. The layers below them were unbroken, lit vividly by the stars and the world's moons. An undulating carpet of mingled silver and green rippled towards the curve of the horizon. The two of them might have been in another dimension of the universe, locked away from the world and sustained only by starlight and infinity.

I feel your wrath, sang Draukhain. *The last time you summoned me you were angry. Is this how it will be from now on?*

Imladrik laughed harshly. The wind raced through his bronze hair. *Your spirit is wrathful too.*

Because you are, kalamn-talaen. *You are angry; so am I.*

Imladrik had kept his son's sword with his own and the two scabbards hung at his belt, clattering against Draukhain's heaving hide. The dragon flew very, very fast. Every so often Draukhain would unleash his potency to the full. Even after centuries steeped in dragons and their ways, Imladrik could still be taken aback by it.

You awaken this in me, Imladrik sang. *You are wild.*

Draukhain grunted, dropping low and skimming across the landscape of vapour. *Believe that if you wish*, he sang, inflecting the harmonies with sceptical humour.

On Ulthuan I am equable, sang Imladrik. *I live a modest life. I sleep on the ground beside my troops.*

You say that as if it were something to be proud of.

It is.

Mortals, snorted Draukhain contemptuously. *Modesty is perverse. Revel in the superiority you have been given.*

Imladrik laughed again. *And be more like you.*

It would improve you.

It would improve my mood.

Master of Dragons

They hurtled into the north-east, swinging far out over the cloud-wreathed ocean. They had left the rugged shoreline of Chrace behind them a long time ago; now all that remained below the cloud-veil was open sea, black as pitch. No birds flew so far out, no ships plied those waters.

I have been ordered to the east, said Imladrik.

Good. I grow tired of the Annulii.

It is against my will. Duty compels me.

Draukhain let a long stream of fire wash over his body, rolling amongst it as he powered through the air. *I will never understand your obsession with duty.*

I know you won't.

You could disobey.

I could. It would break Ulthuan apart, and the druchii are not slow to take advantage of weakness.

At the mention of the dark kin, Draukhain let fly with a furious spout of smoke-edged flame. Nothing, save perhaps the daemons of the earth, was more likely to rouse a drake to fury than the mention of the druchii, who enslaved and broke dragons whenever they were able.

That is the one thing I will miss, sang Draukhain. *Every druchii that dies under my claws makes me live a little more.*

You may find some to kill in Elthin Arvan.

Not enough of them. But still – I am glad we are going. I will bring terror to the wilds.

Imladrik smiled grimly. Draukhain was perfectly capable of that. All the dragons under his command brought terror in their wake. They were perhaps the only weapons they had that the dawi didn't understand.

But dragons were not 'weapons' – he had admonished his brother for saying the same thing.

I will not fight this war the way he wishes me to, Imladrik sang. *He thinks the dawi will crumble on the first charge. I know they will not. I have seen their stone halls. We could break against those holds for eternity and they would never crack.*

Draukhain rolled to one side, pulling across a buffeting squall of wind and angling expertly along in its wake. *I would relish taking apart a hold*, he sang. *It would be vengeance for all my kind they have slaughtered. They think of us as beasts – did you know that?*

I did. And many asur think the same way about them. He looked up at the stars above them, cold, distant and uncaring. *That is the easiest step to take: to see one's enemy as an animal.* He thought of Thoriol, and winced inside. *None of us are brutes. We should not even be fighting.*

But we are. That cannot be changed now.

Perhaps, perhaps not. That shall be my first battle.

Draukhain began to sheer downwards, dragging his wings closer to the thick carpet of moonlit cloud. *So when shall we commence this? Shall I bear you to Elthin Arvan this night?*

Imladrik shook his head. *Not yet, great one*, he sang. His mind-voice became low, almost reluctant. *Did I say my first battle? No, I have one more ahead of me before I leave. Take me to Tor Vael.*

Yethanial awoke with the first rays of sunlight bursting through open shutters. She had slept poorly – just a couple of hours, her mind unable to break itself away from the worries that circled endlessly in her head. For a moment she stared groggily at the pale grey arched window. She could smell salt on the breeze, and something else too: charred metal.

She pushed herself free of the sheets abruptly, suddenly worried that something in the kitchens had been left to burn. Then she remembered what else in her life routinely smelled of a blacksmith's forge.

'My lady,' said Imladrik from behind her.

She turned to face him. 'How long have you been there?'

Imladrik came over to join her on the bed. 'Not long. I did not wish to wake you before the dawn did.'

Yethanial smiled cautiously. 'My lord,' she said and reached for him.

Imladrik pulled back.

Yethanial frowned. 'What is it?'

Imladrik rarely looked truly uncertain. He had an understated confidence that resonated with those around him; it was one reason why he was popular with his troops. In the absence of that, Yethanial felt her anxiety return.

'Where is Thoriol?' he asked.

'I thought he was with you, in Kor Evril.'

'He did not come back here?'

'No. What happened?'

Imladrik seemed to slump inside. 'He failed with a drake. He blames me. He may be right to. It was not the proper time.'

Yethanial reached for his hand. 'He will recover, though? It does not always succeed the first time – that is what you told me.'

'I do not know. For the first time, I begin to doubt.' He looked up at her. Again, uncertainty was etched deep on his face. 'He might never do it.'

'He is young. He can turn his mind to anything.' She tried to smile, to make light of it. 'Perhaps he might become a scholar. Would that be so bad?'

'It might have been something I did. Perhaps I pushed him too fast. The summonings come easily to me; I forget that others need more time.'

'You are hard on yourself. Did your father ever give as much time to you? You have devoted yourself to that child, and when he comes to his senses the two of you will speak and this will be forgotten.'

'We will not speak.'

'Why not?'

'Because I will not be here.' Imladrik's face took on a grimmer aspect; it was the way he looked before taking his leave for the next battle.

Yethanial withdrew her hand. Caradryel's final words to her entered her mind. 'What do you mean?'

Imladrik looked at her steadily. 'I have been ordered back to Elthin Arvan.'

Yethanial felt as if her stomach had been turned inside out. 'Refuse,' she said, her voice hard. 'Refuse him.'

'I cannot.'

'You can.' Her shock made her sharp. 'You can refuse anything you like. You command *legions*. You command mages, you command ships, you command dragons. Tell Caledor to finish his sordid war for himself.'

Imladrik looked back at her, his face an agony of understanding. He did not need to be told such things. 'That is why I cannot refuse. He will not change his mind. If I oppose him, my troops will remain loyal. War will come to Ulthuan. I will not see that.'

Yethanial wanted to rage at him. His resignation was infuriating. 'I don't believe you,' she accused, pushing herself angrily away from him. 'You could do it if you wished.'

'He is the King. He has the mandate of the Flame.'

Yethanial got out of the bed and strode over to where she had discarded her robe the night before. She wrapped it around herself. 'He is your jealous brother. He is a fool.'

'Listen to me.' Imladrik rose too. 'This is a chance to mend the damage he has done. He thinks that by sending me away I will be mired in fighting for years. He thinks I will do as he would, and take the fight to the dawi, but I will not. He does not know them as I do. I can end it. Think on it, Yethanial: I can *end* it.'

She shot him a scornful look, reaching up to tie her hair back. 'Did you think that up on your way here?'

Imladrik stiffened. 'Do not use those words.'

'And what words do you expect me to use?' she shouted, surprising herself with her vehemence. 'Do you expect me to say: my blessings go with you? Is that what you want? You will not get it! You belong here, with me, with those who love you.'

'You think I *wanted* this?' Some colour returned to his cheeks, some wounded pride.

'Yes! Yes, I think you did want this! Half your soul has been there, ever since you came back. You could not scrub its mud from your hands, you could never forget what you did there.'

'Yethanial, you are–'

'You could never forget *her*.'

As soon as she said it, she wished she could gulp the words back down and bury them deep. She stared at Imladrik, her mouth open, her eyes still flashing with anger. Imladrik stared back at her. Silence fell between them, tense and febrile.

'That was unworthy,' said Imladrik at last. His voice was soft, though it too resonated with anger.

'Was it?' asked Yethanial.

'If you understood me at all, you would know it.'

Imladrik pushed his cloak back from where it had fallen over his shoulder. His expression was dangerous – like a thunderhead curdling on the horizon. He said nothing more, just turned and walked from the chamber. As he left, he kicked the door closed behind him, making it slam and shiver in the frame.

Yethanial stayed where she was, frozen by the emotions running through her.

Why did I say it? she thought, as angry and confused with herself as she was at him.

Then she remembered Caradryel again.

He will be sent back to the colonies, my lady. Nothing can prevent it.

She rushed at the door, yanking it open and going after him. There were things she needed to tell him. Parting on such terms would leave a wake of bitterness. It would weaken him, and it would weaken her.

But by the time she had run down the stairways and across the empty hall and pushed her way through the great gates, she was too late. She stood on the wet grass, her robe rippling around her in the morning breeze, watching the long tail of Draukhain disappear into the far distance, already high out over the sea.

She watched the dragon for a little while longer, then the haze of the horizon defeated her.

'Sundered again,' she breathed, ignoring the shouted queries after her welfare from the guards on the walls. She heard them hurrying after her, no doubt with cloaks and hoods to ward against the dawn chill.

She felt cold to her soul, though the elements did nothing to worsen that. Some words, some thoughts, could not easily be taken back.

CHAPTER EIGHT

Caradryel sat alone. The ornate surroundings of Faer-Lyen's private dining hall surrounded him. A long polished table stretched away into the distance, set with polished silverware and decked with terraces of candles. He'd taken pleasure in such things in the past. Now they did nothing but expose his inadequacies.

He would have to find something to occupy him soon, some scheme or diversion. He might arrange an assignation at court – it had been a while – or manage the destruction of a rival's career. The arts of state were like a ritual game, with pieces scattered across the board in complicated webs of power. Move one, and the whole pattern shifted.

Caradryel was good at the game. He knew which cords to pull, which ears to whisper in, which beds to slip into and out of and which palms to press with gold, jewels or daggers. The fact that his father saw no value in such prowess was neither here nor there; slowly, with glacial patience, Caradryel had built up a formidable cadre of loyal retainers, dotted around the Houses like thieves in the basement of a

110   *Chris Wraight*

grand old mansion. One day he would call the favours in. It amused him sometimes to contemplate what would happen after that. Perhaps he would find himself exiled from Ulthuan in disgrace, perhaps end up on the Throne.

He knew the source of his ennui. The affair with Yethanial, he could see now, had been a miscalculation. It was no good trying courtly suavity on the likes of her – she was a scholar, a dealer in the purity of words and thoughts. He should have been more humble, less cocksure, then perhaps he might have swung it.

It was a shame. He had managed to persuade himself that a spell in Elthin Arvan would be just the thing; he could have ingratiated himself with his new master and extended his network of patronage to the colonies. He could have observed the war first-hand and gauged how best to take advantage of the many opportunities that such things invariably delivered. Most of all, he knew he would have enjoyed the simple pleasures of seeing something different. Even Ulthuan, the most spectacular and varied realm in all the world, became dull after a while.

He took a sip of wine, and a low chime sounded from the far end of the dining chamber.

'Come,' he said lazily, only mildly interested.

The doors opened and a servant padded in.

'Your pardon, lord,' he said, bowing. 'A lady awaits.'

Caradryel's lids barely lifted. 'Mirielle? She's early.'

'From Tor Vael, lord.'

Caradryel's heart skipped a beat. 'Khaine's eyes, you fool, show her in.'

By the time the servant had withdrawn, summoned Yethanial and brought her up to the dining chamber, Caradryel had seen that the table was cleared of food and the platters replaced with a heap of serious-looking scrolls.

He rose to greet her as she entered, affecting a look of disinterested welcome. Yethanial wore grey robes and a grey

Master of Dragons 111

hood, making her look almost ghostly. She didn't so much as glance at the piles of parchment he'd carefully arranged.

'This is a surprise, my lady,' he said.

'Is it?' she asked, her voice resigned. 'I thought you knew everything.'

'By no means. Are you well?'

Yethanial laughed sourly. 'He has gone. Just as you said he would.'

'Ah, I'm sorry. I didn't think it would come so soon.'

'I hope you can take some satisfaction from being right.'

'Believe me, that's not how I take satisfaction.' Caradryel motioned towards a chair. 'Will you sit?'

'I had much to think about after he left,' said Yethanial, ignoring the offer. 'At first I determined to ignore you. I supposed that if, as you told me, knowledge of Caledor's orders was widely shared, then you were nothing more than the boldest of any number of gossip-merchants.'

Caradryel bowed humbly.

'But then I gave the matter thought,' she went on. 'I have a tendency to disregard your sort. I find the games played in Lothern tiresome, and so assume that all the highborn do. This has evidently been a mistake. Perhaps I should have paid them more attention, and thus avoided a snare.'

'I am flattered that you think so.'

'I asked around about you. Believe it or not, I have contacts of my own, some of whom have the ear of the powerful.'

'I do not doubt it. What did they say?'

'Listen to me now. Do not interrupt. My husband is heading to Elthin Arvan alone. He wishes to end the war, not to prolong it, and for this reason those already there will resist him at every turn. He has respect from those who fight but few allies among those who command. You offered your services to me. Having no better options, I am taking up the offer. I wish you to go to Tor Alessi and work for Tor Caled. I can pay you anything you wish.'

'That will not be nec–'

'I said do not interrupt. If you accept, you will be required to perform three duties. First, advise the Lord Imladrik. Follow his commands, see that he achieves what he has set out to, give him sound counsel. Second, report back to me on all matters of import. Ships ply between Lothern and Tor Alessi, so this should not be difficult, though do it secretly. My husband is no schemer. You may struggle to understand this, but he has a noble soul and will do nothing unless he sees the good for Ulthuan in it.'

'So I under–'

'Third, I wish to hear details of anything concerning the dragon riders. There is a mage among them, her name is Liandra. At one time she and my husband... worked together. No doubt she is still active in the defence of the colonies. Other riders will follow my husband to Elthin Arvan, and they should be watched too. Make this a priority. Dragon riders are a strange breed, hot-blooded and affected by the wills of the beasts they ride. They must not have influence over him.'

'Liandra? Of the House of Athinol?'

Yethanial gave him a wintry smile. 'You seem well-informed. I hope, for your sake, that you are. I find this work, this *deception*, distasteful. It would not take much for me to change my mind and call a halt. Should you prove unequal to the challenge, or should you not fulfil these orders in every particular, I shall have no hesitation in cutting you off and leaving you stranded there.'

'I have no doubt of it.'

'Make no mistake, Caradryel of Faer-Lyen: when in the right mood, the Lord Imladrik is the most dangerous warrior of this age of the world. Though I may not look it, I have strengths of my own and am quite capable of visiting retribution on those who would harm us. We make a formidable pairing, and we will continue to do so, whatever fleeting

Master of Dragons 113

difficulties may come between us. You should be aware of this before agreeing to take the assignment. You should be aware of your peril.'

Caradryel had to fight to stop himself smiling. The notion, so recently entertained, that he might struggle with boredom over the coming months now seemed impossibly quaint.

'I understand,' he said, his face as serious as his mood was buoyant. 'And I have already given the matter all the thought I plan to. So here is my answer: you may consider me, my lady of Tor Vael, your most humble servant.'

Liandra strode along the curving corridors of the Tower of Winds. The quality of the stonework around her was finer than at Kor Vanaeth, but still far cruder than that found in Ulthuan. Tor Alessi was the largest and the mightiest of the asur settlements in the east, but it still couldn't mimic the elegance found in her race's homeland. The whole place had been built for defence, with three concentric circles of high walls and heavy bulwarks over the gates, and the aesthetics had suffered as a result. The city had been besieged three times since the war had broken out and each battle had left its scars. In the lulls between fighting the walls had been made thicker and higher, every time further ruining what symmetry remained.

The Tower of Winds stood at the westernmost point of the city, where the walls ran up to the sea and enclosed the deep harbour below. It had survived mostly unscathed, being too far from the perimeter for the dawi's catapults and stone-throwers to make much impact. Even so, the lack of finish in its interior spoke of the hard times that had fallen on the city. Metal finishings had been stripped out and melted down for weapons, glass had been pushed out of window frames and replaced with iron grilles, sacred images of the gods had been removed from their proud stations on the walls and taken into the catacombs for safekeeping. What remained in place was stark, functional, pared-down.

For all that, the white stone still shone in the light of the setting sun, and the banners of the gathered armies still fluttered proudly in the sea-wind. The city had never been more heavily populated – as the principal landing for the Phoenix King's armies, it hummed with the constant tramp of soldiers' boots and the clatter of unloading cargo.

Tor Alessi was battered, roughened at the edges, but still proud.

Like us all, thought Liandra.

She reached the twin doors to the Council Chamber, where two Sea Guard sentries waited on either side. They pushed the doors open immediately, and she went inside.

The Council Chamber took up the full width of the Tower's topmost storey. The floor was polished marble, deep black and veined with silver, and the rune Ceyl had been engraved in the centre of the floor, picked out in iron and inlaid with pearl. Five thrones surrounded the rune, each one facing inwards, each hewn from obsidian and surmounted with the crest of a royal house. Sunlight poured in through narrow barred windows.

Four of the thrones were occupied: Lady Aelis of House Lamael, Lord Salendor of House Tor Achare, Lord Caerwal of House Ophel and Lord Gelthar of House Derreth. One remained to be filled.

'Welcome, Liandra,' said Aelis, rising from her throne. The Mistress of Tor Alessi was wand-thin, with dark hair pulled back from an austere face and bound with silver wire. 'We are glad you decided to make us complete.'

Liandra bowed. 'I was honoured to be asked,' she said, taking her seat as Aelis resumed hers. 'Have I missed much?'

'We were waiting for you,' said Salendor. His stocky frame made him look too big for his seat, and his dun-red cloak was still caked with mud, as were his tall leather boots. His magestaff rested loosely in his hand.

Master of Dragons

'I came as swiftly as I could,' she said. 'Much needed to be done at Kor Vanaeth.'

'You wasted your time, then,' replied Salendor. 'It will never stand a second attack.'

Liandra retained her composure. She knew what he was doing; in a way, it was a compliment. *He tests me. He wishes only warriors on this Council.*

'We will be ready, when they come again,' she insisted, her voice quiet but firm. 'We have been blooded once, and may bleed again, but we will never retreat.'

They held one another's gaze for a moment, her blue eyes locked with his. Then he grunted and looked away.

'That is why we are all here,' interjected Aelis calmly. 'We know they are coming again. A month, a few weeks, maybe. The question is: how shall we respond?'

Liandra stole a glance at the other two members of the Council. Caerwal and Gelthar were both the very image of asur nobility: slim, impeccably dressed, their robes lined with gold and their lean faces placid. They did not look like they would rush into battle with the relish of Salendor. For that matter, they did not look like they would do anything with relish.

So that is how this works: Salendor and myself are the hotheads, they are the cautious, and Aelis will adjudicate.

'We have more power in Elthin Arvan now than when the King was here,' said Gelthar, speaking ponderously. 'We must install the legions here, in Athel Maraya, Athel Toralien. Then we wait.'

Salendor snorted. 'We *wait*. Your counsel never changes, Gelthar. What would it take to prompt action from you?'

Gelthar remained implacable. 'Why give up our advantage? Let them wear themselves out in endless sieges.'

'Each siege has cost us,' said Liandra.

'It has,' said Caerwal bitterly. 'Gods, it has.'

'And when did this become the asur way of war?' demanded

Salendor, exasperated. 'This is craven counsel.'

Gelthar pursed his lips. 'Enlighten us, then. What is yours?'

Salendor sat forward in his throne. 'Muster the legions at Athel Maraya. Strike now. Meet them under Loren Lacoi before they get to us here.' He shot a furtive glance at Liandra, as if already looking for her agreement. 'They move slower than a crippled carthorse. We can choose where to engage them, how we engage them.' He smiled rakishly. 'If we choose, we can *crush* them.'

Gelthar sniffed. 'Your counsel, too, never changes.'

Aelis looked at Liandra. 'Your people have suffered as ours have. What is your view?'

Here it is. My chance to play the part assigned to me.

'My view?' she asked. She could feel Salendor's impatience, and ignored him. 'It is this: whenever our race has been threatened, we have ridden out. We have never waited for our lands to be burned first. We are the masters of the world; if we do not defend what is ours, then we do not deserve the title.' She allowed herself to look at Salendor and caught the look of approval in his face. 'We must strike first. Caledor has bought us this brief lull. Let us use it.'

Salendor could barely contain himself. '*Hear* her, my lady,' he urged Aelis. 'It is only caution that keeps us back. They sowed the seeds of this war; now let them reap the harvest.'

'And throw away our greatest asset,' said Gelthar wearily. 'The walls they have never yet breached.'

'We *wither* inside them!' cried Salendor.

'They preserve us,' said Gelthar.

'They did not preserve Athel Numiel,' said Caerwal coldly. 'It had high walls, but they did not stop the slaughter there. They *murdered* my–'

'Enough.' Aelis held up her hand again, stilling the argument. She inclined her head to one side, as if listening for something.

'Do not stifle–' started Salendor, but Aelis silenced him with a glare.

Master of Dragons 117

'Be still,' she said. 'Do you not hear it?'

For a moment, Liandra sensed nothing. The first thing she noticed was a tremor in her mind-harmony with Vranesh. She felt the dragon's sudden emotion flowing into her body, as if the resonance of a musical instrument had made the hairs on her neck rise. The sentiment was a powerful one; at first, she assumed it spoke of alarm, and she half-rose in her seat.

Then she discerned its true character – *joy*, of a pure kind, like a child recognising its mother and rushing to greet her.

By then the noises that Aelis had heard had become more obvious. From far below the Council Chamber, dim but growing in volume, crowds were crying out in fear and wonder.

Liandra pushed herself from the throne and rushed to the western wall of the chamber, followed by the others. She pulled open a pair of doors leading to the tower's balcony and stepped out into fresh air.

The five of them lined up on the balcony's narrow platform, suspended high above Tor Alessi's narrow, teeming streets. Below them, a tangle of whitewashed buildings crowded and clustered its way towards the harbour, a half-ring of stone enclosing a basin of deep blue water. Dozens of warships swayed on the waves, their masts seesawing as they were buffeted. Across the entire city, from the high ringed walls to the summits of its many spires, tight-packed throngs peered up into the skies.

High over the harbour, buoyed by the downbeats of splayed wings, six dragons hovered in mid-air. Vranesh shot up to greet them, snaking around the newcomers and sending columns of flame shooting out in elation.

Liandra knew the dragons' names: Rafuel, Khalamor, Gaudringnar, Telagis, Mornavere. Their mind-voices sang to her like a choir, overlapping and pushing against one another. They were magnificent, as huge as watchtowers and blazing with colours: gold, emerald, ivory, amethyst, wine-red. The air around them shimmered with heat and magic, as if they had carved their way into the realm of the senses from beyond the veils of madness. For all that, they were no daemon-kind – they were flesh, bone and blood, as superb and pristine as fallen stars.

All the drakes carried riders, each one wearing heavy plate armour and carrying a rune-tipped blade. They were nearly as splendid as their steeds, and she knew their names too: Heruen of Yvresse; Cademel of Eataine; Selegar, Teranion and Lania of Caledor. She could sense their gathered power, filling the air around her and making it tremble.

One drake hovered apart from the others, and they all paid deference to him. The mighty Draukhain arched his long neck high, holding perfect position with ease. Sunlight flashed from his sapphire hide, making it dazzle and shine like a coat of ithilmar. Even from such a distance Liandra could smell the burnt backwash of his movements. The furnace of his lungs sent out curls of fire and smoke like garlands; the aroma was almost as familiar to her as Vranesh's.

Atop Draukhain's churning shoulder-blades sat the Master of them all, the scion of the Dragontamer, the one whose name she still hesitated to recall lest it brought pain back with it. She tried to look away, but it was futile; her eyes were drawn ever upwards, scanning up to the silver armour with its black runic warding, the crimson cloak that draped across dragonhide, the naked longsword. She thought for an instant that she caught an intense flash of green eyes under a heavy silver helm, and had to grip the railing of the balcony to keep her poise.

She had forgotten the aura of power that he carried with him. None but a fellow dragon rider could truly know the command Imladrik possessed; only one of their esoteric fraternity could understand what it took to earn the allegiance of a creature like Draukhain.

Master of Dragons

119

Once, long ago, Vranesh had told her how her own kind saw Imladrik.

He is the dawn and the dusk, she had sung, respectfully, with none of her usual flippancy. *He is the sun and the moon. Where he goes, we will go; when he passes, so shall we. He is the kalamn-talaen. He is the Master.*

Liandra tried to look away, and failed. She felt old emotions rising to the surface, breaking the mask of certainty she had learned to wear over the last thirty years.

Salendor, standing at her side, seemed to feel nothing but elation. He turned to her, his face alive with fresh hope. 'Imladrik!' he cried. 'Drakes! The King has sent us rare weapons! Now the dawi shall know fear!'

Liandra tried to smile. All she could think about was the figure atop the sapphire dragon: what he had been to her before, what his return to Elthin Arvan foreboded.

'They are not weapons,' she said faintly, her heart already twisting in anguish.

II
DRAGONFIRE

CHAPTER NINE

The time had come.

The wait had passed quickly by the reckoning of his people, but still every day spent in preparation and argument had seemed like an age. The mountain-realm was huge and sprawling, home to hundreds of holds, mines, bulwarks, citadels and quarries. It took time to reach them all, to pass on the news, to wait for anger to boil up within the deliberate minds of the dawi.

But now the time had come. Given enough of it to consider the wrong, given enough to reflect on it and compare it to the wrongs of the past, they became angry. They started muttering in the deep places, hammering away at the walls in unsettling rhythms. They chanted in the lightless halls and stoked the eternal fires of the forges. They smelted iron and beat gromril, they marched along the winding ways of the Ungdrin, they poured out onto the causeways of the great Karaks, their faces masked by helms, accompanied by the booming call of war-horns.

He had kindled a fire in the deep vaults. Then he had

watched it grow, rippling out into every corner of the dawi empire until it became a roaring inferno. The Lords of the Dwarfs had been roused from their torpor. No dissenting voices had been raised, no old grudges had been unearthed, no rival claim to the leadership of this anger had emerged. They were united in slow, cold fury and the rock itself rang from their ironshod treads. A dozen armies already marched; more would follow.

The time had come.

First hundreds came, then thousands, then tens of thousands. His own host snaked along the ice-bitten road to Karaz-a-Karak and down towards the forest-lands of the elgi who had brought such hatred upon their own heads.

Morgrim Bargrum, kin of the High King, cousin to the slain Snorri Halfhand, the Uniter, the one they were already calling the Doom of the Elves, stood on a high spur of rock and watched his army grind its way west.

The sky above him was leaden and bloated with rain. Lightning flickered across the northern horizon, broken by the massive shoulders of far peaks. Dull light glinted from chainmail, from axes, from the tips of quarrels and from the iron of the great standard poles.

Morgrim rested on his axe-handle, his chin jutting and his beard spilling over his crossed hands. His bunched-muscle arms, each one tattooed and laced with scars, studs and iron rings, flexed in time with the tramp of boots. His heavy helm sat low on his brow, pocked with precious stones and draped with a curtain of fine mail.

Like all his kind, he was hard, angular, solid, immovable. The cross-hatch rune *zhazad* had been daubed on his forehead in his own blood, now dried a dark brown by the chill mountain wind. His eyes glittered darkly under the shadow of furrowed brows. His boots were planted firmly, locked against the stone as if one with it.

The host was immense. Not since the days of forgotten

Master of Dragons

wars had so many of the dawi marched under one banner. Many of them had torn their beards, ripping hair from flesh in savage mockery of what had been done to the ambassadors in Ulthuan. Many more had painted their armour plates with blood, just as Morgrim had done. Dwarf blood was thick. It dried fast, cleaving to steel like lacquer. Even as the rain fell, coursing over hunched shoulders in runnels, those bloodstains remained vivid.

Morgrim watched his regiments creep down towards the lowlands. He watched the tight squares huddle together, ringed with shields and toothed with speartips. He watched grim formations of longbeards, roused from their lethargy by the anger he had birthed. They marched slowly, their grey eyes fixed unwaveringly on the horizon, their lips unmoving. He watched smaller formations of bulkier warriors covered from head to toe in thick plates of gromril, clanking like infernal machinery. He watched hammer-holders stride down the causeway, each one thronged around a great lord of battle. He watched heavy battle standards swinging among them, all adorned with the runic emblems of holds picked out in gold and bronze.

It was just one army of many. More would follow, gathered together in the booming halls of deep fastnesses and sent forth into an unsuspecting world.

All of this Morgrim watched in silence. It was not an army of containment, or of exploration, or of defence. It had no other purpose than destruction.

In my name, cousin, he mouthed silently. *You will be avenged.* The time had come.

'*Tromm*, lord,' came a throaty voice at his shoulder. Morgrim did not need to turn to see who it was.

'*Tromm*, Morek,' he said, all the while watching the host march on. It would be many hours before the vanguard cleared the foothills, and many more hours before the rearguard passed his vantage. 'Have you come to summon me down?'

'Summon you? I would not dare.'

The Master Runesmith was far older than Morgrim. His beard was flecked with grey like the down of a hunting peregrine, and his eyes were sunk deep into leather-tough skin the colour of burnished copper. He carried an ancient runestaff topped with gromril and wore master-crafted armour of interlocking plates.

'Look out on them,' said Morgrim, his voice as gruff and spare as a *drakk*'s exhalation. 'Look at what we have done, then tell me: what does your heart say?'

Morek did as he was bid. He cast his deep-set eyes over the slowly moving host. It looked like a river of molten iron creeping down the flank of the mountains. As the light began to fail and the shadows lengthened, the iron darkened.

'It says that this thing cannot be stopped,' Morek said. 'It tells me Halfhand did not die in vain. He saw through the elgi – even his father did not see so clearly. They set this fate in motion, they shall bear the pain of it.'

Morgrim grunted. He could feel the dull thuds of a thousand footfalls, echoing up through the stone beneath his feet.

We have made the mountains tremble.

'I did not want this,' Morgrim said, his voice low and dark, as it had been ever since Snorri had died. 'Let the records state that.'

'They will.'

'But now it is settled, I feel the blood of the ancients grow hot within me.'

'As do we all.'

Morgrim bared his teeth – a tight, warlike grimace, one that made the lined skin of his face crack and flex. 'My axe thirsts.'

Morek glanced at the blade. Its runes were inert. 'It has not been proved yet.'

'You made it. It will answer.'

Morek hawked a gobbet of spittle up and spat on the ground. 'And Drogor?'

Morgrim's expression briefly faltered. 'What of him?'

'Where is he? None have seen him for months.'

'I care not.' Morgrim found the mention of Drogor an irritant. He did not want to be reminded of that baleful presence, one that had hung around his cousin like the stench of carrion. There had always been something strange about Drogor, though it had been hard to say quite what it was. His eyes had been… dull.

'He came from nowhere,' said Morek. 'Now he returns to nowhere, and no one, it seems, wishes to speak of it.'

'I never liked him,' said Morgrim dismissively. 'Snorri listened too closely to him. Those who remain are pure.'

Morek pursed a pair of cracked lips. 'That they are – for now. But beware: your armies will hold in one piece only as long as their anger remains. You must bind your thanes strongly until they can face the enemy. Even Gotrek struggled to control them, and while he remains grieving he cannot help you.'

'Fear not,' growled Morgrim, his slab-heavy face glowering under the sky. 'They sought a leader, one who would deliver their axes to the elgi. With Snorri's passing, that is all I live to do.' His lips twisted into a half-snarl then, disfiguring features that had once been mild-tempered. 'I will permit the elgi to leave these shores, if they choose the path of sense. But if they stay to fight, then I swear by Grimnir I will choke them all in their own thin blood.'

Morek nodded sagely.

'That would be worth seeing,' he said, his voice thick with relish.

Imladrik stood before the Council of Five. They regarded him with a mix of wariness and awe. At least, four of them did; the fifth didn't lift her eyes from the floor.

'So here we are together,' said Aelis, clasping her hands. 'At last.'

Imladrik regarded her coolly.

She thinks I should have made this Council my priority. Let her think away; the world has changed, and they will have to get used to it.

'My apologies for the delay,' he said. 'You'll understand I had many things to detain me.'

The chamber around them was deep in the Old City, down in the heart of the first colonists' settlement. The stonework was more refined than in the Tower of Winds, the wood more cleanly carved, for it had been raised in a more carefree time when the thought of war between close allies would have been impossible to conceive.

'You have kept us waiting, my lord,' said Salendor. 'We have armies garrisoned here, in Athel Maraya, in forward stations. All they need is orders.'

Imladrik knew he had to be careful around Salendor. The warrior was clearly itching for a fight and no doubt saw him as the one to deliver it. Imladrik could sense the brutality coiled within him, the eagerness to spill blood, and he could also sense the fine-honed mind, the moral clarity. Salendor was a serious proposition, but a dangerous one.

'I know where our armies are,' Imladrik said. 'And they will wait a little longer for orders.' He turned to Aelis. 'The defences here are impressive. Everything you have done is impressive. I have not come to sweep it away and start again – I am here to work with you, not against you.'

'That is good to hear,' said Aelis. 'We have not always had… wise governance out here.'

Imladrik just resisted the temptation, nagging away at him since he'd entered the chamber, to glance over at Liandra. She hovered, dressed in crimson as ever, on the edge of his vision. They had not spoken since his arrival. Though he would never have admitted it to anyone, that was the true reason he had put off meeting the Council – Yethanial's words still burned in his memory.

'There has been division between you,' Imladrik said. 'This cannot continue – we must speak with one voice.'

'We have all we need,' said Caerwal. 'One choice remains: to meet them here, or march east and face them in the wilds.'

'The judgement is a fine one,' said Aelis.

Imladrik could sense Liandra's mind-voice on the margins. He didn't need to ask what side of the debate she was on. 'Yes, it would be,' he said, 'were we committed to war.'

Silence followed that. Imladrik waited for his words to sink in.

'My lord,' started Salendor cautiously, 'we have been at war for nearly thirty years.'

'Hardly,' said Imladrik calmly. 'We have been shown only a tithe of their strength.'

Salendor looked perplexed. 'These are the opening moves of the game. We are ready for what will come.'

'We are ready?' asked Imladrik. 'You sound sure. I hope you are. I hope you remain sure when your woods begin to burn. I hope you remain sure when our people begin to die in earnest, and I hope you remain sure when the corpses are piled high between the ocean and Karaz-a-Karak.'

Salendor looked taken aback. Still Imladrik did not seek to catch Liandra's eye.

'This is a lull,' Imladrik continued. 'My brother's victory wounded them, but we know it will not last. You gave me two choices, but I give you a third: pull back from the precipice. Close the wound. Talk to the dawi.'

Again, silence. When the next voice broke in, Imladrik had to work hard to keep his expression neutral.

'They will not listen,' said Liandra.

Her speech was just as he remembered it – hard-edged, louder than most, flavoured with the rough tones that spoke of a long time away from home. For a moment he could have been dragged back in time, to the long conversations they had shared while on the wing together, the tips of their steeds' pinions nearly touching. He could have recalled how her mind-voice had sparred with his, approaching that strange intimacy that a dragon rider shared with his steed.

It was harder than he had expected, to hear that voice again.

'You are sure?' he asked, unwilling to contradict her directly. Not yet.

'With respect, we have tried this,' interjected Salendor, clearly making an effort to retain his temper. 'They do not talk. They slaughter.'

Caerwal also looked unconvinced. 'That is the truth. If you had been here during these last years–'

'I have been in the colonies longer than any of you,' said Imladrik firmly. 'I founded Oeragor in the east before the towers of this city were raised, beside which thirty years away is nothing. You are free to dispute with me, Caerwal, but never presume that I know not of what I speak.'

Caerwal looked chastened, and fell quiet.

'War may come,' Imladrik went on. 'It may be too late to prevent it, but I will try. That is my first order: keep the defences in order, but no armies will march. Messages will be sent to the dawi. Snorri Halfhand is dead, but I knew his cousin in happier times – if I understand anything of them, he will be the first to seek vengeance, and of all of them he was always the mildest.'

Salendor shook his head in frustration. 'Your brother killed Halfhand. You know how they are – his rage will blind him now. The father, too.'

'Perhaps,' conceded Imladrik. 'If so, it will be a mark against us, for Snorri was a noble warrior when I knew him. For that reason I will make the attempt. We *must* make the attempt: we cannot be as blind as them, for we are the children of Aenarion and the fates hold us to a higher standard.'

Master of Dragons

He saw Aelis looking at him doubtfully. None of the others spoke in support of him. He had not expected them to do so; this counsel was always going to be unpopular with those who had suffered most.

'Then how will you achieve this?' asked Liandra. The tone of her voice was strange. 'The dawi kill any of us they come across, even under banners of truce. The rules of war have long since ceased to apply in Elthin Arvan.'

Imladrik turned to her. Her face was just as he remembered it – framed by a shock of copper hair, pale and vigorous, her blue eyes rich and glittering.

'It will not be easy,' he admitted, 'but no paths are free of danger, and I will not believe their minds are fully closed, not yet, not until I have seen it with my own eyes. They were a proud people, one in which honour once dwelt.'

'So you always counselled,' replied Liandra, 'even before the war started. Things change, though, my lord. People change.'

Imladrik held her gaze. 'The core of them remains the same. That never alters.'

'Does it not, my lord?'

'It cannot.'

They looked at one another for a little longer. Imladrik thought she might speak to him directly, mind to mind, just as they had once done freely.

In the event, she said nothing, and her eyes fell away.

'If this is the will of the Crown,' said Aelis slowly, breaking the awkward silence, 'then of course it shall be done, just as you command.'

Imladrik nodded. 'Good. Then our business is concluded here. This is our last chance for peace, my lords; let us ensure it does not fail.'

'And, despite all, if it should?' asked Salendor sceptically.

'Then, my Lord of Tor Achare, you shall have the slaughter you desire,' said Imladrik wearily. 'And when that is done, when the world lies in ashes around us, we can reflect at length on what follies may be committed by the wise, and what horror may be unleashed by those who once only worshipped beauty.'

After the Council had dispersed Imladrik made his way to his chambers. He had taken up residence in one of the smaller towers, pressed tight against the inner wall as it curved round towards the harbour. Its windows faced west, back across the seas to Ulthuan. The accommodation within was modest: a few rooms in the lower levels in which to receive guests, a couple more devoted to charts and ledgers, a private suite at the summit in which he slept and meditated.

Tor Alessi's citizens treated him with a muted reverence. They parted to allow him passage along the narrow streets. Mothers brought their children out to witness his presence, as if that would confer some sort of protection on them. Soldiers bowed low; mages doffed their staffs.

He found the whole exercise ridiculous and irritating. His father, ever the consummate mythmaker, had appreciated deference, viewing it as an essential tool of kingship. His brother loved it for other reasons – it eased the constant doubt that nagged at his jealous soul. Imladrik, who had never wanted anything more than solitude and the clear air of black-flanked mountains, had come to hate it. In that, at least, he was of a mind with his wife.

Yethanial had been in his dreams ever since he had left Tor Vael. After their last meeting he had headed first to Lothern to take counsel from the commanders of the fleet, then to Caledor to summon his dragon riders. Only then, days later, had he embarked across the ocean at the head of the speartip of drakes.

In the days since then he had thrown himself into making sense of the sprawling web of armies committed to the

Master of Dragons

defence of the asur territories. Communications in the wilds were difficult and estimates of the enemy strength, their movements and deployments, were confusing and contradictory. All that had kept him busy, which was good.

But if his days were full, his nights were empty. He would lie for hours on his shallow bunk, knowing sleep was far away, remembering Yethanial's look of reproach. He would turn her words over in his mind endlessly, worrying at them, picking them apart. He had never felt more alone. Draukhain was no comfort; like all dragons, he found mortal attachments trivial.

They are a fortunate breed, Imladrik thought. *To care only for freedom, to care nothing for confinement. As for us, we are nothing but the sum of our confinements.*

Imladrik reached the doors to his tower. The guards bowed low long before they needed to.

'My lord, tidings from Ulthuan,' reported one of them, a tall Sea Guard officer with a competent, soldierly look. 'Sent by swift dispatch from Cothique.'

Imladrik raised an eyebrow. 'Very swift. What news?'

'A single passenger. He awaits within. I checked his credentials.'

'Very good. No disturbances, please.'

'By your will.'

Imladrik passed inside and the doors locked closed behind him. Though he could not see them, he knew that archers had been stationed all around the tower. Units of spearmen were deployed nearby and a mage was on duty at all times in a neighbouring spire, all of them watching against attack. Centuries of warfare, open and clandestine, against the druchii had made the asur protective of their commanders.

His guest waited for him in the room beyond the entrance hall, lounging in a low chair by the fire. As soon as Imladrik entered he got to his feet, showing off a flurry of damask robes decorated with fabulously complicated images of serpents and seawyrms. His hair was straw-blond and arranged impeccably across slender shoulders. His face had a certain sharpness to it, but his smile came readily enough.

'My Lord Imladrik,' he said, bowing floridly.

Imladrik looked at him steadily. 'You were sent from Ulthuan? Who sent you?'

'I sent myself.'

Imladrik drew a seat up before the fire.

'You had better explain.'

'My name is Caradryel of the House of Reveniol, latterly in the service of Tor Caled. Though you will not remember it, we have met before. You did me the not insignificant service of saving my life when our ship was attacked by druchii. That placed me in your debt; since then, I have been searching for a way to repay it.'

Imladrik regarded Caradryel doubtfully. His speech was polished, but there was something… slippery about it.

'Latterly, though, I was fortunate enough to be presented with a way to remedy matters,' Caradryel went on. 'I learned you had no counsellor. This is, you might say, my speciality. I have a facility for the arts of state – negotiation, diplomacy, persuasion and inveiglement. I flatter myself, but to my mind there really is none better. So there it is: in this, you have my service.'

Imladrik couldn't suppress a twitching smile. Caradryel had front, that was certain.

'Interesting,' Imladrik said. 'Perhaps you can tell me why I should prefer your service to my officials stationed here, all of whom have sworn oaths to the Crown and to my security?'

Caradryel shrugged. 'They are competent enough, no doubt. Two things count against them. First, they are loyal to the Crown, not to you. I have no especial fondness for your royal brother, if I am truly honest, but have every personal reason to see you prosper. You might even say that it has become my vocation.'

'And the second?'

Caradryel smiled. 'None of them are as good as me. Not remotely.'

'You are not short of confidence.'

'Modesty is a waste of everyone's time.'

'I know someone who would agree with you,' said Imladrik. 'Myself, I have always thought it the mark of nobility.'

'I make no claim to be noble. Far from it. Still, I am the best offer you'll have out here.'

'So you clearly believe.'

'Perhaps you should ask how I got myself in here. Do you really think I had anything like the right credentials? Other supplicants have been waiting days for an audience and yet I arrived on the quayside yesterday evening with little more than the clothes on my back.' He smiled to himself, drawing a few tattered leaves of parchment from his robes' pocket. 'Your guards are thorough and honest, but they need to check the provenance of official seals more carefully. Honestly, I could have been *anyone.*'

'So you are a trickster,' concluded Imladrik. 'Tor Alessi has a thousand of them. Work quickly: your audience is drawing to its conclusion.'

Caradryel nodded to himself. 'You dislike subterfuge. Easy enough, for someone who can walk into any chamber in Ulthuan he pleases, though it has its uses for the rest of us. Here, though: perhaps this will speak more eloquently on my behalf.'

Caradryel took one of the leaves of parchment and handed it over.

Only a few words had been written on it, in a clear, elegant hand that Imladrik recognised only too well.

* * *

Though we parted at odds, my thoughts remain with you. The bearer of this message comes with my blessing. He is boastful and tiresome, but will serve you. Y.

Imladrik looked at it long and hard. Though none but he would have known it, the Eltharin characters had been written in such a way as to conceal a second meaning amid the words, something that Yethanial had long delighted in doing. *Trust him*, the hidden text said, lost amongst the swirls and loops of the runic script.

'Boastful *and* tiresome,' said Caradryel ruefully. 'I thought that a little harsh.'

'She finds the company of most people tiresome,' said Imladrik, reading the message again. 'Do not take it personally.'

Seeing Yethanial's calligraphy before him sharpened the sense of loss. He could imagine her, bent low over the writing desk, painstakingly drawing each character with the attention to propriety and order that characterised all her work. Beauty existed in everything she did – the kind of raw, bleak beauty that was prized in windswept Cothique.

'We spoke at length before I set sail,' said Caradryel. 'She understood what I understand: that Tor Alessi is a den of wolves, ready to tear apart your plans as soon as you make them clear.'

'My wife does not concern herself with statecraft.'

'Perhaps not,' said Caradryel, 'but she is a good judge of character. I approached her thinking I would persuade her easily; by the end, I was the one being examined. She is a formidable soul, if you will forgive me saying.'

'She is. She always has been.' Imladrik leaned back in his chair, feeling fatigue bite at his shoulders and wondering what to make of the figure before him. 'If she had not vouched for you, all your honey-tongued words would have made little difference. But she did, and so you give me much to think on.'

Master of Dragons

Caradryel's face become serious. 'Think on it as much as you wish, my lord, but time is not on our side. I know what is happening here. I know that you wish to halt the war, but most in this city do not – they will work to frustrate you at every turn, even as they smile to your face and bow before you. You cannot fight them openly, because they will not contest you openly. Salendor is one; there may be others. If you truly wish to bend the city to your will, then we need to act now.'

'I have done so. The orders have been issued.'

'Ah, but will they be carried out?'

Imladrik smiled coldly. 'Have a care, Caradryel. I am not some simpleton ripe to be lectured – I am your master. Remember that.'

'Master?' asked Caradryel, slyly. 'So we do have an arrangement?'

'Perhaps. Some tasks that need to be performed are difficult; I had not yet decided who to assign them to. One in particular might serve as a test: perform it well, and I will look on your application with favour. I need to contact someone. It must be done quietly, and it must be done quickly. It will be dangerous.'

'Perfect,' said Caradryel. 'Who?'

'His name is Morgrim Bargrum,' said Imladrik. 'He was a friend, once.'

'A dwarf?'

'If our scouts have it right, he is marching towards us even as we sit here. He will not be coming to talk.'

Caradryel smiled, though a little less assuredly. 'A challenge, then. We will have to change his mind.'

'To change a dwarf's mind,' Imladrik remarked dryly. 'If you can achieve that, my friend, then I may start to believe your boasts.'

⤙ CHAPTER TEN ⤚

Thoriol woke late. The sunlight hurt his eyes and he squinted against it, holding his hand up to the window. There were no drapes. He had no idea why.

He felt sick, as though the floor were pitching under him, and let slip a weak groan of wine-sickness.

He opened his eyes wider, getting used to the glare slowly. It was then that he realised the floor really was moving. For a few moments he had no idea what was happening. A stab of panic shot through his stomach.

Then he smelled salt, saw the narrow window in one wall of the chamber, and felt the rough planks of decking beneath him.

At sea, he realised, which made him scarcely less panicked. *How, in the name of Isha…?*

He pushed himself into a seated position, head hammering from the rush of blood. The wine-sickness at least was no illusion – he felt like vomiting.

So he did. He managed to get to the far corner of the tiny cabin before his guts rebelled, then retched for a long time, leaving a foul puddle of saliva-strung bile against the curved wall of the ship's hull.

Finishing made him feel only a little better. His whole body felt shivery and feverish. He had a dim recollection of a female elf with silk-like hair offering him something, but he couldn't remember what it was. It had smelled good, that he did recall.

Hands shaking, he clawed his way back to where he'd awoken. He'd slept in his robes, the same ones he'd worn coming down from the Dragonspine. He peered cautiously at the window again. The movement of the horizon made his nausea worse.

What day is this? How long have I been asleep?

He got to his feet, bracing uncertainly against the movement of the cabin around him. The space was barely big enough to house him and he cracked his head on the low roof. Cursing, he fumbled for the clasp on the door. After a few false starts, he managed to push it open, and staggered out into a larger space beyond.

Three figures turned to face him, all seated around a long table covered in charts. Leaf-shaped windows ran down the two sides of a larger cabin, each running with spray as the ship pitched.

'Good morning,' said one of them, looking at Thoriol with a smile.

Thoriol stared back at him. The elf had strangely familiar features: a scar on his right cheek and a blunt, tanned face. For a minute he was taken back to that evening in the House of Pleasure. How long ago was that? Last night?

'Who are you?' Thoriol managed to blurt out. He had to grasp the doorframe to keep from falling. 'Where am I?'

The elf with the scar motioned to his companions, who rose silently and left the cabin by a door at the other end. Then Scar-face beckoned Thoriol to join him at the table.

'Come,' he said. His voice had an earthy quality, rich with

the accent of Chrace. 'You look like you could use a seat.'

In the absence of better options, Thoriol tottered over to the table, collapsed onto the bench and slumped to his elbows.

'Who are you?' he asked again, feeling like he might be sick a second time.

'Baelian.'

Thoriol stared stupidly, wondering if that should mean something to him. 'That all?'

Baelian shrugged. 'What do you want to know? This is my ship. The archers aboard are my company. As are you, of course.'

'As am I,' Thoriol repeated. He felt thick-headed. Some of what Baelian said resonated faintly with him, as if he'd dreamed of it a long time ago. 'I have no idea what has happened, but I warn you, sir, my father is–'

'Yes, you explained all of that,' said Baelian. 'Do you not remember?'

Thoriol managed to summon up the energy for a cold look. 'Obviously not.'

'You had taken a lot of it. Your first time, perhaps? It can do that to the unwary.'

As Baelian spoke, some recollection began to filter back through Thoriol's addled mind. *The dream-philtre. The poppy.*

'How long have I been out?' he asked nervously.

'Three days.'

Thoriol felt dizzy. He stared at the rough grain of the wood, trying to latch on to something certain. 'If you have taken me against my will,' he said, as deliberately as he was able, 'you will suffer for it.'

Baelian laughed. He pushed back, hands behind his head. 'Do I look like the kind? This is what you *wanted*, lad. You may not remember it now, but you will.'

As Baelian spoke Thoriol began to have the horrible feeling that he had done something very rash. His memory

142   *Chris Wraight*

began to come back in slivers – he recalled speaking to Baelian in the House, watching the scar with fascination in the light of the lanterns.

'Why don't you remind me?' Thoriol suggested. 'That might save some time.'

'As you wish.' Baelian reached across the table and rifled through some leaves of parchment before drawing one out. He pushed it across to Thoriol. 'Your scroll of warrant. You signed it before we left Lothern.'

Thoriol stared at the sheet. It was covered with a dense screed of runes and had a wax seal at its base. Just above the seal he could see his own scrawled handwriting.

'We spoke for a long time,' explained Baelian. 'You wanted to escape, I made you a proposal. You were very keen to take it up. It'll all come back in time.'

'What does this mean?' Thoriol asked, struggling to decipher what he'd been given – the words seemed to swim before his eyes.

'You are a member of my company of archers. You've had the training, you know how to use a longbow. The pay's good, and in gold. You'll get it, too: ask anyone. Nothing to worry about, lad. You wanted to escape, and this is your chance.'

Thoriol ran a shaking hand through his blond-grey hair. His nausea got worse with every revelation. Some of what Baelian told him resonated, some of it didn't.

'You took advantage,' Thoriol accused, putting as much authority as he could into his voice. 'I was not in my right mind. You have no hold over me.'

Baelian looked amused. 'Is that right? That's not what the parchment says.'

'I had taken a… dream-philtre.'

'A dream-philtre? I'm shocked. You know they're prohibited?'

Thoriol looked up into Baelian's eyes and saw the mockery there. 'So that's how this works.'

Master of Dragons

Baelian sighed. 'Look, lad, this can be as easy or hard as you make it. You're one of the company. You can't change that, not until I release you, but you're no slave. Like I say, you'll be paid, you'll be trained. The captains aren't too picky about who serves these days, not with two wars running at once, so you'll be fine. Anyway, I look after my own.'

Thoriol barely listened. Already thoughts of his father's vengeance were running through his head. He guessed that this Baelian didn't fully understand who he'd taken on; telling him again would do no good, as he'd surely not convince him now. A familiar voice of derision echoed through his head.

You are a failure. You have failed again. And this time you are on your own.

'So where are we going?' he asked. He had to plan, to think, to recover. He was of the House of Tor Caled, the lineage of the Dragontamer – something would turn up.

'Where do you think? Where the fighting is.'

For a moment, Thoriol had a terrifying vision of Naggaroth – a land he had only heard about in hushed whispers. He knew that his father had campaigned in the seas off the frozen coasts, and there were rumours that asur raiding parties had penetrated the interior. Even before Baelian spoke again, though, he realised how stupid that idea was.

'The *colonies*, lad,' said Baelian. 'A long way from Ulthuan. You should be happy – you can make a fine fortune in the east, and whatever you're running away from back home won't follow you out there.'

Thoriol nodded wearily. So that was that – a single night's indiscretion, and he'd allowed himself to be hoodwinked into a stint in the wilderness. Once the ship made landfall he'd have to think hard on how to get out of it.

'Tor Alessi?' he asked, trying to picture how the next few weeks were likely to unfold.

'Where else?' said Baelian. 'Or, as you'll start to think of it soon, home.'

Thoriol smiled acidly. The stench of vomit was beginning to seep from his cabin, mirroring his mood. It was hard to think of a way in which he could have got things more badly wrong.

Of course, there was one silver lining; though by means he'd never have chosen, he was getting almost as far away from his father as possible.

That was something.

'You will *break!*' screamed Drutheira, slamming her staff on the rock at her feet.

Bloodfang reared up before her, forty feet in the air, its body snapping and twisting like a fish caught on a wire. Flames gusted and flickered, covering the black dragon in a nimbus of ash and light.

From her cliff-edge vantage high over the northern scarps of the Arluii, Drutheira could see its anguish – its jaws were twisted and torn, its eyes stared wildly. Every so often it would swoop down, flames licking at the corners of its mouth, ready to snap her up in a single bite.

She stood firm, staff raised and feet apart, knowing the creature could not break its magical bonds. Bloodfang would always pull out at the last moment, doubling back on its length, screaming with frustration and shooting back into the sky.

The beast's misery radiated out in front of her, a pall of anguish that seemed to stain the air itself, the agony of a great and noble mind laid to waste by the slow arts of the Witch King. Though she knew little of dragon-lore, she understood well enough what a mighty feat it must have been to enslave one of the famed fire-drakes of Caledor.

She wondered what exactly must have been done to break its spirit. Had it been raised from an egg by Malekith and tortured from birth? Or had it somehow been lured into the Witch King's clutches once full-grown and imprisoned

Master of Dragons 145

in secret? She could not imagine what torments must have been applied, perhaps over decades, to turn what had been born as a creature of ecstatic fire into such a twisted, ruined horror.

Bloodfang's wings were ragged and punched with holes. Some bore the marks of hooks or iron rings. Its scaly hide was dull, as if caked with soot. Only its eyes still flashed with intensity – they were a white-less silver, and were painful to gaze at for too long.

Black and silver: Malekith's favourite colours. Truly, he had left his imprint heavily on the world.

'Break!' she commanded again.

Purple-edge lightning forked out from the tip of her staff, crackling around the hovering dragon and causing it to roar in fresh pain.

'You *know* my voice now,' hissed Drutheira, applying more power to the halo of dark energy dancing around her. 'Resisting will only bring you *more pain*.'

Bloodfang screamed at her, flicking the barbed point of its tail within a few feet of her face. Pain was the only thing its ruined mind truly understood.

Drutheira withdrew the sorcerous lightning, freeing Bloodfang from the lash of it for a few moments.

'Come, now,' she said, her voice softer. 'This can end. What remains for you, should you resist? You cannot go back to your kind now – they would rend you wing from wing. We are your guardians now. We are your protectors.'

That made Bloodfang scream again, though the strangled tone was different – almost a sob, albeit one generated from iron-cast lungs. Its wings beat a little less firmly; its body writhed with a little less frenzy. Its huge head, gnarled with tumours of black bone and horn, slumped lower.

Drutheira smiled. 'That is better. We may yet come to understand one another. Come closer.'

Malchior and Ashniel were nearby – she could sense their

sullen presence – but neither came out into the open, for they had neither the power nor the will for this work and did not wish to risk inflaming the dragon more than necessary.

It hates us, thought Drutheira as the battered creature sank a fraction further in the sky. *It hates us, and needs us. Truly Malekith has excelled himself with this: he has taken our self-loathing and given it form.*

She lowered her staff and the last of the lightning flickered away, dancing across the bare stone like scattered embers. Drutheira took a single step towards the dragon, which continued to descend even though its fear and anger had clearly not gone away.

'Give in,' Drutheira urged.

Despite herself, she couldn't resist admiring the beast's damaged magnificence. Up close its sheer size was daunting. It stank of charred flesh and old blood, every downdraft of its wings sending a charnel mixture of ancient kills to waft over her. The thought of enslaving such power was faintly ridiculous – the beast could slay her with a casual twitch of its talons.

But it wouldn't. That was the genius of sorcery.

'Give *in*,' she breathed, watching the long neck bow in exhausted submission before her.

It came closer. She saw long trails of hot tears running down its cheeks and almost let slip a cry of joy. Her whole body tensed, ready for the most dangerous moment – Bloodfang's will had been ground down further, but the spark of rebellion had not been entirely extinguished.

Just a little closer, she thought, inhaling deeply as the wings washed pungent air across her. *A little… closer…*

Bloodfang's jaws reached the level of her shoulders. She snatched the staff up again and it blazed into purple-tinged life. The dragon tried to jerk away but it was too late – snaking curls of aethyric matter locked on to its neck, lashing fast like tentacles.

Drutheira launched herself into the air, leaping high and pulled upward by the crackling lines of force. The long whips of coruscation acted like grapple-lines, hauling her onto the creature's bucking neck and over to the rider's mount at the junction of its shoulders.

It all happened so quickly; before Bloodfang could lurch away from the cliff-edge Drutheira had straddled its nape. She planted her staff firmly, driving the spiked heel into the dragon's flesh. It screamed again, snapping its body like an unbroken steer's, trying to dislodge the goading presence on its back.

'Ha!' roared Drutheira, her eyes shining. She held her position, hanging on tight to the wing-sinews that jutted out on either side of her.

Bloodfang raced into the air, corkscrewing up into the heavens, screaming all the while in an incoherent mess of anguish. The wind raced past, pulling Drutheira's white hair behind her and making her robes ripple wildly.

She grabbed the golden chain that ran from the dragon's huge neck and yanked as hard as she could. Bloodfang's collar jerked back, wrenching the drake's head up and slowing its ascent.

Drutheira felt a hot surge of elation. The beast's scent filled her nostrils; its agony filled her mind. She could almost hear the creature's inner voice echoing in her own thoughts – a jumbled, maddened stream of half-thoughts and half-words.

'You know your master!' she cried, seizing the staff again with her right hand and twisting the spike in further.

Bloodfang roared in pain, but its spasms grew less violent. It came around, swinging back towards the cliff edge. Below them the land fell away in a steep drop towards the range's northern fringes. Drutheira caught glimpses of huge swathes of land spreading out into the distance – tracts of forest bisected by the grey ribbon of a mighty river snaking west towards the sea. The view thrilled her. Never before had she

148   *Chris Wraight*

seen so far. It felt like she was the queen of the earth.

Far below, she saw Ashniel and Malchior creep from their hiding places to stand and gawp at her. She laughed to see that – they looked tiny, like insects crawling across dirt.

'And what do you say now?' she cried, hoping her voice would carry over the continued bellowing from her enraged mount.

They said nothing. Perhaps they could not hear her, or perhaps they had nothing to say. Drutheira turned away from them, uncaring. She had the vindication she needed: the dragon had been broken again. It would take time to learn how to command it properly, to force it to fight again, to trust it to respond to her commands.

In the meantime, the ascent into the heavens continued to make her heart beat with elation. She yanked on the chain, forcing Bloodfang to climb higher. The mountains extended out below her, a rumpled landscape of broken granite and snow-streaked summits. The wind around her was as cold as Naggaroth, as pure as hate.

Unbreakable, she thought to herself, sensing the massive power undulating beneath her and already planning what she would do with it. *Unstoppable.*

Sevekai crouched low, feeling his boots sink into the soft earth. They had been badly worn by the months he had spent in the wilds – the leather had split along the soles, letting in water and irritating the sores that clustered on his feet.

He was still sick. His chest gave him spasms of pain every time he breathed and his left leg was badly swollen. Vision had only properly returned to one eye; the other wept constantly. He was famished, chilled, often delirious.

For all that, things had improved since his awakening at the base of the gorge. Water had been plentiful in that dank, sodden chasm, so his strength had returned in gradual slivers,

Master of Dragons 149

eventually enabling him to drag himself down under the cover of the trees. Refusing to countenance even the possibility of dying, he had grimly pulled himself like a worm along the forest floor, sniffing out anything that looked remotely edible.

He had had some successes – a thicket of wild rythweed that he'd been able to chew on, followed by a collection of sour crab apples left rotting under wind-shaken boughs. He'd made some mistakes, too: an appealing clump of milk-white fungi bulging in the shadow of a rotting log had made his stomach turn and given him blinding headaches and two days of vomiting.

Still, with every tortured step he'd taken since then a little more of his native strength had returned. His ordeal had begun to feel almost like purification – his body had been driven down to a whipcord-lean frame of sinew. When he stooped to drink at a stream, he saw a sunken, cadaverous visage staring back at him from the water and only slowly recognised the reflection of his own face. Everything came to him vividly, as if the world had been scrubbed clean and somehow made more real.

When not travelling he slept for long periods, drained by even the most mundane tasks. When he slept his dreams were lurid. He saw Drutheira in them often, and imagined they were still together.

'I am glad you survived, my love,' she told him.

'Where are you?' he asked.

'Far away,' she said. 'Keep moving. Keep walking.'

Sevekai did as his dreams commanded. Sometimes crawling, sometimes limping, he picked his way down from the gorge. The landscape of the Arluii never stopped being unforgiving: as soon as he negotiated one rock-filled defile he would be faced with a fresh wall of broken cliffs. Get around that, and he would have to plunge back into thick tangles of knotweed or negotiate treacherous, icy river-courses. A circlet of blunt peaks reared over him the whole time, vast and uncaring, cutting off the light of the sun and making his bones ache from the cold. He began to hate them.

Time passed in a strange way. He started to suspect he was sleeping for much longer than he ought to. Sometimes he would awaken and the world around him would look altered, as if too much time had passed, or sometimes not enough. Whenever he saw more clumps of mushrooms he ignored them; even his ever-present hunger did not make him desperate enough to risk more sickness.

Gradually, painfully, the severity of the mountains began to lessen. He staggered into a hinterland rising from a bare land of blasted grass and tumbled boulders. The wind moaned across them, snagging at the stone. He stumbled onwards, barely noticing which direction he was heading in, his feet falling in front of one another in a numb, automatic procession.

When he finally dropped to his knees he was faintly surprised to feel soft earth under his flesh, not rock. He lifted his head groggily and saw a hillside running away from him, fading eventually into a wide valley studded with scraggly vegetation. He twisted his neck to peer over his shoulder, back to where the outriders of the Arluii loomed up hugely against a darkening horizon.

Where am I? he asked himself, knowing that he had no means of answering.

He looked back down the slope. Ahead of him, a few hundred yards away, the scrub began to thicken into the tight foliage of Elthin Arvan's forest country. The further he went, he knew, the thicker it would get. Elthin Arvan was covered in forest, a cloak of wizened and grasping branches.

Such landscape was all he knew of forests – few trees grew in Naggaroth, and he was too young to have witnessed the blessed glades of Avelorn. When Drutheira had scorned the ugliness of the east, Sevekai had seldom understood her;

Master of Dragons   151

next to the icy wastes of home, Elthin Arvan was teeming with life. Something about the smell of it appealed to him – the mulchy, sedimentary tang that never left the air.

He curled his fingers into the earth, watching the black soil part between them.

I can barely remember Naggaroth. And if I could… He smiled grimly, making his swollen gums ache. *Would I want to go back?*

A sudden noise ripped him from his thoughts. He instantly adopted a defensive crouch, ignoring the protests from his tortured limbs. For a few moments, he couldn't see what had made it.

He screwed his eyes tight, scanning the scrubland before him. His left hand reached down for the throwing dagger strapped to his boot. He hadn't heard the sound of a single living thing since waking. The sensation was strangely unnerving. His heart raced; his hand trembled slightly.

Then it came again, from ahead of him and to the left, a hundred yards away, lodged amid the jumble of bushes and boulders – like a hoarse cough, but far lower and richer than a druchii's voice.

Slowly, Sevekai crept towards the sound, keeping low, staring hard at the thicket of branches ahead. The lessons of his long training returned to him. His heart-rate slowed; his hands stilled.

Then he saw it: a stag, standing still amid a thicket of briars. It was young, its limbs slender and its flanks glossy. It looked directly at him, antlers half-lowered in challenge, nostrils flaring.

Sevekai froze. He could smell its musk and the scent made him salivate – it must have been weeks since he'd eaten more than berries. He clutched the hilt of his dagger tightly, preparing his muscles to throw.

Something nagged at him. Something was wrong. The stag just stood there, watching him. It should have bounded away, darting back into the cover of the trees.

Sevekai reached down gingerly and pulled a second dagger from his belt. A blade in each hand, he slunk a little closer, keeping as low and silent as possible.

He needn't have bothered. The stag stayed where it was, perfectly aware of his presence. Two black, deeply liquid eyes regarded him steadily. Its ribcage shivered as it breathed.

What are you waiting for?

Sevekai paused. Everything felt disconnected, as if he was in a dream. He sniffed. He picked up no taint of Dhar, but then he hardly had Drutheira's facility for sensing it.

A few more steps and he was into throwing range. He hesitated for a moment longer, perturbed by the creature's lack of movement.

Something is wrong.

Then, sharp as a snake-strike, he threw. The first dagger went cartwheeling through the air before *thunking* heavily into the beast's shoulder. The stag buckled, baying, and at last kicked free of the briars.

By then Sevekai was already moving. One hand loosed the second dagger, the other reached for a third. Every throw was perfectly aimed: one after the other, the long steel blades bit deep, carving through the beast's hide.

The stag managed to stagger on for a few more yards before tripping over its buckling legs and collapsing heavily to the ground. Sevekai caught up with it, grabbing it by its shaggy nape and using the last of his blades to slit its throat. He pulled the knife across its flesh viciously and a jet of hot, wine-dark blood gushed out, drenching his clothes.

The smell of it intoxicated him. He grew dizzy, both from the exertion and from the thick, viscous musk enveloping him. He reeled, falling down against the animal's heaving shoulders.

Blood splashed against his chin. Almost unconsciously, he sucked greedily on it. As soon as the hot liquor passed his

Master of Dragons 153

lips he felt a sudden swell of energy. He plunged forwards, cupping his hands under the torrent and gulping more blood down.

The thick, earthy taste of it made his vision swim, but he kept going – it felt as if life were flowing into his limbs again, heating him, strengthening him. He drank and drank, tearing at the wound's edge with his teeth, gnawing at the raw flesh in his famishment.

He did not stop until the flow had slowed to a dribble and the stag's eyes had gone glassy. Then he pulled free, his hands shaking again, chin sticky with residue.

He felt nauseous. He sank down on his haunches and stared about him. The empty land gazed back, still scoured by the wind, still as broken and grey-edged as it had been. In the distance loomed the Arluii, a wall of solid darkness against the low sky. Behind him, the land fell away into the bosom of the gathering woodland.

It took a long time for his breathing to return to normal. Practical thoughts began to enter his head – to make a fire, to butcher the carcass, to preserve more for later, to clean the blades.

He did none of those things. He just sat, his face and hands as bloody as Khaine's. Something like vitality had returned, though it was bitter and hard to absorb.

The blood of the land.

He didn't know where those words came from. They entered his head unbidden, just as so much had entered his head unbidden since the fall.

Now you have drunk the blood of the land.

He began to shiver again, and wondered if some of the poison from his blades had got into the stag's bloodstream. His stomach began to cramp, and he curled over, coiled up next to the corpse of the stag in a bizarrely tender embrace. A curtain of shadow fell across his eyes. The shaking got worse. He tried to still his teeth's chattering, and failed.

So cold.

His eyes fluttered closed, his fists balled, his neck-cords strained. Cradled amid the limbs of the beast he had killed, Sevekai screamed. Then he screamed again.

It was hard to tell how long the screaming lasted. He nearly blacked out from it, but when the spasms finally eased he found he could lift his head. Lines of saliva hung, trembling, from his bloody chin.

Ahead of him, no more than ten paces distant, a crow was perched on a briar. It stared at him just as the stag had done, eerily unmoving.

Sevekai looked at it for a long time. Then, without quite knowing why, he held up his hand. The crow flapped across, alighting on his wrist and digging its talons in.

'Well met, crow,' said Sevekai, his voice cracked and hoarse. It sounded like someone else's.

The crow nodded its sleek head. Then, unconcerned, it began to preen.

Sevekai got to his feet. His head was light but the worst of the blood-agony had passed. He stood for a while, looking down into the valley, holding the crow like a falconer holds his hunting-bird.

For the first time, perhaps, in many years, something like certainty descended over him.

'It has changed,' he said, surprising himself. 'Blood of Khaine, everything has changed.'

CHAPTER ELEVEN

The chamber was dark, lit only by a few wall-mounted candles. Four bare walls enclosed an empty stone floor, a single door served as entrance and exit, and there were no windows.

Liandra waited impatiently. It was hard to resist the urge to pace up and down, like some prisoner in a cell. It wasn't just her current surroundings; ever since arriving at Tor Alessi she had felt confined. The huge city bore down on her, shutting her in, cramping her movement. Every so often she had fled the walls for a short time, taking Vranesh out on the sudden, vigorous flights the dragon loved. They had circled high up, going as far east as they dared, hoping against hope to see the first glimpse of the dwarf army marching through the forest.

But she could not always be on the wing. Membership of the Council brought duties with it: fresh troops arriving at the harbourside every day, and every shipful needing to be garrisoned and supplied.

It had initially been exhilarating to see the huge strength of the asur legions being landed at Tor Alessi. It had felt for a time as if the real power she had craved for so long had finally fallen into her lap.

That feeling had not lasted. She was not in command, not truly; Imladrik gave the orders, locked away in his isolated tower overlooking the sea, taking no advice and heeding no requests for fresh Council meetings. The enormous strength at his disposal was kept behind the walls. No armies were sent out into the wilds. No regiments were spared for outlying fortresses such as her own Kor Vanaeth.

For a long time she had held her tongue, biding her time. Surely, she reasoned, Imladrik would come to her. As the long days passed, however, it became clear that he would not.

Liandra had almost gone to the tower herself. She had walked halfway there, rehearsing what arguments she would make to him.

'Kor Vanaeth can be defended,' she had planned to say. 'Give leave for two regiments, that is all – two regiments and a battery of bolt throwers. The rest I can manage.'

She had never made it. As she had walked, her pride had got the better of her. Liandra had never begged, not even to him. Her father, still in Ulthuan fighting the druchii, had taught her that. If Imladrik had softened and turned away from the sacred savagery of his calling, then that was his loss; she would play no part in it.

Since then she had made no fresh attempt to contact him. She had festered, her frustration with enforced inaction growing with every wasted day. At times it felt like her heart was hammering at her ribcage, inflamed by imprisonment.

If he had not come back we would be marching by now, she thought, watching the candles burn low. *If he had not come back, the battles would have started.*

She heard a noise outside the door. Boots shuffled for a moment, then a key rattled in the lock. The door opened, exposing a cowled silhouette.

Master of Dragons

'Did anyone mark you?' asked Liandra.

'What do you take me for?' replied Salendor, slipping inside and closing the door. He pushed the cowl back, revealing coarse, battle-scarred features.

'As yet, I don't know,' said Liandra irritably. She hadn't wanted a meeting with him, not outside the confines of the Council and certainly not in the city, but Salendor was not an easy person to delay for long.

'I know your mind, Liandra,' he said, leaning against the wall. 'You and me, we are spirits of the same temper.'

'So you believe.'

'I can see it in your face. You chafe here. You've fought the dawi, just as I have, and you know what must be done.'

'And if I do?' Liandra stared at him defiantly. 'What does it matter? We have our orders.'

Salendor laughed. 'You care nothing for orders.'

Liandra bristled. It was tiresome to have a reputation for impetuosity, forever likely to tear off on some reckless charge into danger. Doubly so when it was true.

'Dragon riders,' Salendor went on casually. 'Gluttons for bloodshed, the lot of you. All but him. Why is that?'

'He is capable of it,' said Liandra.

'So they tell me, but I've seen no evidence. If not for his bloodline, I might suspect he had no stomach for a fight.'

'Then you would be a fool.'

Salendor shot her a shrewd look. 'None know him better than you, eh? I heard that too. Tell me, what passed between you when he was last here?'

'Why did you wish to see me, Salendor?'

'You know why. Peace is not possible. He might put off war for a few months, maybe years, but not forever.'

Liandra said nothing. Salendor was right, of course, but there was no point in confirming it.

'So we have two choices,' Salendor went on. 'First, we can change his mind.'

158   *Chris Wraight*

'Impossible,' said Liandra. Despite herself, a little sadness sank into her voice. 'Trust me, there is no turning it.'

'Then you know what must be done: we make other arrangements.'

'That could mean anything.'

'It means *acting*,' said Salendor. 'He can talk with them for as long as he wishes, but there will be no peace if we do not allow it.'

'You would not dare.'

'*We*, Liandra. You and me. Forget the rest of the Council – they would not stir if the world was ending around their ears. Gelthar is obsessed with defence and Caerwal... I do not understand Caerwal. His people have been butchered and still he hesitates. But you know the truth – we are *warriors*. We have already blooded the dawi, we will do so again. Think on it: my forces will follow my orders. Add yours, and near half the armies of Tor Alessi would march on our word.'

Liandra closed her eyes wearily. She could already see images parading before her – legions of spearmen coursing through open gates, picking up speed as they charged towards dug-in ranks of iron and bronze, surmounted by the raging wingbeats of dragons sweeping east. She saw herself at the head of it, as glorious and unstoppable as Isha, festooned in flame and underpinned by fields of steel.

'You do not know me,' she said softly.

Salendor lost his smile. 'What?'

Liandra opened her eyes. 'If you came here asking me to oppose him, then you do not know me.'

'So you spurn the offer.'

'It is no offer!' she said, her eyes flashing with anger. 'You give me nothing but revolt, something the humblest archer captain would blush to consider. I had heard you were a tactician, my lord, not a gutter-thief.'

Salendor pushed clear of the wall, suddenly looking dangerous. 'You dare to–'

Master of Dragons

'I dare nothing!' cried Liandra. 'And neither do you – we are just following our instincts, doing what we were trained to do. Do you think Imladrik is a simpleton? His troops would fight for him until their last breaths – *none of them* will stir to support you. You might as well ask them to fight with the druchii.'

Salendor took a single step towards her, his right fist clenching. For the first time Liandra saw just how powerfully built he was. 'Then you are in his thrall, just as I feared,' he said. 'What were you, then – his lover? His whore?'

'Say no more,' hissed Liandra, her own fists balling. A stray flicker of fire rippled over her flesh. 'I swear by holy Isha if you say another word I will kill you.'

They stood facing one another, hearts beating powerfully, eyes locked together. Liandra saw the desperation in Salendor's battle-scarred face. For a moment she thought he might goad her further, just to test whether her threats meant anything.

Then, slowly, grudgingly, he backed down. 'They were unworthy words,' he muttered. 'I should not have spoken them.'

Liandra unclenched her own hands, feeling the burn from where her fingernails had dug in. He had dragged her close.

Salendor shook his head with frustration, looking like he wanted to punch the walls. 'But by Khaine,' he spat, 'he drives me to it. He does not answer my pleas. He will not bend. He will damn us all.'

Liandra looked at him coldly. All at once, Salendor's rage seemed ignoble to her, like the rantings of a child kept from his sweetmeats rather than the noble fury of a son of Ulthuan.

'You have said what you came to say,' she said. 'No word of it shall come from my lips. Now go.'

Salendor hesitated. 'I will not make the offer again,' he warned.

'You should not have done so now.' Liandra ran her hands

through her hair. She felt weary, tainted. Despite the insult, some of what he had said hit near the mark. 'Salendor, I know why you suffer. On another day, in another war, perhaps I might have listened. But know this: I can never oppose him.'

Salendor looked at her grimly. 'So there it is. I made the attempt.' He started to leave, then halted. 'He has some hold over you, I see that. I will not ask you again, but beware. Memories are a poor guide.'

Liandra didn't reply. Salendor shrugged, withdrew down the length of the chamber and stalked back outside.

She waited for a long time after that, standing still as the candles burned down, leaving a suitable interval before following him out into the city. She had lost track of time and had no idea whether the sun had gone down.

It didn't matter. Salendor's words still echoed in her mind.

He has some hold over you, I see that.

Perhaps he had, once, but that was a long time ago. The more she thought about it, the more she doubted whether it had ever been true.

Caradryel rode uneasily. The guards Imladrik had sent to escort him were from his own personal retinue: Caledorian, each with a dragon-winged helm and riding a powerful black charger. Twenty rode within Caradryel's eyeshot; twice that were in bow-range, fanning out through the trees in a wide, almost silent arc.

Even to Caradryel's untrained eyes they were quite obviously deadly. Their captain, a sour-faced killer named Feliadh, had made no secret of his contempt for his feckless-looking charge. Feliadh had ridden ahead during the entire journey, conversing with his troops in a local dialect and avoiding standard Eltharin. The days had thus passed in a procession of weary, wordless rides followed by lonely and windswept camps.

Master of Dragons

Every so often the party would encounter bands of scouts returning from the east. Some looked relatively unscathed; others had been savaged, down to one or two survivors. Feliadh would ask them for news, which was always the same.

'They're on the march,' the scouts would say, voices wary. 'They're cutting down the trees as they come. We couldn't see an end to them. No end at all.'

Feliadh would calmly ask them the most direct route towards the dawi vanguard, ignoring the incredulous looks on the scouts' faces.

'If you really wish to…' they would begin, and then reluctantly offer directions.

Caradryel had lost count of how many such encounters they had had. Six, seven, maybe. With each one they passed a little further away from the security of Tor Alessi's hinterland and a little further into the dark, uncharted morass of Loren Lacoi.

The Great Forest, they called it. 'Great' referred to its size, not its beauty. Caradryel had been prepared for neither: the utterly huge expanse, nor the stinking ugliness of it. His horse's hooves sank deep into sucking slicks of mud. They ploughed through swarms of biting flies and had to cut through choking walls of briars. Strange noises welled up out of the shadows, echoing in the murk like laughter.

It was worse at night. Caradryel slept badly, huddled in his damp cloak and trying not to hear the whoops and calls of the distant gloom.

'Why are we fighting over this?' he muttered once to himself.

Feliadh overheard him. 'You have not been to Athel Maraya, my lord,' he said.

'Should I have?'

'Lord Salendor's realm,' Feliadh said, his voice full of admiration. 'Filled with the light of a thousand lanterns. Only Avelorn is more beautiful. One day this whole forest will be as Athel Maraya is now.' He glanced around them, scanning across the gnarled and bloated knuckles of the tree-branches. 'That is why we came here: to turn this filth into something that reflects honour to Asuryan. Do you not see that?'

Caradryel grunted something like agreement, though the pious tone in Feliadh's voice annoyed him.

That had been days ago. Since then they had pressed on, skirting south of the sprawling port-city of Sith Rionnasc and along the northern shores of the wide River Anurein. On the south-western horizon loomed the distant Arluii; ahead of them was nothing but forest.

They came across no further bands of scouts, and no living settlements. Once they passed through an abandoned Kor, its walls black and broken. Another day they stumbled across mine workings, long since deserted though still bearing the angular runes of the dawi over heavy stone lintels. Feliadh went cautiously through the ruins, wary of an ambush. None came. The war had driven its old inhabitants away long ago, just as it had in all the smaller dwellings. Now only the great fortified cities remained – islands in a sea of unbroken wilderness, guarded by high walls and watchful towers.

They passed into a long, snaking valley overshadowed by marching terraces of pines. A stream, half-stopped with rocks and silt, ran uncertainly down its base. Above them the sun struggled to clear a screen of white-grey cloud, casting grey light weakly over a dripping vista.

Caradryel shivered. Feliadh remained up ahead, his shoulders rolling easily with the gait of his steed. The Caledorian horses trod with uncanny skill, making almost no sound as they moved along the valley floor. The only noise was the faint moan of distant wind and the crack of twigs under hooves.

He tried to relax in the saddle. The trek was beginning to exhaust him. If it went on much longer, he might have to speak to Feliadh and demand a change of tack.

The first quarrels came out of nowhere – the first Caradryel

Master of Dragons 163

knew of them was when a Caledorian outrider bent double, clutching at his breast and coughing blood.

The guards around him immediately drew their blades.

'Truce!' Feliadh roared, his harsh voice outraged. The captain's standard-bearer brandished the white flag wildly.

Caradryel struggled to control his mount. More quarrels scythed across the open space, sending the beast into a panic. Cries rang out as the darts found their targets. Caledorian outriders spurred their horses up the slopes, seeking out the sources.

'Where *are* they?' Caradryel blurted out loud, drawing his sword but seeing nothing to attack. The enemy must have been dug in, waiting for them with the patience of statues.

'We come under flag of truce!' shouted Feliadh again. Caradryel saw him spur his horse onwards, pushing further down the valley. He made no attempt to hide.

Typical Caledorian, thought Caradryel grimly. *More bravery than brains.*

He dug his heels in, forcing his skittish horse to stagger up the stony incline away from the river. Pine trunks surrounded him, mottled with shadows. He heard the dull *clink-thunk* of a crossbow mechanism working. Without thinking, he threw his body forwards, causing his steed to stumble. A dart whistled past his left shoulder, tearing the fabric of his cloak.

Caradryel hauled on the reins, yanking his mount's head around. For a split second he thought he caught a glint of armour in the undergrowth, but then it was gone, lost in a swirl of movement and shadows.

The Caledorian knights were more successful in unearthing hidden attackers, and the clash of steel against iron rang down from the upper slopes. Caradryel heard one of them shouting out an Eltharin battle cry before it was drowned by a sudden shout of *Khazuk! Khazuk!*

Nothing was in the open; everything was hidden. The Caledorians made heavy work of the defence, hampered by the trees and the terrain. Caradryel saw another one go down, the shaft of a quarrel shivering in his neck, but others gained higher ground and began to hunt down the crossbowmen.

'Truce!' bellowed Feliadh from further ahead, his voice increasingly forlorn amid the cries of aggression from all around. More quarrels fizzed between the trees, some clanging from shields or thudding into the trunks.

A few moments more and the encounter would be a blood-bath. The dawi either couldn't hear Feliadh or didn't care. Caradryel felt fear rise up his throat, ready to choke him. That would be a disaster – only he had the means of preventing a slaughter, and he was almost too scared to try it.

'Khazukhan!' he cried, standing in the stirrups and flinging his cloak back. If a dart were aimed at him now, he'd stand no chance. 'Imladriki a elgi tarum a grikhaz Morgrim Bargrum! Morgrim Bargrum! Imladriki a elgi!'

Almost as soon as the words left his mouth, a horn sounded from high up the valley slopes. It was an unearthly sound – a brazen dirge that made the ground vibrate.

The rain of quarrels stopped immediately. Some of the Caledorians responded with cries of victory, thinking their counter-charge had routed the attackers, but Feliadh was astute enough to see what was going on.

'Hold fast!' he ordered, hauling his own steed round and hastening over to Caradryel's position. 'Do not pursue! Pull back!'

The rest of the riders did likewise, drawing together again, their swords still drawn and their manner wary. Three did not return; several more carried wounds or dented armour plates.

For a long, terrible period, nothing happened. The dwarfs seemed to melt back into the earth. The wind moaned down the valley, the needles rustled in the pines.

'What was that?' whispered Feliadh, keeping his eyes on the forest around them.

Master of Dragons

'Honest answer?' replied Caradryel, his heart still beating hard. 'I'm not exactly sure. Imladrik made me memorise it.'

Feliadh raised an eyebrow. 'Well memorised, then.'

Another horn-note sounded, a fraction higher, still with the thrumming reverberation that seemed to lodge in the bones. All around them, from just a few paces away to a hundred yards up the wooded slopes, dwarfs rose from the undergrowth. There must have been over a hundred of them.

'By the Flame,' breathed Feliadh, gazing at them.

Caradryel felt slightly sick. The trap had been artfully laid. If the Caledorians had kept up the pursuit they would have been overwhelmed, however bravely they fought. He had never seen such a display of stealth.

The dwarfs said nothing. They stood like graven images amid the bracken. Caradryel found it hard to tell one from another: they were all stocky, broad-shouldered, bearded and clad in thick plates of armour that overlapped across their burly chests. Dark eyes glinted from under the brow of iron helms.

Now that he saw them in the flesh, Caradryel at last understood some of what Imladrik had told him in Tor Alessi. When the asur called them the 'stunted folk', that implied something missing, something unfinished. He saw how false that was: they were almost as broad as they were tall, as sturdy as tree-roots and as heavy as ingots of pig-iron. They stared back at him without the slightest shred of fear or wonder. No doubt existed in those dark stares, just disciplined, regimented hatred.

They will never forgive, he realised. *They will never give in. They do not know how to.*

Eventually, one of dawi made a move. The dwarf broke ranks and waded towards them through knee-high undergrowth that reached his waist. His beard was steel-grey, plaited and folded up in a baroque array of knots and tassels. His exposed biceps were a patchwork of scars, tattoos and iron studs. Unlike the crossbow-wielders, he carried a war-hammer, the head of which was beautifully engraved with runes and dragon-head knotwork. His helm was open-faced and crowned with drake-wings just like the Caledorians, though his were bulky and blunt in comparison.

When he was a few paces away he rested the hammerhead on the ground before him, folded his hands over the hilt, and leaned on it. His eyes, sunk deep under bristling brows, surveyed Feliadh's troops with calm disdain.

'Who here speaks Khazalid?' he demanded. His voice was deep and hoarse, as if clogged with coal-dust.

Caradryel swallowed. His usual self-assurance would not help him here. 'None do,' he said, edging his horse to the fore of the Caledorian group. 'I was given the words by another.'

The dwarf chuckled. It sounded like loose stones tumbling down a ravine. 'So I thought. You speak like a stupid child. We barely understood you.'

Caradryel bowed in apology. 'Forgive me. I had little time to learn. I had hoped to speak in… other circumstances.'

'No doubt,' said the dwarf. 'Thank your pale gods that we heard the name Imladrik – that is all that saved you.'

'He wishes to pass a message to his friend, Morgrim Bargrum,' said Caradryel. 'We had hoped to find him here.'

The dwarf scowled. 'If they were friends once, they are friends no longer. But if you carry terms of surrender we will hear them.'

Caradryel paused. This was difficult. 'Imladrik's tidings are for Lord Morgrim alone,' he said, trying to sound authoritative without being haughty. 'Unless, that is, it is he to whom I am speaking.'

The dwarfs broke into a barking, growling fit of laughter, filling the valley with their bizarre and guttural mirth. Caradryel could feel Feliadh's annoyance, and placed a hand on his forearm to restrain him.

Laughter is good, he thought, studying the chortling dwarf

Master of Dragons

before him carefully. *I will endure a thousand insults if it gets us to where we need to be.*

'Your mind is as slow as your speech, elgi,' mocked the dwarf. 'You think we would risk Morgrim in the vanguard? You speak to Grondil of Zhufbar, slayer of your sickly kin-folk, and I ask you again: what are your tidings?'

Caradryel recalled what Imladrik had told him of the dawi.

'They despise weakness, and they despise arrogance,' Imladrik had told him. 'Steer a path between the two: never show frailty, but never insult them. Everything they do is a challenge. Give in to it, and they will hold you in contempt; ignore it and they will assume you mock them. Remember: they kill anything that mocks them.'

Caradryel swallowed.

'Grondil of Zhufbar,' he said. 'I am Caradryel of the House of Reveniol. I serve Imladrik of House Tor Caled. He commands me to speak only to Morgrim. You have us at your mercy and may slay us at your pleasure, but for all that none among us will break our vows. I will speak with Morgrim alone, or I will die here in this valley. They are the choices: you, my lord, have the decision.'

For a moment, silence. Caradryel felt a chill run up his arms. His stomach felt weak. The words 'die here in this valley' had slipped out rather easily.

Then Grondil chuckled again, and shook his head. 'Elgi amuse me,' he said. 'So serious, all the time. And you love your fine words.'

He shot Caradryel a sly, intelligent look.

'I'll take you to Morgrim,' Grondil said. 'Though you'll have to watch your scrawny backs with him – he doesn't have my sense of humour.'

Thoriol emerged into the sunlight, blinking and stumbling. He carried his gear slung across his back, just like the others. They were dressed the same way: loose-fitting white robes trimmed with a deep crimson. Baelian's company shouldered their longbows casually, used to the cumbersome lengths of yew and silk-spun bowstrings. Thoriol remembered enough of his training to use the weapon but struggled to look proficient with it.

'It'll come,' Baelian had told him during the crossing, grinning as ever. 'Soon you'll forget what it was like not to carry one.'

Thoriol gazed up at the soaring spires of Tor Alessi, glistening white in the strong sunlight. Gull-shrieks filled the air. Behind him, the length of a gangplank away, the *Resurviel* bobbed on the quayside. Harbour-hands were already crawling all over her, furling sails and stowing lines.

Baelian's company assembled on the stone quay, all twenty-four of them. Crowds pushed past them as Baelian attempted to call them to order and speak to the harbour official. Everything in the waterfront seemed to be in constant motion – a carnival of unloading, loading, shouting, moving and hauling. The wind was stiff and thick with salt. The aroma of it was different to Ulthuan – fewer spice fragrances and somehow… dirtier.

While Baelian argued with the official, Thoriol let his eyes wander across to the towers rearing up ahead. Some of them still bore the scars of ballista strikes. Banners of the King and various noble houses rippled in the breeze, exposing images of trees, horses, sea-serpents and hawks.

Everything was martial, hard-edged and poorly finished. Tor Alessi seemed to have no purpose to it but war.

Eventually Baelian turned away from the official, his scarred face tight with irritation.

'Fools,' he spat, rolling up some parchment and stowing it under his robes. 'This place is full to bursting and they're running around like startled pheasants. Useless.' He started to storm off, then turned and gave Thoriol a significant glance. 'Stay together. I've got us lodgings in the lower Eliamar quarter. Let's not get lost in the crush, eh?'

Master of Dragons 169

Thoriol smiled dryly. The captain had little to worry about – Thoriol had no plans to make an escape any time soon. Despite himself, he had found himself rather enjoying his reacquaintance with the archery he had learned as a youth. He'd taken a surprising degree of pleasure in handling the long yew bow, in stringing it and leaning in to the pull.

It came back quickly. He remembered how he'd taken hunting bows into the forests west of Tor Vael, and how proficient he'd become at bringing back a haul for the larders. He'd always had a quick eye, and enjoyed the lightweight spring of the weapon; far more elegant than a sword or an axe. Only later had that enjoyment faded, and he'd never had the chance to become expert with the battlefield weapons of the asur companies – long, slender bows with a range of over two hundred yards and a fearful delivery. The effort required just to bend those bows was considerable, and after days of practice on the ship he was only capable of matching his counterparts' most elementary efforts.

For all that, the process had been oddly cathartic. The others had accepted him readily, showing little or no interest in his origins but willing to help him learn. They shared watered-down wine, bread, hard cheese and olives, discussing the potential for riches in the east, the prospects for the war against the druchii, tales – implausible or otherwise – of love affairs in Saphery and Avelorn.

After the worst of his sickness had abated, Thoriol had found himself more at ease in their company than he would have imagined possible. His early reticence had earned him the moniker of 'the Silent'. Despite opening up a little since then, the name had stuck, and he saw no harm in it.

He had made friends: Loeth, the tall one from Tiranoc; Taemon, the intense brooder from Chrace; Rovil and Florean from Eataine, good-natured, jovial and as close as brothers.

They did not judge him, except in jest. They accepted the strange gaps in his history without question, for most of them had similar missing pieces from their own half-told lives. They did not talk of arcane matters or the deep counsel of kings, but they laughed often, and seemed to have few cares beyond the acquisition of prestige, the payment in gold coin every month, and the care of their bows and quivers – about which they were all fastidious.

So the crossing had not been as arduous as Thoriol had feared. He still rankled over the deception that had brought him there, and remained wary of the ever-smirking Baelian, but he could not pretend that it had been unbearable.

Now, looking at the teeming mass of asur around him, letting the rough-edged splendour of Tor Alessi sink in, feeling the firmness of solid ground under his feet for the first time since passing out in Lothern, he smiled ruefully.

The world was a strange place. For the time being, he would see where the current path led. Thoriol the Scholar was long dead, confined to a past that he could not talk about. Thoriol the Dragon rider had always been a fiction, something that he'd known deep down would never amount to much.

Thoriol the Archer, though. It had a certain ring to it. Perhaps not enough for him to tarry with it for more than a few weeks, but a certain ring nonetheless.

'Lost in thought?' came a familiar voice just ahead of him. Rovil was grinning at him.

'Always lost in thought,' said Taemon sharply.

'Or seasick,' said Loeth. 'Though that won't be a problem now.'

Thoriol said nothing, happy to live up to his new name, but smiled back amiably.

Then he pulled his hood up against the chill sea-wind, taking care to avoid the crush of bodies around him, and followed his companions up the winding streets from the waterfront to whatever future awaited him in the city.

CHAPTER TWELVE

Caradryel sat on a low, rough-hewn bench, resisting the urge to scratch his neck. He kept his back straight and his hands clasped loosely in his lap, trying to project the kind of elegant disinterest that he supposed the dawi would expect him to display.

Since arriving at the dwarf camp he had felt eyes all over him, scouring him like some slab of precious metal ready for the hammer. They were subtle, though; they never looked at him straight on, but only from under heavily lidded eyes. He could never quite meet their gaze – they turned away, quick as cats, muttering impenetrably into their plaited beards.

He'd done his best to observe them in return, making mental notes of their habits and demeanour. Their physicality was quite astonishing, from the tightly corded muscles of their exposed forearms to the heavy tread of their ironshod boots. They crashed through the undergrowth like bulls, growling, expectorating and grumbling the whole time. Yet, when they truly wanted to, they could slip into the shadows like wraiths, sinking into an almost trancelike stillness.

They smelled strongly, though not in the bestial, unclean way he'd imagined they would, but more of burned things: metal, leather, embers. If anything, they reminded him of the faint aroma he'd detected from Imladrik, the residue from the drakes he rode.

They had treated their guests well enough – curtly, with plenty of snide remarks on elgi weakness and moral cowardice, but no physical violence. That gave Caradryel at least some hope that things were not as far gone as they might have been. Grondil had escorted him and the Caledorians to a clearing some five miles from where the ambush had been laid. On the way they'd passed several heavily armoured columns of dwarfs marching west. They didn't so much march through the forest as annihilate it, smashing aside the grasping branches and treading the splinters into the mud. Now Caradryel sat alongside Feliadh and the others, waiting; ignored by the dozens of dawi warriors that came and went across the clearing, though their hostility was palpable on the air, hanging like a stink of contagion.

Perhaps, he admitted ruefully, thinking back on his grand plans for ingratiation, *on this occasion at least, I may have overreached myself.*

'Who is the one sent by Imladrik?' came a voice then from the far side of the clearing.

Caradryel's head snapped up. A dwarf had emerged from the trees, flanked on either side by a retinue of axe-wielders in iron battle plate. Unlike most of the others he wore no helm, and his black beard spilled openly across his finely worked breastplate.

Something about his eyes, the way he looked straight at Caradryel in the way that none of the others did, gave away his status. Those grey eyes had the fixed certainty of command that he'd only witnessed before in Imladrik. Like him, this dwarf walked with a kind of unconscious air of confidence. Also like him, there was a bleakness to him, an

Master of Dragons

austere mien that lined his face and gave his wrinkled skin a greyish sheen.

'I am,' Caradryel said, rising from the bench and bowing.

The dwarf lord looked at him for some time before snorting. 'You're no warrior,' he observed.

'Indeed not.'

'Why did he send you?'

'I perform these things for him. My service is with words, not with blades.'

'I can see that.'

Caradryel worked hard to maintain a deferential manner, fully aware of his danger. Out of the corner of his eye he saw the heavily armoured guards regarding him carefully, as if yearning to find an excuse to strike.

'Imladrik spoke to me highly of the dawi,' Caradryel said.

The dwarf lord grunted. 'Imladrik,' he repeated slowly, as if savouring the bitter taste of the word. 'He is here again, on this side of the ocean?'

'He is at Tor Alessi.'

'Why did he not come himself?'

'For the same reason, I imagine, that you do not walk in the vanguard.'

The dwarf nodded slowly. 'Once he rode freely all the way to Karaz-a-Karak. He was our guest at the Everpeak. Did you know that?'

'They were freer times.'

'They were.'

The dwarf lord gestured to his retinue – the faintest movement of a finger – and the armoured warriors withdrew a few paces, crossing their arms and glowering on the edge of the clearing.

'These are my *bazan-khazakrum*,' he said to Caradryel. 'Each has sworn a death-oath and would lay down his life a dozen times over before any harm came to me. They find your presence an insult.'

Caradryel resisted the urge to glance at them. 'I regret that.'

'Perhaps you think that your status will be enough to protect you.'

Caradryel could sense Feliadh and the others tensing up and willed them not to do anything stupid. Caledorian hot-bloodedness was an asset on the battlefield but a handicap for this sort of work.

'I understand the point you are making,' he said.

'Do you?' The dwarf lord drew closer to him. 'What point am I making?'

'What happened to your ambassadors was shameful,' said Caradryel. Those words, at least, were no deception – Caledor had been stupid to humiliate the dwarf embassy and all but the most blinkered of his ministers knew it. 'Imladrik regards it as an unforgivable crime.'

'Unforgivable, eh?' The dwarf lord came closer still. His forehead came up to Caradryel's chest, but somehow the disparity in height did nothing to alter the unequal relationship of threat that existed. Caradryel felt ludicrously skinny next to the solid mass of flesh and iron that stood before him. He could smell the dwarf's breath – a meaty, beery aroma. 'Imladrik knows we never forgive anything, so that's not saying very much.'

Suddenly, with a jerk of speed, the dwarf grabbed Caradryel's long blond hair and yanked him down to his knees.

'Shall I rip these golden locks from your head?' he hissed, pushing his face towards Caradryel's in a snarl. 'Shall I shave your head and send you limping back to Tor Alessi?'

Caradryel grimaced, feeling his scalp flex, hoping Feliadh had remained completely still. The dwarf twisted his fist further, half-pulling a clump free, making Caradryel gasp.

Then the pressure released. The dwarf let him go, shaking a few loose tresses from his gauntlet in disgust.

'We do not do such things,' he muttered. 'We leave that to savages.'

Master of Dragons

Caradryel caught his breath, still on his knees.

The dwarf lord glared at him coldly. 'So what do you have to say to me?'

Caradryel looked up. 'You are Morgrim?'

'I am.'

'Then I am instructed to tell you this. Imladrik knows of the wrongs done to your people. He laments the death of Snorri Halfhand. He grieves for the loss of trust between our peoples, and understands that much blood has been shed on both sides, but still believes that an unwinnable war between us may be averted. He wishes to speak to you, as he once did, to explain what we know of this conflict's origins.'

Morgrim looked at him wearily, as if he'd hoped for something better, but did not interrupt.

'There are things about my race you do not know,' Caradryel went on. 'We are divided. This war is part of that.'

Morgrim laughed harshly. 'You say this now, when your cities are besieged. You say this now, when our strength is revealed and you realise the folly of shaming us.'

Caradryel wanted to stop him there, to point out that however strong the dwarf legions were they had nothing to compare with the flights of dragons, and that Imladrik's embassy was sent not from weakness but from strength, and that Tor Alessi had been turned into an anvil on which even the mightiest of hosts would break like foaming surf.

But he said none of that – it would have done no good.

'So what can Imladrik offer?' demanded Morgrim, his eyes flashing with anger. 'My cousin lies dead. Some of my people now live only to see the elgi driven into the sea – what shall I say to them?'

Caradryel clambered back to his feet, brushing the soil from his robes. Just as he had done before, he aimed to find the balance – not craven, not arrogant, not supine, not threatening.

'Imladrik knows you will march on the city. He knows

your people demand vengeance and knows you are sworn to deliver it. All he asks is that, for the sake of your old friendship, you speak to him once before giving the final order. He will meet you, under flag of truce. He requests nothing more – no assurances, no treaties – just the chance to speak.'

Morgrim's grey eyes flickered, for the first time, with less than certainty.

'That's all?' he asked.

Caradryel risked a nod. 'If he has any further tidings, he has not shared them with me.'

Morgrim shook his head and turned away. 'This army is drawn from all the holds,' he muttered. 'There is no dam capable of holding it back now.' He snapped his gaze back to Caradryel. 'It is too late. It cannot be stopped.'

Caradryel met his glare evenly. 'He told me you would say that, and so told me to reply thus: The runes never lie, but nor do they compel. Nothing is fated.'

That held Morgrim's attention. The dwarf pondered the words for what seemed like an age.

Caradryel watched him, saying nothing. He had heard it said that dawi minds were slow, like those of simpletons or children, but he saw the lie in that immediately. Morgrim was no fool, and if his thoughts worked with more deliberation than an elf's then perhaps that was to his credit. Caledor had a quick tongue and a ready wit, but it had not made him a wise king.

Finally Morgrim's face lifted again.

'The march continues,' he announced. 'I swore an oath to bring this army to Tor Alessi and I will not break it.'

He drew close to Caradryel again, the familiar breath-stink of meat and ale wafting over him.

'But I will think on your words,' Morgrim said, making it sound more like a threat. 'By the time you smell sea-salt, you will know my answer to them.'

* * *

Final preparations had been made. The great hawkships of the fleet put to sea again, packed with ballistae and Sea Guard units to keep the supply routes open. The last repairs were made to the city's battlements and bulwarks. Standards bearing the runes of war – Charoi, Ceyl, Minaith, Urithair – were slung from every parapet and balcony, rippling down the pale stone in a riot of blues, reds and emeralds. Tor Alessi's many walls stood proudly against the desolation of the land about them, rising up like spars of dirty bone from the scorched and scoured earth below.

They will drown in their own blood, observed Draukhain, wheeling high above the tallest of the towers. *The city is impregnable.*

Imladrik gazed down at the sprawling fortress below, not sharing the dragon's assessment. To be sure, the defences were awe-inspiring – taller, thicker and more heavily manned than at any time since the city's foundation – but he'd seen what the dwarfs could do when their blood was raging.

Our strength is not in the walls, he sang. *I hope, though, that they will prove enough of a deterrent.*

Draukhain laughed, pulling hard round and swinging over the sea. The long, maundering coasts extended far into the north, their smooth strands broken by rocky dune country.

So restrained, the drake mocked. *You really are not much sport.*

The sun blazed strongly, making the sea sparkle and lifting the worst of the gloom from the nearby forest. Imladrik turned his head to the east, watching curls of mist rise from the brooding treeline. It looked like the woodland had somehow contracted, pulling together like an inhalation before the storm.

Just on the edge of sensation, he almost felt something, like a faint whiff of burning, or the distance-muffled sound of iron boots crashing through rotten wood.

Consumed by it, he missed Liandra's approach, coming

out of the sun-glare some hundred feet above him, riding the high airs with her habitual carefree abandon. He only sensed her at the last minute, just as she swung alongside him, her red steed trailing a long line of hot smoke behind her.

'My lord!' cried Liandra, saluting him. Her copper hair buffeted out behind her, her robes tugging at her body in the wind.

He saw her then just as he remembered her – a creature of fire, a spirit of the raw heavens, unbound and vivacious. It was as if the past had suddenly come alive before him, his memories crystallising out of empty skies.

'My lady,' he responded, immediately wincing as he remembered how he and Yethanial played at such exchanges. 'I did not know you were aloft.'

Liandra laughed. She was close enough now for him to see her face light up in amusement – the narrowing of her eyes, the wrinkling of her freckled skin.

'No,' she replied. 'I don't suppose you did. You've been busy since you got here, lord. Too busy to speak to me, it seems, or to know very much of what I am doing – no doubt you've had weightier matters on your mind.'

The familiar insolence – he'd missed it.

'I have been busy,' he admitted, giving Draukhain his head and speeding further up the coastline. Vranesh struggled to match the pace and was soon spitting sparks of effort from her flame-red maw. 'As you should have been too.'

'Oh, my duties have been many. I have thousands of spears under my command, all waiting for orders to march. They have been waiting a long time.'

'I know,' said Imladrik. He was not blind to their frustration. 'And if I have my way they will be waiting longer still.'

Do you really think you can halt it? Liandra sang, her voice appearing in his mind as suddenly and as clearly as Draukhain's did.

Master of Dragons

That stung him. It was an intrusion, an unwelcome reminder of how they'd once conversed.

'You always wanted to fight them, Liandra,' he responded aloud, pushing Draukhain harder. The wind raced against him, making his crimson cloak ripple. 'You wanted it even before Kor Vanaeth.'

'No,' she replied, shaking her head vigorously. 'I did not. I came with you to the mountains and tried to understand them. Remember this – they started the killing.'

Imladrik let slip a weary laugh. 'Oh, they *started* it. Then that makes everything clear.'

You make it sound as if our races are equals, she sang. *You make it sound as if they could actually hurt us, if we had a mind to prevent it.*

Draukhain swung round again, enjoying the speed and exchange. He seemed to be goading his younger counterpart a little, daring her to match his mastery of the air. Imladrik let him.

'You are all the same,' said Imladrik wearily. 'You, Salendor, my brother: you think we are bound to destroy them. You are all wrong.'

Are we? Or is it you, my lord, who is afraid?

Imladrik spun around, hauling Draukhain back on himself in mid-air, rearing up in the sky like a charger on the battlefield.

'Afraid?' he asked, incredulous.

Liandra laughed again. 'Of battle? You know I do not mean that.' She was struggling to keep Vranesh on a counter-trajectory to match Draukhain's dazzling change of angles. *You are fearful of what would happen if you unleashed yourself, if you allowed yourself – for one moment – to let slip the shackles she has placed on you and became what you know you should be.*

Only then did Draukhain's flight dip from perfection. Imladrik's mind flickered, momentarily, out of focus.

What do you mean? he sang, inflecting the harmony with warning.

That you are a dragon rider, lord. You always have been. You have fire in your blood but you will not light the kindling. As Liandra spoke her eyes glittered, as if she was both thrilled and appalled by what she was saying. *You think you love her – you have persuaded yourself you do – but you are wrong. She has tamed you.*

Imladrik rose in the saddle, angling his staff towards her, feeling a hot wash of anger building behind his eyes.

'Foreswear those words!' he cried, feeling Draukhain respond instantly. The dragon's vast wings fanned the air into a whirl of ashes and flame-flickers. Raw aethyr-fire rippled along his staff-length, crackling angrily.

Liandra glared back at him, her face twisted in both delight and fear.

'I take back nothing, lord!' she shouted across the gap between steeds. 'The truth needs to be told!'

Imladrik spurred Draukhain towards Vranesh, and for a moment, just a moment, he teetered on the edge of attack. He could already see the outcome – the tangled clash of talons, laced with the quick burn of actinic magic. He had a splintered image of himself, wreathed in anger and lightning-crowned majesty, cleaving the air apart and casting the Sun Dragon down and into the sea.

At the last moment he pulled away. Draukhain turned, pulling out of the encounter and swinging back out seawards, and he caught a glimpse of Liandra's defiant, terrified face staring right at him.

The dragons spun apart, wings beating and tails writhing. Draukhain quickly took up the dominant position, his shadow falling over the smaller Vranesh and turning her vivid red scales into a dull, dried-blood colour.

Is this what you intended? Imladrik sang, controlling his mighty steed with some difficulty. *To make me angry? You would risk that, knowing what it means?*

Master of Dragons

Liandra's resolve dissolved then – she was like a child who'd pulled at the tail of a cat and now had to contend with the claws.

'Something had to stir you!' she cried aloud. 'You are *dead!* You treat me with contempt, like some lordly conquest which now means nothing to you – a toy, thrown aside now that you have taken up loftier things.'

'I never dishonoured you,' said Imladrik.

Then Liandra laughed for a third time, and the sound was bitter. 'No, you did not. I do not believe a day has passed when you have not kept your honour, my lord.'

Imladrik said nothing. The words cut him deeply, especially coming from her. He knew what they all wanted of him, and he also knew what *she* wanted of him – the two things were much the same. Just as he had done years ago, he felt the tug of desire, the pull towards oblivion. The dragon responded to it, growling like a blast furnace lighting up.

It would be so easy. He could give in this time, forgetting about windswept Tor Vael, forgetting about Ulthuan and its survival. The two of them could do what they had resisted before and take the fight to the enemy together. They could sweep east at the head of Caledor's armies, burning a furrow through the forest until the flames licked the very ramparts of Karaz-a-Karak.

He saw Draukhain and Vranesh flying in dreadful unison, the Master and Mistress of Dragons searing through the air like vengeful gods, cracking open the halls of the dwarfs and exposing the deeps within. He could cut loose at last, unlocking the cage that kept his true nature sealed behind layers of control. He could unfurl, giving into the second soul that whispered within him and finally, just for once, forget duty and embrace *pleasure*.

He felt the words form in his mind, ready for the song that would seal things.

I long for it. I long to bring ruin on them, with you by my side.

I would wage war until the end of the world with you, caring for nothing but death and splendour.

In the end, though, it was Liandra that turned away, as if suddenly afraid of what she might goad him into doing. Vranesh's head dipped, and the two of them started to circle back down, gliding through the twisting air currents.

'But you are right, of course,' she said bleakly. 'You are always right.'

Imladrik followed her. The fury ebbed from him, but only slowly.

You deserved better than silence, he sang.

That halted her. Vranesh slid round, angling so that Liandra could look back up at him. She gave him a proud look.

'I did.'

'And do not think, even for a moment, that I had forgotten.' Imladrik came down to her level, easing Draukhain's bulk alongside the slender Vranesh. 'We are all the children of Aenarion, Liandra. That is our downfall. We have only ever been defeated by ourselves.'

Tor Alessi was by then barely visible, a speck of white stonework on the long shore. They could have been alone, the two of them, lost in an edgeless sky.

'Do you not think it would be easier for me to give Salendor what he wishes?' Imladrik asked softly. 'I know what it would bring – victories, to begin with. For a time we would hurt them. Our thirst for vengeance would be slaked, and we would revel in it.'

Draukhain was circling Vranesh now, turning in a wide falconer's arc as Imladrik kept speaking.

'But then the long grind would begin. Athel Maraya would burn. Athel Toralien, Sith Rionnasc, Oeragor – they would all burn. We would throw our finest into those flames and they would wither. Even the dragons would grow sick of it as the years wore on; they would no longer heed our songs, leaving us alone against an empire of mindless fury.'

Master of Dragons

Liandra listened warily, as if he was spinning some deception around her.

'And who would gain from this?' asked Imladrik. 'You know whose hand was behind the war – the same that grasps the sceptre in Naggaroth. I will not see that happen. I will not let our desire for vengeance give him what he desires.'

She never looked away. Her expression never changed: sceptical, bruised, disappointed.

'You sell us short,' she said.

'That is your judgement,' said Imladrik.

'Then I must warn you, lord,' said Liandra, nudging Vranesh closer. 'You are wrong. This course leads to ruin. We must strike now before they gather more strength.'

Imladrik nodded. 'I know your view, though it changes nothing.'

'So what, then, of us?'

Imladrik felt his stomach twist. The burn of desire was still there – for another life, one that he had only glimpsed in brief intense snatches. Above it all, though, hovered Yethanial's calm presence, the one who had sustained him, the one his true soul cleaved to when away from the heady madness of the dragon.

'That moment has gone, *feleth-amina*,' he said, forcing the words out. 'We have both taken vows.'

Liandra looked at him for a little longer, her face flushed. He couldn't decipher her expression – it could have been anger, or maybe humiliation, or simply disbelief. They hung there for a while longer, their steeds' wings making the air thrum, before her expression finally hardened again.

'You may have done, my lord,' she said. 'For myself, I vow nothing.'

Then Vranesh arched, twisted, and shot down towards the sea. She went quickly, like a falling stone, plunging down towards the sparkling waters.

Imladrik watched her go, motionless in the air, letting

Draukhain hold position and giving him no orders.

For a long time he said nothing at all. The wind pulled at his hair. He felt wretched, more wretched than he could remember being – even the brisk push of the salty air felt stale and old.

I like her, sang Draukhain eventually. *I always did – she has a heart after our own. Are you sure you are right in this, kalamn-talaen?*

Imladrik's eyes remained locked on the diminishing figure of the flame-red dragon as she spiralled out over the ocean.

No, great one, he sang bleakly. *I am not sure about anything.*

'Draw!'

Thoriol bent into the pull, using his whole body to lever the arrow on to the string. Alongside him on the battlements his company did likewise; alongside them a hundred other companies the same. With a ripple of steel points, the battalions of an entire wall-section pulled their bowstrings tight, angling the heavy yew shafts and holding position.

Thoriol felt his muscles tremble as the tension bit. He'd become far more proficient than he had been, but the effort of using the longbow was considerable and he was less comfortable with it than his companions. They could work a longbow for an hour and register little fatigue, whereas he was struggling after several flights.

He gritted his teeth, desperate not to lose face. Loeth stood beside him, calm as ever.

'Release!'

The order was a relief – Thoriol loosed his arrow with the others, watching as the dense hail of darts soared up into the sky and arced down to the plain beyond.

The sight was a stirring one. Their wall-section was nearly fifty feet above the level of the plain, facing due east. The arrows clustered together in a thick cloud, whistling through the air before jabbing down into the sodden earth far below.

Master of Dragons

The range was impressive – over a hundred and fifty yards, with each dart falling within a wide band. Thousands of arrows already stood at angles in the mud, the results of many previous volleys.

'Draw!'

If Thoriol had counted correctly, this should be the last one. He'd already reached for his arrow in the rack before him and had it ready. He grasped the string with three fingers, feeling the single-feather fletch brush against his knuckle. The nock slid up against the silken string, and he pulled it tight using his bodyweight as a counterbalance.

At such ranges the aim was not as important as the timing. The task was to fill the air with a thick cloud of arrows, all hammering earthwards in a single block. The defenders of Tor Alessi knew from experience that dwarf armour was extremely tough and so single shots were rarely effective. The only thing that troubled units clad in steel plate was a veritable flood of darts, clogging the air and rattling down against them in a dense cloud. At such concentrations there was every chance of hitting an exposed joint or sliding through a narrow eye-slit, and, even if the majority of arrows wouldn't register a kill, the flight as a whole would badly hamper any advancing formation.

'Release!'

Thoriol let fly, watching with satisfaction as his arrow soared upwards with the others. The air thickened with shafts again before they swooped down in unison, tracing a steep arch towards the plain below.

It was a sight to gladden the heart of any true son of Ulthuan. When the final assault came it would be even grander – thousands of archers arranged across the entire stretch of parapets, raining steel-tipped ruin on the advancing host. To that would be added the shuddering flights of ballista bolts and the arcane snarl of magecraft.

Thoriol smiled. For the attackers, it would be like walking

into a hurricane. He found himself almost desperate for them to arrive, just so he could witness it.

'Stand down!'

The order rang out from the tower at the far end of the parapet. All along the battlements archer companies leaned heavily against the stone, shaking down aching arms and counting their remaining arrows. A trumpet sounded as dozens of basket-carrying menials hurried out of the gates below, ready for the laborious process of retrieving the arrows and carting them back up to the armoury for re-use.

Loeth smiled at him amiably. 'You're keeping up, Silent.'

Thoriol nodded. 'Seems that way.'

Baelian pushed his way towards them, moving carefully along the crowded parapet.

'It'll be harder when we're doing it for real,' he warned, looking with guarded approval at Thoriol and the others. 'Think your arms are aching now? They'll be shredded by the end, and that's before you see what the bastards will be hurling up at us the whole time.'

Rovil laughed. 'From fifty feet down?'

'Don't be a fool,' snapped Baelian. 'Last time they breached the walls in nine places before we drove them out.' He swept his scarred gaze across them, wagging a calloused finger in their direction like an old loremaster with his pupils. 'Be *careful*. Remember your training. If they break through any-where close to you, reach for your knives and fall back in good order. It's not your task to stop them up close – that's what the knights are there for.'

Thoriol looked away then, his mind already wandering – Baelian had given them the same speech many times.

As he did so, he caught a familiar whiff on the air, like burning embers. He craned his head, shading his eyes with one hand against the glare of the sun. He'd known ever since arriving that dragon riders were among Tor Alessi's defend-ers but he'd made no effort to find out anything about them

– the memory of the Dragonspine was still too raw for that and he'd had plenty to occupy him with the archery work.

But as he looked up then, though, he saw it – the massive sapphire drake, the one he'd seen over Tor Vael and Tor Caled a hundred times. It was dropping fast, descending into the forest of spires behind them with an echoing clap of huge wings. A moment later and it was gone, lost in the vastness of the upper city.

He felt his stomach twist.

'That is Imladrik's dragon,' he said, blurting it out even as Baelian was still speaking.

'So it is,' smiled Loeth. 'What did you expect? I've seen him aloft twice since we dropped anchor.'

Florean nodded enthusiastically. 'A monster. A true monster.'

Thoriol turned to Baelian. 'Then... he's here?'

'Of course he is.' Baelian looked at him steadily. 'He commands the army.'

Thoriol almost felt like laughing, but not from mirth. Even the simple task of escaping his father seemed to be beyond him. A familiar sinking sensation fell over him: the embrace of failure.

He started to say something, but Baelian's look silenced him. The archery captain shot him a glare, the meaning of which was obvious.

No one needs to know but you and me.

Thoriol clammed up.

'Are you all right, Silent?' asked Florean. 'You've gone pale.'

'I'm fine,' replied Thoriol. 'Gods, but my arms are sore.'

They could believe that, and so the moment passed. The archers gathered up their arrows into quivers and checked their strings for damage. Loeth reached for a pot of beeswax and began to rub at a splintered section of his longbow – it would need to be replaced, but the bowyers were already working flat out and spares were hard to come by.

As the company fell into its familiar routines Baelian drew Thoriol to one side.

'You've made a place for yourself here, lad,' he said, his voice low. 'Don't do anything foolish.'

Thoriol didn't know how to reply. Thoughts of escape had faded days ago, replaced by the enjoyment of – for the first time – actually doing something worthwhile well. The fact that his father was in the city, no doubt preoccupied with the enormous task of organising its defences, shouldn't have made a difference to anything.

But it did, of course. It tarnished the whole exercise, putting into relief just how incongruous it was that he, the son of the King's brother, had ended up serving in the rank and file of his armies.

He was about to mumble something inconsequential when his attention was broken for a second time. Clarions, whole groups of them, began to sound from the tops of the highest towers. A rustle of movement followed, then the rising clamour of voices raised all along the battlements.

Thoriol looked out across the plain just in time to see the collectors hurrying back to the gates, escorted by spear-carrying riders who hadn't been there a moment ago. The clarions continued to sound, joined soon afterwards by ringing blasts from the city's huge central keep.

His gaze snapped up to the edge of the forest, only a few miles distant but hazy in the strong sun. He saw nothing moving there, but the sight nevertheless filled him with foreboding.

'So they've been sighted,' Thoriol said quietly.

Baelian stared out in the same direction, eyes fixed on the horizon.

'Sounds like it,' he agreed. 'Better get those arms limber again, lad. Looks like you'll be using them soon.'

CHAPTER THIRTEEN

The dwarfs on the march were like a slow avalanche battering its way down a mountainside. They made little effort to skirt around obstacles or difficult terrain – they ploughed through it, never changing pace, keeping their heads low and their arms swinging in unison. In their wake they left a wasteland of hacked stumps and trampled-down foliage, a scar on the forest as wide as fifty warriors marching shoulder to shoulder.

Behind those pioneers came the builders. Wooden bridges were thrown up over gorges; earthworks were hurriedly put up to shore the road's margins; the stubbornest obstacles were simply demolished by a whole phalanx of bare-chested workers using axes, hammers, shovels and long-handled hods.

Caradryel had plenty of time to watch the dawi at work, and what he saw gave him plenty to think about. Even the lowliest worker applied himself with almost fanatical zeal. He saw dwarfs staggering under their own weight in rubble, shining with sweat, refusing any help until their portion of the labour was done. He saw others carrying atrocious wounds and still working on, shrugging off levels of pain that would have had him in bed for a week.

The dwarfs seemed consumed by a kind of low-level mania that drove them west, ever west, obliterating anything they came across on the way. He found their single-mindedness both repellent and admirable. An elf would have found a more elegant route, taking care to conserve strength for the battle ahead. Something about the dawi's utter disregard for such considerations made him uneasy.

He had spoken to Morgrim on and off during the trek towards Tor Alessi. The dwarf lord was busy for most of the time with his thanes and warlords and spared himself as little as they did, marching to and fro amongst the armoured columns tirelessly, taking counsel and ruminating with them long into the night. Dwarf discussions seemed to involve an inordinate amount of beard-tugging, ale-drinking and low grunting – even about seemingly trivial matters.

Slowly Caradryel had come to realise why Morgrim kept himself so busy. The dwarf army, which was far, far bigger than he'd been led to believe, was composed of forces from many different holds. Each one was led by its own prince or thane, many of whom were older than Morgrim and had trenchant views of their own. Seniority was a powerful thing with them, and Morgrim had to work incessantly to keep the whole messy, fractious, temperamental caravan on the road.

Caradryel found himself admiring the dour warrior. Morgrim was driven and irascible, obviously haunted by the death of his cousin and the need for blood-vengeance, but he could keep his head when he needed to, cajoling and arguing with a deft mix of forcefulness and tact.

'Does it make you nervous?' Morgrim had asked Caradryel on one of their few conversations together.

'What, lord?'

'Being surrounded by those who wish to kill you.'

Caradryel thought for a moment. 'In truth, I have never found myself to be universally popular,' he said eventually. 'So, no.'

Morgrim didn't smile. It was rare to see him smile, and when he did it was a cynical gesture, bereft of warmth.

'Morek tells me I am wasting my time with you,' said Morgrim. 'He says you should have been sent back to Tor Alessi with an iron collar round your neck.'

'Morek is your counsellor?'

'My runelord.'

'I'm glad you didn't listen to him.'

Morgrim picked his nose and flicked the results to the floor. 'You know what I despise about you elgi?'

Caradryel didn't offer a suggestion.

'Your lack of seriousness,' said Morgrim. He held up his axe. 'This is Morek's finest work. He spent decades crafting the symbols into this metal. He bent his neck over it, honing, tapping, seeking. He never smiled, never made an unworthy remark – he worked until it was done. Now the power within it almost scares me.'

Caradryel thought of all the wasted, half-finished endeavours he'd embarked upon in his life, only to discard them when something more appealing came his way.

'This land rewards such work,' Morgrim went on. 'It is a serious land. You can carve a living here, if you work at it, but it will never repay sloth. I've seen the way you people look at the grime under the leaves and I know what you think of it, but we cherish every shadow, every pit. It is our place. You should not have come here.'

'We have been in Elthin Arvan for a thousand years,' countered Caradryel carefully. 'There is room enough for both of us, is there not?'

Morgrim hawked up a gobbet of phlegm and spat it messily. 'I don't think so,' he said.

Caradryel paused before speaking again. 'If I may, then, lord – a question.'

Morgrim grunted his assent.

'Why are you not sending me back to Imladrik? Why are you entertaining his proposal at all?'

'Because of who he is.' Morgrim drew in a long breath. The leather-tough skin around his eyes creased as he remembered. 'He never looked down on us. He did not scorn our food, nor our caverns, nor call us stunted. When I showed him the vaults of the Everpeak he remained silent. He bowed before the great image of Grimnir, and for a moment I could not tell whether it was elgi or dawi who stood there.'

When Morgrim spoke of Imladrik, his harsh voice softened a little, losing its cold edge of disdain.

'I looked at him and I saw one of us,' Morgrim said. 'A soul that understood the path of duty.' Morgrim glanced at Caradryel. 'He learned Khazalid. He spoke it well, for an elgi. It took him twenty years, he told me, to master the greeting-forms, but he did it. I know of no others of your kind who have even tried, let alone succeeded.'

As Morgrim spoke, Caradryel remembered the ephemera of Yethanial's patient scholarship at Tor Vael. He had wondered at the relationship between the two of them back then, struck by how pale and grey she seemed next to his vigorous dynamism, but perhaps there was something more profound there than appearances.

'His brother is a fool and my people will rejoice when his neck is cut,' continued Morgrim. 'But my cousin was not wise-tempered either.' The dwarf's nose crinkled as he attempted what passed with him for a smile. 'What might have been, if Imladrik and I had been the heirs? Perhaps none of this foolishness.'

He looked sidelong at Caradryel.

'But all we have are the things set before us, and I will tell

Master of Dragons 193

you this: I respect him for the reason I do not respect you. He is *serious*.'

Caradryel remembered how, despite himself, that accusation had wounded him. Alone among all the insults and contempt he'd faced from that dawi, that one had somehow struck home.

Perhaps, he thought, *if I somehow make it out of here alive, I will have to address this. Perhaps I have been playing at life for too long.*

Now though, days later, the march was coming to an end. Caradryel had taken his place beside Feliadh again. He and the other Caledorians walked by his side, leading their horses, looking dishevelled from the long trek but otherwise unharmed. For the last few hours the trees had been thinning out around them, gradually giving way to a bleak country of grass, sea-wind and loamy earth.

The dwarf vanguard pulled together, forming up into squares of impeccably ordered warriors. Morgrim and his *bazan-khazakrum* hearthguard had forged their way to the forefront, taking the combined standards of the army with them – a heavy-set collection of banners bearing stylised images of forges, hammers, flames and mountains.

'Now we see where this game has led us,' whispered Feliadh to Caradryel.

Caradryel nodded, keeping a careful watch on Morgrim's progress ahead.

'We will indeed.'

They crested a low tussock of tufted grass and sucking mud, beyond which the plains running down the sea suddenly opened out before them. Caradryel breathed in deeply, relishing the brine on the brisk air.

The sun was low in the east behind them, still pulling clear of the morning mists over the forest. Elthin Arvan's coastline was visible in the distance, a line of barred silver crowned with piled seaborne clouds. The huge, proud outline of Tor

Alessi broke its emptiness, jutting up from the plain in a mass of spear-sharp towers and soaring walls. Runes on its walls could be made out even from such a distance, picked out in gold and emerald, glowing warmly as the waxing sun caught the gilt tapestry.

Caradryel saw the city then as the dwarfs around him must have seen it – huge, bristling with arms and magic, a fastness unrivalled by any the elves had built in all their colonial lands. It looked indomitable, as solid as the Phoenix Throne itself.

If Caradryel had been one of those dour-faced, iron-clad warriors his spirits might have faltered then. Somehow, he doubted theirs would.

'So what do we do now?' asked Feliadh. The Caledorian had started treating him with a good deal more respect since the events of the ambush.

'The Doom of the Elves has made his arrival,' Caradryel said dryly. 'Now we wait for the Master of Dragons to make his.'

Alviar walked along Kor Vanaeth's main thoroughfare. Loose soil and straw clung to his boots – the stone paving that had once made the roads a pleasure to walk on had long since been ripped up for repairs to the walls and citadel. Everything that had any military use had been taken, including ornamental stone lintels, bronze statues, even articles from the temples.

Alviar had disapproved of that at the time, as had most of the citizens. Liandra had been most insistent, though. She always was.

If he was honest, Alviar had never truly agreed with the decision to repopulate Kor Vanaeth. It was too small, too isolated, too enclosed by the forest. He would have been happy enough to follow Liandra to Tor Alessi or Athel Toralien, to start a new life in one of the truly big fortresses, the only places where a modicum of safety was still preserved.

He smiled as he remembered how Liandra had replied when he'd first suggested that, years ago. He'd never been able to repeat what she said in front of his four children, but the sight of her with eyes blazing, cheeks scarlet and spittle flying remained seared on his memory. She hadn't agreed.

Given all of that, it had been a disappointment when she'd accepted the summons at last to go to Tor Alessi. Right up until the end he had hoped she'd find a way to ignore it, but then Alviar supposed that it was hard to resist the Council for long.

She'd been torn about it, at least, which boded well for her return.

'I will come back,' she had promised him.

'I know you will, lady,' he had replied.

'And I will bring reinforcements too. It's long past time Tor Alessi released some of its defenders – they can hardly house the troops they've got.'

'That would be good, my lady.'

Then she had gone, taking wing on that flame-red dragon of hers. Alviar had watched her go, wondering if anything she'd promised would be delivered.

Since then, nothing. Vague reports had reached them of dwarf armies on the move again, but all had been from the north. Alviar had done what he could in the meantime: overseeing the last of the repairs to the walls, ensuring the soldiers he did possess were in a good state of readiness for whatever might come. They knew that attack was likely, particularly if the dwarf forces started to splinter as they had done so many times in the past, so he'd sent messages to Tor Alessi warning of the imminent danger, despite little faith they would be received.

He looked up at the citadel ahead of him. It rose from the patchwork of houses like a tree-stump from the soil, streaked black from old fires. If all failed, the entire population could retreat to that redoubt, the only part of the old fortress that had remained intact after the dwarf attacks.

Alviar narrowed his eyes, running his gaze along the battlements. He thought he should really send someone up to ensure the ballistae were all in perfect condition and safely stowed before the next storm came in.

He was about to turn away, making a note to himself to have a word with the watch commander, when something else caught his eye. It was high up in the eastern sky – a lone bird with a strange, halting flight.

He paused, wondering for a moment what it was. Then, as the speck of darkness grew larger, his heart missed a beat. For all its ungainliness it was coming at them fast. Far, far too fast.

'Sound the alarm!' he shouted, breaking into a run. 'Man the walls!'

He made it as far as the citadel gates before it hit them. The stench was incredible – a rolling wash of hot putrescence, like a boiled corpse. He staggered, losing his footing and colliding heavily with the stone doorframe. From behind him he heard screams as others looked up into the skies and saw what was bearing down on them.

Hands trembling, Alviar pushed his way through the citadel doors and scrambled up the spiral stairway beyond. As he raced up the steps they seemed to shiver underneath him.

He reached the bell tower and caught hold of the long chain, yanking it frantically. That was the signal – it should bring the soldiers to their stations on the walls and summon everyone else to the sanctuary of the citadel.

Alviar rang it furiously for a few seconds longer, his heart pounding and his pulse racing.

It had been huge. Huge, and… *wrong*.

Then he tore out of the chamber and up to the citadel's summit. As he ran he started praying that the ballistae were manned and that they'd managed to get a few bolts away.

He didn't know whether anything they had would do much against that monster, but they should at least attempt a defence.

He burst out into the open at the top of the stairwell, slamming the wooden door back on its hinges as he emerged on to the wide, flat rooftop. He was instantly reassured – several dozen guards were already there on the ramparts, hauling the heavy ballistae and bolt throwers into firing angles and shouting furiously at one another. The wind whipped across him, as hot as a desert sandstorm and flecked with eerie snarls of flame.

'Where is it?' he yelled, twisting around as he ran, his neck craned up into the skies.

It was a superfluous question. The black dragon headed straight at them, less than a hundred feet away and tearing towards the citadel's summit. Green and purple energies laced around it, dripping like molten metal from its outstretched maw. Alviar caught a blurred impression of massive jaws pulled wide and a pair of silver eyes blazing with madness before he threw himself on to the stone and covered his head with his hands.

He heard a throttling roar that made the stone beneath his chest judder, then felt a sudden rush of air being inhaled into massive lungs. The stink intensified – a foul mix of mortuary scraps and magic. Amid all the roaring and the terror he thought he caught a woman's voice, screaming out words that he couldn't understand but that somehow amplified the paralysing dread that gripped him tight.

That, though, was the last of Alviar's fear-fractured impressions. A second later the jets of flame came, tempests of addled fire that crashed across the citadel's battlements like breakers against a prow, immolating everything like the vengeance of Khaine and sealing, for a second time, the doom of Kor Vanaeth.

* * *

The doors were barred with spiked iron bands and weighed the same as a fully laden trade cutter. Somewhere within the cavernous gatehouse, chains the width of wine barrels clanked taut around wheels, then pulled.

Imladrik watched them draw to the full – first a slit, then a window of daylight, then the wide vista of the plains beyond.

His mount was skittish under him. The horse could smell dragon, and that always unsettled them. He placed a reassuring hand on its neck and whispered the calming words that Yethanial had taught him.

Twenty ceremonial riders passed through the archway ahead of him, each decked in dazzling ithilmar and carrying pennants with the emblems of Ulthuan and Caledor. Aelis rode on his left side, Salendor on his right. Gelthar and Caerwal came behind, along with three battle-mages.

Liandra had still not returned from wherever Vranesh had taken her. Imladrik could have remained preoccupied, but the time had passed for that.

One battle at a time.

They rode out. Ahead of them, a mile from the walls, the dwarfs had taken up positions. Their army stretched across the eastern limit of the plain in a long arc. Imladrik could see regiments digging in: some carrying huge warhammers two-handed, others with axes or stubby crossbows. Their armour glinted dully in the sun, exposing intricate knotwork engraving on the helms and pauldron plates.

He tried to estimate numbers. Fifty thousand? Sixty? There might be more still marching through the forest to join them. In any case, it was a brutally large muster.

Thin columns of smoke were already rising from the dwarf encampment, marking the fires that they would drink and eat around, working one another up into battle-readiness with old tales of heroism and grudgement. Once those tales might have concerned Malekith and Snorri Whitebeard,

Master of Dragons

though they would do so no longer, and for that Imladrik was thankful.

The Sundering was largely unknown to the dwarfs. If they had ever been curious about the affairs of Ulthuan they would no doubt have uncovered the truth soon enough, but they were an insular race with little concern for internal elgi politics. For their part the asur had never made reference to it. In the early days many assumed Malekith would be defeated quickly. Only slowly had the dreadful truth become apparent – that the split would linger for as long as any could foresee, and that the Witch King was far too powerful to be reliably defended against, let alone destroyed.

After that the asur kept the truth from the outside world, guarding their shame like an oil lantern in the wind, sheltering it from prying eyes and hoping that, somehow, it could be contained. When the strife in Elthin Arvan had first come, Imladrik had sent Gotrek letters, hinting at the truth, still constrained by the need for secrecy and veiled with vagueness. Perhaps he should have been more explicit.

Ahead of him the dawi banners hung limply. Everything about them was blunt, grim, heavy. As the elves approached the dwarf lines, crossbow-bearing guards stomped out to greet them. Behind them came a company of foot soldiers wearing thick plates over chainmail, their helms carved into grotesque representations of dragon-faces. Imladrik pulled the reins gently, and the party came to a halt.

The dwarfs assembled, crossbows levelled, saying nothing. An uneasy silence descended, broken only by the distant sounds of campfires crackling and supply wagons being unloaded.

Imladrik removed his high helm, exposing his face to the enemy.

'*Tromm, dawinarri,*' he said, bowing respectfully. '*Ka ghurraz Imladriki na Kaledor.*'

The wind whistled. For many heartbeats, no one spoke.

'Your accent has got worse.'

The voice came from behind the lines, hidden by the grim wall of steel and iron. Imladrik thought it sounded harsher than it had once done; back then, Snorri had always been the angry one, his cousin the voice of calm.

'I have not had much time to practise,' Imladrik called out, resisting the urge to scan along the lines to see where Morgrim was hidden.

He did not have to wait for long. The guards shuffled to one side, and the iron-clad hearthguard replaced them. Then their ranks parted, exposing two figures standing within their midst.

One was grizzled with age, his long beard flecked grey and his stance hunched. He carried a thick-shafted stave crowned with an iron anvil, the head of which seemed to shimmer as if in a heat-haze. Imladrik did not recognise him, though he knew well enough the marks of a runesmith.

The other one he certainly knew, though time had not been kind to the memory. Morgrim's helm and armour were smeared with blood, daubed in ritual marks of vengeance. His eyes had darkened and his previously open face had withdrawn into a scarred, tight visage of distrust. His boots and cloak were travel-worn, his fine armour splattered with the mud of the road. He carried an ornate axe, studded with runes. It looked new-forged.

Imladrik dismounted, though even on foot he still towered over the dwarf lord.

Morgrim did not bow. 'You sent me a fool,' he said.

'He came to me recommended,' said Imladrik.

'By whom?'

'Someone I trust.'

Morgrim grunted. 'We did not harm him,' he said, in a voice that indicated he regretted the fact.

'Then what of his tidings? Do we have leave to talk?'

'My thanes counsel against it. They are hungry to see your

Master of Dragons

walls in rubble. They ask me what you can tell us that we haven't heard before.'

'Little, perhaps,' admitted Imladrik. 'But not nothing. We used to speak often, you and I. Back then your cousin was the one who wouldn't listen.'

A shadow fell across Morgrim's face. 'His death is the cause of this.'

'He should have been buried in the Everpeak with honour. He should have taken his place beside Grimnir, and should have done so intact.'

As Imladrik spoke, one of his guards dismounted and bore him a rosewood box inlaid with silver renditions of the dwarfen runes of kingship. Imladrik passed it to Morgrim, stooping as he delivered it.

'I brought this from Lothern, where it should never have been taken. It is presented to you in reverence, in the hope that it may be returned to where it belongs.'

Morgrim glared up at him suspiciously for a moment. Then he opened the catch. A withered hand lay within, cushioned on silk and bound with fine linen. Its fingers had been severed at the first knuckle.

Morgrim stared at it for a long time. When he next spoke, his voice was thick.

'I would have brought our armies to Ulthuan to retrieve this.'

'I know.'

'And you think you can buy my goodwill with it?'

'It was not intended to buy anything,' said Imladrik, knowing the danger of mortal insult. 'I give it to you now before fighting makes it impossible, so it may be returned to his father in Karaz-a-Karak and interred with the *grondaz* rites. I would have it known that Snorri Halfhand, greatest of dawi princes, can still grasp an axe in the afterlife.'

Morgrim nodded slowly. 'Aye,' he said grimly. 'It would be fitting.'

Then he glared up at Imladrik again.

'It can never go back to how it was,' he said. 'My army will remain on these plains, preparing for battle. But I will listen. Perhaps you can tell me something new, perhaps not: I make no promises.'

Imladrik bowed, feeling a surge of relief wash over him. He felt like thanking Morgrim, knowing the risks the dwarf lord ran to make such a concession, but that would have been fatal – dwarfs cared nothing for gratitude, only debts, loyalty and payment.

So instead he rose to his full height and withdrew slowly, never taking his eyes off Morgrim's conflicted face.

'So be it,' he said. 'The last chance to end this madness. By Asuryan, let us not waste it.'

CHAPTER FOURTEEN

Liandra drove Vranesh hard, pushing her towards the far-off peaks of the Arluii. Her steed was happy to comply. As ever, their moods were intertwined, amplified and echoed in one another's minds with every movement and gesture.

She knew she should turn back. Her foray out over Loren Lacoi had given her a hawk's eye view of dawi columns moving close to Tor Alessi's hinterland – the vanguard of the main force would not be far behind it. On another day, she might have ordered Vranesh down, raking the slow-moving formations with a burst of dragonfire. She would have enjoyed that – it would have been a release after so long holding back.

Imladrik, of course, wouldn't have allowed it. His restraint was maddening. Liandra knew what he was capable of if he chose to unlock the power coiled tight within that proud, buttoned-up exterior. She had seen it for herself, and the memory still burned within her.

But she had made herself weary now telling others of his potential, even Salendor had stopped believing her.

'It doesn't matter how much you *tell* me this,' he'd complained, smarting after her rejection of him. 'Weak elves tell good stories.'

Salendor was within his rights to be sceptical – very few had ever seen dragon riders in action. The drakes were rare and majestic beasts, kept away from the battlefield by their riders unless the need was great. Salendor could have no idea what would happen when they were let loose. He could have no idea how contemptuously Draukhain or Vranesh could carve through the mightiest of defences, leaving nothing but molten armour fragments in their wake.

The dawi did not understand it either. It was centuries since dragons had gone to war in Elthin Arvan – no dwarfs now lived who would have witnessed them unleashed to the full. They had only ever hunted miserable cave-dwelling wyrms of the eastern mountains – the colossally powerful Star Dragons of the Annulii were another proposition entirely.

It was all so *frustrating*.

He is a fool, sang Vranesh in sympathy.

Liandra laughed bitterly. *You've changed your tune.*

Who but a fool would spurn the chance to mate with you?

It is not about mating, she sang back, affronted. *Gods, you can be crude sometimes.*

Then what is it? Vranesh sounded genuinely interested.

I see the things we could accomplish together. It was hard to conceal emotions from the dragons – they sniffed them out like prey. *He sees it too, but holds back.*

Because he is promised to another?

That is not all. Liandra's mind-voice was hesitant; she didn't like thinking of Imladrik's motivations. *He has his father's example to think of.*

Imrik, sang Vranesh with approval.

Indeed. Think on the lesson of Imrik, and you will understand both his sons.

Vranesh dipped a little lower, pulling clear of a long grey cloudbank. Ahead of them, still many leagues distant, the grey profile of the Arluii pocked the southern horizon.

His father refused to draw the Sword of Khaine, even though it would have ended the war, sang Liandra. *Caledor believes this was weak, and has spent his life trying to erase the shame of it. He would go to war with his own shadow if it offended him.*

And kalamn-talaen?

He thinks otherwise. Liandra looked out at the vast spread of Elthin Arvan, regarding it with the mix of hatred and devotion that she had always felt. *He thinks we carry the seeds of our destruction within us. He yearns for nothing more than to give free rein to the dragon, but dreads what it will do to him. He does not want to become another Aenarion.*

Liandra gripped her staff tightly. *I am his Sword of Khaine,* she sang. *That is the problem.*

Vranesh snorted her contempt. *Foolish.*

Liandra nodded slowly. *It is. We are a foolish race.*

Vranesh angled steeply, pulling closer to the land below. Liandra peered over the creature's shoulder, scouring the unbroken forest for signs of movement.

When will you order me back to the city? sang Vranesh. *Not that I am in a hurry – I enjoy the chance to stretch my pinions.*

Liandra was about to reply, to begin the long journey back, when something suddenly struck at her soul: a sharp pain, like a dagger-thrust. She winced, tensing in the saddle.

'What is that?' she asked aloud, voice tight with pain.

Vranesh had felt it too – the dragon instantly gained altitude, powering aloft with an urgency she hadn't employed for a long time.

East, Vranesh sang.

Liandra twisted around, feeling the pain intensify. Only slowly did she recognise the cause: echoes of agony in the aethyr, souls shrieking in pain, all wrapped in the poisonous embrace of Dhar magic.

'Kor Vanaeth,' she breathed, her heart suddenly chilling. 'Blood of Isha – my people.'

By then Vranesh was already flying hard, thrusting east, picking up speed with every powerful wingbeat.

Liandra reeled, clutching her breast as more waves of misery impacted.

She had always had a sympathetic link with her adopted home, but this was different. The pain was being shouted out across the aethyr like a beacon in the night. Someone wanted her to feel it.

Abomination, snarled Vranesh. The dragon's voice was twisted in fury. *I sense it.*

Find it, gasped Liandra, trying to shake off the sickening pain and summon up her own anger. *Find it, run it down. By Isha's tears, you shall have the bloodshed you seek.*

The tent's canvas walls swayed in the wind, buffeted by gusts that came off the western ocean and straight across the plain. It was an elaborate construction, a storeyed collection of fabric-walled chambers erected around a scaffold of thick wooden poles and taut hemp ropes. Imladrik had had it prepared weeks ago, hoping that it would be used for such a purpose; erecting it had taken just a few hours.

The site was equidistant between the dwarf camp and the city walls. No more than a hundred delegates were permitted within half a mile of it, fifty from each opposing force. Despite the precautions, the atmosphere of tense antagonism was palpable. Dwarfs glowered at their elgi counterparts; the asur glared back at them with equal suspicion.

Imladrik didn't like to see it, but he wasn't surprised.

So are the dreams of our fathers diminished.

He sat at the centre of a long table covered in white linen. He had come in his ceremonial robes rather than armour as a gesture of trust. Aelis, Gelthar, Caerwal and Salendor sat on either side of him, all similarly garbed.

Master of Dragons

There was still no sign of Liandra. He had sent messages to her quarters. She might, of course, have been unaware that the dawi had finally arrived, but he doubted it. Whatever her feelings about remaining in his presence, she should not have stayed away.

Perhaps that vindicated everything he had done. He wished he could feel surer.

Opposite them, sitting at a similar table, were the dwarfs. Three lords, in addition to the runesmith, sat with Morgrim. Imladrik didn't know them or recognise their livery; they had been introduced as Frei of Karak Drazh, Grondil of Zhufbar and Eldig of Karak Varn. They were neither princes nor kings, but thanes, advisers to their hold-master. Each looked ancient, as knotted and weathered as oak-stumps.

For all of their grandeur, there could be no doubt who dominated the chamber. Morgrim brooded in the midst of them, his countenance hanging like a funeral pall over the proceedings. He still wore his fabulously ornate battle plate with its swirling curves of knotwork decoration and bronze-limned detail, looking ready to unclasp his axe at any moment.

Still, he was there. That was something.

'So,' Imladrik said, inclining his head toward Morgrim, who made no move in return. 'Three sieges have taken place here. It is my hope we may avoid a fourth.'

Grondil grunted, Eldig looked bored, but none of them spoke. From either side of him Imladrik could sense the wariness of his own side: Salendor disdainful, Gelthar wary, Caerwal silently hostile.

'We came here for vengeance,' replied Morgrim. 'It will not be halted by words we have heard before.'

'Things have changed,' said Imladrik. 'I suspect much.'

'Suspect?' Morgrim's tone was dismissive.

'More than suspect.' Imladrik motioned to one of the servants standing in the margins of the chamber, who unfurled a long sheet of parchment and held it aloft.

'This is a map of our homeland,' said Imladrik. 'I had it drawn with every detail. You can see the extent of Ulthuan here. Note the scarcity of land between the mountains and the sea. So it was that the asur first came to Elthin Arvan, to escape the boundaries that fate had enclosed us in.'

Morgrim's eyes flickered over the parchment, taking in the detail quickly.

'Observe the land to the north-west,' Imladrik went on. 'The race who live there we name the druchii, the dark ones. They are driven by a pleasure creed which turns their minds, blighting them with sadism. For seven centuries we have warred with them. For more than a generation we have kept this war secret, shamed by it even as we strive to end it. Over the years it has changed us: we have become a harder people. We remember our fight against the daemons with pride, but this secret war has caused us nothing but shame.'

Morgrim looked back at him doubtfully. 'What is shameful about war?'

'Because the druchii were once one with us,' said Imladrik. Admitting it, even after so long, was still painful. 'Their master was our greatest captain. He will be known to you in your annals. His name is Malekith.'

The runesmith Morek grunted in recognition. 'We do remember. He was a friend of the dawi.'

'He was once,' said Imladrik. 'He was many things, once.'

Morgrim placed his gauntlets on the table before him with a soft *clunk*. 'This is your business, elgi. We have no concern what battles you make for yourselves.'

'So it would be, had the war not spread to Elthin Arvan. We have always tried to prevent it. Even in times of peace we maintained a watch on the seas, knowing that the Witch King would covet our cities here just as he covets those in Ulthuan. Athel Toralien was his once, and he is jealous over what he believes has been taken from him.'

As he spoke, Imladrik kept a wary eye on the dwarfs before

Master of Dragons

him. They made very few gestures and gave away almost nothing, though they were still listening, which was good.

'Druchii can pass as asur with some ease; even my own kind cannot always tell them apart. I tried to warn Gotrek of it, but by then he was in no mood to listen. They have certainly been here, perhaps in small numbers, but enough for what they were sent for.'

Morgrim leaned forward. 'And what is that? Enough hints – tell us what you suspect.'

'Agrin Fireheart,' said Imladrik. 'The spark that started this. They killed him, not us. The trade caravans, the first attacks; we were not responsible.'

That brought a change: Grondil shook his head angrily, Frei rolled his eyes. Morek leaned over to Morgrim and whispered something in his ear.

'You're telling me that these… druchii were to blame?' Morgrim asked, pushing the runelord away. He pronounced the word awkwardly.

'In the beginning, yes.'

'There were a hundred skirmishes,' said Morgrim sceptically. 'Dozens of attacks in the first years. We *know* they came from your colonies.'

'That did happen. Tempers flared, some lords were foolish.'

'Foolish!' snorted Grondil.

'And we also were attacked by dwarfs,' said Salendor, his eyes flat with hostility.

'All suffered,' admitted Imladrik, giving the Lord of Athel Maraya a sharp look. 'All of us did.' He turned to address Morgrim directly. 'You remember how much your High King tried to restrain your warriors, how much I attempted to keep my own back, and how we both failed – could that have happened if other forces were not at work? Think back: were there no voices in the holds whispering from the start? Strangers, perhaps, who somehow gained the ears of the already-willing?'

210   *Chris Wraight*

He might have imagined it, but Imladrik thought he caught a flicker of recognition from Morek then – the briefest of sidelong glances.

'I will not try to convince you we were not to blame,' said Imladrik. 'Believe me, I regret plenty, including things that happened before I went to Ulthuan. All I will say is this: other powers were active, powers that have wished to see us brought low ever since the Sundering. And if that is the case, should we not stand back, just for a moment, and consider what that means?'

His eyes remained fixed on Morgrim's.

'Warriors have died,' Imladrik said. 'Some fights have been without honour, and I understand the need for grudgement, but the *Dammaz Kron* makes provision for deception, does it not? This is my case, lords. Deception has taken place, poisoning the way between us. We can restore it, if we choose – it requires patient work, a little more understanding.'

Imladrik sat back, waiting for the response. He hardly dared to breathe. It would have been in character for the dawi to flatly refuse any further discussion – the information was new to them and they did not like tidings they could not personally verify.

The runesmith leaned over to Morgrim and they conferred for a few moments in whispers. They needn't have lowered their voices – even Imladrik could not understand much of the Khazalid they used. After that, Morgrim took views from the three other thanes. They took their time, grumbling and muttering in their guttural tongue with stabbing gestures from armoured fingers.

Imladrik watched all the while. None of his companions said anything; they sat erect in their seats, their faces calm. Of all of them, Caerwal looked the most uneasy, which surprised him. Salendor's hostility, for the moment, had been replaced by curiosity.

Eventually Morgrim leaned forward again. His expression,

Master of Dragons

as much of it as could be read under the ironwork of his helm, had not changed.

'We are not stupid,' he said. 'Nor are we blind. We know that you have your divisions. Perhaps we did not appreciate how deep they ran.'

Morgrim didn't bother looking at or addressing the others; he spoke to Imladrik alone.

'But you cannot think this is enough. Halfhand was slain by your own Phoenix King. The blood has been bad for too long to wave away with half-truths.'

Imladrik bristled. 'They are not half-truths.'

'Then prove them.'

Imladrik was about to ask, wearily, what would satisfy him when Morgrim shot him a rare look, one almost reminiscent of the way he used to be before, free of the patina of bitterness that now clouded his every move.

'But neither let it be said that the dawi do not know their own laws,' he said. 'You are right about the *Dammaz Kron*.'

He still didn't smile, though. Perhaps he was no longer capable of it.

'So tell us more about the druchii.'

Drutheira brought Bloodfang around for another pass, thundering towards the devastation that had once been Kor Vanaeth. The dragon had exceeded her expectations – once given a channel for its misery it had poured the full measure of woe on to its target, ravaging the asur settlement as if the place were somehow responsible for its life of torment.

The defenders had done their best. Some had even managed to loose a few bolts from eagle-shaped launchers atop the citadel's central tower. One had sheered close, nearly punching a fresh hole in Bloodfang's already ragged wings, but that was the best they had managed before the dragon had razed the rooftops, sweeping the whole rabble of artillery pieces from their places in a single, scything run.

After that the battle was ludicrously one-sided, something Drutheira took an exquisite pleasure in. The dragon's columns of flame ripped roofs clean from walls; its raking claws tore deep into towers and bulwarks, collapsing masonry into clouds of spiralling rubble. Arrows clattered uselessly from its armoured hide, igniting as they shot through the waves of flame that swathed the beast.

Drutheira hung on tight throughout, clutching the bone-spur before her one-handed and enjoying the violent swerve of the plunging attack. Her other hand brandished her staff, but aside from adding a few aesthetic touches she left the destruction to the dragon.

Magnificent, she thought, lurching to one side as Bloodfang shouldered aside another watchtower, crushing it into clouds of flaming dust. *Truly magnificent.*

By then little remained of Kor Vanaeth aside from its crudely fashioned central citadel. Shattered walls and dwellings lay smouldering and stinking. Whole streets had been demolished in the rush of claws and fire, their inhabitants roasted as they scampered for sanctuary. A porcine smell of cooked flesh hung over the sorry remnants, sweet and cloying and utterly delicious.

'The fastness,' Drutheira snarled, cracking her staff over Bloodfang's writhing neck.

The dragon roared its hatred, twisting its long jaws around and snapping at her, but the defiance was all for show – Drutheira dominated the creature entirely now, like a kicked cur goaded into the hunt. Bloodfang rolled awkwardly in the air, twisting its sinuous body and powering towards the citadel.

The survivors of the first attacks had barricaded themselves in there, trusting in its thick walls and heavy-beamed roof. Retreat had been the only strategy open to them, but it hemmed them in and sealed their doom. Bloodfang threw itself at the citadel's smoke-darkened flanks, hurling cascades of fire across the stonework. Narrow windows exploded as

Master of Dragons

213

raw dragonflame washed across them, showering the ruins below with blood-coloured glass. The dragon reared up and slammed directly into the walls, latching on with all four claws and grinding into the stone.

Drutheira was nearly thrown from her seat by the impact and had to scrabble to hold her place. 'Not so clumsy!' she cried.

By then, though, there was no stopping it. Perched halfway up the steep citadel walls, the dragon started to tear its way towards the soft interior, ripping the thick shell open and sending stone blocks thudding to earth.

A buttress collapsed, sending cracks racing across the reeling fortifications. A huge sandstone lintel dissolved into debris as Bloodfang's tail slammed into it, further weakening the structure. Drutheira heard muffled screams from within.

They would be cowering now, huddled in the deepest recesses and praying for deliverance. That was fine – it was what she wanted them to do. To turn those screams into aethyr-born echoes was the most trivial exercise of her art. The preparations had already been made, the blood-sacrifices performed. The death of Kor Vanaeth would echo in the hearts of any who cared for it.

Bloodfang grabbed a mighty block of wall-section in its jaws, ripped it free and flung it to one side. The heavy chunk of stonework sailed through the air before thumping down amid the destruction, rolling twice and toppling into the skeletal frame of some burned-out dwelling.

That left a gaping wound in the citadel's outer fortifications. Drutheira could make out torchlit movement within – a score of desperate defenders with what looked like long pikes, backing up in the face of Bloodfang's bludgeoning entry.

Drutheira couldn't help but laugh. It was like watching ants rush to staunch the breaches in their nest. She ran her fingers along her staff, pondering about adding some agony of her own to Bloodfang's relentless assault – perhaps they would be more amusing to watch with their skins pulled inside out.

'Burn them,' she ordered, her eyes going flat with delight.

But Bloodfang did not obey. The dragon pounced clear, dragging half the wall-section with it. The sudden movement caught Drutheira off-guard, and she rocked in her seat, nearly slipping for a second time.

'What are you *doing?*' she shrieked, snatching her staff up to strike the creature's flesh.

Bloodfang climbed fast, pulling away from the burning wreckage, its huge lungs wheezing from the sudden effort. Drutheira felt a shudder pass through its body, like a ship turning too rashly in a hard swell. She twisted around, scanning the rapidly tipping horizon for what had got the creature spooked.

It didn't take long. She wondered how she hadn't sensed it earlier.

'There she is,' she hissed, projecting witch-sight into the north-west.

Still far off, half-lost in the gloom of the dusk, a scarlet dragon was tearing towards them, burning up the air around it in its haste and fury. The creature came on fast. Terrifyingly fast.

Drutheira felt a sharp thrill of excitement shudder through her. A *real* dragon, not the ruined, sorcery-spoiled monster she had charge of. This should be interesting.

'Away,' she ordered, seizing control again, swinging around and into the south-east. Bloodfang responded, weeping fire and anguish, its silver eyes rolling with battle-madness. Together they raced from the ruins, out over the forest and towards the Arluii.

Drutheira looked over her shoulder. She no longer needed witch-sight to see the blazing dragon on her tail – it devoured the air between them, racing along hungrily, its wings a smoke-clouded blur.

Come to me, then, thought Drutheira greedily, watching the dragon rider's vengeful progress. *The last time you pursued me I was alone, but now I have such delightful toys.*

She struck Bloodfang hard, goading it onwards.

To the mountains, you and I. For the reckoning.

CHAPTER FIFTEEN

The meeting broke up in the evening, just as the shadows began to lengthen. Caradryel had watched it all with interest, hanging back in the margins and taking care not to become conspicuous.

It was good to be back among the civilised; the stench of the dawi had become wearisome. The food they had given him had been all but inedible – heavy sourdough breads slathered in some form of meat dripping washed down with the bitterest, darkest, foamiest liquid he had ever imbibed. He'd struggled to keep it in his stomach, though he couldn't deny it had given him endurance to keep marching.

Imladrik had been appreciative of his efforts in bringing Morgrim to the table, though there had been little time for the two of them to confer since his return. Caradryel had not been able to pass on properly his worries over division within the dwarf ranks, though Imladrik would surely have guessed much of it. Most of the dawi army was thirsting for blood still; it would take only the merest hint of a spark to light the fire again.

'Worry about our own people,' Imladrik had told him. 'That is your task now.'

Since then Caradryel's eyes had been firmly fixed on the asur delegation. He'd watched Gelthar try his best to hide his uneasiness, Caerwal his impotent hostility, Aelis her frustration at being sidelined. They were all of them chafing for one reason or another, though their noble-born discipline worked hard against rebellion.

As he had been from the start, Salendor remained the worry. The warrior-mage had scowled and frowned his way through the proceedings, interjecting unhelpfully and coming perilously close to overriding Imladrik twice. The dwarfs must have noticed, though of course they gave no sign of it.

Now, as the various contingents left the main tent and made their way warily back to their respective camps, the fragile air of amity withered again. Asur guards looked on stonily as the dawi trudged out of the marquee and back to their increasingly settled battle-lines.

Morgrim was the last to go.

'Until tomorrow,' Imladrik told him, bowing.

'Until then,' Morgrim replied, nodding brusquely.

After that the tent remained occupied only by asur council members. Servants milled around them, removing the linen drapes and the pitchers and salvers that had been served during the day. Caerwal talked animatedly with Aelis – something about reparations for Athel Numiel – Gelthar with Imladrik. Only Salendor was missing.

Caradryel withdrew from the tent and made his way across the rutted plain towards the city. In the failing light Tor Alessi looked even more massive and unlovely than it had when he'd left it. He reached the gates, showed his medallion of office to the guards and passed under the archway.

Inside the walls Tor Alessi hummed with activity. Its streets were crowded, just as always, swollen with soldiers hurrying to their stations or back to barracks. Caradryel pushed his way through the jostling throngs. No one paid him any attention – he was just one more official on just one more errand.

Salendor's mansion close to the quayside was well-guarded and not easy to observe unseen. By the time Caradryel reached it – an extensive, many-towered edifice near the waterfront, encircled by high walls – torches were being lit against the gathering dark. He could see the masts of ships in the harbour, black against deep blue.

Caradryel pulled back, letting the shadows of the nearside wall envelop him. The roads were still busy, dense with movement just like every street and alleyway in the entire fortress. He watched the gates of Salendor's mansion for a few moments. No one came in or out. A soft glow of lanterns spilled from the upper windows, but no figures were silhouetted against the glass.

He withdrew, walking back the way he had come until he reached a nondescript-looking building set back from the quayside road, three storeys tall, square and heavily built. The smell of grain emanated from it and piles of empty sacking slumped against the stone. Like so many of the harbourside buildings it had long since been commandeered for supply storage, which made it ideal for the purposes Caradryel had put it to.

He slipped a key into the lock and went inside, climbing up a steep stairwell past stacked grainsacks and wine barrels. The third floor was largely empty. As he entered, a figure at the window turned hurriedly to look at him.

'It's me,' said Caradryel, joining him. 'Anything to report?'

Geleth, one of his many agents in the city, relaxed. 'He's had visitors.'

'From Athel Maraya?'

'Hard to tell.'

Caradryel peered out of the window, keeping his head low against the sill. Salendor's mansion was quiet, enclosed within its high walls and insulated from the bustle outside.

'How long has he been back?'

'He arrived just ahead of you.'

Caradryel nodded. There was nothing, nothing at all, suspicious about Salendor's movements – every member of the Council had supplicants and counsellors calling in a steady stream, even more so since the preparations for battle had been stepped up. Unusual, though, to receive them here, rather than his formal lodgings near the Tower of Winds.

Caradryel scanned the mansion frontage. It was an old design, less functional than the buildings on either side of it, with something of the old flamboyance of Athinol. It looked like the two wings ran back a long way from the frontage, part-hidden by the walls of the mansion's neighbours. He could just make out lantern-glows from a long way back, though the windows themselves were almost totally obscured.

'How many guests entered by the main gates?' Caradryel asked.

'A dozen or so.'

'And left?'

'Half that.'

Caradryel nodded. 'So they're being put up, or there's another way out.' He pushed himself to his feet. 'Keep watching the gates. Try to spy an insignia if you can.'

He walked back down to street level, wondering where best to start in the maze of alleyways and narrow streets that zigzagged around the mansion. He matched the unconcerned gait of those around him, letting his eyes wander over the buildings that loomed up into the early evening sky.

It would have been pleasant to linger, had circumstances been different. The soft light on the stone, the chatter of the crowds, the smell of cooking from a dozen different windows, it was all agreeable enough.

Following a hunch, Caradryel ambled into a very narrow

Master of Dragons

alleyway that ran at an angle away from the main street. Just as he had expected, after a while it doubled back, enclosed on either side by tall stone walls with few overlooking windows. He smelled the dank, briny smell of seawater puddles and felt layers of moist dust under his boots. Soon he was in a labyrinth of capillary footways, all of them hemmed in by a close press of tenements. The hubbub of the main thoroughfares fell away into a low, distant hum.

Then, fifty yards ahead, he saw a shadow flit from a side door, a door that might very well have led out from one of the mansion's rear wings. Caradryel lengthened his stride. The shadow went ahead of him, neither hurrying nor tarrying. It wore a cloak with a red lining.

Caradryel began to catch up, and checked his pace – he needed to see where Salendor's guests were coming from before he challenged them. He slipped around a sharp corner only to stare down an empty path. Too late, he realised he'd missed a narrow opening twenty paces back, and retraced his steps just in time to see his quarry reach the end of another meandering alleyway.

Caradryel broke into a jog, cursing himself for carelessness. The end of the alleyway opened out on to the main quayside thoroughfare, as busy as all the others. Caradryel emerged breathlessly from the shadows, peering back and forth.

Crowds milled close by, a mix of soldiers in full armour and harbour workers in loose woollen tunics. Caradryel pushed his way through them, trying to catch sight of the figure he'd been chasing.

Sure enough, a way ahead and separated by a throng of unconcerned passers-by, he caught half a glimpse of scarlet fabric, quickly lost in the press. He pushed towards it, shoving his way past those in his path, but it soon became hopeless – the volume of bodies around him reduced his progress to a crawl.

Mouthing a curse under his breath, Caradryel elbowed

his way over to the waterfront where the mass of bodies was thinner, trying to decide if he'd learned anything of importance.

He concluded that he probably hadn't, not enough to report back to Imladrik with at any rate. Something was going on. He resolved to make enquiries on his return as to the whereabouts of the dragon rider Liandra. If she was still missing by the morning and messengers were colluding with Salendor, wearing what might or might not be the livery of Kor Vanaeth... well, that would be of some interest.

It would not be worth divulging to anyone else, at least not in the absence of anything like proof, but it was the start of something, something that might grow.

His face fixed in a frown of concentration, Caradryel started walking again. He had much to think on before the dawn.

Fatigue had no hold on Liandra, nor on Vranesh. The dragon tore through the night sky as fast as she had ever flown, eating up the leagues in an attempt to run down the abomination before them. There was no complaint nor query from her mind-voice, just a blank, animal hatred that crowded out all else.

It is ruined! Vranesh cried out, her song discordant with pain. *What have they done to it?*

The horror in Vranesh's mind polluted Liandra's own, making her hands shake with rage.

I know not, great one, she sang back, holding back tears of empathetic anger. *Believe me, we shall end it.*

Kor Vanaeth's desolation still hung in her mind's eye, inescapable and damning. She had hardly paused over the ruins, unwilling to lose the abomination's trail. The city was gone now, destroyed for a second time, and from this there would be no rebirth. The walls might have survived an attack by the dawi, but a dragon was another matter. The wreckage of the assault spread for miles into the forest – there had even been signs of a slaughtered dwarf warband amid the trees. The fact that the creature's rampage had been indiscriminate gave no comfort.

The stink of Dhar hung over the dragon's trail, tainting the air with a residue of putrid over-sweetness. The aroma was horribly familiar to Liandra, instantly bringing back memories of a hunt she had ended a long time ago. Like a nightmare dragged back into the world of wakefulness the same stink of sorcery had re-emerged, more spiteful than before and now borne on tattered, tortured wings.

Death will be a mercy for it, Vranesh sang, still enraged.

Mercy for the beast, replied Liandra grimly. *For her, nothing.*

The abomination was still fast. It must have once been a truly magnificent creature, a rare scion of the Dragonspine with few peers, for the black arts of the Witch King had not robbed it of its native speed. Even Vranesh, counted among the swiftest of the drakes, closed on it only slowly.

The hours passed in a bleak procession, marked only by twin flames in the night, the two of them tearing across the sleeping world like burning stars. When the clouds rolled over them at last, cutting out the light of the moons and dousing them in perfect darkness, it felt as if the earth and sky had been swept away, leaving them alone in a void of pure hatred, pursuer and pursued, hunter and prey.

Only with the dawn did the gap close. The black dragon seemed to tire as the sky in the east lightened, finally slow-ing as the mist-pooled mountains below were picked out by the shafts of gold. The two drakes came together, poised over the high peaks, wings splayed and claws unfurled.

Now we have them, Vranesh sang, her mind-voice little more than a growl.

Liandra leaned forward in her seat, sending flickers of aethyr-fire snaking along her staff.

Fight well, beloved, she sang.

Fight well, feleth-amina, came the reply.

Imladrik slept little, troubled by dreams in which both Yethanial and Thoriol had appeared before him accusing him of things he had done and things he had not. Waking from them to find himself in a besieged city on the edge of eternal war was almost a relief.

Dawn brought a sobering vision to the east of his tower. Morgrim's host had continued to grow, digging in across several miles of open countryside. Massive engines of war had been dragged up out of the trees – ballistae, trebuchets, siege towers, as well as other huge constructions he had never seen before. Whole regiments of infantry engaged in exhaustive dawn-drills before his eyes, swinging hammers and axes in unison across ranks a hundred wide. Every so often booming war-horns would sound, prompting a massed *Khazuk!* response which made the earth shake.

Imladrik watched them for a long time, scouring for signs of weakness, marvelling at the vast swell of bodies, all encased in thick armour or draped in coats of close-fitting mail. They went with a swagger, fully aware of their destructive potential. Self-doubt did not come easily to a dwarf – they knew just how deadly they were when gathered together in numbers.

After that he dressed and prepared for the day. He made his way down to the plain in the company of his ceremonial guard. Caradryel was waiting for him at the gatehouse, and the two of them walked out to the great tent together.

'Any news from Liandra?' Caradryel asked.

'Not yet. I am choosing to be generous, and assume she does not know that the dawi are here.'

Caradryel looked sceptical. 'It is still a desertion, is it not?'

'As I say, I am choosing to be generous.'

'Have you asked Salendor about her?'

Master of Dragons

Imladrik gave him a hard look. 'Why would I do that?'

'Perhaps you should. Just gently.' Caradryel looked ahead to where the cluster of tents shivered in the early morning wind, and grimaced. 'Another day of this. Blood of Khaine, I wonder if I'd prefer the fighting.'

'What of Salendor?'

'He's been busy, talking to all sorts of people.' He gave Imladrik a wary look. 'I think he's close to the edge.'

'Then keep an eye on him. I can handle the others, but I still need your eyes and ears. Do you need more money?'

Caradryel looked mildly insulted. 'I'll come to you if I do.'

They reached the tent, its canvas walls glossy with dew. Two guards in the livery of Silver Helms stood to attention, clasping their fists against their chests in homage.

'Does it ever get wearing?' asked Caradryel as they passed within. 'Being saluted by everyone?'

'I live for it,' said Imladrik, not really in the mood for Caradryel's flippancy.

The dwarfs were waiting for them in the central chamber, sat as they had been the day before, looking just as mutely murderous. Aelis, Salendor, Gelthar and Caerwal were there likewise, waiting for Imladrik to take his place.

'My lords,' he acknowledged as the elves rose to greet him. He bowed to Morgrim and the dwarfs, then took his seat. Caradryel took his place on the margins, sliding effortlessly into his habitual state of near-invisibility.

Imladrik reached for a pewter goblet filled with watered-down wine and took a sip. Then he clasped his hands before him and drew in a long, quiet breath.

'So,' he said, already feeling weary. 'Let us begin again.'

The black dragon coiled in the air ahead of them, no longer trying to escape and adopting a defensive posture. Its long ebony body snaked in an S-curve before hunching over, claws raised and jaws open.

Vranesh gave it no time to prepare – she hurtled straight at it, preceding her attack with a wall of crimson flame. The dragons collided in a blaze of mingled energy, lighting up the peaks in vivid, crimson-edged relief.

Vranesh powered through the inferno, raking out with her foreclaws, but the other dragon twisted away, doubling back on itself to escape the rush of talons. Liandra caught a fleeting glimpse of her opponent – an ivory-skinned druchii in torn robes. The sorceress looked emaciated, her staring eyes hollow with fatigue and deprivation.

They tumbled apart, each creature already coiling for the return. Vranesh was quicker, and managed to loose another gout of magma-hot flame before the abomination could bring its jaws around.

The blast hurt it – Liandra heard its screaming even over Vranesh's frenzied roars – but the black dragon somehow pushed through the intense heat and loosed a barrage of its own. Vranesh plummeted, letting dragonfire shoot over her arching spine before thrusting back up for a bite at the enemy's trailing tail. By then the abomination had powered away again, swinging about in mid-air and drawing in breath for a third fire-blast.

The speed of it, the intensity of it, the *noise* of it – was incredible. At first Liandra could do little more than hang on as Vranesh wheeled, bellowed and dived. Her counterpart seemed even more unsteady. Perhaps she was still new to the dragon; if so, that gave Liandra an edge.

In close, great one, she urged, regaining her balance and angling her staff for attack. *The rider is the weakness.*

Vranesh hardly needed telling. The dragon shot forwards, tail flicking out and her wings slamming back. As the enemy raced in close, Liandra unleashed her art.

'*Malamayna elitha terayas!*' she cried, feeling her staff shudder as lightning crackled out from its tip.

Golden aethyr-fire shattered across the abomination's

mottled hide, showering both creatures in clouds of stinking black blood. The beast screamed again, this time with genuine excruciation, and launched itself directly at Liandra, evading Vranesh's jaws and aiming to pluck her clean from her mount.

Vranesh was equal to the move, plunging down again and rolling away, but only just – Liandra had to throw herself to one side to evade the talons before Vranesh pulled them both out of danger.

Again, Liandra commanded, pushing singed hair from her face and righting herself for a second pass. Her heart was thumping, her eyes shining. The mountains wheeled and swung below them, lit by the angry glow of the dawn sun. Vranesh swooped, angling her attack to scrape across the abomination's wings.

Then Liandra felt it: a sudden plunge of pain in her spine, as if a metal bolt had been hammered in. Vranesh sensed it and tried to pull out at the last moment, but it was too late. As if forewarned, the black dragon pounced, ripping its foreclaws across Vranesh's extended neck.

Liandra reeled, feeling herself go dizzy. The abomination made the most of the confusion, tearing and clawing, trying to bring its ragged maw to bear.

Her vision swimming, it was all Liandra could do to summon a fresh brace of lightning-bolts and hurl them into the monster's face. That knocked it back, giving Vranesh the chance to pull out of the attack.

The witch, sang the dragon.

No, gasped Liandra, tottering in her seat and peering down at the mountains below. *From the earth.*

Vranesh immediately plunged towards the horizon, blood trailing behind her in a long stream. Liandra could feel the depth of the wound in the dragon's neck as clearly as she felt the pain in her own body.

Forcing herself to concentrate, she scoured the landscape

below. Rocky crags sped by beneath them, snow-crowned and empty. She could hear the wheezing breath of the dragon racing after them and ignored it.

She is not alone, Liandra sang, gaspingly. *She drew us here. We must withdraw.*

No! The vehemence of her denial surprised even her. *This is the chance – I will not lose it.*

Even as she sang the words she saw them – two robed figures standing on the very lip of a high crag below them, each one chanting, their staffs running with black-purple illumination.

Vranesh thrust towards them immediately, corkscrewing and undulating to avoid the abomination's pursuing fire. Liandra felt fresh stabs of pure pain explode within her and fought to maintain consciousness. Her staff felt impossibly heavy in her hand, and an almost overwhelming urge came over her to let it fall away.

Fight it! sang Vranesh, bucking hard to her left to evade a spitting column of dragonfire.

Liandra gritted her teeth, feeling sweat sluice down the nape of her neck. Her hands shook as she summoned aethyr-fire back to her.

You are a daughter of Isha, she recited to herself as the edge of the crag raced towards her. *You are a daughter of Isha.*

She could see their faces now – two druchii sorcerers, one male, one female, each bedecked in tongues of dark fire. At the last minute, faced with the crimson hurricane of fire and flesh barrelling towards them, they broke, sprinting back along the crag-top and seeking shelter.

The sudden cessation of their pain-magic revived Liandra. Her staff sprang back to life, shimmering with pent-up golden fire.

'Asuryan!' she cried aloud, swinging her staff around her head before hurling its tip in the direction of the fleeing sorcerers.

Master of Dragons

The air shook as the fire blazed free, streaking after the druchii and detonating around them in a hard crack. The entire crag-top exploded in a roar of shattering stone.

Vranesh pulled up at the last moment, claws scrabbling through the breaking summit. With an echoing boom the crag began to collapse, dragging whole chunks of slush and granite down the far side. Liandra swayed in her seat as Vranesh's momentum carried them both over. The pain had gone, but the abomination was still hurtling after them, snarling close on Vranesh's tail.

Did we get them? she asked, twisting her head to catch sight of the sorceress – she could smell and hear the dragon but no longer see it.

Vranesh didn't reply. Her huge breaths were strained. A hot aroma of burned copper rose from her torn neck-scales as she thrust up skywards, more laboured than before.

Then Liandra caught sight of the enemy, still close but hovering forty feet clear, strangely indecisive, as if the loss of the sorcerers had given its rider doubtful pause.

Liandra's eyes narrowed. She crouched low across Vranesh's straining shoulders, her staff still rippling with power.

Now we take her, she snarled.

CHAPTER SIXTEEN

'You have given us *nothing!*' accused Grondil, flecks of spittle flying. 'You say you do not think of us as fools. Well, you have a strange way of showing it.'

Caradryel watched the dwarf lord rage. The display was impressive, full of the red-cheeked, fist-slamming bravado the dwarfs employed when they wished to get a point across. Grondil had stood up to speak, though the difference in height, as far as Caradryel could see, was slight.

Caradryel glanced over at Imladrik, sitting calmly waiting for the tirade to finish.

'What would you have me do?' Imladrik replied. 'Summon the druchii before you?'

Grondil glowered. 'It would be a start.'

'Enough,' muttered Morgrim irritably. 'You have made your point.'

Grondil glared at Morgrim for a moment. Then, grudgingly, he sat down again.

Morgrim looked tired. Caradryel guessed that he had been engaged in many long sessions of argument with his thanes during the night. Morgrim had very little to gain from any cessation in hostilities but plenty to lose; perhaps the strain was getting to him.

'Grondil speaks the truth,' said Morgrim. 'We can talk around this as much as we like, but we will always come back to the same issue. You ask us to believe you, to trust you, yet trust is just the thing we do not have.'

Imladrik raised his hands in a gesture of hopelessness. 'We've talked ourselves hollow over this. Your people in the high places, mine in the lowlands. There is room for us to live alongside one another.'

'For now, perhaps,' said Morgrim. 'But in a year, when memories have faded? What shall I tell the High King – that we had the chance to destroy our enemy when he was weak and instead let him recover to come after us again?' He shook his head. 'You must give us more. There is a blood-debt on your head.'

Caradryel had been watching Imladrik's exchanges for so long that he'd almost forgotten the other members of the Council. Against the odds, it was Caerwal who spoke up then, his blank face uncharacteristically animated.

'Blood-debt?' he demanded bitterly. 'What of my people? Who will pay the price for the slain at Athel Numiel?'

Eldig snorted. 'Perhaps it was not dawi who killed them. Perhaps it was these druchii. After all, who can tell?'

Caerwal shot to his feet. 'Do *not* dishonour them!' he shouted, his cheeks flushing.

Grondil and Eldig both stood up and started to shout back. Caradryel glanced at Imladrik again and their eyes met. Imladrik gave him a weary look that said *this is hopeless*.

Then, just as the entire chamber dissolved – again – into a series of bawling matches, a lone elf slipped in to the tent from the asur side and sidled up to Salendor. He wore the livery of Athel Maraya, and in all the commotion no one gave him a second glance.

No one, except, for Caradryel, who observed carefully. The elf stooped low and whispered something in Salendor's ear. Then, just as silently and with as much discretion as before, he rose to his feet and ghosted back out. Salendor sat for a while, pensive, no longer paying much attention to what was going on around him but staring down at his hands.

'And so what do we have left to talk about?' demanded the runelord Morek amongst the hubbub, his old voice cracked and cynical.

'Everything, *rhunki*,' urged Imladrik, still trying to rescue something from the wreckage. 'If we could just calm ourselves...'

'That is wise counsel,' said Salendor, suddenly lifting his head up and looking around the chamber. At the sound of his voice, the space fell quiet. 'We have been arguing for hours and achieving nothing. Perhaps some time apart would be beneficial.' He glanced over at Imladrik, seeking his approval. 'Some wine, some food.'

Imladrik considered that for a moment, seemingly torn between pressing on and cutting things short before they descended into a brawl.

'Very well,' he said resignedly. 'We will adjourn. But, my lords, I implore you to *consider* what has been offered here. Reflect on it. Let us hope we may convene in a better temper.'

The session rose. As servants filed into the chamber with refreshments, Salendor quietly made his way to the entrance and walked outside.

Caradryel got up and followed him. As he neared the canvas opening, Imladrik broke free of an animated discussion with Caerwal and called him back.

'Where are you going?' he asked.

Caradryel nodded in the direction of the city. 'Salendor,' he said, and that was all that was needed.

Imladrik looked distracted, no doubt already thinking of ways to salvage the upcoming session. 'Are you sure you're–'

'Leave him to me,' Caradryel said. 'You worry about the dawi.'

Imladrik nodded. 'Very well, but if he's ready to move...' He paused, his face looking almost haggard for a moment before hardening again.

'You know what to do,' he said, and turned away.

The land raced past in a blur. The two drakes dived and soared, each snapping at the other as they tried to find purchase, neither landing the decisive blow.

Drutheira had been reduced to hanging on grimly. The crimson mage was far more powerful than she'd guessed. A dragon – a *real* dragon – was also far more powerful than she'd guessed. Her own mount was bigger and more steeped in sorcery, but its erratic mind made it a haphazard and flailing combatant.

She had no idea where they were. The hours of flying had left her disorientated and exhausted. The Arluii were long behind them, a hateful memory now consigned to the north. Seeing her companions on the mountaintop swatted aside so easily had been like taking a kick to the stomach – they should have been able to cripple the mage at least. Perhaps their powers had withered during the long years of the hunt, or perhaps they had just got careless.

A sun-hot burst of flame rushed past her. Bloodfang wheeled down to its right, tilting clear of the blast, its chains clanking as it spun away from the danger.

'Back!' she cried, driving the spike-point of her staff into the creature's neck again, though it did little good. 'Do not run!'

Bloodfang had long since ceased responding to her commands. The beast had been badly mauled, first by dragonfire and then by talons – the pain seemed to have driven what little sanity it possessed into abeyance.

Drutheira glanced over her shoulder. The red mage was

close behind, just as she had been since the fight over the mountains, her face fixed in a mask of hatred, her staff still glittering with nascent sunbursts of power.

Drutheira raised her own staff, dragging up yet another gobbet of raw Dhar potency, dreading the pain it would bring her.

'Kheledh-dhar teliakh feroil!' she shrieked, her voice cracking, and launched a trio of spinning black stars at the red dragon.

The creature evaded two of them, pulling up high with a sudden thrust of its wings and arching over the star-bolts, but one impacted, cracking into its exposed chest. The bolt detonated with a sick *snap*, making the air around it shudder and bleeding out lines of oil-black force. The star-bolt clamped on, sprouting slick tentacles that gripped and ripped like a living thing.

The red dragon bucked and twisted, bellowing in pain, nearly throwing its rider off and falling further behind.

'Now!' Drutheira screamed at her wayward steed, wishing she could grab the monster's head and force it to see what she had done. 'While it is wounded!'

The red dragon's roars of pain must have penetrated into even Bloodfang's pain-curdled mind, for it responded at last, switching back mid-air and inhaling for a fresh blast of dragonfire.

By then the asur mage had done her warding work, ripping the sorcerous matter clear of her mount's flesh and casting it away. Bloodfang lurched into range, its massive wings thrusting like bellows, fire kindling between its open rows of yellow teeth. The red dragon responded as best it could, uncoiling its wracked body and summoning up flame-curls of its own.

Bloodfang slammed into it, hurling a raging stream of dragonfire at its torso and following up with scything swipes from its extended forelegs. The two beasts crunched together, meeting with an echoing crack of bone.

Drutheira's mount ripped into the other drake's already ravaged neck-armour. Claws and tail-barbs flew back and forth, dragging and biting. The two creatures grappled with one another, rolling over and over in the skies, retching fresh dragonfire into one another even as their jaws bit deep into fissured armour.

Blood splashed across Drutheira's face as she gripped tight, trying to keep her head as the world whirled around her. She caught fractured glimpses of her adversary doing the same thing, lost in the savagery of the dragons unleashed at close quarters.

Drutheira had lived through a hundred battles, but the viciousness of this one took her breath away. Both creatures were consumed with primal bloodlust, far beyond reason or mortal understanding, roaring into one another like hounds on a stag. Bloodfang was the bigger, the heavier and the more powerful – its muscles rippled under steel-hard armour as its claws punched out – but the crimson dragon was still the quicker and more cunning, writhing out of the reach of its enemy's jaws and biting back with attacks of its own.

Drutheira swung around in her mounted vantage, getting a brief glimpse of open water far below them, but dared not shift position further to get a better look. She gripped Bloodfang's bucking neck two-handed, no longer able to use her staff, summon magic, or do anything other than weather the storm.

'Elemen-dyan tel feliamor!'

The words somehow rose above the deafening roars, piercing the confusion like a sudden shaft of sunlight. Drutheira snapped her head back up and what she saw took her breath away.

The red mage was standing – *standing* – on her steed's back, bracing herself with one hand while the other whirled her staff around her head. Her poise and balance were incredible, as if she could somehow anticipate every movement her mount was making and adjust for it ahead of time.

Drutheira tried to drag herself into an attacking posture, to kindle her staff and summon up some kind of response, but Bloodfang's violent movements made it impossible and she fell back heavily against a bulge of heaving wing-muscles.

Then the world exploded around her. The red mage launched her magic: a coruscating bloom that blistered the air and ripped into the glimmering world of the aethyr beyond. Drutheira heard a sudden clap, followed by a howl of wind and the tart stink of burning. Bloodfang, agonised by a sudden burst of aethyr-brilliance, twisted its massive head over to bite at the source.

'No!' cried Drutheira, hauling on the beast's chains. 'Do not–'

It was too late. Bloodfang's massive, sore-encrusted jowls closed on the mage's incandescent staff-tip even as she thrust it out. Its point drove up through the roof of the creature's mouth cavity, searing clean through flesh, gristle and bone.

The red dragon spun away, breaking free of Bloodfang's throttling embrace and powering back into the open sky, leaving the mage's flaming staff embedded in the black dragon's maw.

Drutheira tried to clamber up towards her steed's head to retrieve the lodged staff, but it was hopeless – she had no command of such work, and Bloodfang had been driven into a frenzy of spasms.

The length of spell-wound ash kept burning away, crackling like lit blackpowder. Bloodfang's mouth was now smoking, and not from the creature's native fire-breath. It arched, clawing at its own face, lost in a hell of pain and confusion as the staff worked its way in towards the brain.

Drutheira clung on, hoping against hope to find some way to pull things back from the brink. The scarlet dragon made no attempt to come at them again – Drutheira caught a fragmentary glimpse of it limping through the air, bleeding profusely, head lolling with exhaustion.

That was the last she saw of it, for Bloodfang plummeted further, losing height with every jerking wingbeat. Its neck thrashed about, its head shook back and forth, its limbs extended rigidly, stiff with pain.

'Fight it!' screamed Drutheira, seeing how fast the world below was racing up to meet them. Now it was clear where they were – out over a wide strand of water that glittered in the sun. Bloodfang was heading right for it, perhaps unable to gain loft, perhaps somehow aiming to douse the agonising fire that raged in its skull.

Drutheira watched helplessly as the dragon's eyes turned from silver to gold before exploding in a splatter of flaming liquid. The skin around its jaws broke open, exposing taut cords of sinew within. Bloodfang's own furnace-like innards now worked against it, feeding the inferno that raged down its neck and into its lungs, hollowing it out, purging the ancient sorcery that had sustained it and turning it into a flesh-bound caldera.

Drutheira had seen enough. Struggling still against the dragon's tumbling flight, she pushed herself out over a shoulder-spur, almost losing her staff in the process. With a sickening lurch she saw how far she had to fall – over sixty feet, though dropping fast.

Bloodfang seemed to sense that she was abandoning it and twisted its blind head round a final time. Even amid its anguish the dragon managed a final burst of fireborn hatred. Drutheira pushed herself clear, leaping from her steed as the flames screamed over her. The heat was intense, sweeping across her back and shoulders, but mercifully brief. For a terrifying moment she felt the world open up below her and the whistling surge of the air racing past her cartwheeling limbs.

Then came the splash and booming rush of impact. She

Master of Dragons

plunged deep below the surface, her robes billowing around her, bubbles swarming into her face and making her gag. She had a sudden terrible fear of hitting the bottom and tried to kick against her momentum. Something snagged against her left ankle and her heart-rate spiked, driven by panic.

Somehow, though, she managed to push up again. She thrashed her way to the surface and her head broke through. She drew in a desperate breath before ducking under again, gulping and spluttering, then pushed back up, her cheeks puffing.

As she emerged she saw Bloodfang go down. The creature was howling, wailing in abject degradation as its face melted away from the bone. Its wings had gone limp, fluttering like a shroud as its chained body rolled earthwards.

The dragon hit the water a hundred feet from her, crashing down with a gargling roar and sending out waves like the wake of a warship. Foam surged up around it, vapourising instantly as its sorcerous flames were finally doused. Its huge tail whipped out a final time, sending spray flying high, before it too was dragged under.

Drutheira caught a final glimpse of the dragon's ruined head, gasping for air, before the hissing waves closed over it, then all was lost in a welter of steam and bloody froth.

The waves from the impact hit her next, nearly swamping her and sending her back under. Her limbs felt like lead weights and her flame-seared flesh smarted – it was all she could do to flail away, blundering towards where she supposed the shore must be.

The sky above her remained empty, with no sign nor sound of the red mage. She swam on, doggedly pulling into calmer waters. Soon she was amongst reeds, then she felt soft mud under her feet. She hauled herself upright, wading through the shallows, breathing heavily.

Standing knee-deep, she looked around her. The shoreline was empty – a parched scrubland of ochre soils and meagre bushes. The sun beat down hard from a clear blue sky, already warming her sodden body.

Her breathing began to calm down, the shaking in her hands eased. There was still no sign of the red mage. The asur's steed had been horribly wounded; perhaps it too had fallen to earth.

Bloodfang, though, was gone. Against all expectation, Drutheira felt a pang of remorse at that.

She shook her head irritably.

It was a beast, she remonstrated with herself. *A dumb, mad beast. May the day come when all the dragons are so enslaved.*

She started to wade again. A silty beach drew closer, covered in a scum of algae and beset by clouds of flies. Beyond that, desolate land stretched away from her. She could see bare hills on the eastern horizon, their crowns baked butter-yellow and dotted with sparse vegetation. Already she felt thirsty, and the heat was growing. The sky remained empty, devoid even of birds.

Perhaps I killed them both.

Her head was light. Already the past two days of unremitting combat felt like some crazed, poppy-fuelled dream, and she still didn't know quite what to make of it.

It had not gone how she had expected, and certainly not as she had planned, but she was alive. That was the important thing: she was bruised, alone, exhausted, but alive.

'So then,' she said out loud, sweeping her dark, hollow eyes across the strange landscape before her. 'What now?'

Caradryel made his way quickly to the city. Just inside the gatehouse he caught up with Feliadh, who was waiting for him with a dozen of his troops in tow.

'Is it time?' Feliadh asked.

'It is,' replied Caradryel. 'Where did he go?'

'Into the Merchants' Quarter.'

Caradryel nodded. 'Then we follow him there.'

Master of Dragons

They went swiftly. Caradryel let his hand stray down to the long knife at his belt, and cursed himself for not bringing something a little more useful.

The Merchants' Quarter was not far, though the name had long since ceased to signify anything meaningfully mercantile. The old storehouses and market squares had been given over to supply depots and training grounds, and like everywhere else in the city the place was crawling with soldiers.

'Who has responsibility for this place?' asked Caradryel as they made their way deeper into the warren of streets.

'The Lord Caerwal,' said Feliadh.

'Really? Interesting.'

They reached a ramshackle courtyard near the centre of what had been the clothiers' market. One of Feliadh's soldiers was waiting for them at the junction of two narrow streets.

'He went in there,' said the soldier, pointing to a nondescript tower a few yards down the left-hand street. 'I counted six with him.'

Caradryel glanced at Feliadh. 'I'd rather not wait. Can you handle six?'

Feliadh smiled condescendingly. 'Worry not,' he said, patting the hilt of his ornate Caledorian longsword.

The captain took the lead. Feliadh walked up to the tower and tried the door. It swung ajar as he pushed it, revealing a shadowy hallway on the other side.

Caradryel took a deep breath. This kind of work was not something he enjoyed – the prospect of blood, real blood, being shed made him nervous in a way that was hard to hide.

'Let's try to make this clean,' he said, drawing his knife. 'Remember – Imladrik wants proof before we take him in.'

Feliadh gestured with a forefinger and his troops drew their blades.

'For Ulthuan,' he said quietly.

Then he plunged inside, barging the door open and charging into the hallway. Caradryel followed closely, trying his best not to impede the movements of the Caledorians around him.

The space beyond the doorway was deserted, but a stairway rose up steeply on the far side. Light and noise came from the upper storey – the sound of voices raised in anger.

Feliadh raced up the stairway two steps at a time, reaching another landing with a heavy wooden door on the far side. An elf was slumped on the floorboards, unconscious. As Caradryel jogged past him he noticed the crimson edge-livery on his rumpled cloak, then Feliadh shouldered the door open.

'Lower your blades!' he roared as he and his soldiers bundled inside. 'In the name of Imladrik of Caledor, lower your blades!'

Caradryel was next inside, his heart thumping heavily.

It was a large, sunlit chamber. A long table ran down its centre at which half a dozen elves in loremasters' robes were seated. Maps, campaign plans and other documents covered the surface. Six soldiers in the armour and colours of Athel Maraya stood protectively around the loremasters, their swords hastily raised at the intrusion.

Salendor stood at the head of the table with mage-staff in hand. He looked furious.

'What is this?' he demanded.

Caradryel pushed his way to the front of his party. The Caledorians fanned out defensively around him.

'My apologies, lord, but I have been tasked with ending this.'

Salendor looked at him incredulously. 'And who are you?'

Caradryel stiffened. The contempt in Salendor's voice was withering.

'Imladrik's agent,' he replied, producing the seal of office he'd been given. 'Please do not resist – it will be easier on everyone.'

Master of Dragons

For a moment Salendor looked too outraged to speak. Caradryel worked hard to retain eye contact with him, painfully aware of how dangerous the mage could be and hoping Feliadh's troops would have his measure if things turned difficult.

'Do not *resist?*' Salendor laughed harshly. 'Blood of Khaine, you have no idea what you've stumbled into.'

Caradryel walked over to the table and grabbed a handful of parchment pieces. He could see instructions scrawled in Eltharin outlining attack routes, all leading to the dawi lines. It was a pre-emptive strike, one designed to destroy the fragile truce.

'This is the proof, my lord,' said Caradryel. 'I have been observing you for some time.'

Salendor raised an eyebrow, and a dark humour played across his lips. 'Have you, now? And you truly think you can bring me in?'

Caradryel swallowed. 'Know that I will do my duty,' he said, gripping his knife tightly.

Then Salendor laughed. He motioned to his guards, who all stood down and sheathed their weapons.

'You're a damn fool,' Salendor sighed. 'And two steps behind me.'

Even as Salendor spoke, Caradryel noticed that the seated figures were not in the same livery as those standing – all of them wore cloaks lined with red, just like the one slumped on the landing outside. They also looked horribly afraid.

'I don't–' he started, suddenly doubtful.

'No, you don't,' said Salendor. 'Tell your Caledorian savages to put their knives away. We are on the same side.'

Caradryel hesitated, unwilling to lose the initiative, but as he looked more closely at the situation his confidence drained away.

'I was alerted to this by one of Caerwal's adjutants,' said Salendor, leaning against the table. 'A loyal one, but I took some time to establish that, because it is important to be *sure*, is it not?'

Caradryel began to feel distinctly foolish. 'The messenger at your mansion.'

'So you have been watching me. I suppose I should be flattered.' Salendor looked over the rows of seated loremasters and his expression changed to contempt. 'I argued against Imladrik's plans – you'll know that. I tried to persuade the others to join me – you might know that too. But you think I'd be stupid enough to try *this*?'

Caradryel stared down at the attack plans. They involved named regiments from the city. 'Then who–'

'Caerwal. Have you not seen the way he is? He lost half his people at Athel Numiel and will never forgive it. Even as he sits in that tent his loremasters have been planning to end it all.'

Caradryel sheathed his knife, feeling a little nauseous, and motioned for Feliadh and his company to do the same. 'When?'

'Any time. Six regiments, all sent against the dawi right flank. Suicidal, but it would have brought the war he wanted. Look, you can see the plans here. You can even check the garrison sigils if you wish.'

Caradryel looked down at his hands. 'My lord, I owe you–'

'Do not insult me. Learn from it.'

Caradryel really had very little idea what to do after that. He felt deeply, profoundly foolish – like a child suddenly exposed at playing in an adult world. Various responses ran through his head, none of them remotely satisfactory.

He started to say something, but the walls suddenly shook, rocked by a new sound that burst in from outside. Caradryel reached for his knife again, staring around him to find the source.

Salendor tensed, as did his guards. An abrupt tumult rose up from the plain. Horn-calls followed it, harsh and dissonant, and the volume of noise quickly mounted.

Caradryel hastened over to the window, followed by Salendor. He opened one of the heavy lead clasps and pushed it open.

Up on the parapets, sentries were rushing to the bell-towers. Their hurried movements spoke of surprise, perhaps some fear. A great boom of drums rang out from the east, soon joined by rolling repetitions. He knew what that was, just as every asur who had spent any length of time in Elthin Arvan did.

Caradryel turned to Salendor, his smooth face going pale. 'The dawi,' he murmured.

Salendor nodded. 'Indeed,' he said, closing the window and making for the door.

'Where are you going?' asked Caradryel, hurrying after him.

Salendor halted at the doorway. The disdain had not left his face. 'It was always bound to end like this. Caerwal has not succeeded, but someone else has. Do what you will – I have more important tasks now.'

As he spoke, the floor throbbed from the chorus of low drumming that now rolled at them from beyond the walls. Caradryel heard the tinny response of clarions, followed by the metallic clatter of soldiers beating to quarters in the streets outside.

Salendor strode out of the chamber, his cloak swirling imperiously around his ankles. His guards followed him.

Feliadh glanced enquiringly at Caradryel. 'What now?'

Caradryel looked around him. Caerwal's loremasters all waited, mute and fearful, knowing the penalty for what they had done. Outside, the drumbeats picked up in tempo and volume, matched by the strident tones of bronze war-horns.

Caradryel's shoulders slumped. Everything he had worked for had just dissolved, and for reasons he did not yet even understand.

246 Chris Wraight

'Chain them,' he said miserably, drawing his knife again and looking distractedly at the dull edge. 'Then report to me.'

Feliadh saluted smartly. 'And where will you be, lord?'

Caradryel smiled coldly. 'On the walls,' he said, already moving. 'Fighting.'

CHAPTER SEVENTEEN

The pain was astonishing. It wasn't physical, though her body had been battered badly on the way down. It was spiritual torture, as exquisite as any devised by the debased courts of Naggaroth. Liandra wanted to scream out loud, to rage against the fortune that had brought her such agony, but somehow managed to bite her tongue.

Tell me you can restore yourself, Liandra sang.

Vranesh could barely summon the strength to open her eye. It stared at Liandra from just a few feet away, immense and glossy like a golden pearl.

Do not be foolish, the dragon replied. *My fire is gone.*

Liandra caressed the dragon's long neck. It felt like her heart was being torn out. She could feel Vranesh's mortal pain, burning in her own body like an echo.

I would go there with you, Liandra sang.

You cannot.

I would be the first.

Vranesh attempted a laugh. A rolling pall of greyish smoke

spilled from her open jawline, sinking into the dry earth and drifting away.

She was right – the fire had gone.

What it is like? asked Liandra, desperate to keep speaking, as if that alone could somehow postpone the moment.

We are there as we were before you entered the world, sang Vranesh. *Before the shaan-tar came to tutor you, before strife came from the outer dark. The eldest of us remember. I will see them again, the names of legend.*

Liandra inhaled deeply, breathing in the remnants of Vranesh's scent. The ember-charred musk was weaker, tinged with the hot stink of blood. The dragon was covered in it, its scales sticky and matt with clogged dust.

The land they had crashed into was a desolate one: sun-hardened plains of baked earth and sparse-brush hills. The heat was oppressive, as if sunk into the air like dye in cloth.

Liandra had little idea where they were. For the long hours of pursuit all that had mattered was vengeance – running down the druchii witch. At least that had been achieved.

Vranesh's voice entered her mind again then, reading her thoughts.

She is not dead.

I saw her hit the water.

The abomination, yes, sang Vranesh. *Not the rider.*

You are sure?

I can hear her still. Vranesh's long mouth twisted at the corners in a reptilian grimace. *She is fearful and alone, but alive.*

Liandra almost stood up then. She almost walked straight out into the heat-shimmer plain, once more driven with that thirst for revenge that had dogged her since first taking the drake-saddle.

But she didn't. She remained where she was, cradled in the massive claws of her mount like a child in the arms of her mother. Her cloak lay about her in singed tatters.

We will hunt her, then. When you are ready.

Master of Dragons 249

Vranesh did not smile that time. The dragon let out a long, long sigh, as sibilant as steel sliding across steel. *You do not listen. You have never listened.*

I do not–

Silence! Vranesh snapped. *No time remains.* The dragon tried to lift her head and failed. More blood bubbled in the corners of its mouth, popping like tar. *Kill the witch if you must, but remember where the real battle lies. All that matters is the song sung between our peoples. If the kalamn-talaen falls then the bond will be broken.*

Liandra did not want to hear the words. Imladrik, for so long an obsession with her, had become an unwelcome reminder of the past, something to be put away and forgotten.

He will not–

Listen! He is the last. Though maybe you can learn. Vranesh blinked – a slippery movement with a leathery inner eyelid – and fixed her obsidian pupil on Liandra. *Do not waste yourself out here. You will be needed. Preserve yourself.*

Liandra felt the words stab at her. *I would follow you*, she said again, tears of anger spiking in her eyes.

Perhaps you might. Perhaps you, out of all of them, might.

Then more grey smoke poured out of Vranesh's blackened nostrils, flecked with black motes. The huge eye lost its glossiness, and a sigh like winter wind escaped from blood-stained jaws.

I loved you, fire-child, Vranesh sang.

Then she was gone. The mind-presence disappeared from Liandra's thoughts, snuffed out in an instant. Although the pain went with it, the hollowness that came in its place was almost unbearable.

Liandra rocked to and fro, balling her fists. For a moment it felt as if she were going mad, or maybe sinking into the same death-trance as her mount.

The tears would not come. She had never been able to

cry from grief, only from anger or frustration. Now, alone, stranded on the edge of the world, her companion sundered from her at last, she just rocked steadily, eyes staring, consumed by horror.

Only much later did the first howl come – a rending wail that burst raw from her throat. Then more cries, each shaking with loss, each sent up into the uncaring, empty skies above.

She lost track of herself, consumed by a grief so total if felt as if the world were swallowing her into its heart. It might have been hours before she returned to her senses.

When she finally did so the heat was still there with the harsh sunlight, and the yellow earth that was as dull and lifeless as the corpse of the dragon beside her.

Liandra rose unsteadily to her feet. She stared at Vranesh. The dragon's crimson wings were ripped and limp; the mighty chest deflated.

There were rites for such occasions, ways of preparing the body for the afterlife, but they required time, strength and the use of a magestaff, none of which she still possessed. In their absence Vranesh's mortal shell was ripe for carrion or plunder.

Liandra collected herself, stilling the shuddering that made her breaths short. She extricated herself from the dragon's clutches, working quickly now that she had some purpose, moving her hands in old patterns, murmuring words she had not used for decades. Even so, they came back quickly to her, just as if they had always been waiting.

The air around Vranesh's corpse seemed to thicken, to fill up, to clog. The raw blood-colour faded, replaced by a dun-yellow miasma. The serrated curve of the creature's spine sank, fading into the profile of the sandy dune beyond. The claws, talons and eyes disappeared, replaced by the shadow of rocks or the straggle of desiccated vegetation.

By the time she was finished all that remained was a vague hump in the landscape, bulbous in places but otherwise one with the stark earth around it.

Master of Dragons

The deception was a minor cantrip – no determined traveller would be fooled by it, and it would dissolve at the first hint of a counter-spell. Liandra guessed that few travellers passed through such a place, though, let alone mages. By the time her illusion wore off, only heat-bleached bones would remain, themselves already sinking into the sand.

She brushed her hands on her robes. Her blood pumped a little less strongly now, anguish replaced by a sense of exhaustion. Her mind still felt empty, bereft of the voice that had once shared it. Her intense grief, for all it might have been weak, had also been cathartic.

She looked around her. To the south lay the long firth where the abomination had gone down. To the north and east lay a wasteland, as vile as it was hot.

She would need to find drinking water, some shade, possibly food. Her arts would help her a little, but not much – she would need to work hard to stay alive.

Liandra started to walk, heading towards the nearby reedbeds. She guessed it was an inlet of seawater, but it was a start. As she went, she struggled to turn her thoughts away from Vranesh and on to the task at hand.

It wasn't easy, but it was possible.

'First, to survive,' she breathed out loud, picking up her pace and leaving the dragon-corpse behind. 'Recover strength. Learn what manner of place this is.'

Her eyes glittered darkly, remembering the witch.

'Then vengeance.'

The summit chamber of the Tower of Winds was full. Armed guards posted themselves wherever there was room; mages shuffled about, preparing spells that would not be ready for hours. A few loremasters tried to stay out of everyone else's way, apologetically shuffling parchment maps and requisition ledgers.

None of them dared to take a step within the inner circle

of thrones. Four figures stood there, ignoring the seats, seemingly oblivious to the hubbub around them.

Both Aelis and Gelthar seemed subdued. Imladrik couldn't have cared less about the wretched Caerwal, whose plans would have been uncovered by Caradryel if they hadn't been by Salendor. The only consolation he took from the whole sorry affair was that his most potent general had remained loyal and still stood at his side. As things had turned out, that might prove the most important point of all.

But Liandra – where was Liandra? Her disappearance had gone from being regrettable, to curious, to worrying. She had always been impulsive, but Imladrik couldn't believe she would have actually deserted, not when things were so poised.

It was too late to do anything about that now.

'Are they marching yet?' demanded Salendor, his blunt expression hard to read.

'They will be soon,' said Aelis.

'What changed?' asked Gelthar, obviously still shocked. 'We were talking. I thought we might be getting somewhere.'

Imladrik shook his head. It felt as if events were running away from him. 'We were.' He slammed his fist into his gauntlet, a gesture born of pure frustration. 'This was not Caerwal's work – something else has riled them.'

'We can find out,' said Salendor.

Imladrik turned on him. 'How?'

'A sending. It may do no good, mind.'

Imladrik felt like laughing. It could hardly make things worse.

'Make it,' he ordered. 'I must speak with him, just one more time.'

Salendor placed his staff before him, holding it two-handed and resting the heel against the marble floor. He closed his eyes and rested his forehead against the tip. A greenish bloom rode up from the centre of the marble,

Master of Dragons

coiling like oily smoke. Strange noises echoed from it – the clash of metal against metal, shouting in a strange tongue, the rush of wind from another place.

Imladrik watched distastefully. A sending was a crude thing, a simulacrum and a sham, but it was the only course left to him. The plain beyond the walls now seethed with dwarfen warriors and the great tent had been abandoned. With the gates having been sealed, no elf now walked outside the walls.

Perhaps, he thought, they should have stood firmer – made some kind of principled stand at the site of the talks. But Imladrik had seen the looks in the eyes of the dawi once the war-horns had started blowing, a look he recognised from a long time ago. There had been no time, no means of responding. The only sensible thing to do had been to withdraw to the city until it was clear what had changed.

Sensible, but hardly heroic.

Salendor's spell took firmer shape. The green cloud reached chest height and spread out across the floor. Within the swirling centre images began to clarify. Like an eye sweeping across a confused panorama, fleeting glimpses of dour faces flickered in and out of focus. The harsh tones of Khazalid rose and fell, fading as the roving search cast about for its target.

Salendor began to sweat. 'They are aware of me,' he said, his eyes still closed. 'That damned runesmith…'

'Do not lose it,' warned Imladrik.

The cloud's restless movement paused and the images within its centre sharpened. Imladrik saw faces looming up out of the gloom, like weeds slowly rising to the surface of a lake.

One swam to the forefront.

'Master Runelord,' said Imladrik, recognising Morek's grim visage.

The dwarf glared back at him, eyes out of focus, as if struggling to see through the sending's magical depths. He raised his runestaff and the anvil-head sparked with energy.

Then Morek's face was gone, replaced by a blurry image of Morgrim. The dwarf lord glowered at Imladrik, squinting hard.

'Sorcery,' he spat. 'This will not be forgotten.'

'What is happening, Morgrim?' asked Imladrik. 'Your warhorns are sounding. Your warriors are moving.'

Coarse laughter sounded from somewhere behind Morgrim; perhaps Morek's.

'I believed you,' Morgrim said. 'For the sake of the past, I believed you. Grimnir's beard, I should have known better.'

Imladrik drew closer, peering with difficulty through the miasma. 'I don't understand. What has changed?'

Morgrim didn't reply immediately. He gazed back at Imladrik, scrutinising him as if for a sign of deception. Then, finally, he spat on the ground and shook his head.

'Maybe you do not know,' he growled. 'Warriors from Karak Varn, attacked as they marched to the muster, their bodies still lying unburied in the great forest.'

They were the words Imladrik had dreaded hearing.

'This was not our doing,' he said, though he knew it would sound empty.

'No, nothing in this war seems to be,' said Morgrim dryly.

Imladrik could hear hurried mutterings all around him as his loremasters tried to ascertain the truth of what Morgrim was saying. It was a futile quest – no reports of a break in the truce had come in, not even rumours.

'Tell me where,' said Imladrik. 'I will investigate, you have my word. If there has been–'

'North of Kor Vanaeth,' said Morgrim. 'A woman – a sorcerer – on a dragon. She came on our warriors with no warning.' Morgrim jabbed a stumpy finger in accusation. 'Who but the asur ride dragons? Who among you commands them?' He was getting angrier with every word. 'This is the greatest insult – I *believed* you. For just a moment, you made me trust again.'

Imladrik felt light-headed.

Liandra.

'I did not order this,' he protested. 'Why would I?'

'You know what?' said Morgrim, his voice as bitter as wormwood. 'I no longer care. I listened to your excuses for two days. I told my thanes to keep their blades in their sheaths. I told them that you were in control of your forces, that you alone were worthy of respect among your faithless people. I told them to listen while you spun stories of druchii, even as others warned me that it was lies and fakery designed to buy time to land more legions.'

Morgrim was getting worked up, his eyes burning and his movements agitated. He had been made to look a fool in front of his thanes, something Imladrik knew he could never forgive.

'If you can't control your beasts, then you are to blame,' Morgrim went on. 'I sacrificed much for you, but no longer. Enough talk. We are coming for you with axe and hammer now. We are doing what we came to do: raze your walls and destroy your city.'

Imladrik saw the mania in his eyes even through the distortions of the sending. Morgrim was in his full battle-rage now, fuelled by the burning sense of injustice his race took so much trouble to cultivate.

'It was one dragon rider, Morgrim,' said Imladrik quietly, though he knew it was almost certainly futile. 'Just one. Can you vouch for all the warriors under your command?'

Morgrim nodded angrily. 'I can. They are already marching, elgi. A blood-debt of a thousand gold ingots hangs around your neck. I plan to claim it myself: for Snorri, who was right about you from the start.'

Even as he finished speaking, the sending began to

dissolve. Imladrik heard chanting from somewhere – the runelord, now working to banish the hated elgi magic from his presence.

'This is the end, Morgrim!' Imladrik cried. 'You give Malekith what he wants!'

'No, *govandrakken*,' snarled Morgrim, his face fracturing into flame-like slivers as Salendor's magic finally gave out. 'It is what *I* want.'

Then the images gusted away, snuffed into curls of emerald smoke by Morek's command of the runes.

After that, no one spoke. Salendor recovered his poise, breathing heavily. All in the chamber had heard the words. They stood still, waiting for Imladrik's response.

Imladrik stared at the floor. Nothing but despair came to him. The hard truth, the one he had tried so hard to resist, had asserted itself once more.

This was the moment. This was when it all turned. No fellowship would exist between the two races again, not after this. He would be the last of his kind to gaze on the giant, rune-engraved images of Grimnir and Grungni, to peer into the gromril shafts and see the glittering metal hacked from the very base of the earth, to witness the ancient iron-bound tomes in the libraries of the runelords.

The world would be poorer for it. It would be colder, darker and less glorious. Even as he contemplated it, reflecting on a future bereft of harmony and riven with suspicion, he could feel the cold vice of hopelessness around his heart.

Imladrik lifted his head, looking first at Salendor.

'We tried,' he said, quietly. 'When I stand before Asuryan I can at least say that.'

Salendor nodded perfunctorily, but it was clear his counsel had not changed. 'And now, lord?'

'The path is clear,' Imladrik replied, his voice heavy. 'Look to the walls. Ensure the bolt throwers are trained. Let us hope they withdraw when our strength becomes obvious.'

'And if they do not?'

'Then they will die, Salendor,' said Imladrik coldly. 'If they force me, to the last warrior I will kill them all.'

CHAPTER EIGHTEEN

Thoriol ran up the steep stairway, taking the steps two at a time. Moving fast was difficult with bow in one hand and quiver in the other – the constant jostling from those around him made it even harder. The entire city was in motion, with troops rushing to their stations under the echoing blare of trumpets. The noise from the war-drums outside was deafening – a grinding, rolling hammer-beat that made the air shake.

The rest of Baelian's company raced alongside him, Florean in the lead with Loeth close behind. The captain brought up the rear carrying his own bow, a heavy yew-shaft tipped with silver that he'd carried into battle for sixty years.

They ran up another winding stairwell, making the torches gutter as they swept past, before spilling out on to the east-facing outer wall. The ramparts were wide – over twelve feet – but were already filling with bodies.

'Down here!' cried Baelian, his voice impatient, directing the company to their allocated place. 'Faster!'

Tor Alessi's walls rose up in three concentric layers: an outer curtain that soared up from the plain for over a hundred feet, smooth and pale with only one land-facing gatehouse; then an inner sanctuary wall that rose even higher, ringing the inner city with its clustered spires and mage-towers; and finally the ultimate bastion, a truly cyclopean cliff of ice-white masonry that protected the mightiest central citadel.

The mages had been stationed up there, their bright-coloured cloaks rippling in the wind and their staffs already shimmering with power. Eagle-winged bolt throwers had been mounted on the next tier down. Some of those war machines were gigantic, carrying darts hewn from single tree trunks and bowcords the diameter of a clenched fist. The archers were stationed on the outer perimeter, thousands of them rammed close along the long, winding parapets.

It was a daunting sight, a majestic display of Ulthuan's glory. The banners of the King and the many asur kingdoms blazed clear under the powerful evening sun, draping the walls in a garland of vivid runes. Thoriol knew thousands more warriors waited within the cover of the walls, ready to advance swiftly if the perimeter were breached. Many of those were regular spearmen detachments, but he'd seen more heavily armed companies waiting in reserve, all clad in high silver helms and wearing ithilmar-plate armour. The entire city was teeming with violence, suppressed for so long but ready, at last, to unleash.

Thoriol slammed his quiver on the stone in front of him, hefted his bow to shoulder height and adjusted position, placing his left foot forward and preparing for the first draw. Only then did he look out beyond the battlements, across the plains that had been until that day empty of life and movement.

All had changed. Marching figures now filled the wasteland, teeming like flies. They were advancing slowly, arranged in long ranks of tight-packed infantry. He couldn't begin to guess how many there were – the entire eastern fringe of

Master of Dragons

261

the plain was dark with them. They marched in rhythm to the incessant beat of the war-drums, swaying in perfect unison under stone-dark banners. Some regiments were clad entirely in close-fitting metal plates; others had donned chainmail hauberks; still more wore heavy breastplates over leather jerkins, their warhammers and battle-axes clutched two-handed.

Behind the front ranks came the war machines – huge and grotesque devices of iron, bronze and wood, dragged into position on massive spiked wheels or metal-bound rollers. Thoriol saw stone-throwers, pitch-lobbers, trebuchets, ballistae, battlefield crossbows, grapnel hurlers and other things he had no name for. Each was massive, towering over the hordes that milled around them, crowned with beaten warmasks and mighty iron rune-plates.

Brazier pans glowed angrily under the open sky, polluting the clear blue with snaking columns of dirty brown. The war-horns kept on blaring, overlapping with one another in a cacophony of hard-edged, intimidatory clamour. None of the dwarfs spoke. None of them chanted or sang – they just tramped across the plain, sweeping with remorseless slowness, surrounding the city in a closing vice.

Thoriol swallowed. He could feel his heart racing. Those on either side of him tensed, ready for the order to draw. Some of the archers were veterans of a hundred engagements and kept their faces stony with resolve; others were scarce more experienced than Thoriol and their nerves were evident even as they attempted to hide them.

The dwarfs came on, closing to five hundred yards of the walls. At such a distance Thoriol could clearly see the details on their armour – the sigils, the battle-runes, the daubs and spots of blood. Every tattooed and bearded face was twisted into hatred, warped by a single-minded desire to break the walls, to drag them down, to drown the city in blood.

So many.

Then, with no obvious order given, the host stopped. Every dwarf halted his march and stood perfectly still. The wardrums ceased. The horns stopped. For an awful moment, the entire plain sank into a fragile silence.

It seemed to go on forever. As if in some bizarre dream, the two armies faced one another across the empty land, uttering no words and issuing no challenge.

Then, as suddenly as the dwarfs had stopped, each raised his weapon above his head. Tens of thousands of mauls, axes, short-swords, flails, warhammers and crossbows pointed directly at the walls, each one aimed in ritual denunciation.

Khazuk! came the cry – an immense, rolling, booming challenge. Every wrong, every grievance, was distilled into that one word and hurled up at the white walls of the city like a curse.

Khazuk!

The din of it was incredible, a roar that seemed to fill the heavens and the earth. Thoriol had to work hard not to fall back from the parapet edge, to creep into the cool shade of the stone and escape the horror of it.

Khazuk!

The third shout was the greatest, a mighty bellow that felt as if it would shatter crystal and dent stone. In its wake the war-horns started up again, underpinned by the frenzied beating of drums. The host began to move once more, but this time the shouts of challenge did not stop. Tor Alessi was besieged by it, surrounded by the maelstrom.

'Hold fast,' warned Baelian. His voice was as steady as the granite around them. Thoriol wondered if anything scared him.

Four hundred yards. Trumpets sounded on the elven battlements, almost drowned by the surge of noise out on the plain.

'Prepare,' ordered Baelian, just as hundreds of other company captains did the same. Tens of thousands of archers stooped for their first arrow, fixing it against the string and preparing for the draw.

Three hundred yards; just on the edge of their range. Thoriol held his stance, feeling like his muscles were about to seize up. He felt nauseous, and swallowed hard.

A second trumpet-blast rang out.

'Draw,' ordered Baelian, notching his own arrow.

Thoriol heaved the string to his cheek. He held it tight, feeling the feathers of the arrow's fletching against his forefinger.

Two hundred and fifty yards. Optimal range. The dwarfs must have known it, but they just kept on marching, still chanting, shouting, challenging and making no effort to evade the storm to come.

This was it. This was the culmination of everything he'd been working for, the final fruits of a foolish flight to Lothern away from the deadening hopes of his father.

Perhaps he might catch sight of me in all this, thought Thoriol dryly. *Perhaps he might approve. Perhaps, for once, I might make him proud.*

Then the final trumpet-blast, the signal to release. Up until now it had all been a mere shadow-play, a rehearsal, a toothless precursor.

'Let fly!' ordered Baelian.

As one they loosed their arrows, and the sky went dark.

Drutheira woke with a start. For a moment she had no idea where she was or what she was doing. Sevekai's face had been in her dreams again, chiding her for leaving him. She hadn't had visions of him for a long time, not since Bloodfang's presence had been in her mind.

It unsettled her. Sevekai was gone, dead, his body rotting at the foot of a mountain gorge. He had no business still affecting her, skulking in her dreams like a spectre of Hag Graef.

It was dark – pitch dark. For a moment she feared she'd slept far into the night, but then, as her awareness returned, she remembered having to tie strips of her cloak around her eyes to blot out the sun. She ripped them off and the light came back as intensely as ever, burning like a brand thrust into her face.

Blinking heavily, she gradually remembered where she was: a shaded hollow under a tumbled cliff of red-brown stone, the best shade she'd been able to find. The cliff wound its way south-east, following the course of an old dried-up river. She'd followed it, unable to stomach the brackish sea-water where she had waded ashore and unable to find more promising tributaries.

So far all she'd found was damp mud caking in the heat. The need for liquid was becoming pressing – despite the oppressive warmth she was no longer sweating, and her head felt thick and clogged.

It had been foolish to fall asleep. More than foolish – dangerous.

She looked around her, squinting against the hard light on the rocks. No sign of movement, pursuit or tracks.

Drutheira pushed herself to her feet, collecting her staff and leaning on it heavily. For the first time ever she regretted having spent so long cultivating the arts of Dhar at the expense of all else. It might have been nice to conjure up something to drink. She could have fooled herself easily enough with chimeras of wine or ice-cool water but the effects would not last. The only things her sorcery could genuinely construct out of nothing were destructive – the bolts of aethyr-lightning that tore through armour, the snarls of unnatural flame that crisped flesh and melted eyes.

It suddenly struck her as so pointless, so *wasteful*. Out here, in the parched hinterland, she was no better than any mortal.

Drutheira started to limp, keeping to the shade of the cliff to her left. Ahead of her the path wound along the foot of the cliff, choked with loose stone. To her right ran the base

Master of Dragons

265

of the dry riverbed, the far shore of which rose up again a few hundred yards distant in another cliff face. Its twin rock-tumbled edges were far apart, enclosing a shallow dusty bowl between them, but they gradually drew closer together the further she went.

In time the riverbed narrowed to a gorge. The sun sailed westward, still horrendously hot. Drutheira's mouth became too dry to open without pain. Her lips cracked and bled, and she breathed through her nostrils as sparingly as possible.

The passing hours gave her no fresh indication of where she was. She remembered vague rumours of a vast land to the south of Elthin Arvan. Malekith had been interested in it, saying that he sensed some strange and potent magic brewing there, but that had been decades ago and Drutheira suspected he didn't truly understand what he was speaking of. As far as she was concerned the place she was in had no magic about it at all, let alone strange and potent magic. It was a forgotten land, a between-place wedged amid greater realms, no doubt destined to remain barren forever.

She caught sight of bushes clustered in the lee of the nearside gorge-wall. They were harsh, dense things – black-leaved, bristling, no more than five feet tall – but it was a hopeful sign. It might even mean water.

She picked up her pace, ignoring the protests from her strained leg-muscles and forcing herself to keep going. She had another day, perhaps two, before the thirst would get her, and she had absolutely no intention of meeting her end in such an undistinguished place.

It was then that she sensed it, hovering close, barely notice-able but wholly unmistakable.

Drutheira crouched low, hugging the rock wall once more and letting its shadow slip over her. She scanned the land-scape around her, sniffing, her eyes wide and her senses working hard.

She is close, she thought, recognising the stink of the asur.

She could not see or hear any sign of the dragon, but the aethyr-presence of the red mage was definitely hanging on the wind.

The sunlight made it hard to see much at distance – dazzling out in the open, causing the air to shake and shimmer. Drutheira did not move for a long time, hoping her adversary would betray herself first.

Can she detect me? she wondered. It was possible that, in her diminished state, Drutheira's aura would be less obvious to a fellow magician than in the normal run of things. Dangerous to rely on the chance, but something not to ignore either.

She crept onwards, hugging the shadow of the gorge, her eyes sweeping around at all times, her staff ready. The scent faded, replaced by the wearyingly familiar tang of burned earth. Perhaps she had been mistaken, or perhaps the dragon rider was still aloft, miles away now, her scent carried by the wind.

Then she saw something else, lodged in the thick tangle of black-leaved bushes ahead – a flicker of red, barely visible, quickly withdrawn. Drutheira tensed, wondering if she had the strength for a summoning.

The asur mage was there, somewhere, crouching or lying among those dark branches. Was she waiting for her? Or was she, too, lost in the wilds and seeking some respite from the beating sun?

The more Drutheira watched, the more her conviction grew. She screwed her eyes up, letting a little sorcery augment her already-sharp vision. Something was hidden in the bushy cover, clad in red, prone on the ground as if exhausted. Drutheira tasted the nauseating tang of Ulthuan mingled with the hot metal aroma of dragon.

Drutheira broke into a lope, going as silently as her training enabled. She flitted across the gorge-floor, body crouched low and robes whispering about her.

Master of Dragons

She was soon amongst the bushes, ignoring the sharp jabs from the thorns as they ripped through her clothes. She raised her staff quickly, kindling dark fire. Ahead of her, only half-obscured by a tight lattice of thorns, was her enemy: out cold on her back, her pale freckled face staring up at the sky, unmoving.

Drutheira pounced, forgetting her fatigue as she crashed through the final curtain of spines, jabbing her staff-heel down at her enemy's heart.

The metal tip hit the ground hard, jarring Drutheira's arms. It bit into nothing – where Drutheira had seen a body, there was now just a stained patch of earth, as dry and desolate as every patch of earth in the whole Khaine-damned place.

Too late she caught a fresh stink of magic, tart in her nostrils like acid.

Illusion!

She felt something hard crack into the back of her head and staggered to her knees. She tried to get up again, to twist around and bring her staff to bear, but another blow followed, flooring her.

Tasting blood in her mouth, she rolled over, feeling the staff slip from numb fingers. Her vision was swimming, already shrinking down to blood-tinged blackness.

Standing above her, real this time, loomed the red mage, her hair hanging limp in the hot air, her face streaked with dust, smoke and gore. She looked half-dead. Her right hand clutched a fist-sized rock, one that dripped with Drutheira's own blood.

'I–' started Drutheira, not knowing what to say, her voice cracked and empty.

That was all she managed. The red mage slammed the rock down again, this time into Drutheira's forehead, snapping her skull back against the ground and making her mind reel in pain.

The last thing she heard before passing out was Eltharin,

the hated tongue of her enemy, but one which she unfortunately understood all too well.

'At last,' hissed Liandra, her voice heavy with exhilaration, readying the rock again. '*At last.*'

Imladrik stood alongside Salendor at the summit of the inner parapet, watching grimly as the dwarfs assaulted all along the eastern walls. The two of them had said little for a long time.

The dawi had assaulted Tor Alessi three times in the past and had been driven back three times. In the early years of the war, though, the armies on both sides had been smaller and expectations different. The dwarfs had expected to demolish the walls; the elves had expected to defend them with ease. In the event the walls had always held, but at terrible cost in desperate defence and hurried counter-attacks. The proud dawi infantry had been mauled by the volume of arrows, while the equally proud asur knights had been hacked apart whenever they had been caught in the open.

Other cities and holds had suffered, but both sides knew that Tor Alessi was the key to the war. While the deepwater harbour endured the Phoenix King could land fresh troops in Elthin Arvan at will; if it fell then the remaining elven Athels and Tors would be vulnerable, each one ripe to be picked apart in turn. So it was that the dwarfs had come for it again and again, scarcely heeding what it cost in blood and gold.

'Will they break in this time?' mused Salendor, watching as more siege engines were hauled into range through a veritable hail of arrows. Some of the asur darts were flaming, and where they kindled the massive war machines collapsed in columns of burning ruin. The battlefield was studded with them, like sacrificial pyres to uncaring gods.

Imladrik shook his head. 'Not while I command.'

Far below them, a heavily armoured column of dwarf

Master of Dragons

infantry was getting bogged down as it tried to force a passage to the gates. The dawi held their shields above their heads, making painful progress with admirable determination, but still they came up short, choked by their own dead and mired in the bloody mud.

'Arrows will not hold them forever,' observed Salendor.

A volley of bolt throwers on the second level opened up, hurling their payloads through the smoky air. The bolts ploughed into the advancing infantry ranks, or lanced into war engines, or collapsed trebuchets in welters of splintered timber.

'Trust to the walls,' said Imladrik calmly.

Salendor looked sceptical. 'Perhaps.'

Even as he spoke, the first stone-throwers reached their positions. Imladrik watched dwarfs run out bracing cables and hammer them into the yielding soil. They threw up massive bronze shields in front of the delicate mechanisms before loading rough-cut stones into the cages and pulling the iron chains tight.

Three of them loosed, almost together. Their lead weights thumped down and their hurling-arms swung high. Three rocks, each the size of a hawkship's prow, sailed through the air before crashing into the parapet of the outer wall. One exploded into fragments without causing much damage. The second smashed a rent in the outer cladding before sliding down the smooth exterior. The third punched straight through the ramparts, dragging dozens of archers with it and careering on into the towers and winding streets beyond.

'That's just the start,' said Salendor bleakly. 'They have bigger ones.'

'Then you had better instruct the mages to take them out, had you not?'

Salendor gave him a significant glance. 'Dragons would do it faster.'

'Yes, they would.' Imladrik did not look at Salendor as

he spoke. The plain was pressed tight with bodies, punctuated by rains of arrows and returning strikes from the war engines. Soon the dawi would gain enough ground to install bolt throwers of their own. They might even force their way to within axe-range of the stonework.

'Will you go aloft, then?' asked Salendor, doing well to control his impatience.

Imladrik pressed his lips together calmly, and kept watching. Salendor had no idea what he was asking. None of them did.

'Instruct the mages to take down the stone-throwers,' Imladrik said coldly. 'Leave worrying about the rest to me.'

More war engines swayed into position. Several were blasted apart by strikes from the wall-mounted bolt throwers, others were fatally pinned by hundreds of flaming arrows, but more than a dozen made it to join the first three and then the onslaught began in earnest. Rocks, spiked iron balls, flaming phials of runesmith-blessed fire, all were flung at the walls in a swinging, pivoting barrage.

The dwarf advance, though bloody, had not been reckless. The most heavily armoured infantry units had soaked up the earliest swathes of arrow-flights, risking casualties but secure in the knowledge that many of the iron-clad warriors would endure. That had bought time to establish the heavier wall-breaking engines. Now that the defenders had been forced to concentrate on multiple targets, the intensity of the dart-storms at ground level lessened, and the iron-clad battalions began to crawl forwards once more.

Tor Alessi began to burn. As the sun wheeled westward, fires kindled by the rain of rune-fire projectiles erupted into life, resisting every effort to put them out. Explosions flared up on the walls where they impacted, adding columns of twisting smoke to the growing film of murk in the air; others burst out within the city itself, drawing troops away from the perimeter to fight the stubbornly persistent blazes.

Master of Dragons

Morgrim watched the carnage unfold from his vantage in the centre of the plain. He could not lie – it made his heart swell.

The bickering and hesitation was over. He didn't know what he would have done if the elgi had not broken the ceasefire. He knew full well that warlords within his own host had been planning similar acts of sabotage, but remained confident he could have prevented them.

Perhaps there was something to Imladrik's fanciful tales. It didn't matter any more. So many acts of cruelty had been committed that the need for grudgement was now overwhelming. Even if he had withdrawn his own army from Tor Alessi, others would have come in time. He knew of musters in the mountains to the east, each one already setting off toward other asur outposts – Athel Toralien, Athel Maraya, Oeragor. There was no way he could have stopped all of them even if he had wanted to.

And he did not want to. He wanted the dwarf armies, all of them, to succeed. He wanted the elgi gone, banished back to their strange and unnatural island, their taint wiped from the honest earth of the dawi homeland. Only then could the wounds of the past be healed, old poisons withdrawn, new mines delved.

It all starts here, he thought grimly. *May Grimnir curse us if we falter now.*

Morek lumbered up to him, his staff acrid with discharged energies.

'*Tromm*, lord,' said the runelord, bowing low.

Morgrim nodded in acknowledgement. As he did so, strange flashes of light lashed out from Tor Alessi's summit. Morek and Morgrim watched as magefire in all hues – emeralds, sapphires, rubies – spiralled down into the dawi front lines, tearing them up like ploughs turning a field.

Morek regarded the development sourly. 'Their magic is as flighty as they are,' he muttered.

A siege tower, the first to come near the city's gate-house, ignited, its crown exploding as magefire kindled and bloomed on its protected shell. Flames raced unnaturally through the heavy leather shrouds and timber bracing-beams, streaking down the structure's core. A few seconds later and it was little more than charred scaffolding, its deadly cargo leaping to safety as the wooden platforms and ladders disintegrated around them. More trundled onward to take its place.

'Deadly, though,' observed Morgrim.

His voice was distracted. For some reason he couldn't take the loss of a few siege towers and trebuchets as seriously as he ought. Something nagged at him, dragging his mind from the conduct of the battle.

'Where are the dragons?' he asked at last, out loud though not speaking to anyone but himself. Everything he had been led to believe, not least from Imladrik himself, told him that the drakes were the most potent weapon the asur had.

Morek looked up at the walls contemptuously. 'We have killed wyrms before.'

The grip around the city tightened. Morgrim saw miners finally reach the base of the walls just south of the gatehouse. He saw more war engines pull into position and begin to unload their deadly contents. He saw fires burst into life on the parapets, sending smoke boiling up into a wearing sky. The light was beginning to wane and turn golden as the sun began its long slow descent towards the ocean. As the shadows lengthened, Tor Alessi looked battered, proud, and doomed, ringed by a veritable sea of ground-deep loathing.

'So we have,' he said softly. 'But keep your runesmiths aware, *rhunki*. The drakes will fly. Only then we shall truly see Imladrik's mettle.'

CHAPTER NINETEEN

'They're coming!'

The shouts of panic were superfluous – Thoriol could see perfectly well that they were coming. Everyone along that section of the parapet could see that they were coming. That didn't stop the shouts, though. Loosing arrows into the skies was one thing; going face to face with the enemy was another.

Magefire rippled through the air like strands of crystallised starlight, spinning and flickering in the dying day. Arrows still flew, though less thickly than they had done. Thoriol wondered just how many thousands of darts had been loosed – how many warehouses had been emptied and how many quivers discarded. His own arm muscles were raw with effort despite the increasingly frequent breaks the company had been forced to take. Using a longbow was not like twanging a hunting bow – it was exhausting, backbending work.

The endless flights had hurt the enemy. He could see the piles of dead on the flat below, bent double, twisted. No enemy, no matter how well armoured or disciplined, could march through such a storm without taking damage.

But the advance had not been halted. The dwarfs had come closer and closer, wading stoically through their own dead, shrugging off the slamming impacts of mage-bolts and quarrel-shots, all the while hurling their strange guttural abuse up at the defenders.

Now the outer walls were reeling. Some sections had been shattered by the stone-throwers, opening breaches that were desperately reinforced by thick knots of spearmen. The dwarf vanguard brought ladders and grapnels with them; once the parapets were blasted clear by the trebuchets a hundred hands would start to climb and a hundred pickaxes would begin to swing. As soon as one ladder was knocked back another two would lurch up again, propelled by burly arms from the boiling mass of bodies on the plain.

Thoriol's own wall-section had weathered the storm. No impacts had shaken their parapet and no rune-magic had been slammed against the foundations. Throughout it all, several hundred archers had been able to maintain regular volleys against the throng below with only their own exhaustion to fight.

It couldn't have lasted. The next big impact was less than a hundred yards from Thoriol's position. He felt the whole wall shudder as the battlements were shattered by a tumbling ball of rock. Cracks snaked like lightning along the stone, and a massive chunk of masonry toppled inwards, breaking up and raining down on the buildings below. The screams of those caught in the disintegration were mercifully short-lived.

Dwarfs homed in on the damaged section. Bolt-thrower quarrels lanced into the crumbling stonework, smashing more pieces free. Arcane-looking caskets crashed amid the residue, bursting with the hateful fire that seemed to kindle on anything. Grapnels followed, some thrown up to haul

Master of Dragons

warriors onto the walls, others used to drag more slabs of facing stone away. With terrible speed the breach was widened and lowered, enough for siege-ladders to start clattering into position against the trailing edge.

The asur defenders were not idle, though. Spearmen from the city's interior clambered up across the ruins, forming dense spear-lines just in the lee of the breach. They spread out across the rubble, overlooked on either side by the still-standing wall-ends. Soon asur and dawi were fighting furiously amid collapsed stonework, just as they were doing across a dozen other breaches.

'For Ulthuan!' roared Baelian, rushing along the parapet to gain a vantage over the broken section. Other archers did the same, eager not to let the spearmen down below take the brunt of the dwarf assault unaided.

Thoriol was swept along in the crush. He barely had time to snatch his quiver before he was standing on the brink, his boots grazing the edge of the precipitous drop. His companions closed by on either shoulder, all drawing their bows.

'Aim well!' cried Baelian.

The wall had not come down cleanly, and long slopes of detritus lay on either side of the breach, serving as a ramp for troops of both sides. Dwarfs clambered up one side, spearmen the other.

Thoriol notched his first arrow and pulled the string taut. The dwarfs were a few dozen yards below him, their attention fixed on the spearmen ahead of them. Thoriol screwed his right eye closed and lowered the point of his arrow just in front of a dwarf warrior lumbering up the steep bank of rubble. He let fly, and the dart thunked heavily into the dwarf's chest. It was enough to send him toppling backwards and into his comrades.

More arrows fizzed down from both sides of the breach. Baelian sent a shaft into the eye-socket of a bellowing dwarf champion – a breathtaking feat of marksmanship. Other darts found their mark, pinning the dwarf advance back and giving the spearmen space to advance across the open wound and pull reinforcements up in their wake.

Thoriol's heart pumped strongly again. Fear ran hard through his veins, though tempered with something else, something wilder and more elemental.

Excitement? Am I truly exhilarated by this?

He could smell them, they were so close. He could hear the wet *shlicks* of the arrows biting into flesh. At such range the elven shafts were utterly deadly, capable of stabbing through all but the very thickest plates of armour.

He notched a second arrow, then a third, watching with grim satisfaction as each found its target.

But the dwarfs were not liable to stumble blindly into a slaughter. Crossbow-wielding warriors crouched low in the rubble and aimed up at the archers on either flank. Soon the air was filled with the snap and whistle of bolts. Thoriol ducked down as one flew past him, almost snagging his trailing shoulder.

Still kneeling, he notched another arrow. Just as he lifted his bow to take aim, he heard a strangled cry. Turning to his right he saw Baelian stumble forwards, a quarrel sticking proudly from his throat. The company captain, at the forefront as always, must have presented a tempting target.

Baelian managed a final look in Thoriol's direction. The scars on his face writhed as he struggled to breathe. Then he collapsed, falling over the edge of the parapet and down into the rock-choked breach below. His body hit the rubble hard; soon it would be under the boots of the advancing dwarfs.

For a second, Thoriol was dumbstruck. Baelian had seemed invincible, immune from the fear and filth of battle.

'Let fly!' came Loeth's voice, thick with rage.

The others leapt to obey. Thoriol felt fury surge up in his breast. For the first time, he was angry rather than scared or thrilled.

Master of Dragons

Ignoring the danger, he stood up straight, drawing his bow with a savage expertise he would never have considered possible during the crossing from Lothern.

'For Ulthuan!' he cried, sending another arrow spinning into the line of advancing dwarfs. Even before it had found its target, he was reaching for another.

Salendor rose up to his full height at the very edge of the precipice. Below him the walls fell away in three vertiginous cliffs, each one towering over an ocean of fire and turmoil. He felt the hot wind rush across his face, laced with ashes and magic. As the sky darkened to dusk he felt power well up within him once more, swelling to the flood, ripe to burst from the tips of his calloused fingers.

The winds of magic raced around him, swirling and eddying with increasing force. Aethyr-essence crackled in the air, snarling with semi-sentient fervour. On either side of him other mages cast their battle-spells. Bolts of vivid, rubescent force shot out into the gathering dark, sweeping past the burning towers and slamming through siege towers, clusters of ladders and knots of enemy fighters.

For all its potency, the magefire was not unopposed. Salendor could feel the deadening effects of the dwarfen runesmiths countering every attempt to raise fresh magic. He could sense their dreary chanting, stilling the vital winds of magic and making them listless. In the wake of such work it was hard to pull the requisite power from the aethyr, to drag it into the world of the senses and make it do its work.

Salendor grimaced, feeling the physical pain of the summoning. His lungs ached from chanting the words, his hands bled from gripping his staff. The siege had become a gruelling test of endurance, a clash of two equally deadly and equally implacable enemies. The entire lower levels of the city were now furiously contested, the many breaches in the walls glowing like a ring of embers. Vast blankets of smoke hung over the lower city, brooding across sites of slaughter. Every so often another war engine would ignite, exploding in an angry bloom of crimson, or another watch-tower would crumble under the relentless onslaught of the stone-throwers, dissolving into yet more shattered masonry.

Salendor whirled his staff around his head, using the growing momentum to add to his summoning. The winds whipped up around him, sparking and surging. Soon he had his target: a battering ram being dragged up to the main gates, covered in metalwork protection and warded by powerful runes of destruction. Though the sigils were carved in the dawi tongue Salendor could sense their malign power well enough.

'*Othial na-Telememnon fariel!*' he shouted, dragging an aethyr-mark out from behind the veil. His staff burst into blazing silver light and he loosed the fire, sending it snaking down through the burning towers. The magical beams homed in on their distant target unerringly, spiralling through the chaos before smashing into glittering shards across the battering ram's housing. Each shard burrowed deeper into the metal plates, dissolving iron and pulverising timber.

Lit up by silver explosions, the battering ram made an appealing target for the surviving archers. First a flaming bolt hit it, then several pitch-dipped arrows impacted. With its thick outer shell compromised, the barbs tore deeper into the mechanism within.

The battering ram's progress ground to a halt. Soon the entire structure was listing, its immense axles broken, its back aflame.

Salendor grunted with satisfaction. That would set them back.

His satisfaction did not last long. The gatehouse was relatively secure, but elsewhere the situation was deteriorating. More breaches in the outer perimeter had been inflicted. One looked particularly bad – a huge gouge in the

Master of Dragons

stonework with dawi actually clambering up the ruins. He could just make out valiant clusters of archers clinging to the two ragged edges, pinning the invaders back. A bold stand, but precarious.

His fellow mages were tiring. One of them, Eialessa of Eataine, as powerful a spellcaster as he had ever seen, looked out on her feet. Several of the others had pale faces and sunken eyes.

'Where are the damned dragons?' Salendor asked aloud, tilting his head to the heavens. Imladrik had been gone for hours – it was becoming absurd. 'Where is the lord of this city?'

Nothing but darkness and tattered clouds answered him. The sky was streaked with sullen red glows, interspersed with occasional sharp flashes of magelight.

But then, finally, he sensed a change on the air. Something stirred, a rush from the west, the echo of something very, very high up.

He saw nothing. The sky remained dark and mottled. The fires continued to burn, adorning Tor Alessi in a corona of sullen anger.

For all that, Salendor could not suppress a smile.

'Ah,' he breathed, raising his staff once more, forgetting his fatigue and remembering anticipation. 'Now, my stunted friends, we shall see.'

Imladrik pushed Draukhain higher. The first pinpoints of starlight clustered on the extreme eastern horizon, glowing in a deepening sky. It was perishingly cold. The other dragons coursed and wheeling around him, wings rigid for the glide. Telagis's emerald wings glinted in the dusk as he swept past Draukhain, bowing his head in submission as the greater drake's shadow fell across him. Imladrik could sense the dragonsong of the other riders, whispering to their mounts, holding their immense power in check.

Down below, far below, his city burned. He could see the flare and pulse of the flames, barred by black lines of smog and ruin. The sun still shone in the west but was setting fast, making the tips of the waves looked like burnished bronze.

Why do we wait? sang Draukhain. The kill-lust was high in him; Imladrik could sense it pressing on his own mind.

I am preparing myself, Imladrik replied. *It has been a long time since you and I went to war.*

Nonsense. We have been killing druchii for months.

They are different.

Draukhain snorted. *Bonier, perhaps.*

Imladrik looked down, peering through the layers of drifting smoke. The vision was hellish, like the opening maw of Mirai in the depths of the gathering night.

The dragon knew well enough why they paused. Draukhain knew almost everything about him – the shape of his moods, the tenor of his thoughts. Sometimes Imladrik wondered if keeping secrets from his mount was even possible. Some things had been surrendered a long time ago – the right to a solitary mind, the right to an undisturbed sequence of mortal thoughts.

I do not wish this to be a slaughter, Imladrik sang.

Then do not ask me to unfurl my claws at all.

I am serious. We must drive them from the walls, but limit our wrath to that.

Draukhain flexed his pinions, preparing for the dive that would take them hurtling into the battle below. *Even now, you harbour dreams of ending this?*

Imladrik smiled bitterly. *Not any more, but they are not daemons. Kill in proportion: that is the maxim.*

Proportion! sang Draukhain contemptuously. *Aenarion would have laughed to hear it.*

And look what became of him.

Draukhain spilled a savage, metal-grating noise from his smoking jawline. *Then we hunt.*

Imladrik rested his blade on the dragon's shoulder bone-spur and tensed for the shift.

Aye, Draukhain – we hunt.

He gave the mental order. His mind connected with those of the five other riders, and for a moment they were locked in silent communion. He felt the hot presence of the Caledorians, so similar to his own; he felt Heruen and Cademel prepare for the dive. He saw the varicoloured wings pull in tight, their iridescence furled.

For a moment all six dragons teetered on the brink, their riders sitting back in the saddle. Then the steepling fall began, and the drakes shot earthwards.

Imladrik felt the wind race past him. Draukhain took the lead position, racing down like some gigantic falcon, already breathing heavily with an iron-furnace rattle in his lungs. Gaudringnar followed closely, shadowed by the swift Rafuel.

Tor Alessi rushed up towards them, rapidly growing in size. Imladrik held his position carefully, watching as the three lines of walls separated and became individually visible. He picked out the flashes of magefire in the pinnacles and the staccato delivery of the bolt throwers. He saw the fires burning along the parapets in the lower city, throbbing and flaring in the gathering dusk.

Draukhain growled with joy. By then he could smell the dawi. He extended his wings again and began to sweep into the attack run.

Hunt well, sang Imladrik to his companions, knowing that once the dragons were amongst the enemy they would each fight alone. That was ever the way with them: they were solitary predators.

The summit of the Tower of Winds shot past, the first of the tall towers to be reached. The drakes split, cascading like lightning across the city. Imladrik caught sight of Salendor standing on one of the highest platforms. The mage-warrior looked elated, and saluted him as he passed.

Then Draukhain plunged down further, snaking through the thud and shriek of projectiles and beating his wings harder.

The walls, sang Imladrik, gripping tight against the push of the wind. *Drive them from the walls.*

Draukhain powered towards the nearest breach, the clap of his wingbeats like thunderbolts. The dawi did not see him coming until far too late. Even then, what could they have done? Run? None of them were fast enough. They had scoffed at the legend of the drakes and now their mockery would kill them.

Imladrik guided the dragon towards the largest of the rents in the eastern flank of the city – a huge hole in the stonework the width of a hawkship's sails. Dwarfs were battering away at a thinning line of elven defenders, pushing gradually into the lower city.

Draukhain *roared*, making the residual bulwarks of the twin wall-ends shake further. In a spiralling flurry of dislodged stone, he crashed into the dwarf front rank.

It was like being hit by a tornado. Dawi were hurled into the air by the impact, plucked and dragged from the rubble by Draukhain's claws or slammed clear by savage downbeats. The lashing tail accounted for dozens more, sweeping them from their positions and sending them cartwheeling, broken-backed, into the seething mass beyond the walls.

Then the fire came. Draukhain twisted around, still airborne, spewing a massive, writhing column of dragonfire that crashed across the stonework like clouds tearing around a mountain summit. Even the staunchest of the dwarfs fell back in the face of that, clawing at terrible burns as they staggered clear.

Imladrik rose higher in his seat, riding the swerve of his mount. He bent his mind to the task of dragonriding, adding his consciousness to Draukhain's own, melding his awareness with that of the mighty drake. They were like twin

Master of Dragons

entities bound within a single gigantic physical frame.

Draukhain snapped his wings back and thrust clear of the breach, leaving a trail of smouldering carnage in his wake before pushing out into the horde of dawi beyond. Staying low, he punched into them like a ploughshare breaking into soil, blasting blue-tinged sheets of flame across the reeling lines before plucking the most defiant of them from the earth and flinging them high.

All across the beleaguered city the tale was the same. Each dragon hit the attacking armies at once, devastating the vanguard and driving deep into the supporting troops behind. These drakes were no drowsy, gold-hoarding wyrms of the eastern mountains – they were Star and Moon dragons, the most powerful beasts in all natural creation, sheer engines of destruction, avatars of primordial devastation. The dawi had never seen the like, and they shredded them.

Imladrik felt the lust for killing swell up within him. The taste of dawi blood came to his lips as splatters of gore streaked across his silver helm. A savage smile half-twitched on his lips, teetering on the brink of spreading.

Retain control, he sang, guiding Draukhain further into the press of dwarf bodies. He could see siege towers up ahead, all ripe for destruction.

Draukhain hurtled low over the battlefield, raking the oncoming hordes. The dwarfs who attempted to rally were first bludgeoned with dragonfire, then gouged by Draukhain's jaws and talons, then swept aside with the disdainful flicks of his immense tail. Crossbow bolts clattered harmlessly from the dragon's scaled hide. Axes and warhammers were wielded too slowly to make an impact; even those that connected did little more than bruise Draukhain's armour.

Imladrik nudged his mount and the dragon climbed a little higher, thrusting clear of the struggling infantry lines and up towards the first siege tower. The dwarfs mounted on its flanks behaved with characteristically insane bravery, holding their positions and loosing a whole flock of quarrels at the approaching monster.

The pitiful scatter didn't even slow them. Draukhain flew straight into it, smashing through the upper platforms and bursting clear of the far side in a rain of broken spars and planks. The entire structure blew apart, flayed into splinters by the thrashing tail and crushing wings. By the time the dragon wheeled back around for a return pass, nothing remained but dust, corpses and crackling firewood.

Back to the walls, sang Imladrik, struggling not to give in to the powerful urge to slay with abandon. Part of him wished to drive onwards, to carve a gorge of slaughter between the bloated flanks of the enemy all the way to the baggage trains. Part of him wished to push on towards Morgrim himself, to punish him for his lack of imagination.

You become the dragon; the dragon becomes you.

But he had to resist, to retain command. Draukhain swung about, angling hard over the disarrayed dwarfs and powering back towards the burning city. Imladrik spied another breach in the outer walls and marked it mentally. He could make out iron-clad infantry labouring in the ruins, driving up a long slope of rubble to get into the city beyond. He saw lines of elven spearmen facing them from the interior, supported by archers perched precariously on the half-ruined walls either side.

This would be simple – another clean sweep, driving the dwarfs back out onto the plain and picking them off. After that the assault could slow: the walls would be secured and the dragons could take up stations above them. The lesson in power would be enough – even Morgrim, stubborn as he was, would have to pull back in the face of it.

As Draukhain arrived at the breach, though, the dragon suddenly pulled up sharply.

What is it? sang Imladrik, looking about him concernedly

Master of Dragons

in case some stray barb had somehow penetrated the dragon's armour.

Your blood is on the walls.

For a second, Imladrik had no idea what he meant. The dragon soared higher, clearing the breach before banking tightly over the eastern wall-end.

Imladrik looked down. Several dozen archers still manned the intact ramparts overlooking the ruined section. Several more lay on the parapet surface, their light armour pierced with quarrels.

I do not under– began Imladrik, then broke off.

Draukhain dipped lower and broke into a hover, his massive body held immobile with all the poise of a kestrel.

I sensed it, sang Draukhain. For once, his voice was neither sarcastic nor wrathful. *Your blood.*

Reluctantly, fearing already what he would see, Imladrik peered into the lambent shadows. One of the archers, the one closest to him, had had his helm knocked from his head. Imladrik recognised the face even amid the fire and murk. For a horrific moment he thought he spied Yethanial there, her bruised features twisted in pain.

Then, in a moment of no less horror, he saw the truth. It was Thoriol, prone, his robes wet with blood, his eyes closed and unmoving.

'What madness–' he started, before being shocked into silence.

The surviving asur on the walls stared up at him, their faces fearful. The surviving dwarfs beat a hasty retreat under the whirling shadow of Draukhain's wings, summoned away by frantic signals from the battlefield.

Imladrik was unable to take his eyes from the scene. Thoriol lay awkwardly on a broken slab of marble, his hand still half-holding a longbow. He was dressed in the manner of a common archer. The last time Imladrik had seen him he'd been arrayed in the acolyte's robes of Tor Caled.

He should have been in Caledor. He should have been *safe*.

Draukhain began to labour in the skies. Imladrik could sense the itch for combat become restive. He looked back over his shoulder, over to where the sea of dwarfen warriors marched, their momentum stalled but their numbers still formidable. The other dragons wheeled and dived at them, lighting up the dusk with blooms of consuming fire.

And then, distracted, Imladrik felt his long-kindled blood-lust boil over. He felt the spirit of the dragon surge through his limbs, animating them with a dark, cold fire. He saw the pale, bruised face of his only son before his eyes.

They have done this. They dragged me here. They caused this war. They laid waste to this land. Damn them! Damn their stubborn, ignorant, savage minds!

Draukhain responded instantly, rising higher against the backdrop of swirling smoke. The beast's animal spirits burst into feral overabundance. Fires sparked into life between his curved fangs. His pinions spread, splaying out like a death shroud.

'Damn them!' roared Imladrik, giving in at last, feeling the hot rush of exhilaration take him over. '*Damn them!*'

His blade became hot in his gauntlets, searing like the cursed steel of the Widowmaker itself. He felt the blood of Aenarion throb in his temples. The runes on his ancient armour glowed an angry arterial red, responding instantly to the preternatural powers unleashed across the sacred silver.

Draukhain pounced, sweeping out into the dark with a magisterial surge. Imladrik levelled his sword-tip over the ocean of souls before him. He no longer saw them as worthy adversaries to be curtailed. All he saw in that moment, his soul twisted with blood-madness, was *prey*.

The other dragons sensed the change in mood. They dived into the enemy with renewed fervour. The lowering sky fractured with bursts of fresh flame and cries of dawi agony. The asur behind the walls, also sensing the vice of restraint lifting, began to pour out through the gaps in the walls. They spilled out on to the plain, murder glittering in their eyes.

Amid them all and above them all, mightier than all others between the mountains and the sea, came the Master of Dragons, unleashed at last, his brow wreathed with darkness, his countenance as severe as Asuryan's, his soul burning with the madness of Khaine.

They have done this, he sang, his mind-voice icy. *Leave none alive.*

CHAPTER TWENTY

Grondil strode onwards through the morass of blood and churned-up mud. It swilled over his shins, dragging at him, though he barely noticed the pull.

Up ahead the walls of Tor Alessi burned a vivid red in the darkness. Trails of fire shot up from the trebuchets and bolt throwers, streaking out in the night. The noise of battle was deafening – a frenzied melange of drums, shouting, screams, magefire explosions.

'To the breach!' he roared, blind to all else. His hearth-guard strode with him, weathering the storm of arrows that whined and clattered about them. He had no idea how many had managed to follow him thus far. The battleground had dissolved into a vast scrum of straining bodies and labouring war engines, all formation lost in the churning melee at the base of the walls.

The sudden arrival of the dragons had changed nothing. They soared and dived into the host, lighting up the sky with flashes of iridescence. Their power looked phenomenal, but that did not concern Grondil. No opponent, however towering or malevolent, had ever truly concerned Grondil. They all drew breath; they could all be killed.

His contingent was still fifty yards short of the walls and making heavy weather of the march. The shells of ruined trebuchets burned in the mud around him, grisly monuments amid a press of straining bodies. The attack was faltering; it needed something decisive to turn the tide.

'The breach!' he bellowed again, swinging his warhammer around his head. The walls ahead had been hammered into semi-ruins, exposing the soft innards of the city within. If a salient could be pushed into the city's perimeter, sheltered by the walls and out of the sweep of the dragons, that might be enough. Grondil could already see the jagged edges of the stonework picked out in the firelight, swarming with defenders trying frantically to shore up the defences. Axeblades flickered in the half-light, rising and falling like picks at a coal-face.

He tried to run, to break into the charge that would carry him to the fighting. His armour clattered around him, weighing him down. He stumbled, falling to one knee, tripped by jutting debris left in the mire. Hot air rushed across his back, scorching him under his armour. A tart stench of ashes clogged his nostrils, followed by a sharp scent of blood.

Cursing, he twisted round to beckon his contingent onward, and his jaw dropped.

They had gone. They had all gone, swept away as if scooped out of the ground by the hands of some daemon of the earth. All that remained was a vast crater of scorched soil, thick with blackened corpses. In the centre of it writhed a gigantic creature, a golden dragon with wings unfurled, its serpentine tail coiling around it, its long neck arched above him.

Up close, it was colossal. Grondil had never seen a living thing so enormous. He almost lost his grip on his hammer.

The rider on the dragon's back lowered a sword in his

direction. It danced with a strange, elusive light that made Grondil's eyes smart.

He didn't wait for it to explode into life. He pushed himself up from the mud and broke into a charge.

'Grimnir!' he bellowed, holding his weapon two-handed and scouring the creature's hide for a weak spot. All he saw was a screen of glistening golden armour, flawless in its protective coverage, splattered with great streaks of dwarfen blood like honour markings.

Before he could get within strike-range the dragon belched a searing blast of flame. It overwhelmed him, raging across his plate armour, worming its way into every joint and crevice. He staggered on for a few more paces, blinded by the heat, hoping to land at least one blow before his strength gave out.

The heat suddenly ebbed. Grondil reeled, trying to squint through the pain, to somehow get into position for a swipe.

But the dragon had taken flight again, hovering just a few yards above the wreckage of Grondil's company. The down-draft of its huge wings was acrid and gore-flecked. For a moment longer Grondil stayed on his feet. He dimly heard shouts of alarm, of retreat. Somewhere close by, something exploded with a dull *boom* – a siege engine, perhaps.

The beast loomed over him, magnificent and terrible, out of reach of his warhammer, impervious to anything he could throw at it. Blood sluiced down Grondil's armour. Delayed by shock, he felt the onset of the burns he'd taken, waves of pain that swelled across his whole body. Then, as if as an afterthought, the dragon turned in the air, switching back sinuously, its tail sweeping round in a casual arc. The heavy end-spine caught Grondil square in the chest, hurling him back through the air, driving his breastplate in and crushing the ribs beneath.

Grondil thudded back to earth twenty paces distant, sliding on his back, his spine arched in pain. Through blood-wet eyes he saw the dragon climb higher into the air, its body a dazzling mottle-pattern of crimson and gold. It snaked higher, graceful and unconcerned, its rider already searching for fresh prey.

Grondil felt oblivion creep up on him. His limbs went cold. He couldn't lift his hammer. The whirl of battle around him became muffled, as if underwater. He kept his eyes fixed on the heavens, trying not to slip away too soon.

He would have raged then, if he had been able. Not against his own death, which meant little to him, but for what the dragon had done to the army about him.

Grungni's beard, he thought, aghast at the cold realisation even as his mind slipped into darkness. *We cannot beat them.*

Morgrim watched the dragons with a slow and growing sense of awe. He had witnessed such creatures before, of course. He had even come close to riding one – the very sapphire monster that was currently ripping his armies into shreds – but he had never seen one unshackled in battle. Only his ancestors in the days of glory, back when Malekith had fought alongside Snorri Whitebeard, would have witnessed such terrible carnage.

He stood grimly amid his faltering legions, resting on his axe, staring fixedly at the bloodshed.

'We cannot hold them!' cried one of his thanes – he did not even notice which one. Warriors were hurrying into position all around him, reserves suddenly pressed into action and charging out across the battlefield. He heard the bellows of captains exhorting their troops to move faster, to fight harder, to bring the damned *drakk* down.

None of them, not one, considered falling back. Faced with a terror greater than any living dwarf had faced, they just kept advancing, hurling themselves into the fiery maw of it with death-oaths spilling from their lips.

We never learn.

Morek limped up to him out of the darkness. The runelord's grey beard was flecked with ash and blood, his staff leaking a thick dirty smoke.

'The *drakk*...' he began, his gnarled face wide with shock.

Morgrim nodded. 'I can see, *rhunki*. I can see it all.'

Out across the far side of the raging battle, the elgi had pushed out of their citadel, emerging in strength from the breaches his own war engines had carved into the outer walls. Their infantry were formidable enough – well-organised squares of mail-clad spearmen supported by cavalry squadrons that moved steadily across the ceded ground. On their own such soldiers would have been a worthy test.

But the dragons... they were something else. Morgrim stayed where he was, saying nothing, in silent awe of their supremacy, their matchless arrogance, their contempt.

Some madness had taken hold of them. They crashed to earth in flailing whirls of claws and tails, crushing everything beneath them, before launching back into the skies with broken bodies trailing in their wake. They smashed siege engines apart. They belched gobbets of coruscation that melted all but the gromril masks of his best equipped elite. Bolts fell harmlessly from their armour. No axe or blade seemed to bite. Those that stood up to them died and, since no dwarf ever ran from danger, that meant whole regiments were wiped out with horrifying speed.

As the sun finally met the western horizon, casting crimson rays across the fields of death and sending long barred shadows streaking out from the base of the towers, the dragons still glittered like jewelled spears, their scales flashing vividly like the coloured glass in the shrine of Grungni.

He remembered Imladrik telling him of the Star Dragons. Morgrim had scoffed at the description.

'We know how to kill *drakk*,' he had said.

Imladrik had laughed. Back then, they had often laughed together. 'Even daemons struggle to live against a Star Dragon,' he had replied. 'On this occasion, my friend, you do not know of what you speak.'

I did not. Truly, I did not.

The runesmiths were struggling as they attempted to drag up rune-wards that would do something to halt the dragons' rampage, the elgi mages in the city were freed up to send their own magics whirling and bursting into the shattered dawi formations. Everything had been overhauled, turning with agonising swiftness from the long grind of a city siege into the sudden slaughter of a rout.

'We cannot fight this,' said Morgrim quietly. With every second that passed more of his host was being hammered into the ground. He could smell the blood on the air, thick as woodsmoke.

'There must be a way,' Morek insisted, still breathing heavily from whatever summoning he had been attempting. His staff looked as if it had been retrieved from a magma-pit; even Morgrim could see that the power had been burned away from it.

'There will be a way,' agreed Morgrim. 'But not this day.'

Morek looked at him doubtfully. 'The thanes will not retreat.'

'They will, because I will order them to.' As he spoke, Morgrim felt a sense of resolution he had never felt before, not even after Snorri's death. The bloodshed inflicted by the asur was so outrageous, so wild, performed with such abandon that he could scarcely believe he had once entertained notions of making peace with them. Under their veneer of superiority they were as bloodthirsty as any lurking creature of the mountains. They were animals.

Morgrim drew his axe and held the blade up before him. It reflected the gold dusk-light dully, picking out the intricate knotwork on the metal. He pointed it up at the distant figure of the sapphire dragon, still tearing across the battlefield and lashing tongues of flame down on the warriors beneath its massive span.

Master of Dragons

'I *curse* you,' he cried, his voice as withering as gall. 'I curse you in the name of immortal Grimnir and the spilled blood of my people. By my blade, I shall find you. By my blade, I shall hunt you down and I shall end you. This is my oath, made in the name of my cousin, made in the name of vengeance, which shall bind us both until death finds us.'

Morgrim's arm shook as he spoke, not from weakness but from fervour. His battle-axe whispered its own response – a sibilant *yes*, barely audible over the clamour of the field. The runes glowed angrily, throbbing from the steel like torchlight. Morek watched, awe-struck.

'It is alive,' he said, staring at the blade. 'You have awakened it.'

Morgrim felt the truth of that. The dragons had kindled something, unlocked something. He remembered Ranuld's prophecy, the mumbled words under the mountain. He could feel Azdrakghar humming between his fingers.

The battle was already lost, ripped from his fingers by the arrival of the dragons, but other battles would come. The dawi would learn, growing stronger and more deadly even as the elgi crowed over their reckless slaughter.

'Do what you can to shield the fighters,' he said coldly. 'We will retreat – for now. Vengeance will come.'

Even as he said it, the word struck him as absurd. How many causes for vengeance had there already been in this messy, dirty war? How many more would come before the end, piling on one another in an overlapping maze of grudges and resentments?

It mattered not. For the present, all that mattered was keeping what remained of his forces intact, preserving them and holding them together. Then the counsels would begin, the recriminations, the renewed oaths. All of them would home on to one thing, and one thing only.

How do we kill the dragons?

Morek hesitated a moment longer, loath to be part of

296   *Chris Wraight*

anything but pure defiance. To fall back, even temporarily, was anathema. Eventually, though, even he bowed his grizzled head.

'It will be done,' he said.

By then, Morgrim was no longer listening. He had turned his mournful gaze back over the battlefield. It was rapidly turning into a charnel-pit.

We will learn, vowed Morgrim, watching the blistering attack runs of the sapphire drake and marvelling at its unmatched destruction. *We will learn, and then we will come back.*

He felt the axe shiver in his fist.

This is not the end.

Imladrik had no idea how much time had passed. Hours seemed to go by in which he had no awareness of anything at all, though they might well have been mere moments amid the combat. Everything melded into a blur, a long smear of violence. His vision was ringed with black, filmy with the blood that had splashed into his face and across his helm. All he heard was the rush and roar of the dragon, the mighty wall of noise that thrummed and raged in his ears.

The sun had gone. Flying through the flamelit dark was like flying through the recesses of a dream. Brilliant explosions of dragonfire and magelight briefly exposed a desolate waste of mud, bone and broken weapons. Tattered standards flew from splintered poles, bearing the images of mountain holds. Every so often Draukhain would spy a living soul and go after it, bearing down like a falcon pouncing on a hare.

The core regiments had gone. They had been smashed open, first by the dragons and then by the vengeful spear battalions that had emerged in their wake. The battlefield had been thinned out, harrowed, flensed.

He remembered the screams. Hearing dwarfs scream had been a strange experience – it took a lot to make a son of the

Master of Dragons

earth open his throat and give away his agony.

All of them had fought. He had admired the hardened units in the centre of the advance on the gate – they had resisted for the longest, striding towards him with utter fearlessness as he glided in for the kill. Their thick plate armour had given them some protection from dragonfire and their blunt warhammers and mauls had been able to crack with some force into the hides of the ravening drakes.

He didn't remember how long it had taken to kill them all. The whole recollection was little more than a mix of blind wrath and delirium. Draukhain had raked into them again and again, tearing up the ground beneath their feet and shaking them in his jaws like a dog with its quarry. Imladrik had been a part of that, guiding him, fuelling his rage, amplifying the annihilation.

At some point the war-horns had sounded again, marking the retreat. That didn't stop the killing. The dragons raced after the withdrawing columns, harrying them, picking off the outliers and tearing them to pieces in mid-air. The dwarfs never turned their backs. They left the field in good order, facing the enemy the whole time, stumbling backwards over terrain made treacherous by blood-slicks. They left behind huge baggage trains, each composed of dozens of heavily laden wains and upturned carts. When the dragons got in amongst the ale-barrels, the night was lit up with fresh explosions and racing channels of quick-burning fire.

Only when they reached the cover of the trees did the worst of the slaughter break off. The dragons wheeled up and around again, hunting down those still out in the open. The asur infantry, seeing the assault begin to ebb, established positions out on the plain, unwilling to break formation by pursuing the dawi into the shadows of the forest.

It was then, slowly, that Imladrik began to recover his equilibrium. He felt the swell and dip of the mighty muscles beneath him and smelled the smoky copper stench of his mount. He saw the stars spin above him and the gore-sodden earth stretch away below. For the first time since the kill-lust had taken him, he truly took in the scale of the destruction.

He allowed Draukhain to carry him across the face of the plain. They flew in silence, the roars and battle-cries stilled.

He could not count the dead. Thousands lay in the mire, spines broken and armour cracked. They stretched from the walls right up to the eaves of the trees, half-buried in muck and slowly cooling gore.

Draukhain still flew strongly. His spirit burned hot. A palpable sense of satisfaction emanated from his blood-streaked body.

Imladrik said nothing. His heart was still beating far faster than usual. His breathing was shallow and rapid. His palms were scorched even through his gauntlets and his sword still glowed red.

The dragon did not slow until they reached the walls again. He flew low over the asur on the plain, who whooped and saluted as they soared overhead, before rising up towards the Tower of Winds.

No, sang Imladrik, his first words since giving the order to unleash the drakes. *The walls.*

Draukhain understood, and banked steeply, heading back towards the breach where he had first sensed Thoriol. In a few moments he had found the spot again and hovered over it. Menials were already at work clearing the bodies from the stonework, labouring under the light of torches brought up from the lower city.

Imladrik guided Draukhain to the breach. The parapets were almost clear; only a few sentries from the archer companies remained, and they cowered in the dragon's shadow, awe-struck.

'Where are the archers who were stationed here?' demanded Imladrik, finding it strange to hear his mortal voice out loud again. His throat was raw and painful.

Master of Dragons

One of the sentries, shading his eyes against the fiery presence above him, stammered a response.

'Th-they withdrew to the healing house. With the others.'

'Their wounded?'

'They took them. The captain died. Two others died.'

'Who lived?'

'Loeth did, lord, and the Silent, and–'

'The who?'

'Thoriol, the Silent, lord.'

A desperate hope kindled. 'Go to the healing house now. Find the captain of the guard and tell him to place a watch on it. Tell him that Imladrik orders it, and will be with him soon.'

The sentry bowed, and fled.

Then Draukhain rose up once more, spiralling higher, his tail curling around the charred and semi-ruined spires.

Where now? the dragon asked.

Imladrik drew in a long, weary breath. He felt sick. He saw Yethanial's face before his mind, calm and grey. Then he saw Liandra's, the polar opposite. He wanted to be furious with her still, but sheer exhaustion got the better of him.

The Tower of Winds, he sang gloomily.

He knew why such torpor affected him: it was always the same after the brief releases of power. Every action had its price, and losing control exacted a heavy burden.

Draukhain thrust upwards, his flight as effortless as ever. The dragon could have flown for days and never grown weary. He was a force of nature, a shard of the world's energy captured and given form; for such as him a night's carnage was of little consequence.

You have done what they asked of you, Draukhain sang, in a rare concession to Imladrik's disquiet. *This is the end. We shall hunt them all the way back to their caves now.*

Imladrik laughed hollowly. *Ah, great one. No, this is not the end. This is just the start.*

Draukhain's long neck swung to and fro in a gesture uncannily like a mortal shaking his head. *You will never be satisfied.*

No, probably not.

They reached the open platform just below the tower's topmost pinnacle. Salendor was there, as were Aelis, Gelthar and many other mages. The spellcasters looked on the edge of collapsing. A raw aroma of aethyric discharge hung on the air like snuffed candles.

Salendor was the first to salute Imladrik. He looked genuinely impressed, his hard expression softening into something close to relieved remorse.

'Hail, lord! You did as you promised.'

Draukhain drew close to the platform's edge. Imladrik pushed himself from his mount, stumbling awkwardly as he touched down on to the stone. His joints were raw and stiff, his limbs wooden. Servants rushed to aid him and he waved them away.

'You doubted the drakes,' Imladrik replied, allowing himself to take a little satisfaction in Salendor's rare humility.

To his credit, Salendor bowed. 'I did. And their master.'

Imladrik turned to Aelis. 'Any word of Liandra?'

Aelis shook her head. As she did so, Imladrik felt a warmth at his back, running up his spine. The air stirred, rustled by an ember-hot wind.

He turned. All six of the dragons were suspended above the platform, five of them still bearing their riders. They held position in a semicircle, heads lowered, spines arched steeply. They hung in perfect formation, huge and terrible, making the robes of the mages bloom and flap from the beat of their wings.

Before the battle each one had been a different colour, as glorious as new-mined precious gems. Now they were all red, covered in the blood of the slain, dripping as if dipped in vats of it, glistening in the light of the fires like raw sides of meat.

Master of Dragons   301

'They salute you, lord,' said Aelis, her eyes shining with wonder.

Imladrik saw then how he must look to the others. He too was drenched from head to toe in blood. He too looked like a visitation from some other world, one of reckless savagery and unlocked murder.

He didn't know what to say. The dragons' fealty, for the first time, embarrassed him. In the light of what he had done, his failure, his loss of control – it felt like a mockery.

You become the dragon, the dragon becomes you.

'Enough,' he said, turning away from them and beginning to walk. His heart was heavy, his footprints dull crimson smudges on the marble. 'My son is here. The boy has need of me.'

III
DRAGONSOUL

CHAPTER TWENTY-ONE

Yethanial woke suddenly. She had only been asleep for a short time, retiring early after a long and gruelling session at her writing desk. Ever since Imladrik had gone her mind had struggled to retain its focus. She dreamed of him often, imagining him at the heart of battle, mounted on that damned creature that made his moods wild and dark.

Her chamber was still lit by half-burned candles. The windows rattled from the wind, a strong easterly. She sat up, rubbing her eyes. Sleep, she knew, would be elusive now.

It could not go on. She had tried to pretend that all was well for too long. She reached out to the table by her bed and rang a small brass bell.

A few moments later her maidservant entered, bowing as she drew close to the bed.

'I asked you for word of my son,' said Yethanial.

'There has been none, lady. Not for many days. The master-at-arms believes...' The girl trailed off, uncertain whether she should go on.

'That he is no longer on Ulthuan,' said Yethanial. She had

come to the same conclusion herself, but unwillingness to countenance it had prevented her from acting. 'We must accept that he is right. And if he is not on Ulthuan, then there is only one place in the world he would have fled to.'

She reached for a scrap of parchment – there were always several lying close to her bed – and began to write with an old quill and half-clotted ink.

'I have stayed here long enough, pining like some useless wife. I am not some useless wife. I am a daughter of Isha with the blood of princes in my veins.'

She handed the parchment to her servant. 'Take this to the harbourmaster at Cothmar. Ensure he finds me a good ship – fast, and with room for a dozen guards. Take my house seal so he knows who asks him. I will travel tomorrow and will be at the quayside by noon.'

The maidservant bowed again, taking the parchment. 'How long will you be gone, lady?'

Yethanial sat back against her bolsters, dreading the long night ahead.

'I have no idea. Long enough.'

The maidservant left, hurrying as she went. Yethanial heard her echoing steps as she skipped down the stairs. Soon after she heard the slam of doors and the creak of the great gates, followed by the drum of horses' hooves in the night.

She hated the thought of leaving. She hated not being in Ulthuan, and hated the thought of a long and dangerous sea crossing. Caledor, had he known, would almost certainly have forbidden it.

Yethanial lay back, pulling the sheets around her. It could not be helped. Even if she had not had such dreams she would have made the crossing, for the sake of her son if for nothing else.

It had always been Thoriol who had drawn them together – he, in the end, remained the strongest bond between them.

One by one, the candles in her chamber blew out,

Master of Dragons

gradually clothing the room in darkness. Yethanial lay there, her mind alert and unsleeping, her hands loosely clasped over the counterpane. Even when the last one guttered out, little more than a pool of wax in the silver holder, she was still awake, her grey eyes shining with resolve.

Liandra shaded her eyes against the horizon-glare. For a moment she didn't believe it – just another mirage on the baking world's edge, a false hope born from desperation.

Then it didn't go away. She looked closer, squinting into the distance. It stayed put, tantalisingly so.

A city. *The* city. One she had never visited but had known must be close: Oeragor, Imladrik's own, thrust out into the utter margins of asur territory in Elthin Arvan and raised from the choking desert in defiance of all reason.

Drutheira didn't say anything. It would have been hard for her to do so with a gag ripped from her own robes wrapped tightly around her jaw. The druchii's eyes were red-rimmed, her stance slumped in the heat.

Every so often on the long trek east she had fallen, no doubt from genuine fatigue. On those occasions Liandra had waited patiently for her to get up, neither helping nor hindering. The druchii witch didn't like to show weakness and would struggle to her feet again when she could. With her arms bound tightly, her tongue clamped and her staff shattered she was no longer a threat, just an encumbrance.

Killing her would have given a modicum of satisfaction. Over the past two days Liandra had come close. Once, in the middle of the night as the campfire burned low, she had reached over to the witch's slumbering form, knife in hand, just a hair's breadth away from plunging the point into her throat.

It had not been mercy that had held her back. In a strange, shadowy way Liandra felt like the dark elf had been part of her life for a long time, an integral part of the struggling tale of the colonies. Drutheira was a dark mirror to her, a spectral counterpart of Liandra's own fiery presence.

When she had first come round from her deep unconsciousness, the witch had smiled thinly.

'So you won,' she had said, as if that was all there was to it.

It had been unutterably eerie to look into the violet eyes of her quarry. The hatred Liandra felt for her was too intense to generate even a token response. She stayed her dagger-hand, though.

Perhaps she had learned something from Imladrik after all, and saw the larger canvas spread out before her. The witch *knew* things: she knew why the druchii had been active, why they had been sent, how many were still in Elthin Arvan. Her very existence was the proof Imladrik needed. If Liandra could bring her back to Tor Alessi alive then the dream of a settlement was not yet dead.

All of which, though, meant nothing if she failed to keep her alive.

Liandra hauled Drutheira along behind her on a length of cord taken from her belt. The witch was in a far worse state than her, ravaged by what must have been months out in the wild. Liandra never untied her and never let her speak again, but soon stopped fearing her powers.

The first day was the worst. Plagued by terrible headaches from the sun, progress amounted to little more than putting one foot in front of the other. All Liandra had to guide her was old memories and a vague sense of *rightness* – like all the asur mageborn she could sense the echoes and resonances of her kind even from immense distances, shimmering amid the aethyr like the whispers of overheard conversations. Many times on that trek she stood still, eyes closed, letting her mind rove ahead of her, seeking out the source of the faint aura of familiarity.

Such work was easier in the absence of Vranesh's huge influence. With the dragon gone, Liandra's mind seemed to

Master of Dragons 309

work more surely. Once the worst of the grief had subsided she found her moods calming down, settling into the analytical patterns required for survival. She still missed the drake's voice – unbearably so, at times – but it was impossible not to also notice how much freer she felt once out of its shadow.

It wasn't until the third day that she began to give up hope. The hard land yawned away from her in every direction, a semi-desert of scree, dust and thorny bushes that gave neither shelter nor moisture. Both of them suffered. Drutheira's eyes were permanently half-closed and puffy, her breathing little more than a soft rattle. They spent most of the morning struggling down a winding defile and having to clamber over boulders twice their size. Only at the end of it, after miles of solid torture, did the landscape finally open up again.

Liandra looked east, and her heart sank: the land was as featureless and barren as the rest. But then she saw them, hard on the edge of her vision: spires, hazy in the distance, glinting like ivory in the sun.

'Oeragor,' she breathed. It was the first word she had spoken aloud for three days.

Drutheira stood beside her, swaying, looking like she had barely any awareness of where she was. Liandra glanced coldly at her. 'They will welcome you there, witch. Always a chamber to be found for the druchii.'

They started to walk again. After the initial euphoria wore off the precariousness of their position reasserted itself. Liandra went steadily, trying not to breathe too heavily, feeling the solid heat hammer at her back and shoulders. She had wound fabric from her cloak over her head, but though it protected her skin from the worst of the sun, it made her feel claustrophobic and stuffy. Every time she looked up the spires seemed to be just where they had been the last time – too far away.

After several hours of trudging she realised she wouldn't make it. Her heart was labouring like an old carthorse's. Her throat was so bone-dry she could no longer swallow and her lips were split and bleeding. The towers remained just where they had been all along: within eyesight, still too far.

Drutheira was in even worse shape. When Liandra stopped the witch fell to the ground and stayed there. Liandra couldn't be sure she was breathing and couldn't be sure that she cared. She sank to her knees, wondering just how long it would take for the sun to fry her into wizened ashes. There was no shelter, no moisture, just open miles of horrific, bleary, seamy heat.

She closed her eyes. After a while, oddly, she began to feel better. The heat on her shoulders felt a little less intense, the air a little less stultifying. Perhaps, she thought, this was what dying felt like.

She opened her eyes again and looked up, half expecting to see the skies unravelling into waves of pure sunlight. Instead she stared straight up into the jaws of a huge creature, hovering above her on massive wings like a golden eagle's. A cruel curved beak snapped at her less than an arm's length from her face. She smelled the tart scent of animal breath on the wind.

For a moment she thought she was hallucinating. Then she saw the rider mounted on the back of the beast – asur armour lined with black and bronze – and realised what it was: a griffon, magnificent in leonine splendour.

'I would have slain you for a dwarf,' called the rider, shading her with his beast's wings. He landed and dismounted, bringing a gourd of water with him. Liandra saw the sigil of Oeragor – a black griffon rampant on an argent field – embroidered on the fabric, and would have smiled if her mouth still worked.

She drank, just a little, letting the griffon-rider hold the gourd for her. The water was cool, almost painfully so.

'We do not see many travellers out in the Blight,' he said. 'If I had not been aloft–'

'Don't,' croaked Liandra. 'I do not wish to think on that.'

'And your companion?'

'Druchii.'

The griffon rider started, hand leaping to the hilt of his sword, but Liandra shook her head weakly.

'Captive,' she rasped, forcing the words out. She began to feel dizzy again, and struggled to keep her poise. 'Bringing… to the city. Take us there. Lord… Imladrik…'

That was all she got out. Black spots appeared before her eyes and she felt her head go thick.

The griffon-rider gazed at Drutheira doubtfully, then back to Liandra.

'I can take you to the city,' he said, tipping the gourd up for her again. 'Though Imladrik is not here, nor has been for many years.' The rider had a young, lean face, one that was both serious and mournful. 'Would that he were. I fear you have not found much sanctuary here.'

Liandra drank greedily. She barely heard the words; all she knew was that she had cheated death – again. That made her happy, almost deliriously so.

'There is little time,' she said painfully. 'Use it well. Take us both.'

A fire burned in the heart of the forest, as tall and broad as the great oaks that crowded around the edges of the clearing. It roared and crackled, sending sparks trailing high up into the night sky and skirling above the treetops.

During the journey west the dwarfs had lit no fires, mindful then of the need for stealth. Now that need had passed.

Morgrim's surviving thanes sat around the blaze, their armour limned a deep orange. Grondil had gone, last seen charging into the path of a golden wyrm, swinging his warhammer wildly around his head and yelling obscenities at the top of his voice. Frei had survived but his arms were both broken, rendering him furiously weaponless. Many others were lost.

Those who remained stared moodily into the flames. Morgrim could see the wounds they had all sustained – deep wounds from speartips or dragon-claws. Frei had lost almost all of his incredibly finely crafted armour, ripped from his back by one of the beasts. He'd been lucky to survive, broken arms or no, though Morgrim knew Frei didn't see things quite like that.

They were consumed with shame. Their cheeks glowed red, their hands rubbed one another, knuckle over knuckle, wearing at their anguish. The dirges had not stopped; even now Morgrim could hear them from the trees, murmured around lesser campfires by the warriors he had brought to the face of ruin.

As for himself, Morgrim felt nothing but resolution. He had felt it ever since leaving the mountains – only Imladrik's doomed attempts to halt the violence had shaken that certainty. There was a kind of purity in adversity and, now that they had been so comprehensively ravaged, all that remained was to fight on. There was nowhere to go, no further questions to ask, nothing left but unbreakable stubbornness.

Which is, after all, what we are known for.

'And so what now?' asked Frei, his voice thick with weariness.

Morek spat on the earth. 'Back to the holds. Muster again, then we strike. Like a hammer on the metal, they will break eventually.'

'No, *rhunki*,' said Morgrim quietly. He remained staring at the flames, appreciating the heat of them against his exposed skin. 'We will not go back.'

Morek looked at him with surprise. To contradict a runelord was rare.

'What do you think will happen when we return?' Morgrim asked, speaking slowly, almost sonorously. 'We could assemble a host three times the size and the result would be the same. The *drakk* are too strong. I should have listened to Imladrik. I took it for boasting, but he was too noble for that. Grimnir's eyes, he was trying to *warn* me.'

The other thanes looked at him warily. They didn't like talk like this.

'We cannot fight them like this,' Morgrim said. 'We must find another way.'

Frei laughed bitterly. 'And what way would that be? Can you now fly in the air? Can you shoot flame from earth to sky?'

'Don't write that off,' said Morgrim, utterly serious. 'But for now? We must forswear Tor Alessi. We must, for the moment, forget the oaths we took there.'

The thanes began to mutter amongst themselves. Even Morek looked perturbed. 'We cannot forget them,' he warned.

'We can let them rest. There are other ways to hurt them.' Morgrim never took his eyes off the flames. They were reassuringly alive to him, like flickering remnants of the ancestor gods he had worshipped his whole life. 'How many *drakk* do they have? I saw six. If others exist, they are over the sea. In one place, those six can destroy any army we create.'

As he spoke he lifted his eyes from the fire and studied the reaction of his surviving thanes. 'That is the key: one place. They cannot be everywhere. They cannot defend Tor Alessi and Athel Toralien, Athel Maraya and Sith Rionnasc, Tor Reven, Kor Peledan or the hundred other fortresses they have built. If we cannot defeat them in one battle then we shall defeat them in a thousand small ones. We must split ourselves, fracture our armies into pieces. Every King shall lead his host, every hold shall work on its own; no grand host will be assembled, not until the very end.'

Morgrim's jaw clenched. 'This is *our land*. Why do we fight like they do, out under the sky, lined up to face their magics? We are *tunnellers*. We can melt into the stone, sink back into the soil. We need no hosts pulled together in the open for the *drakk* to fly at.'

His eyes went flat as he envisioned it.

'We can mount endless attacks, one after the other, directed at every fortress they possess. They will turn most of them back. They will kill many more of us. But some will get through. One by one, the walls will fall. We can make this world a hell for them, one in which the suffering never ceases. They fight well, the elgi. They fight better than any warriors I have ever seen. But do they *suffer* well? No one suffers like the dawi. We will make *this* the battleground – they will be broken on the anvil of our suffering.'

He finished. The silence was broken by the low roar of the fire and the murmur of the dirges. The thanes listened. They digested. They reflected.

Morgrim leaned back, clasping his hands together. They would need time. The High King would need time, as would the other warlords and captains who were already marching towards their future battles. Word would spread out, travelling like wildfire along the mud-thick lanes of the deep forest, gradually spreading from mouth to mouth until the whole world was running with it.

Morek shook his head. 'I don't know,' he muttered.

That was good. A runelord would never simply agree; there needed to be deliberation, debate, rumination. As a start, given the circumstances, Morek's stance was admirably open.

Morgrim determined to say no more that night. He would listen to the others, knowing that in time his counsel would prevail. He had seen the way the war must now be fought. In time the others would too.

A thousand tiny battles, each one grinding into the bedrock of the earth, each one a new wound on the weary face of the elgi empire.

He was already planning his next move. Before dusk the following day he would be marching. His army would splinter, each shard heading in a different direction, and he

Master of Dragons   315

would make his own way among them, no longer the leader of many holds but the warlord of one.

He could see the spires of his prey in his mind, rising from the dry lands to the south, the fragile citadel created by his enemy.

For revenge, for the deaths of Tor Alessi, that one would be the first to burn.

Sunlight angled into the marble chamber from high glass windows. Low beds ran along the walls, dozens of them, each occupied by a wounded highborn. Incense burned in suspended thuribles, a soft fragrance of lavender and marjoram designed to mask the underlying tang of blood. Attendants came and went, feet shuffling on the stone, pale robes brushing.

Thoriol lay on his back, staring at the ceiling. His whole side throbbed with a dull pain, worse when he moved. His chest and stomach were swathed in bandages, some of them bloody.

He had only sketchy memories of how he had arrived there. He didn't remember falling during the battle; he had pushed to the forefront, determined to avenge Baelian's death. He'd loosed two, maybe three, arrows, thinking that they'd all found their marks.

After that, very little. The dwarfs had been massing in numbers and one of them must have loosed a crossbow bolt at him. He had dim recollections of a burning night, of shouting and hurrying. He'd awoken briefly in a crowded chamber, its floor strewn with bloody straw and smoking candles. Someone had leaned over him, pulling his face around to get a better look. He remembered the pain being much worse then.

Then he'd awoken in the marble chamber with very little idea how much time had passed. His dressings had been changed and healing oils applied to his wounds. The attendants had treated him with the sort of unconscious respect he'd enjoyed as a dragon rider's acolyte in Tor Caled, not with the peremptory instruction an archer enjoyed.

He tried to pull himself further up in his bunk, to ease some of the discomfort in his side. As he did so he saw two figures approach, and his heart sank.

'Awake, then,' said the first of them. The Master Healer was an old man from Yvresse, bald as an infant, prone to smiling, his fingers stained from the herbs he crushed during the night hours. 'I do not think you will be with us much longer.'

Thoriol ignored him; his companion was another matter.

'How did you find out?' Thoriol asked his father.

Imladrik looked tired. Incredibly tired. His skin was raw, as if scrubbed hard with pumice to remove some terrible stain, and his long hair hung listlessly around his face. 'Draukhain recognised you,' he said. 'He can sense the Dragontamer's bloodline.'

Thoriol winced. 'Then you brought me here.'

'Others took you from the walls. I sent for you once I knew you lived.'

'You should not have taken me from my company.'

'If you had not been brought here you would have died,' said the Master Healer placidly. 'Two quarrels pierced your flesh, one deeply.'

Imladrik turned to the Healer. 'Thank you, Taenar. I think I might have some time alone with my son now.'

The Healer bowed and withdrew, his slippers padding on the marble. Once he was gone Imladrik sat at the end of the bed. As he did so his whole body seemed to sag.

'Why, son?' he asked.

Thoriol had dreaded the question ever since he had awoken on that first morning, out at sea with his head hammering. It was all so random, all so unplanned. Not for the first time, he had no good answers.

Master of Dragons

'I was deceived, at the start,' he said, opting to be as truthful as he could. 'Then I thought I'd been given another chance. Where is the rest of my company?'

'I do not know. I can ask Caradryel to bring them to–'

'No!' Thoriol exhaled with irritation. 'No, they will not want that. Do you not understand?'

'No, I do not understand.'

'It would terrify them.' Thoriol didn't want to explain. 'They were all running away, for one reason or another. I will find them myself.'

Imladrik looked at him with concern. It was an expression Thoriol recognised very well – the look of strained worry, of doubt, one that said *are you sure that is wise?*

'You are not one of them,' Imladrik warned. 'You are a prince. It could not have lasted.'

'You do not know them.'

'Of course not. Do you think I know a fraction of those who serve under me?'

Thoriol struggled to control his irritation. 'They were good soldiers.'

'No doubt, but you are better than them.'

'Why? Because I am Tor Caled?'

'Yes.' Imladrik's voice was soft but his expression was unbending. 'We do not choose our path, son. You may think you can deny your bloodline and take up a longbow, forgetting every privilege you have had, but believe me the gods will punish you for it. You were born to higher things.'

Thoriol laughed sourly. 'You saw what happened in the Dragonspine.'

'You failed. Once. Do you think that every rider succeeds on his first attempt? Don't be weak. You are throwing everything away.'

That stung. 'Do you know how many dwarfs I killed on the walls? I was *of service*. For the first time in my life, I did something worthy.'

'I have ten thousand archers,' said Imladrik, still struggling to comprehend. 'I have one son.'

'Yes, you do, so let me choose this.'

'Did you not hear me? Choice is for lovesick swains. There is no choice; there is duty.'

Thoriol felt like screaming. All his life it had been the same, the relentless pressure to fulfil the potential of his ancestors.

'It is not as if I wish to remain idle,' he protested. 'I can fight! I will fight.'

'You placed yourself in danger.'

'But the dragons are dangerous. Magic is dangerous.'

'You do not belong there.'

'I do not–'

'I *will not lose you!*' Imladrik shouted, losing control for just a moment before reeling it in again. He clenched his fists, balling them into the coverlet.

Thoriol said nothing, stunned. His father rarely raised his voice; he rarely needed to.

Imladrik took a deep breath. Fatigue hung heavily under his eyes in black rings.

'You are the destiny of the House,' he said, quietly, recovering himself. 'My brother is a fool and a warmonger – he has no issue and will not live out the storm he has set in motion. Only you will remain, Thoriol. Only you.'

That was hard to hear. It had always been hard to hear. He had never wanted any part of it, though even to think such a thing seemed churlish in the light of the sacrifices that had been made.

That had ever been his curse, ill-fitted for the life the gods had ordained for him. His father would never understand, being so consumed by the path he had taken, so entranced and absorbed in the dragons that gave him his power and his reputation.

Before he could reply, though, Imladrik rose, pushing himself heavily from the bunk as if he carried the weight

Master of Dragons

of the Annulii on his shoulders.

'You need rest.' He looked shaky on his feet. 'Gods, I need rest. I should not have raised my voice. But promise me this: stay here. Do not seek them out. We will talk again and find some way to make sense of all of this.'

Thoriol watched him, wondering if anything he had said, now or at any other time, had ever made much of an impression on his father. Perhaps he should have tried dragonsong.

Imladrik extended a hand awkwardly, then let it drop. 'I am glad you are recovering. For a moment, during the siege…' A wintry smile flickered. 'We will talk again.'

Thoriol nodded weakly, knowing that they would and yet doubting that anything much would be said.

'So we will,' he replied, his voice unenthusiastic.

CHAPTER TWENTY-TWO

Death just wouldn't find Drutheira. She felt as if it had been snapping at her heels for years, but the final cut was never quite made. If she had been of a sentimental disposition she might have suspected fate was preserving her for something or other, but she wasn't, and so she didn't. It was all luck, blind luck, and of a particularly sadistic kind at that.

At least her jailors had given her something to drink. The asur treated her roughly but Liandra had been insistent that she wasn't to be harmed and her orders had been followed with typical assiduousness.

So noble, the asur; so *proper*, in thrall to the rules that bound them into their stultifying patterns of decay. Their reasonableness drove her mad. If the situations had been reversed they would all have been writhing in agony pits by now, their skin hanging from their flesh and their eyes served up on ice for the delectation of the witch elves. They would have begged to tell her everything they knew before the end, which would at least have been amusing for her if not actually useful.

Her detention in Oeragor had been luxurious in comparison. Once she had recovered enough bodily strength to swallow her food unaided she had been strapped into a metal chair deep within the citadel's dungeons. Warding runes had been engraved in the walls, sapping any residual sorcery that might still have lurked in her battered body. A dozen guards stood outside her cell at all times, two of which were always mages. When the asur entered to give her food they glared at her with stony, hatred-filled eyes, clearly itching to do her violence but never giving in.

She could not move, she could not use her art, she could not even speak unless the gag was taken from her scabrous mouth. The whole thing was a humiliation; a spell of honest torture might have been preferable.

Liandra didn't deign to speak to her for two days. When she finally did descend to the dungeon, closing the door behind her with studious relish, Drutheira wondered whether death had found her at last. She certainly didn't blame the mage for wanting to kill her – the antipathy was, after all, entirely mutual.

Once again, though, her expectations were confounded. Liandra looked sleek and rested, freshly supplied with a new staff and pristine mage's robes. She ripped Drutheira's gag free, checked her bonds were secure, then stood before her, arms crossed. For a long time she did nothing but examine her, as if trying to ascertain whether the pitiful creature before her could really have been responsible for so much suffering.

'No questions?' Drutheira croaked eventually. Her strained voice sounded odd in the dank, echoing cell.

'What could you tell me,' said Liandra coolly, 'that I do not already know?'

Liandra's voice was a surprise: it was temperate, restrained even. Everything Drutheira knew about Liandra promised impetuosity, but perhaps being deprived of her creature had bled the fire from her.

Master of Dragons

'Plenty, I judge,' Drutheira said.

Liandra's expression didn't change. It was contemptuous more than anything.

'You were sent to Elthin Arvan by Malekith,' she said. 'We were guarding the sea-lanes, so the best you could do was land in secret. You were here for years, hiding out in the wilds, doing nothing. Only when orders from Naggaroth came did you act, starting the violence that turned the dawi against us. You killed the dawi runelord. You ambushed the trade routes.'

Drutheira couldn't help but smile. When listed like that, the tally of achievement was rather impressive.

'We didn't do it all,' she said. 'Plenty of you wished for war.'

'You are right. I was one of them.'

'Then you should be pleased.'

'How little you understand us.' Liandra crossed her arms, threading the staff under an elbow. 'You sit there, smirking, content in small malice. Nothing you have done here will hasten Malekith's return to the Phoenix Throne. He will remain an outcast for the rest of his days, howling his misery into the ice.'

Drutheira inclined her head in putative agreement. 'Maybe, but he has his war. Nothing can stop that now.'

'You know less than you think. They are talking again, and the dwarfs know of the secret war. All they need now is proof, and that is why you have been suffered to live – so I can drag you to Tor Alessi where, under the hot irons, you will be made to speak. Truth-spells shall be wound around you. All shall hear it. Your last action, before I finally kill you, will be to weep for the ruin of all you have sought to achieve.'

Drutheira couldn't prevent a faint quiver of doubt showing on her face then. Liandra might have been lying, of course, but she sounded unnervingly confident. Recovering, Drutheira glared back defiantly.

'Wishful,' she said. 'You know the chance has long gone. I sense the hatred boiling away within you even from here – you *loathe* the dawi.'

Liandra drew close to her then, so close that Drutheira could smell the fragrance of her robes and make out the freckles on her pale cheeks.

'I do,' Liandra whispered, bending over her almost tenderly. 'I wish to see every last one of them driven back into the mountains, but how much more do I loathe *you.*'

The intensity of hatred then was unmistakable. Drutheira tried to pull her head away but her bonds held her tightly.

'When you burn, witch, I shall be watching,' Liandra whispered coolly. 'For the sake of those you killed, I will *revel* in your agony.'

Drutheira couldn't look away. Two blue eyes glared at her from the gloom, unwavering in their passionate intensity.

For the first time in a long while, no words came to her: no acid riposte, no withering put-down. She was alone, shackled, held in the vice by those who hated her, and there was nothing much left to say.

Then Liandra sneered, her message delivered, and withdrew. The mage swept from the chamber, not looking back, and slammed the heavy door behind her.

Alone again in the darkness, Drutheira heard the bolts lock home. Then silence fell again, as complete as the outer void.

This, I admit, she thought to herself mordantly, *is getting difficult.*

The drum beat with a steady, driving rhythm. Even as the dark trees clustered close, their shaggy branches hanging low across the path, the beat continued – heavy, dull, dour.

Morgrim enjoyed the sound of it. It reminded him of the beating of hammers in the deeps, the ever-present sound of the sunken holds. Its steady pace spoke of certainty, resolve, persistence.

Master of Dragons

He marched in time with it, as did all of his retinue. Five hundred dwarfs of the *bazan-khazakrum* kept up the punishing pace, hour after hour, pausing only for snatched meals of cured meat washed down with strong ale. They carried their supplies on their backs, not waiting for a baggage train to keep up with them. Every warrior matched the stride, none falling behind, none pressing ahead.

The constant exertion helped Morgrim forget. While he was moving, his breathing heavy and his arms swinging, he could consign the memory of Tor Alessi to forgetfulness. Only in the few hours of sleep he allowed himself did the images come back – the flaming fields, the stink of burning flesh, the cries of alarm. He would awake in the cold dawn, his eyes already staring, his fists clenched with anguish.

'Onward,' he would growl, and all those around him would drag themselves to their feet once again.

Dwarfs could cover a phenomenal amount of ground when the occasion demanded. They were not quick in their movements but they were relentless. No other race of the earth had such endurance, such capacity to drive onwards into the night and start again before first light. Freed of the straggling demands of his huge army, Morgrim's warband had made good progress, led from the front and hauled onwards by his indomitable will.

Morek kept pace just as well as the others. He swayed as he strode, his cheeks red and puffing, his brows lowered in a permanent scowl of concentration.

'How many miles?' he asked, several days into the march, the road still thickly overlooked by foliage. His hauberk was thick with mud, his cloak ripped and sodden.

'No idea,' replied Morgrim, maintaining pace to the hammer of the drum. 'Why do you ask?'

Morek snorted. 'Because Tor Alessi is at one end of the world and Oeragor is at the other. I do not mind the exertion, but was there not a closer prize?'

Morgrim hawked up phlegm and spat it noisily into the verge. 'There are many closer prizes. Soon they will all be burning.'

'That is not an answer.'

'Then because it is *his*.' Morgrim's voice shook with vehemence. He was tempted to stop then, to call the march to a halt and remonstrate with the runelord, but resisted. Every minute was vital. 'It is his place, the one he built. It will hurt him.' He glared at Morek. 'Enough of a reason?'

Morek nodded, his breathing getting a little more snatched. 'So it is a private war with you now.'

'It is, and if you have issue with that there are other warbands you could join.'

Morek shook his head wearily. 'Gods, no. I made an oath.'

Morgrim looked ahead again. 'Good. While we march, recite your rune-craft. I will need it.'

He knew he spoke harshly; the runelord deserved more. His mood was dark, though. He could feel Snorri's casket rattling against his jerkin, bound to his chest with chains of iron. Imladrik had no doubt intended the return of Halfhand's remains as a gesture of goodwill. Now, in the aftermath of what had been unleashed, it felt like an insult.

'I sent word to every thane under the mountains,' he muttered. 'They are all marching. Frei has taken half his hold to Sith Rionnasc. Others are heading through the forest. Others are marching under Brynnoth of Barak Varr. His army is the one we will join. He will support the new way of war – he was ever a wily soul and he knows how best to skin the elgi.'

Morgrim didn't mention the other reason he wished to join forces with Brynnoth's armies. Rumours had been whispered through the candlelit corridors of Karaz-a-Karak for months, sometimes with scorn, though often with interest. Brynnoth had done something interesting in Barak Varr, something that held greater promise of taking on the elgi than the campaign of scorched earth he now advocated.

Master of Dragons

He'd heard stories of airborne machines, held aloft only by sacks of air and carrying weapons of fiendish invention. That was interesting. The two of them needed to talk, and to accomplish that he needed to get to Brynnoth.

For now, though, retaliation needed to be decisive, extensive, and, above all, swift.

'You think we will be in time?' asked Morek. 'Last I heard he was close to his muster weeks ago.'

'We will be in time,' said Morgrim dismissively. 'We will make rafts for the river and drive up against the current. We will march into the Ungdrin when we find it again. I will burn myself into the ground if need be, but we will be there.'

Spittle flew from his mouth as he spoke. Anger was only ever a finger's breadth under the surface with him, ever ready to erupt. The axe weighed heavily on his back at such times, as if daring him to draw it.

Morek scratched the back of his neck, still marching, looking as if he had his doubts but was too prudent to voice them.

'The runes,' he said, glancing at the axe. 'Do they still answer?'

Morgrim nodded. Azdrakghar had felt alive since Tor Alessi, resonating through his armour in its strapping. 'It growls like a caged wolf.'

'The *drakk* woke it,' said Morek. 'Snorri thought–'

'Do not mention him,' snapped Morgrim sharply. 'I grow tired of hearing his name. For too long we have used it, making it stoke our anger. Do we not have enough reasons of our own to hate them?'

Morek stared at him. 'I only meant–'

'It is my blade. Snorri was wrong, it was forged for me. It was forged for the *drakk*. You knew this when you made it.'

Morek shook his grizzled head, puffing hard. 'I don't know. Even Ranuld didn't know. If it has a destiny, I cannot see it.'

'I can,' said Morgrim, his grey eyes narrow. He kept marching. 'I see it as clear as moonlight.'

'So here we are again.'

Imladrik sat in his throne at the summit of the Tower of Winds. Three of the other thrones were occupied.

Caerwal was no longer there. Neither was Liandra, whose whereabouts had still not been established. Word had come in regarding the fate of her fortress: Kor Vanaeth lay in ruins, its surviving people heading towards Tor Alessi. A dwarf column nearby had also been destroyed. Both sites, Imladrik had been told, bore the marks of dragonfire.

He didn't know why she'd done it. Hatred – for him or for the dawi – didn't seem enough. The betrayal hurt him deeply, the more so given the uncertainty over her motives. He'd been tempted to take Draukhain east and find her. Perhaps there were still things they had to say to one another.

Or maybe she had extinguished any trust they still had. As surely as if she had slipped a dagger into Morgrim's chest, Liandra had ensured the war could never be stopped.

Whatever I may have done to hurt you, he thought bitterly, *I deserved better than that.*

'We are victorious,' said Aelis. She looked reinvigorated. The flight of the dragons had given them all hope again. 'Thanks to you.'

Gelthar, who sat one place to her left, also looked content. His troops had been first out onto the plain once the dwarf retreat had started.

Of all of them, though, it was Salendor who had been most vindicated by events. The mage-lord was at pains not to make too much of it, but his satisfaction was hard to hide.

'Then the question is: what now?' asked Imladrik.

'Go after them,' said Salendor bluntly. Then he laughed. 'Did you expect any other counsel? Morgrim's army is broken.'

Master of Dragons 329

'They are ripe for destruction,' agreed Gelthar. 'Now is the time.'

Aelis shot her companions a tolerant look. 'Have you learned nothing, lords? We will offer our views here, discuss them for an age, and then Imladrik will overrule us.'

Imladrik smiled wryly. 'So you understand how this works at last.'

In truth, his position was a strange one. His policy of restraint had failed spectacularly, just as they had all warned him it would. On the other hand he had demonstrated the full ambit of power at his command, which had daunted even Salendor. He couldn't decide quite what that made him.

A fool? A saviour? Possibly both.

'You have another idea,' said Salendor.

Imladrik leaned back in his throne. 'Place yourself in the mind of our enemy. What will he be thinking?'

'Vengeance,' said Gelthar. 'They will come back at us.'

'Yes, but how? They are not stupid. We have exposed our greatest strength to them, and they have felt just how powerful that is. They will not repeat their mistake.'

'What can they do?' asked Aelis lightly. 'They have no answer to your drakes.'

'They will find one. Even now they will be thinking on it. As I say, they are not stupid.'

'They will disperse,' said Salendor quietly.

All turned to him. Imladrik nodded fractionally. For all their differences, he had always known that Salendor was the most tactically astute of his captains.

'Six dragons,' Salendor went on, speaking thoughtfully. 'Overwhelming together, but they cannot be everywhere.' His voice grew in certainty as he considered the options. 'I would send my warriors in every direction. Forget this place – they cannot take it now. But what of Athel Maraya, or Athel Toralien?'

'Quite,' said Imladrik. 'If we had a hundred dragons then we could consider engaging them, but even Aenarion did not command such numbers. This is their land – our numbers are divided between here and Ulthuan. We do not know how many warriors they have under arms, but it is surely many times what we can muster.'

Aelis's brow furrowed. 'Then what is to be done?'

'The dragon riders will be sent out,' said Imladrik, 'one to each great fortress. Regiments will travel to the frontier citadels. They must leave immediately, for the dawi move fast when the mood is on them. They disperse; so do we.'

Gelthar looked unconvinced. 'That is thinning our forces. No early victory can come from this.'

'You are right,' said Imladrik. 'We will be fighting for years.' He had resolved not to labour the point, but it was worth stating again, just to underline why he had worked so hard to avoid it. 'This will be the shape of the war now: brawling over scorched earth, each of us as exhausted as the other. History shall judge us harshly for it.' He shook his head in frustration. 'And Liandra most of all.'

The others looked awkwardly at one another.

'You cannot believe that,' said Salendor.

'Then where is she?' Imladrik demanded, trying not to let his frustration spill out too obviously.

'I do not know.'

'She went to Kor Vanaeth. We know this.'

'And only the word of our enemy condemns her,' said Salendor, 'I will not doubt her loyalty, not until we know more.'

'So sure,' observed Imladrik, looking at him carefully. 'No qualm at all?'

Salendor looked back confidently. 'None.'

Part of Imladrik wanted to believe him. Any thread of hope that Liandra was not responsible would be clung to.

For all that, he remembered how she had been when they had last spoken.

We must strike now before they gather more strength.

'The truth will out,' was all he said. 'For now, we have preparations to make. We cannot remain gathered here while the fighting spreads across Loren Lacoi. Salendor, you must leave for Athel Maraya and prepare for attack – they will surely be there soon. Gelthar, take Athel Toralien and order its defences. Aelis, command of Tor Alessi will be returned to you. Each of you shall have dragon riders: two remaining here, two for Athel Maraya, one for Athel Toralien. A lone drake will be a match for all but the mightiest armies, and the memory of their blooding here will not fade quickly.'

Things had changed since he'd first arrived. They nodded readily enough, accepting his orders. Even Salendor voiced no objection.

'And you, lord?' asked Aelis. 'Where will you go?'

Imladrik did not know the answer to that. A dozen places had already sprung to mind: remaining in Tor Alessi; joining Salendor at Athel Maraya; heading to his own citadel of Oeragor on the edge of the wasteland; returning to Ulthuan to petition for more troops and dragon riders. The final option was the least palatable but also the most prudent: it would give them the best chance of survival in the storm to come. It would, though, mean leaving the conduct of the war to others and abasing himself before his brother.

'Where the war takes me,' he said. Even then, though, locked in discussion of strategy, Liandra's fate burned on his mind. 'Asuryan, no doubt, will determine.'

CHAPTER TWENTY-THREE

Liandra headed across the piazza feeling, if not exactly content, then certainly partially satisfied. The days since her recovery had passed quickly, dulling some of her lingering grief over Vranesh. It had taken an almighty effort of will not to kill Drutheira when she had spoken to her last, but the witch's unmistakable reaction to the news of what Liandra intended had almost been worth it on its own. Vengeance would come in time and would be all the sweeter for the wait.

She reached the western end of the piazza, passed under a shaded portico, and ascended a long train of stone stairs. It had not taken long for her to recover from her ordeal out in the wasteland, especially since Oeragor's people had plied her with medicinal draughts and restorative tinctures.

Their care had been welcome, but now impatience was beginning to drive her again. She was mindful of the fact that her disappearance from Tor Alessi had been sudden. Imladrik would not know why she had gone; he might attribute it to her awkward outbursts during their last conversation, perhaps even cowardice in the face of the dwarf advance. The matter needed to be settled quickly, not least as she had no means of knowing how the talks were faring, nor indeed if they were even still in progress.

As ever, the lack of certain knowledge was troubling. For far too long she had been guessing at shadows and half-truths, just as they all had. Such was always the way in Elthin Arvan, a land of enormous distances, choked by forests and hampered by lurking dangers under the shade of every branch.

At the end of her climb she reached a sunlit chamber with arched colonnades around the edges. She passed across a marble floor, up another spiral stair and into the interior of a large octagonal tower. By the time Liandra emerged at the topmost balcony she could feel the pricking of sweat in the small of her back.

She had not quite recovered, then; not yet.

A tall figure in long ivory robes waited for her, standing against the balcony railing and staring out northwards. His hands and face were tanned a rich light brown, much like the rest of Oeragor's population. It was an attractive counterpoint to the washed-out colouring of temperate Ulthuan.

'How is our guest?' the tall elf asked.

'Talkative,' she replied. 'Not that I am much interested in what she has to say.'

Kelemar, Regent of Oeragor, nodded in satisfaction. 'I am glad you're happy, though I warn you my people are not. There has been talk of breaking into the dungeons and dragging her out.'

'I can understand that. Believe me, I will rid you of her as soon as I may.'

Kelemar looked back out over the balcony's edge. 'That would be appreciated, but I don't know how you'll do it.'

Below them lay the tight-packed towers of Oeragor's northern slopes. The city had been built at the heart of the wide, sun-baked plain and the buildings clustered together as if

Master of Dragons

for protection from the elements. Every surface was white-washed. The walls gleamed under the sun, making Liandra's eyes water if she looked at them for too long.

It was not a large settlement. She had often wondered why Imladrik had chosen such a site. Oeragor's foundations had been sited over a deep well of pure spring water, an oasis amid the bleakness; so it did at least have enough to drink, as well as a surplus to irrigate some modest gardens and terraced plantations. The city stood on the site of a truly ancient road, one that predated even the dawi presence in Elthin Arvan, though none could say who had made it or why. Its population numbered some five thousand, almost as small as Kor Vanaeth though far more remote. Even with recent reinforcements it stood at a little over seven thousand, leaving plenty of room within the whitewashed walls for more.

Liandra once asked Imladrik why he had adopted the far-flung location. He hadn't been very forthcoming.

'We cannot restrict ourselves to the coast,' he'd said lightly. 'We must push into the wild places, taming them one by one.'

It wasn't much of an answer. Liandra had always suspected he'd had designs on making the place his home one day, a refuge away from the scheming of Ulthuan and the grimy hardship of the coastal colonies. She could certainly imagine Draukhain out here, coasting effortlessly over the empty lands, his sky-blue hide sparkling in unbroken sunlight.

Even if that were true, though, she knew he'd never be given the freedom to pursue the dream. Caledor had summoned him back to Ulthuan to oversee the everlasting war against the druchii, then given him the command that had taken him to Tor Alessi. One way or another, his brother had frustrated any plans Imladrik might have once had for Oeragor.

And of course there was his wife, the scholar-lady of Tor

Vael. Liandra could not imagine her willingly uprooting and coming to the desert. The relationship between the two of them had always been a mystery to her, one that perhaps only they themselves truly understood.

But that was uncomfortable to think about.

'You say the roads north are still too perilous?' Liandra asked, shading her eyes as she looked out over the honey-yellow landscape.

'The dawi are marching. They have emptied their holds to the east, destroyed our outposts all across the northern edge of the Blight.'

'The Blight. I can see why you called it that.'

'Nothing else seemed appropriate. You were lucky to last out there for as long as you did.'

Liandra pushed a stray length of copper-blonde hair from her face. She could already feel her skin tightening in the heat. 'Why stay here, Kelemar? What keeps you?'

'Because we were ordered to. And because we have our task here: to turn the barren land into a garden.'

Liandra had thought much the same of Kor Vanaeth. Elthin Arvan was dirty, dangerous and feral, but the vision of the colonists had been to tame it, to make it a paradise. If they were fighting for anything noble, that was it.

'And, of course, it is Imladrik's place,' Kelemar went on. 'We are all his people. We would work ourselves into the dust for him.'

Liandra shook her head gently. 'Why is this? He inspires this... devotion.'

Kelemar pursed his lips in modest disapproval. 'In the early days he laboured with us here. He carried stones on his back with the rest of us. He could have followed the life of his brother and lived in a palace in Lothern. Whatever it was that took him away from us, we know he did not choose it.' He smiled regretfully. 'Does that give you your answer?'

'There's some secret to it, to be sure.' She found herself

Master of Dragons 337

wishing to change the subject and withdrew from the balcony's edge, pulling out of the direct sunlight. 'So the passage north is closed, and there is nothing to the south, west and east but empty rock. I need to find some way to reach Tor Alessi.'

'I think you have missed your chance. The dawi will be here soon.'

Liandra looked out north again, seeing no more than haze and heat-shimmer.

'How long?'

'A few days, if we are lucky.'

Liandra drew in a deep breath. Oeragor was a world away from Tor Alessi, where, she had to assume, hostilities were still suspended. To end up stranded in some sweaty skirmish on the margins of civilisation while the real war in the west had been interrupted... The frustration was almost unbearable.

'There will be a way,' Liandra said, doggedly. 'The witch cannot die here. I do not intend to die here. By Isha, there *will* be a way.'

Caradryel pushed back in his chair, feeling irritable and at a loose end. He hadn't slept well for days, kept awake both by his memories of the siege – which were terrible – and his frustration at how the events beforehand had turned out.

Everything he had touched had turned to swill. Confidence, a quality he had never struggled to lay hold of, was in short supply. He had considered speaking to Imladrik about it, perhaps even suggesting that his service had been a mistake and he would be better employed back in Ulthuan.

That, of course, would have been a mistake. Having offered his assistance so brazenly, Caradryel knew there would be no backing out of it now.

In the days since the siege had ended he had barely exchanged a dozen words with his master. Imladrik had looked exhausted in the aftermath of the battle, his face drawn with a dull kind of horror. He'd remained punishingly busy, striding from one end of the city to the other to oversee repairs, rebuilding and restocking. Given the damage inflicted, it would be weeks before full order was restored.

Beyond the walls, the battlefield reeked. Mists rolled in from the sea, turning everything mouldy and sodden. Huge funeral pyres had been constructed to dispose of the dead but they had burned sullenly, leaving thick shrouds of foul-smelling smoke suspended in the air around them. Days later the plain still smouldered under grey clouds, its soils blackened and clotted.

Caradryel had found few things to occupy himself during those days. He had followed up on a few loose ends from the Caerwal affair. He had ensured that his informants were paid, and had kept several of them on to ensure he knew what was going on while the city slowly recovered its equilibrium.

Many of the regiments were now being prepared for marches elsewhere. The dragons flew constantly in the skies over the harbour, as if giving visible reminder of the might of Ulthuan before the troops were sent off into enemy-infested swamps to an uncertain fate. It felt as if everything was unwinding, slowly dissipating like the smoke over the slain.

He tipped his chair on to two legs and swung back on it lazily. When the knock came on the door of his chamber, he nearly sent it – and himself – toppling over.

'Come,' he snapped, righting himself and brushing his robes down.

The door opened and Geleth entered with a female elf in tow. She looked like a beggar, her shift dirty and ragged, her hands and face dirty from the road.

'My lord,' said Geleth, bowing. 'Something I thought you might wish to hear.'

Caradryel shot a superficial smile at the newcomer. 'Welcome. Be seated.'

She remained standing. She had a hunted look in her eyes. Her hands turned over one another in a nervous pattern.

Caradryel glanced at Geleth, who returned a look that said *give her time*.

'Perhaps you would like some wine?' Caradryel tried again. 'Something to eat?'

The elf shook her head. 'Are you Imladrik?'

Caradryel just about suppressed a smile. 'No, not really, but if there is something you wished–'

'I came here for Imladrik.'

'He has many things to worry him. The best way to get a message to him is to entrust it to me. So, let us see if we can get things started. What is your name?'

She looked uncertain. For a minute Caradryel thought she might make a break for the doors.

'Alieth,' she said.

'Good. Alieth, where are you from?'

'Kor Vanaeth.'

Caradryel raised an eyebrow. 'Kor Vanaeth was destroyed.'

Alieth's face flickered with momentary anguish. 'It was. I walked here.'

'On your own?'

'There were others. Not many.'

Caradryel found himself getting interested. Geleth stood calmly by her side, saying nothing.

'You should sit,' Caradryel said, motioning to a chair opposite him. 'You look like you need it.'

Gingerly, Alieth shuffled over to it, perching on the edge as if afraid it would fall apart.

'You are among friends,' Caradryel went on. 'Tell me everything. No dwarf can get to you here.'

She shook her head. 'It wasn't the dwarfs.'

'What do you mean?'

'Kor Vanaeth. It was not destroyed by the dwarfs. We never saw them.'

Caradryel frowned. 'The reports we have–'

'They are wrong. That is why I have to speak to Imladrik. We know he is close to the Lady.'

'Liandra?'

Alieth nodded. 'We came because we had nowhere else to go. When we arrived here we heard rumours.' She frowned. 'Foul rumours. They are saying the Lady broke her commands, that she caused the dwarfs to attack. It is lies.'

Caradryel crossed his legs and leaned forwards, listening carefully. 'Tell me everything. From the beginning. Can you do that?'

'We were attacked. A black dragon ridden by a sorcerer. She destroyed the city. The Lady came to our aid, and they fought above us. I saw it. I saw the red dragon take on the black, driving it out over the mountains.

'A black dragon?' asked Caradryel. He'd never heard of such a thing.

Alieth nodded vigorously. 'A monster, covered in chains. The Lady pursued it. That was the last we saw. Some tried to follow, but they moved too fast.' She started to rub her hands together again. 'Imladrik must know. The Lady is in danger. There were no dwarfs at Kor Vanaeth.'

'Please calm yourself. If what you say is true–'

'It is true.'

'–then I will pass it on to Lord Imladrik. Are you prepared to vouch under oaths to Asuryan?'

Alieth nodded firmly.

Caradryel reached out and rested his hand on hers. It was a tender, reassuring gesture, one he had always been proud of.

'Then I want you to keep remembering,' he said soothingly. 'Think carefully, hold nothing back. Lord Imladrik will be made aware, but first you must tell me what happened next.'

Alieth began to speak again then, a little more fluently as

Master of Dragons

341

she gathered confidence, explaining how she and her companions had survived the onslaught and subsequently made their way through the forest towards the coast.

Caradryel listened, making mental notes of the portions he would pass on to Imladrik. Even as he did so, though, another, more encouraging thought made its presence felt.

This will make me useful again.

So it was that as he listened, despite the impropriety of it, despite his attempts to quell it, Caradryel could not help a furtive smile creeping along the corners of his elegant mouth.

Night fell, though the skies above Tor Alessi remained blood-red from the fires. Labourers worked tirelessly, building as fast as their exhausted limbs would allow. Detachments of soldiers still prowled the streets, though their numbers had been thinned following losses and reassignments.

The world's moons rode high in a cloud-patchworked sky. A lone dragon flew lazily to the north, its black outline stark against the silvery feathering of the heavens.

Thoriol did not spend time watching it. His whole body throbbed. It felt as if his wound had opened up again; a hot, damp sensation had broken out just under his ribs.

He didn't stop walking. He limped through the dusk, ignoring those around him just as they ignored him. He passed fire-scarred walls and piles of rubble. Somewhere in the distance he heard weeping. There had been weeping every night since the siege and the passing of time did little to lessen it.

Thoriol kept going, averting his face from the glow of the torches.

It had been easy to deceive the Master Healer, who was more adept at creating poultices than he was at reading intentions. With all else that had transpired, the few guards there had been preoccupied with other matters and were not looking for a lone charge seeking to evade their attention.

In any case, there was little they could have done to stop him leaving. He was a prince of a noble house, the Dragon-tamer's House no less, and they would have been bound to accept his orders if he'd been forced to give them.

For all that, Thoriol had been glad no confrontation had taken place. Giving orders was not, and had never been, his strength.

He limped down a long, crooked street in the south quarter of the lower city. It looked different to the last time he'd been there. Then again, much of the city looked different. The buildings seemed to crowd a little closer, their pointed roofs angling like furled batwings into the night.

He found the door he was looking for, and paused. Two narrow windows shone with hearth-rich light from within. He could hear voices from the other side, voices he recognised. Someone was laughing; a tankard clinked.

Thoriol smiled. His father was wrong. He did not understand such things. Comradeship, *companionship* – Imladrik had never known such closeness. He'd probably never fought alongside another living soul in his life, save for the great beasts that carried him into war.

Thoriol reached for the door and rapped hard. He heard more laughter, the sound of something being knocked over, then it opened.

'Greetings!' said Thoriol, trying to look carefree against the pain of his wound.

Taemon stood in the doorway. His mouth opened. It took him just a little too long to close it. He stood there, stupidly, a tankard in one hand, the door-latch in the other.

'Well?' asked Thoriol good-naturedly. 'Are you going to let me in?'

Taemon stammered an apology and stood aside. Thoriol limped into a crowded chamber. Loeth sat in a chair by the fire, his leg bandaged and raised on a stool. Rovil stood over the mantelpiece, looking as if he'd just been speaking.

Florean sat across a rough table. He'd been carving the skin from an apple, knife still in hand.

All of them stared at Thoriol as he entered. Their laughter stilled.

'Silent?' asked Loeth, squinting up at him as if unsure it was really him.

Thoriol nodded, grinning. Already he felt better; the marble chambers of the old city now seemed like some kind of fleeting aberration. 'They would not tell me where you were, but I hoped nothing had changed. What happened to your leg?'

Loeth looked down at the bandages, as if seeing them for the first time. 'Dawi quarrel,' he said uncertainly. 'Thigh. But it's healing.'

Thoriol gazed around the room. He smelled the familiar aromas of rough wine, straw, cooked meat.

None of them spoke. The fire spat. Rovil stared at the floor; Florean kept his knife in hand, frozen in the act of peeling appleskin.

'Well?' asked Thoriol, wanting to laugh at their shock. 'Have you all lost your tongues?'

Taemon closed the door and stood against it, arms folded. 'Where have you been?' he asked.

That was the first sign. Taemon's voice was blunt with suspicion.

'They took me to the old city.'

'That's what we heard,' said Rovil.

'But I'm back now,' said Thoriol.

'So you are,' said Taemon.

Thoriol looked back at them all. The chamber felt suddenly chill.

'What is this?' he asked, maintaining a smile with some effort. 'I know Baelian has gone, but–'

'Yes, Baelian has gone,' said Loeth. He plunged his dagger into the table. 'He was not taken to the upper city. He was burned out on the plain.'

'I didn't know that.'

'No, you didn't.' Loeth didn't make eye-contact. He just kept staring at the dagger hilt. 'Why would you?'

'I was wounded.'

'You were highborn,' said Taemon.

Thoriol felt his cheeks flush. They had never spoken like this, not even on their first meeting out at sea. 'Does that matter?'

'Lying does,' said Florean.

'He didn't–' began Rovil, trying to soften the tenseness in the room, but he was soon talked over.

'Did you fancy some sport, then?' asked Florean. 'See how the rustics live? I hope it was worth it.'

Thoriol's heartbeat picked up. 'That's not how it was.'

'Why don't you tell us, then?' asked Loeth. 'How was it?'

'It was Baelian. He was recruiting in Lothern. We spoke, but my memory is hazy. I don't even remember agreeing to join, but–'

Taemon smiled coldly. 'He took advantage. You were wine-stupid and you made promises he held you to.'

'Yes,' said Thoriol. 'That's it. But after that, I worked at it. You saw that I did. It wasn't about lying, it was about being… honest.'

Loeth shook his head dismissively, smiling in disbelief. 'Your *father*, Thoriol. Your father is Imladrik.'

'And?'

'You truly do not see, do you?' murmured Taemon. 'They won't permit this, and when they come after us it won't be you that suffers.'

'I can prevent that.'

Loeth laughed harshly. 'No, you can't. And even if you could, here's the thing. We don't want you here.'

Rovil looked uncomfortable then. Even Florean looked a little embarrassed.

Thoriol felt like he'd been struck in the stomach. His father's last words to him seemed to echo in his mind.

You do not belong there.

With a sinking, almost nauseous feeling in his innards, Thoriol realised how right he had been. Again.

'I don't understand,' he said, though he did, perfectly.

'It's not just a game for us,' said Taemon. 'We can't leave when the blood starts running. You can.'

'And you lied,' said Florean.

'Baelian did too, but he's dead,' said Loeth. 'There's no place for you here any more.'

A tense silence fell. Rovil almost said something, his honest face contorted with unhappiness, but a glare from Florean cut him off again.

'Then it seems I misunderstood,' said Thoriol stiffly. 'You should know this, though: I never lied.'

'You hid the truth,' said Taemon, as unbending as ever. 'What's the difference?'

Thoriol scanned across the room, seeing nothing but hostile faces. They wanted him gone. Not until he left would the drinking start up again, the flow of jests and jibes that would last long into the night. It was a curiously wounding experience, far more so than the quarrel-gash in his side.

'I won't say anything of this,' he mumbled, pulling his robes about him and walking back to the door. 'And… I wish you fortune.'

'And to you,' said Rovil. No one else spoke.

Then Thoriol ducked under the lintel and was out into the night again. The door closed behind him with a dull *click*. Few people were abroad; the street was quiet, no one paid him any attention.

He looked down the mazy passages, the ones that led deeper into the lower city. There was nothing for him there. Then he turned the other way, facing up the slope towards the spires and interconnected towers of the old city. Their pinnacles reared up like stacked arrowheads, sharp black against the sullen red of the sky.

They looked alien to him, like reminders of a harsher world he had almost managed to leave. Now they beckoned him back, as inexorable as the tides.

Not much use fighting it, he thought.

Slowly, his feet heavy, he started to retrace his steps, back up to where the highborn – his people – conducted their lives.

CHAPTER TWENTY-FOUR

The first dwarfs were sighted on a cloudless morning following a rare lull in the heat. A griffon rider circling high above Oeragor's northern marches was able to convey some useful tidings: a dozen lightly armoured scouts moving through the Blight. They weren't going quickly; they were marking out the approaches, frequently stopping and conferring with one another.

After that, three more riders were dispatched north. They all came back with similar stories – the first tendrils of the dawi host were moving within range, creeping down from the foothills and out on the plains. The numbers reported steadily rose: a few dozen, then a few hundred, then many hundred, then more.

On hearing the news Liandra went down to the dungeons again. She did not enter the witch's cell but ensured that Drutheira's guard was doubled and that they would not leave their posts without explicit instructions from her.

'If the dawi get this far, kill her,' she had told them. 'Do not untie her, do not ungag her, just kill her.'

Then she headed back up to the northern watchtower, going as quickly as she could. The noises of preparation followed her all the way there: the thud of hammers, the tinny rattle of swords being drawn from armouries. In a way it was a relief to hear it again: things were moving.

Kelemar was waiting for her at the summit of the tower, along with Celian, captain of the griffon riders. Both were already wearing their armour – light plates of steel over silk undershirts, open-faced helms, no cloaks. The heavier garb of regular spear companies would have been hopelessly impractical in such terrain; lightness and movement were the keys to warfare out in the blighted lands.

'Here at last,' said Kelemar as she arrived. It took Liandra a moment to realise he was referring to the dawi, not her.

'Are they ready for battle?' she asked.

Celian nodded. 'Very much so.'

That was the final confirmation. 'Then it has all been for nothing,' said Liandra wearily. 'Salendor told him the dwarfs would not listen to reason.'

Kelemar reached up to wipe a line of sweat from his brow. 'Maybe this army has not heeded its commands – there is more than one dwarf lord under the mountains.'

'Maybe,' said Liandra grimly, unconvinced.

She felt sweat on her hands as she gripped her staff. Facing the enemy without her dragon would be a new experience, and not one she relished. Even to use magefire without Vranesh alongside her felt… wrong.

'Any numbers yet?' she asked, screwing her eyes up against the glare.

'Twenty thousand,' said Celian flatly.

'Really?'

The captain nodded. 'At least.'

Liandra smiled wanly. 'Perhaps I should not have asked.'

'You could leave,' said Kelemar. 'No oath of fealty compels you.'

Master of Dragons 349

Liandra turned on him, incredulous. 'Are you jesting?'

'I merely–'

'Well, do not. Never again.' Her face hardened. 'I have never run from battle.'

Celian leaned out over the balcony railing, shading his eyes. 'And there they are.'

Liandra and Kelemar turned, following his outstretched hand. There was very little to see – just a faint plume of dust on the north-western horizon. It looked strangely innocuous, a wisp of wind gusting across the powdered earth.

It would grow. Steadily, slowly, just as it had been at Tor Alessi, the dawi would tramp out of the wilderness, their armour caked in filth from the road, their standards hanging heavily in the air.

Liandra thought then of the vast armies that Vranesh had shown her from afar, crawling in the shadow of the peaks, pouring out of the ground like tar sliding up from a well.

'So it starts again,' she said grimly.

Brynnoth, King of Barak Varr, was both irritated and intrigued. The orders had been given, the front ranks of warriors were already within sight of the elven fortress.

He had been looking forward to the fighting. Taking Oeragor would eliminate the elvish presence on his southern flank, freeing up forces for the more serious campaigns in the west. Oeragor might not have had the prestige of Tor Alessi, but it was an important step nonetheless. Brynnoth wanted his name in the book of victories, and he wanted Barak Varr taken seriously alongside the larger holds of the mountains.

He wouldn't have held up the advance if the name he'd been given had been anyone else's. A part of him remained sceptical – Tor Alessi was a long way away. When he finally saw the incoming party hove into view, though, he saw it to be true. Morgrim Elgidum stood before him, sweltering in the heat.

Brynnoth laughed, partly from disbelief.

'You are lost, lord?' he asked.

Morgrim didn't smile. 'You are already attacking?'

'The advance has begun.'

'Then I will fight with you.'

'I thought you were–'

'Things have changed.'

Brynnoth puffed his cheeks out thoughtfully. Morgrim looked fatigued. His whole troop looked fatigued. If they truly had come all the way from the coast... well, he'd have been fatigued too.

'So I see,' Brynnoth said. 'Your axe with mine, then; it will be an honour.'

Morgrim limped closer. 'Do you have the new machines?'

'New machines?'

'The ones that fly.'

Brynnoth smiled. 'Ah, Copperfist's devices. So you've heard about those. No, they're not ready. May never be.'

Morgrim grunted. 'When this is over I need to speak to him.'

Brynnoth decided he didn't like the way he was being addressed. Morgrim was a prince, one held high in the runelords' estimation, but Brynnoth was lord of an entire hold.

'I'll decide that,' he said. 'You could tell me why you wish to. You could also tell me why you're here at all.'

Morgrim looked at him sourly. '*Drakk*. The elgi are using *drakk*.'

Brynnoth snorted. 'And?'

'They kill faster than anything I've ever seen. What war machines do you have?'

'Ballistae. Bolt throwers. They're being rolled up towards the city.'

'Keep them back. Angle them steeply and save them for the skies. We weren't prepared for them – you should be.'

Master of Dragons

Brynnoth narrowed his eyes. 'What happened?'

'They tore us apart.'

Morgrim's expression was thunderous. Brynnoth decided not to press the matter. 'I'll heed the warning then,' he said, 'but there are no *drakk* here.'

'For now.'

Morgrim's own soldiers stood shoulder to shoulder around him, as grim-faced and battered as their master. A runelord leaned on his staff some way distant, looking nearly at the end of his strength.

They didn't look capable of adding much to his own forces, all of whom were in prime condition for the fight. Adding a few hundred exhausted refugees from a failed campaign didn't seem like much of an asset.

Still, it was Morgrim.

'Then we should march,' said Brynnoth. 'Or do you need rest?'

Morgrim gestured to his warriors, all of whom took up their weapons and fell into formation.

'Just show me the elgi,' he growled.

Caradryel raced up the stairs to Imladrik's arming chamber. The news had reached him late that Imladrik was leaving the city; he hoped not too late.

He pushed his way past the guards at the doors and entered the chamber breathlessly. Imladrik was still there, fixing the last silver pauldron in place, his tall helm placed beside him on a stool.

'My lord,' he said, bowing.

Imladrik acknowledged his presence with a curt nod. 'You're out of breath.'

'I didn't know you were leaving so soon.'

Imladrik reached for his long cloak and draped it over his shoulders. 'The dawi are moving. We should too.'

Caradryel sat down heavily on a chest made from varnished

Lustrian hardwood. His breathing took a while to return to normal.

'I have news,' he said.

Imladrik looked at him coolly. 'More reliable than your last?'

Caradryel flushed. He would not be allowed to forget about Salendor any time soon. 'I trust so. It concerns Liandra.'

Imladrik turned on him, suddenly interested.

'Refugees from Kor Vanaeth have got here,' said Caradryel. 'They told me she was in combat with a black dragon and pursued it over the Arluii, heading south-east. They swear on Asuryan's Flame she had nothing to do with the dwarfs killed there.'

'A black dragon?'

'So they said. I've never heard of such a thing.'

Imladrik looked distasteful. 'They exist. Creatures of the druchii.'

'She did not desert, though: that is the important thing.'

For a moment Imladrik's expression became almost desperately hopeful. 'How reliable is this?'

'They all said the same thing. A sorceress on a black dragon, attacking the fortress before being driven off by the red mage. I believe them.'

Imladrik reached for his sword. 'Where did their fight take them?'

'They don't know. South, over the mountains.'

'Anywhere, then.' Imladrik took his helm under his arm and walked towards the doors, fully armoured and ready for his steed.

'Should we not search for her?' asked Caradryel, following him.

'Elthin Arvan is vast.' Imladrik's voice was flat.

'But a druchii dragon! Is that not worth–'

'Just stories. The dawi are real, and they are here.'

'But you cannot–'

'Enough.' Imladrik kept walking, out of the chamber and up another flight of stairs. 'Liandra was always reckless. She should have been here, with us, when the city was under siege. I will not leave the war now.'

Caradryel followed him uneasily. 'Oeragor is out there,' he offered. 'She might have made it that far.'

'And if she has?' Imladrik emerged at the top of the tower and donned his helm. A large courtyard extended out around them, open to the skies. 'I do not choose my battle-grounds on a whim.'

Caradryel looked up just in time to see the giant sapphire dragon descending to the courtyard, its wings a blur of motion. He retreated in the face of it, his robes flapping and his hair streaming. He'd not been so close to it since the first encounter out at sea, and the experience was almost overwhelming. He retreated to the far edge of the courtyard and pressed his back against the railings.

The dragon landed impossibly lightly, its huge talons barely scraping the stone beneath it. Its long, inscrutable face didn't so much as glance in his direction. Imladrik walked up to it casually, placed a foot on its crooked foreleg and hoisted himself up into position.

'So where will you go?' Caradryel called up to him.

Imladrik did reply, but by then the dragon was already moving, thrusting heavily and coiling up into the air. The response was lost in the downdraft of smoke-flecked turbulence.

Caradryel watched him go, overcoming his fear of the beast just enough to admire its smooth, powerful movement up into the heavens. He felt a pang of envy then, just for an instant, seeing the flash of sunlight on the creature's sparkling flanks and hearing the low growl of its breathing.

Soon it had gone, undulating into the distance, thrusting through the heavens with its ever-astonishing speed and grace.

Caradryel pushed back from the railings and walked around the courtyard's edge.

It was a good vantage. He could see out over the plain to the east, the cluster of spires in the old city to the north, the deep blue curve of the ocean to the west. Only one ship broke the waves – a light warship carrying full sail and working hard.

Caradryel screwed his eyes up against the distance. Few ships had come to Tor Alessi since the days of constant reinforcement; more recently the flow had been the other way, with heavy troop galleons setting off up the coast to Athel Toralien and the other coastal fortresses. This ship was heading in from due west, straight out of the open seas.

Caradryel watched it, wondering whether it brought any interesting news. He pondered whether he should head down to the harbourside. He was about to demur when he made out the emblem on the ship's sails: the mark of House Tor Caled, picked out in gold, shining in the sun just as the dragon's scales had done.

It was then he knew who was on that ship, and it made his mind up for him. Hurrying again, he passed down the stairs and into the tower, wondering what possible errand could have brought Yethanial of Tor Vael away from her books and over to Elthin Arvan.

They came out of the dust, a rolling tide of iron and leather, bodies pressed close together, standards swaying to the rhythm of hide drums.

Liandra watched them come, standing on the upper battlements with Kelemar and her fellow mages. Not many of them: just five besides her, and she far surpassed the others in power. Aside from the griffon-riders and some battle-hardened Chracian warriors sent east a decade ago, Oeragor's defences were modest, designed for stray incursions of greenskins.

Master of Dragons

The dwarf army closing in on them was more than an incursion. The front ranks came on quickly, wading through the ochre dust, kicking it up and tramping it down. A vast rolling cloud came with them, rearing above the army like a protective mantle.

They brought wall-breaking engines with them, ballistae mounted on huge platforms and battering rams on rollers. They had crossbow units, axe-wielders, hammer-bearers and ironclad maul-bringers. The mismatch between the attackers and the defenders was almost ludicrous. Oeragor was like a lone spur of rock thrust out into a rising tide, isolated and ripe to be overwhelmed.

Kelemar watched them stoically.

'Signal the archers,' he said. 'Let fly at two hundred yards.'

A messenger ran down to the parapet. Clarions rang out with the signal, and all across the ramparts longbows were notched and raised. The few bolt throwers mounted on the walls were primed, loaded and swung into position.

The gates were the weak point. Even though they had been reinforced with terraces of granite and cross-braced iron beams, that was the place where the outer stone barrier broke its smooth uniformity. Five hundred of Kelemar's best troops waited on the other side of it, crouched in the shade, waiting for the inevitable breakthrough.

Liandra looked up to the skies. The griffons were aloft, hugging the central towers and circling slowly. Their riders would not venture far from the walls once the assault began, restricting themselves to counter-attacking runs until the armies were grappling at close quarters. No sense in being torn to pieces by quarrels before getting a chance to land a claw.

The dwarf vanguard ground closer. The tumult from the drums and war-horns became all-consuming, forcing the captains on the walls to shout at their own troops just to be heard. Infantry squares spread out across the northern face of the city, extending in either direction as far as Liandra could make out through the swirling dust. The air became thick with it, surging up over the ramparts and coating the stone.

'Perhaps he was right,' said Liandra softly to herself, thinking of Imladrik. Now that she saw the scale of the dawi host in the full glare of daylight, the sheer immensity of just one of their many armies, she found herself wondering whether anything could prevail against them for long.

Then the long grind would begin. Athel Maraya would burn. Athel Toralien, Sith Rionnasc, Oeragor – they would all burn.

'Did you say something?' asked Kelemar.

Liandra shook her head. 'Just preparing myself.'

The dwarfs marched to within bowshot. The orders went out, and Liandra watched the archers loose their arrows, angling the shafts high so they plummeted down hard in a solid curtain. It was an impressive enough show, and some dwarfs in the front ranks stumbled.

Not nearly enough, though. The army kept coming through the onslaught, its pace hardly dented. Bolt throwers opened up, sending heavy quarrels whistling directly into the front ranks. Wherever they hit they tore furrows in the infantry formations, scattering dwarfs and throwing up fresh plumes of dust.

They kept coming. The hammer of the drums became almost unbearable. The heat, the dust, the blare of the war-horns – it was like being thrust into the maw of insanity.

Kelemar took up his helm, fixed it in place and drew his longsword. He held the blade up to the obscured sun.

'For Asuryan, Ulthuan and Tor Caled,' he said, his voice steady. All around him his retinue did the same, raising their blades through the murk.

He turned to Liandra, a resigned expression on his face.

'I'll take my place at the gatehouse now,' he said. As he spoke the stonework around him trembled – the front rank

Master of Dragons

of dwarfs had made it to the foundations. 'You have all you need?'

Liandra raised her staff, the one she'd been given after her rescue from the Blight. 'It will do.'

'Then Isha be with you, lady.'

Liandra inclined her head. The first shouts and screams of combat drifted over from the walls.

'And with you, lord.'

As Kelemar left she turned, raised her staff, and kindled the first stirrings of aethyr-fire along its length. Ahead of her rose a sheer wall of rage, a heat-drenched surge of focused violence, repeated in rank after rank of implacable dawi warriors, all now surging towards the walls like jackals crowding a carcass.

She ignored the tight kernel of fear in her breast, ignored the avian scream of the griffons as they swooped into the fray, ignored the murmured spells of the mages around her, and prepared her first summoning.

It was about survival now.

'For Ulthuan!' she cried aloud, and her staff blazed with light.

CHAPTER TWENTY-FIVE

Imladrik rode east. Below him the forest passed in a smear of speed. The endless trees looked like waves on the ocean, infinite and without permanent form, a swathe of dirty grey-green under a cloud-pocked sky.

Draukhain had sung little since their departure from Tor Alessi. The dragon seemed in contemplative mood.

So you will leave, then? the creature sang eventually.

I need more troops, I need more dragon riders. Only the King can grant me those.

He will not do so willingly.

No, he doesn't grant anything willingly.

In the far distance the mountains rose up, their vast peaks little more than claw-shaped marks on the edge of the world. Draukhain exhaled a gobbet of black smoke from his nostrils. He was flying fast, though comfortably within his capability.

You know, of course, that Ulthuan is in the west? he sang, sounding amused with himself.

Imladrik sighed. Like everything he had done since

arriving in Elthin Arvan, his current course felt far from wise. It was driven by necessity, though; by loyalty, and by a hope he hardly dared entertain.

Oeragor is my city. I should have gone there at the start of this.
What can you do there now? Too far to help.

Not for you, great one. Imladrik peered ahead of him, as if he could see out across the Arluii and into the great Blight, the semi-desert that separated the temperate northern lands from the lush and mysterious south. *It should be abandoned, its people escorted to the coast. I will oversee this, then go to Ulthuan. To Tor Vael, then to Lothern. The arguments will begin again.*

Draukhain's head dipped, his shoulders powering smoothly. The ivory-skinned wings worked harder, scything through the air.

Always arguments with you.

So it seems. Imladrik shook his head. *I need to breathe the air of the Dragonspine again, if only for a short time. I need to think.*

Draukhain discharged a growling fireball in approval. *Good. Good. I will breathe it with you.*

Imladrik watched the forest slide underneath him, mile after mile of featureless foliage. The dream of taming it, of turning it into a fragranced land of beauty, now seemed worse than foolish.

This has nothing to do with the fire-child, then? asked Draukhain, impishly.

Nothing.

You mean that?

Imladrik did not reply. It was impossible to lie, almost impossible to dissemble. In truth he didn't know what he would do if Liandra were still alive. The reports of a druchii abomination might have been true, they might have been false. He had tried to persuade himself, and Caradryel, that he didn't care and that his first duty was now to the war, but the arguments were weak. Possibilities wore away at him,

Master of Dragons

361

eating into what little sleep he could muster.

This flight was a final act of duty, a last display of responsibility before the war would consume him utterly. Yethanial had been right – Elthin Arvan made his moods dark, however hard he tried to counteract it. Once Oeragor was evacuated he would return west, rebuilding the bridges he had let fall into ruins. Thoriol, Yethanial, Menlaeth – they were the souls he needed to cleave to. They were his blood-ties, the ones whose faces he saw in his dreams.

This will be the last ride to Oeragor, he sang, remembering how much labour it had been to create and how many plans he had once had for it. It had been years since he had even seen it. *Let us try to enjoy it.*

The gates buckled, struck from the outside by the first kick of the ram.

Kelemar, waiting with his knights in the inner courtyard, steeled himself.

'Stand fast!' he cried, watching the wood tremble and splinter.

Above him on either side the walls rang with the clang and crack of combat. Ladders were already appearing on the ramparts, each one thrown up by iron-clad dawi gauntlets. Rocks sailed high over the parapets, crashing into the towers beyond and sending rubble cascading down to the streets.

The ram thudded into the gates again, bending the bracing-beams inwards with a dull boom.

Kelemar tensed, ready for movement. His best infantry stood around him, all ready for the charge. They would have to meet the dawi at speed, trusting to the charge to repel them. Once the dwarfs were inside the battle was lost.

On either flank of the courtyard stood two rows of archers, bows already bent. In the centre stood the swordsmen. All held position, hearts beating hard, waiting for the inevitable crack of timber.

The third impact broke the braces, sending tremors running along the stone lintel and shivering the doors. Dust spilled out of the cracks in ghostly spirals. The roar of aggression from the far side grew in volume – a hoarse, guttural chant of detestation.

'On my command,' warned Kelemar, seeing the nervous twitches of those around him.

The battering ram crashed into the gates a fourth time, smashing through the centre and slamming the ruined doors back on their tortured hinges. Broken spars tumbled clear, rolling across the stone flags like felled tree trunks.

'Let fly!' cried Kelemar.

The archers sent a volley out at waist height. The arrows spun through the debris, finding their marks with wet *thunks*. Some dwarfs made it through, stumbling into the open over the broken timbers; many more were hurled back, throats and chests impaled.

'For Ulthuan!' roared Kelemar, charging at the breach.

His troops echoed the shout, sweeping alongside him in a close wave of steel. Kelemar made the ruined doors and swung his blade into the reeling face of a dwarf warrior, already hampered by an arrow sticking from his ribs. The sword bit deep, angled between helm and gorget, spraying blood out in a thick whip-line of crimson.

More dwarfs clambered through the ruins bearing axes, mauls, hammers. They pushed the yard-long splinters aside, backed up by the brazen blare of war-horns.

Kelemar barrelled into one of them, kicking him backwards before plunging his blade point-forwards into his stomach. The dwarf's armour deflected the blade, sending it pranging away, and Kelemar nearly stumbled. He caught a cruel-edged maul swinging low at his legs and just managed to twist clear. One of his own knights then cracked a blow across the maul-bearer's face-plate, throwing him on his back where he was finished off by a third.

Master of Dragons

The melee sprawled onward across the ruined gates, a desperate pack of grappling, thrusting and stabbing. The elves gained the initiative, and their charge carried them under the shadow of the gatehouse. Helped by the steady torrent of arrows from the walls, they pushed the dwarf vanguard back out into the sunlight.

Kelemar drove onward, nearly decapitating a dwarf with a vicious backhand strike. Swords whirled on either side of him, spun and thrust with disciplined speed. The counter-attack pressed out further. More dwarfs piled into the breach, charging out of the dust like iron ghosts.

They seemed to fear nothing. They didn't move as fast as his own fighters and their reach was far less, but every blow was struck with a heavy, spiteful intent. Kelemar saw his troops begin to take damage – bones smashed, armour dented, swords shattered.

'Hold here!' he bellowed, hoping they could drive the dawi back far enough for the engineers to erect some kind of barricade across the shattered doorway. He pivoted expertly, using his bodyweight to propel his blade across the chest of another dwarf, biting clean through the chainmail and into flesh beneath.

It was only then that his gaze alighted on the dwarf beyond. This one was taller than the others; broader, too. His armour was all-encompassing, lined with gold and covered in blood and dust. He strode into battle with a dour, heavy tread, a huge axe gripped two-handed. He didn't roar his contempt like the others; he just waded silently through the throng around him, striking out with chill deliberation.

Kelemar rushed to engage him, seeing he was the linchpin and knowing he needed to buy more time. He closed in, throwing a wild swipe across the dwarf's right pauldron.

The dwarf met the strike with his axe and the two weapons rang together, resounding like bells as the metal bit. Kelemar's arms recoiled; it was like hitting an anvil.

The dwarf counter-swung, aiming for Kelemar's midriff. Kelemar got his sword in the way – just. He staggered backwards, aware out of the corner of his eye that his troops were beginning to take a similar beating.

The counter-charge was faltering. Kelemar pressed forward, whirling his blade around to where it could be slid into the dwarf's gorget. The manoeuvre was done well, as quickly as he had ever done it.

It was too slow, though, and too weak. The dwarf thrust his body into the blow, hurling his axe-head savagely upwards. Kelemar's blade was ripped from his grasp by the viciousness of the dwarf's strike.

Bereft of options, Kelemar grabbed a dagger from his belt, aiming for the dwarf helm's narrow eye-slit. By then the axe-head was already sweeping back, careering through the air two-handed. Kelemar didn't even feel pain as the edge cut deep into his chest; only seconds later, as his innards spilled out across the dust, did the raw agony bloom up within.

Kelemar fell, coughing blood, eyes staring sightlessly at the dark runes on the dwarf's axe-blade. If he'd had any self-awareness left he might have consoled himself that to fall to such a master-crafted blade was no shame; he had stood no chance, not against a weapon forged to take down the mightiest of living beasts.

His head cracked against the hard ground, just as those around him fell to the remorseless advance of the dawi vanguard. He didn't see the ladders finally find their purchase on the ramparts above, nor the last of the gate-doors kicked aside, nor the first rank of knights beaten back into the breach.

For a while the dwarf who had slain him stood over the corpse, as if ruminating on the kill. His axe dripped with blood, his breastplate and gauntlets ran thickly with it.

Then Morgrim Bargrum lifted his head, pointed Azdrakghar through the ravaged gatehouse, and broke into his stride once more.

Master of Dragons

'Khazuk!' he roared, at last joining in the wall of noise created by his war-hungry warriors. *'Khazuk!'*

Liandra hurled another flurry of star-bolts into the advancing knot of dwarfs before retreating further up the stairway. The front rank collapsed in a burst of crimson fire, their armour cracking and splitting. Dwarfs tumbled down the steep incline before toppling over the stone balustrade and down to the dust below.

More quickly arrived to replace them. Uttering grim dirges to their ancestor gods, the dawi advanced remorselessly. They stomped their way up the stairs, helm-shaded eyes burning with fury.

Liandra fell back again, already summoning up more aethyr-fire. Her palms were raw, her breathing ragged. The watchtower she'd been aiming for loomed up at the summit of the open stairway. Ahead of her, past the square at the stairs' base, was a scene of pure destruction. She could see dwarfs crawling all over the city's multi-layered thoroughfares and bridges, slaying at will, driving the remaining defenders back into whatever squalid last stands they might be able to muster.

The battle for the walls had been a nightmare – a doomed attempt to hold back whole battalions of implacable attackers. They had clambered over every obstacle, destroyed every barricade, surged up a hundred ladders and demolished entire stretches of wall with their damned stonebreakers.

She had no idea where the other mages were. She'd seen one of them dragged down into the rubble after a wall-collapse, his screams lingering thinly before being suddenly cut off. After the gatehouse had been taken the order had come to abandon the outer perimeter and fall back towards the central tower, but the retreat had been anything but orderly. Blood was everywhere, splattered against the hot stone like a gruesome mural.

Somehow Liandra had made it to the centre of the city, fighting the whole way with her ever-diminishing band of defenders. The Caledorians with her had fought well but they were hopelessly outnumbered. The watchtower was her last refuge – a squat, four-sided building at the summit of the wide stairway, still occupied by archers and with the emblem of Tor Caled hanging limply from the flagpole.

She retreated further up towards the doorway, now less than twenty feet away, her robes ripped and her staff spitting sparks.

Closer to hand, the dawi clustered once more at the base of the stair, ready to pile upwards towards the tower. Liandra slammed her staff on the ground before her.

'*Namale ta celemion!*' she cried, angling the staff-point and dragging more aethyr-energy from the sluggish winds of magic.

A nest of crimson serpents crackled into life, spinning from the tip of her staff and flailing outwards. Liandra swung the staff around twice before hurling the writhing collection down at the dawi labouring up the stairs.

The snakes scattered across the foremost, clamping on to the joints of their armour and burrowing down like leeches. They snapped and slithered as if alive, their unnatural skins blazing with arcane matter.

Liandra didn't wait to see if that would halt them – she knew it wouldn't for long – but turned and scampered up the last few steps. A few dozen guards held the doors open for her.

She slipped inside, heart thudding, feeling the trickle of blood running down her forearm.

'Brace it,' she ordered curtly. Soldiers around her hefted the heavy wooden bars into place.

She pressed on, running up more stairs, a tight-wound spiral that ran up the interior of the watchtower. As she went she passed rooms with archers crouched at the narrow windows.

Master of Dragons

They looked low on arrows, and some were already turning to their knives.

At the top level she joined a disconsolate band of swordsmen, all of them streaked with grime and gore, their robes dishevelled and armour cracked.

'Who's in command here?' Liandra asked, limping over to the outer parapet.

Several of them looked at one another for a moment, as if the idea of 'command' belonged to a different age, before the tallest of them replied, 'You are, lady.'

Liandra smiled humourlessly, and peered through the nearest embrasure.

Dust and smoke rose up from the corpse of Oeragor. The gatehouse was now a gaping scar through which marched an endless stream of dwarf warriors. A few islands of resistance remained – clusters of asur defenders holed up in towers or rooftop terraces.

Even as she watched, a griffon-rider swooped on an advancing column of axe-carriers. The huge beast crashed among them, lashing out with claw and beak. Its wings beat ferociously, sending dozens of dwarfs staggering backwards. For a while its lone assault chewed through the oncoming warriors, crushing those within its grasp, flattening others rushing to help. Eerie shrieks of anger rose up above the howl and holler of the battle, a single voice of defiance amid the wreckage of the city.

Then, slowly, the volume of warriors around it began to tell. Liandra watched axe-wielders crawl closer, one by one getting within swing-range. The griffon managed to slay half a dozen more before the blades began to bite. It tried to pounce back into the air but crossbow bolts suddenly scythed out from the shadows. More dwarfs appeared, drawn by the shouts of combat. The griffon was dragged back to earth, its rider seized from the saddle and buried beneath a riot of fists, axe-handles and cutting blades.

Liandra looked away. The screams of the dying creature were hard to listen to, and they went on for a long time. It might have been the last of them. The griffons had accounted for many of the dwarf dead, but it hadn't been nearly enough.

'What are your orders, lady?' asked one of the swordsmen by her side.

Liandra screwed her eyes up against the glare and peered out beyond the walls. Most of the dwarfs' war engines were still out on the plain and guarded by phalanxes of infantry. Almost none had loosed their deadly, steel-tipped bolts. The chassis of the bolt throwers were angled steeply, pointing directly skyward.

'Why so cautious?' she murmured.

She turned to the swordsman. His youthful face was badly bruised, with a purple swelling under a cut eye.

'Give me a moment,' she told him. 'My power will return. I will stand alongside you.'

From below, she heard the first booms as the doors took the strain. She grimaced; the dawi would be inside soon, and that would be an end to it.

'When they come, you will all do your duty,' she said, sweeping her gaze across the chamber and fixing each swordsman in the eye. 'Stand your ground, do not shame our people by giving in to fear.'

She clutched her staff, feeling the dull stirrings of magic under the surface once more.

'They'll take this place, that we know,' she said grimly. 'But, by Isha, we'll make them bleed for it first.'

For a long time Drutheira had heard nothing. The cell was dark, the walls thick. A few dull booms, some muffled shouting from the corridor outside, not much else.

Hours had passed. She began to get very thirsty. It had been a long time since her captors had brought her anything to

Master of Dragons

eat or drink. No doubt they had other things on their minds.

She tested her bonds again, straining against the metal shackles keeping her ankles and wrists locked tight to the chair. She could only move her head fractionally before the chain around her neck pulled tight, restricting her breathing. She'd nearly passed out a few days ago testing the limits of the restraints, and didn't fancy repeating the experiment.

The asur were not careless about such things, which was a shame.

An ignominious end, she thought to herself. *Buried alive in a city on the edge of the world.*

Then she heard a series of thumps above her. She sat perfectly still, letting her acute senses work.

The slit of light under the cell door flickered. She heard more heavy cracks, like iron-shod boots clattering on marble. Voices were raised in alarm and challenge, followed by a sound she couldn't make out.

Drutheira tensed. Either the asur were coming for her or the dawi had penetrated this far down. Neither eventuality was good for her.

The door shivered as something hard hit it. More voices rose, followed by a sharp, wet sound of steel punching into flesh, then a strangled cry.

Locks slid back, chains rattled. Drutheira stared directly ahead, determined to look whatever was coming in the face. If they made the mistake of ungagging her before they slid the knife in then there might still be some way back for her.

The door creaked open. Two asur dressed in the white robes of the city burst in. One of them looked badly wounded, cradling an arm in a sling. The other seemed to need time to steady himself and adjusted slowly to the near perfect dark of the cell.

Drutheira waited patiently. Through the open doorway she could see bodies lumped against the stone floor.

The nearest guard drew a long knife from a scabbard at his

calf and loomed over her. Drutheira felt the steel against her cheek, cold as night. She didn't move a muscle. She didn't so much as wince as he pulled the blade across her face, severing the gag and freeing her mouth.

She immediately started to speak – words of power that would burst their eyeballs and shrivel their tongues. Before she could get the spell out, though, the guard clamped a hand over her mouth, leaning close. Drutheira looked up at him, almost amused by the effrontery of it.

'Do nothing foolish,' came a familiar voice.

The guard pulled the linen from his face, revealing Malchior's badly sunburned features.

Drutheira's eye flickered to one side. Ashniel leaned against the cell walls.

Malchior withdrew his hand and got to work on the rest of her bonds.

Drutheira swallowed. Her throat was almost too parched to speak.

'How?' she croaked.

'With difficulty,' said Malchior, unlocking the clasps at her ankles.

'We nearly died getting here,' said Ashniel weakly. 'And nearly died after we arrived.'

Drutheira raised an eyebrow. So they hadn't been killed by the dragon. How they had tracked her to such a place, and why, were questions for later. The fact they were before her at all was verging on the impossible.

Malchior released the last of the locks. Drutheira got to her feet shakily. For a moment she thought she would collapse again – the blood rushed painfully through her joints – but she managed to remain on her feet.

'You have your staff?' she asked.

Malchior nodded. 'Take robes from the guards. I can do the rest.'

As Drutheira hobbled from her cell into the corridor

outside she saw the results of their labours: six corpses cooling on the stone. She stooped over the nearest and began to strip his robes from him.

'Where are the dawi?' she asked, pulling them over her head.

'Everywhere,' said Ashniel.

'This city is dead,' said Malchior flatly. 'We might have waited longer, but the dwarfs are killing everything that moves.'

Drutheira smoothed white linen over her druchii garb. The asur fabric smelled foul. 'Then how are we going to get out?'

Malchior looked at her distastefully, as if he regretted coming after her at all but had been persuaded against his better judgement. 'Deceptions are not as mysterious to me as they are to you.'

As he spoke his features rippled like water under a dropped stone. Ashniel's altered too – she became less conspicuous, little more than a shadow in the flickering torchlight. It wasn't much of an illusion, but amid all the confusion it might suffice.

'Lead on, then,' Drutheira said, bowing slightly. Malchior's cockiness was already beginning to irritate her.

From further up ahead she could hear the sounds of combat – horns blaring, asur crying out in pain and aggression, the heavy *clang* of steel on stone. It might have been nice to linger, to watch a while, soaking in the air of misery, but that would be a luxury too far.

They slipped along the corridor and up a narrow torchlit stair, passing more bodies on the way.

'What is your plan?' Drutheira whispered, limping after Malchior. 'You know some way across that desert?'

Malchior turned back. His face was curiously hard to make out, a shimmering reflection just on the edge of vision.

'We don't have long,' he said. 'If you wish to live, just shut up and follow me.'

He didn't wait for a response before pressing on. Ashniel followed after him. She was clearly in some pain, and said nothing.

Drutheira's eyes went flat. On another day she would have flayed the skin from his palms for talking to her like that. This was not another day, though; mere moments ago she had been contemplating the certain prospect of death. She felt like she'd been doing that for a long time.

'Play at this all you want,' she muttered, shuffling after Malchior, her limbs stiff and aching. 'Once we're out, it won't save you.'

CHAPTER TWENTY-SIX

Imladrik spied the smoke from a long way out and immediately knew what it meant.

Dawi, growled Draukhain, picking up speed.

So fast, murmured Imladrik. He had expected it to take far longer for them to regroup after Tor Alessi, but perhaps that had been a foolish hope. It was not in their nature to retreat.

The dragon powered through the air, faster and faster, picking up truly furious momentum. As he surged towards the burning city, Imladrik could see the extent of the dwarf army that surrounded it.

It was huge. The desert floor was covered in a thick, dark layer of bodies, all converging on the embattled spires at their midst. The rolling sound of war-drums made the air thrum.

Draukhain plunged into the heart of it, his wings driving powerful downbeats like hammers, his jaws already kindling with heart-fire.

Imladrik watched the walls race towards him. They were broken in a dozen places, crushed into wreckage and clogged with the bodies of the slain. He couldn't see any asur defenders still on the walls. Here and there banners of Ulthuan and Caledor flew from tower-tops, but it was clear that the city was lost.

We are too late, he sang, his mind-voice filled with horror.

Not yet, snarled Draukhain, angling down towards the battle. He raced towards the dwarf rearguard still out on the plain, swooping into a low glide.

This time, though, the dwarfs were prepared. A barrage of quarrels flew up from the rank of bolt throwers lined up along the approaches to the city. Brynnoth had taken Morgrim's counsel and saved every one of them.

Draukhain banked hard as the darts whistled past him. They were poorly aimed, but there were many of them. A second wave surged up from the earth, making the air thick with barbs. The dragon narrowly missed colliding with a six-foot-long spiked bolt, checking his surging flight and losing precious speed.

No time, urged Imladrik. *To the city.*

Draukhain obeyed instantly, sweeping across the rows of bolt throwers and powering towards the walls. As he went he carpeted the ground before him in a rolling wave of fire. Several of the war engines burst into flame, exploding as their tinder-dry frames ignited. Others kept up the attack, pursuing the dragon as he sped past, aiming to puncture a wing or sever a tendon.

Imladrik barely noticed the rain of darts. His eyes fixed on the burning spires ahead, desperately searching for some sign of defiance. He thought he caught a flash of magefire and his heart leapt – only for it to be sunlight glaring from dawi armour plates.

The centre, he sang, and Draukhain shot over the walls and thrust towards the tallest towers. Bolts, quarrels and arrows followed them, none biting but several coming close.

A cluster of spires loomed up at them, hazy in the

Master of Dragons

kicked-up dust and smoke. Draukhain weaved through them, loosing tight gouts of flame at any dawi exposed on the surface. He spied a whole phalanx of warriors making their way across a high bridge suspended between tower-tops and pounced after them, climbing steeply and vomiting a column of immolation. They scattered, desperately trying to escape the inundation.

At the last minute Draukhain pulled up. His long tail crashed into the slender span as he soared past, slicing straight through it. The bridge collapsed, dissolving into a cataract of powdered stone and sending the surviving dwarfs plummeting to the earth below.

Imladrik scoured the cityscape. At last, he made out some defenders – asur knights engaged in a fighting retreat towards the huge Temple of Asuryan, just a few hundred of them surrounded by a far larger force of dwarfs.

Down there, he commanded.

Draukhain plunged, tipping left to evade the nearest spire and diving hard. By the time he reached ground-level he was travelling very, very fast. He crashed into the dwarfs, scraping his claws along the ground and dragging dozens up with him, then shooting clear and hurling away those he had skewered. Their broken bodies tumbled headlong before slamming into the walls of the buildings they had ruined.

Draukhain immediately banked hard for another pass, narrowly missing the turret of another tower. The confined spaces of Oeragor's fortress heart were hard to manoeuvre in – with every wingbeat Draukhain risked crashing into a solid wall of stone. Whenever he rose above the line of the tower-tops the bolt throwers would open up again, sending a cloud of darts screaming towards them.

This wasn't Tor Alessi; the dwarfs were not facing battalions of mages and spearmen, nor were there other dragons to rake the bolt throwers while Draukhain slaughtered the infantry. They were alone, a sole dragon and his rider against an entire army, grappling over a fortress that had already been lost.

Imladrik felt like screaming. The hot rush of killing hammered in his temples again, the familiar surge of fury that always came when the dragon was unleashed. This time, though, it was tainted by other things: guilt, frustration. He was too late. He had tarried at the coast for too long, tied up with the business of the war there, dragged down by the complaints and concerns of others.

Liandra. Is she here?

Draukhain thundered down a narrow gap between buildings, his wings brushing at the edges of the stone canyon, covering the cowering dwarfs below in vengeful flames. Then he leapt steeply upwards, swerving away from a looming watchtower before hauling his immense body into the clear.

The bolt seemed to come out of nowhere. As if guided by fate, it scythed through the maze of spires and speared clean through Draukhain's right wing. Its steel tip pierced the hard membranous flesh and lodged fast.

The dragon immediately tilted, righting himself a fraction of a second later. The pain of the blow radiated through Imladrik's mind, a sharp echo that felt as if his own right arm had been impaled.

Down lower! he sang urgently.

More quarrels spiralled through the air, a constant barrage, hurled over the towers by the ranks upon ranks of bolt throwers brought up to the city. They shot above and around them, mere yards away.

Imladrik looked about him, despair mounting. He almost gave the order to pull away then, to power clear of the city's edge and seek respite. There was precious little to save in any case – he needed to *think*.

It was Draukhain that prevented him. The wound seemed to enrage him, as if the sheer impertinence of it somehow pricked his immense sense of superiority. The dragon flew harder, barrelling into the sides of buildings around him and

Master of Dragons

377

crushing them into rubble. His flames surged out, cascading like breakers against whole rooftops and street-fronts. He roared and bellowed, his tail thrashed, his jaws gaped.

He would take on the whole army, Imladrik knew. He would fly into it, again and again, until one of them lay broken in the dust.

Imladrik looked down then, through the murk and the dirt, trying to make some sense of the milling confusion at ground level. Dwarfs were everywhere, gazing up in either fury or wonder, some running for cover, others angling crossbows in their direction.

Draukhain broke out of the narrow spaces and swung round into a wide courtyard, pursuing a whole company of fleeing infantry into the open. Hundreds more waited for them there, all heavily armoured in iron plates and carrying huge, ornate warhammers. As soon as he saw them Imladrik realised this was the heart of the dwarf army, the thanes and their elite troops at the forefront of the fighting. Dozens of quarrellers crowded the space, jostling to get the first shot away. Bolt throwers had been erected around the courtyard's edge, each one strung tight and loaded.

Pull away, warned Imladrik, seeing the danger. They couldn't miss. Even a blind bowman with a single arrow couldn't miss in that space. *Pull away!*

Draukhain paid no heed. He fell into attack posture – wings splayed, claws out, jaws open. He flew at them in a blaze of fire and loathing, ripping through their ranks like a wolf loosed amid cattle. Imladrik bucked as the impact came, nearly losing his seat. He saw the walls race around in a blur, broken by scattered dwarf corpses, many on fire, others torn into tatters of bloody flesh.

Draukhain thrust upwards, nearing the far side of the courtyard and needing to climb again. Imladrik felt bolts slice into the dragon's side – two of them, each punching deep within Draukhain's armoured hide.

Draukhain twisted in agony, almost crashing straight into the oncoming wall, hampered by his impaled wing. Flames flared out from his outstretched jaws, bursting across one of the bolt throwers and blasting it into ash.

The dragon tried to gain loft, but a fresh flurry of crossbow bolts slammed into his outstretched wings. They pierced the flesh, sending hot, black blood spotting in the air.

Away! ordered Imladrik, glancing up at the sky above. They were hemmed in, overlooked by walls on all sides. This was no place to get bogged down.

Draukhain's claws brushed against the ground. He pounced back at the dwarfs, almost running, his wings rent and bloody. A ferocious swathe of fire burst from his maw, clearing the ground before him. Dwarfs caught in the blaze staggered away, clawing at their eyes or trying to roll the flames out.

The carnage was terrible – Imladrik saw scores dead, face-down in the dust and blood, their armour charred black – but Draukhain couldn't kill them quickly enough.

More quarrels screamed across at them from the far side of the courtyard. Two more found their mark, biting deep in Draukhain's thrashing neck. Imladrik felt the pain of it again, blinding in intensity.

Caught by the impact, Draukhain skidded to one side, tilting over wildly. His shoulder crashed to the earth, digging deep into the stone flags and tipping them up. Imladrik was thrown clear, leaping at the last moment before his mount careered into the side of a terrace. The impact was huge – a *crack* of breaking stone, a shower of masonry over the prone body of the huge beast. Rocks the size of a dawi's chest thudded into Draukhain's flanks, denting the armoured scales.

Imladrik leapt to his feet and spun around, his sword in hand. He twisted his head to see where Draukhain had landed, and saw with horror the half-buried outline of dragon flesh amid a landslide of rubble.

Master of Dragons 379

Ahead of him, their formation steadily recovering in the wake of the dragon's ruinous descent, stood the dwarfs. They shook themselves down. They gazed up at the beast, now crippled and in their midst. They saw the lone elf standing before him.

They drew their blades.

Draukhain barely moved – perhaps stunned, maybe mortally wounded. His presence in Imladrik's mind was almost imperceptible. Being without it was terrible, even amid all else, like having his memories excised.

He turned to face the enemy. More than a hundred limped towards him, and others were entering the courtyard. Recovering their poise, they spread out, hemming him in. Some of them started to murmur words in Khazalid – battle-curses, old grudges.

Imladrik gripped his sword tight. Ifulvin was ancient, encrusted with runes of power and forged in the age of legend before the coming of the daemons. The ithilmar felt heavy in his gauntlets; he would have to find a way to make it dance.

'Do not approach him,' came a thick, battle-weary voice from the midst of the advancing dwarfs.

They instantly fell back. The speaker emerged from among them, alone. Imladrik recognised him at once – the heavy-set arms, the embellished armour, the dour air of sullen hatred. He carried his huge axe two-handed, and runes showed darkly on the metal.

The two of them faced one another, just yards apart. The remaining dwarfs fanned out, forming a wide semicircle of closed steel around them. Imladrik could hear Draukhain's broken breathing behind him, moist with congealed blood.

'You,' said Imladrik, gazing at Morgrim and wondering if he was some kind of horrific mirage. 'How are you here?'

'Do not worry about that,' Morgrim replied, swinging his axe around him and striding forwards. 'Worry about this.'

* * *

The dragon changed everything. Liandra sensed it coming just before she saw it, magnificent and beautiful, tearing in from the west. For a moment she dared to hope that the others were with him – six dragons would have turned the tide, shattering the dwarf advance and giving them a chance. Even one, though – just *one* – toppled everything on its head.

Then it disappeared, plunging into the mass of spires at the city's heart.

'We have to reach it,' she said, turning from the tower's window and heading for the door. She felt invigorated.

The swordsmen around her stared back in almost comical surprise.

'Lady, do you mean–'

'Do not protest.' She glared at them all, daring one to voice an objection. Only a few dozen remained, plus the archers on the lower levels. They would be lucky to make it half way before being overwhelmed, but that changed nothing. 'Stay with me – I will do what I can to protect you.'

Her staff was already humming with energy. The short respite, combined with Imladrik's presence in Oeragor, gave her fresh hope.

It could be done. They could resist, if only their scattered forces could be given fresh impetus. It wasn't over.

She pushed the door back and jogged down the stairs. The swordsmen came behind her, hastily adjusting their helms. As she descended, Liandra heard the hammering on the outer doors rise in volume. She smelled the musty stink of the dawi on the far side, their ale-heavy sweat and their foul leather jerkins, and felt the thrill of incipient combat burn in her again.

This would be recompense. This would be retribution.

She halted before the doors, watching the timbers vibrate from the impact of the ram. The asur soldiers clustered in her wake, weapons drawn, faces torn between duty and doubt.

Liandra had no doubt. For the first time in a long time she knew exactly what to do.

'*Ravallamora telias heraneth!*' she cried, raising her staff high.

The doors exploded into a welter of light and heat, blasting the shards back and sending the dwarfs on the far side tumbling down the stairway. Sunlight flooded in, dazzling after the shade of the tower.

Liandra charged out, her staff ringing with power, her eyes shining. Behind her came the rest of the troops.

She looked out over Oeragor's ruined towers, and smiled.

'Fighting together, you and I,' she breathed. 'It was always meant to be.'

Imladrik leapt back as Morgrim swung his axe. The swipe was barely controlled – a vicious lunge that nearly sent the dwarf stumbling forwards.

Imladrik backed away warily. For all the hours of flying he felt fresh and in control. Morgrim looked exhausted. To reach Oeragor after the fighting at Tor Alessi he must have marched without pause for days. He had already endured heavy fighting under the punishing heat. Yet, somehow, he was still on his feet.

'You want the honour of killing me yourself,' he said, watching Morgrim come at him again. 'Is that it?'

Morgrim grunted, breathing heavily. 'It is not about honour any more.'

He swung again, moving surprisingly quickly, getting the axe-edge within a few inches of Imladrik's body.

'It is always about honour,' said Imladrik, sidestepping easily. He kept his feet moving fluidly, letting his opponent do the work. 'That is the one thing we share.'

'We share *nothing!*' raged Morgrim, breaking into a charge and switching his axe back suddenly.

Imladrik was forced into a parry, the impact nearly making him gasp. The strength in Morgrim's blows was incredible.

'You are sure about that?' asked Imladrik, pulling his blade away before pressing in close, trusting to the speed of his movements. He battered a few blows across Morgrim's armour before the dwarf pulled away, head lowered.

'You *ride* those creatures,' Morgrim spat. 'You goad them to war. They're vermin. Their minds are poison.'

Imladrik held guard watchfully. Getting through Morgrim's armour would be a challenge – it was all-encompassing, a masterpiece of craftsmanship.

'You should have listened at Tor Alessi,' he said. 'I warned you. Damn you, Morgrim, I *warned* you.'

Morgrim growled, and broke back into a lumbering charge. The two of them exchanged furious blows, one after the other, the steel of their blades sending sparks cascading around them. Imladrik ceded ground, pace by pace, retreating back towards the prone form of Draukhain.

'And I listened!' roared Morgrim. 'By my beard, I listened! That is now my shame.'

Imladrik held his ground, digging in. The blades locked again. This time Morgrim gave ground first. Even his mighty arms, it seemed, were capable of exhaustion.

'Your shame is right here,' panted Imladrik. 'You wanted blood-debt for your cousin, and now you have it.'

'Do not mention him.'

Imladrik parried a fresh thrust and returned a low strike. 'Why not? He blinds you still?'

Morgrim was wheezing now, rolling into contact like a drunken prize-fighter. He said nothing more but worked his axe harder, probing for the way through Imladrik's defence.

'You stubborn soul!' spat Imladrik. 'Snorri has *gone*. He was a fool, just as his killer was a fool.'

They rocked back and forth, trading more blows. Imladrik had to marvel at Morgrim's endurance. Ifulvin nearly buckled under one spiteful lunge, the steel bending under the force of it.

'We had a *chance*,' Imladrik said, breathing hard. 'We could have done better. I told you the truth.'

Morgrim fell back, gasping, his axe held low. 'I watched what your animals did,' he said, his voice ragged. 'You were riding one, so do not preach to me about restraint.'

Then he ploughed into the attack again. The blows were brutal, hurried, devastating. Imladrik fell away, working hard not to be overwhelmed.

'This land is death for you now, elgi,' Morgrim grunted. 'All of you. It will never stop.'

The duel stepped up in intensity. The twin weapons whirled around one another – the axe-blade cumbersome but crushing, the sword-edge rapid but lighter. None intervened, and still Draukhain did not stir, though the city continued to burn around them – a funeral pyre of old hopes.

Imladrik pressed the attack again, his blade blurring with speed. He hammered Morgrim back again, rocking the dwarf on to his heels.

'Caledor will never surrender,' he warned, his voice strained with effort. 'Do you truly think you can kill a Phoenix King?'

Morgrim shorted his disdain. 'His death will end this. Nothing else.'

'And mine?'

'I kill you because I have to. I will kill Caledor for pleasure.'

Imladrik smiled coldly. 'You will have neither.'

He pivoted on his heel, building momentum for a savage crossways swipe. At the last moment he adjusted the trajectory, ducking his blade under Morgrim's lifting guard. Ifulvin cut deep into the dwarf's armour, catching on the chainmail between shifting plates.

Morgrim staggered, and his axe fell by a hand's width. Imladrik hammered another blow in, denting a gromril plate. Ifulvin whirled, moving now with terrible velocity and smashing Morgrim back by another pace. The dwarf's breathing worsened, his head lowered. More strikes scythed down, bludgeoning him back through the dust, nearly causing him to sprawl on his back. Blood splattered across the stone, thick as tar.

It was merciless. None of the assembled dawi moved a muscle – they watched, stony-faced, as their lord was driven across the courtyard. Imladrik kept up the pressure, fighting with peerless artistry, the sun flashing from his helm.

He smashed Morgrim's defence aside with a brutal side-stroke, then rotated his glittering blade on its length, hoisting it over Morgrim's reeling body and holding it point-down. He angled it at the dwarf's shoulder, both hands on the hilt, ready to drive.

As he did so, Draukhain stirred at last, his bloodied head lifting from the rubble of the wall. A wave of hot, bitter air rolled out from his tangled body as he shook his neck, his great eyes cloudy.

The runes of Morgrim's axe suddenly flared. The angular grooves in the metal blazed red-hot amid the bloody patina of the blade. His whole armour surged with power, as if kindled by the awakening of the dragonsoul.

Imladrik plunged Ifulvin down, powering it with all his strength. Morgrim thrust in return, shoving Azdrakghar upwards with both hands, and flames licked along the edge of the blade.

The twin weapons met in a crash of light. A ripple of force shot out from the impact, stirring the dust from the flags. With a crack like ice breaking, Ifulvin shattered. Imladrik felt the force of it radiate up his arms, hard as a hammer on an anvil. He pulled back, amazed, his hands shaking from the impact.

Morgrim roared back at him, heedless, his axe still intact and glowing blood-red. The runes burned like torches. Imladrik saw the blow coming in and desperately jabbed his broken blade in its path, but Ifulvin was swatted aside, its power broken. Morgrim's whole body shook with raw heat-shimmer, a vision of rune-magic unlocked.

Somewhere close by, Draukhain was roaring in thunderous frustration, his coiled body still pinned by wreckage. Imladrik felt the dragon's anger and pain and could have wept from it.

Weaponless, all he could do was watch the axe-head sweep around again, propelled by Morgrim's blind savagery. Its curved edge punched deep into Imladrik's midriff, cutting through the silver armour with a flash of rune-energy. The bite was deep. A wash of pain crashed through him, numbing his limbs. Morgrim pushed the blade in deeper, tearing through muscle.

Imladrik's vision went blurry. He heard Draukhain's strangled roaring behind him even as he sank to his knees. The broken hilt-shards fell from his hand, clattering in the dust.

Morgrim pulled his axe free, dragging a long sluice of blood with it. Imladrik fell forwards, catching himself with his hands.

That brought him level with Morgrim's helm-hidden face. They looked at one another. Imladrik could feel the blood pumping out of him, draining his life away. Morgrim stared back, frozen rigid, as if suddenly shocked by what he had done. He could hear cries of alarm, the discharge of magefire and the groggy snarling of the dragon, still locked in the tangled detritus of its agony.

It was all strangely detached. All he truly saw was Morgrim. Everything else faded into grey.

He wanted to say something. He tried to blurt words out, but none came. Life ebbed from him like water from a sieve.

He closed his eyes. Morgrim was saying something to him, but he couldn't hear it.

He felt the rain of Cothique against his face. He saw the tower of Tor Vael standing against a lowering sky, the light at its summit glowing warmly.

He tried to walk towards it, but even in his delirium he

could not do so. The world folded up on itself in darkness.

The last thing he saw was the outline of a drake, high up over the sea, curving in flight out to the west.

He wanted to follow it, but could no longer move.

Liandra saw him fall.

She was running, sprinting with what remained of her escort, her robes and staff still wreathed in flame. The journey into the heart of the city had been horrific – a constant battle with hordes of dawi, all of whom had turned from their slaughter to waylay her. The swordsmen and archers around her had been cut down mercilessly, valiant to the last but wildly outnumbered. On another day she would have stopped to help them.

Not this day. She tore as fast as her legs would carry her, sending a wave of fire coursing out in front of her, burning and blasting any who stumbled into her path. Her desperation made her strong; not since Vranesh had died had she used her power so freely. Her whole body shimmered with it – it spilled from her eyes and mouth, as fierce as sunlight and as hot as coals.

For all that, she was too late. She careered into the courtyard, her boots skidding on the stone, only to see a vista of devastation open up before her.

Draukhain had been brought down and lay half-buried in wreckage on the far side of the square. Dwarfs were everywhere, hundreds of them, most arranged in a loose semicircle around the stricken dragon. Others streamed into the courtyard, attracted by the sights and sounds of combat.

Liandra looked about her. Only a handful of asur remained by her side, panting with exhaustion, their armour hanging ragged from their shoulders. In their expressions was bewilderment – she had led them through the heart of the battle to their deaths. At least at the tower they might have held out for a few hours longer.

Master of Dragons

'Follow,' she commanded, setting off once more.

Few of the dwarfs noticed her arrival – their attention was on the scene before them. Liandra powered through them, smashing them aside with blasts from her staff. Like a hot iron through water she forged a path towards the centre of the throng, raging words of power throughout, her copper hair flying about her face.

It was only then, right at the end, that she saw him fall. Imladrik collapsed forward, his silver armour dark with blood, his eyes wide with surprise. He didn't see her. It didn't look like he saw anything but the dwarf who had killed him.

Liandra knew who it was – she recognised the armour from a long time ago, though now it bled with the afterglow of unleashed magic.

'Imladrik!' she cried, rushing forwards, heedless of the dwarf arms that reached out to drag her back. The fires about her guttered out, extinguished as suddenly as they had been summoned.

Morgrim barked an order to his warriors. The fighting around her ceased, she was allowed through. Ignoring all else, she fell to her knees, cradling Imladrik's head in her lap, barely feeling the tears that ran down her cheeks.

'Imladrik,' she said again, searching for some small flicker of consciousness.

He was gone. His bruised face was as pale as bone, his unseeing eyes still staring out.

Ahead of her, the vast form of Draukhain struggled to free himself from the wreckage. A foreleg emerged, crusted in dust. The dragon growled menacingly, his eyes flashing with fury.

The dwarfs backed away from it, crossbows raised. Liandra heard the *clunk* of bolt throwers being primed.

Morgrim issued another terse order in Khazalid, and the dwarfs stood down.

Liandra turned on him, half-blind with grief.

'He was your *friend!*' she blurted.

Morgrim looked uncertainly back at her, as if he'd awoken from some dream and no longer knew what it was he'd been striving for. The warriors around him held position, silent as statues.

Liandra turned back to Imladrik, smoothing his eyelids closed. Draukhain managed to drag himself half-free of the rubble, his long tail coiling. The dragon's massive head lowered, dipping over Imladrik's prone body, steam drifting from his nostrils. Even so badly wounded, the beast towered over all else in the square, a crippled leviathan amid the ruins.

Morgrim shook the blood from his axe, stared at it for a moment, then hoisted it across his back.

'This place is ours now,' he said grimly.

Liandra shot him a contemptuous look. 'You could have had it. You could have had anything you demanded. He would have listened.' She turned back to Imladrik. His blood ran across her robes, staining them deep. 'You have killed the only one of us who would have done.'

Draukhain issued a low, grinding growl. The dragon was recovering some of his strength, and pulled another limb from the ruins. He was half-standing now, with only his hindquarters buried.

'Order your beast back, or I will have it killed,' said Morgrim.

Liandra glanced up at Draukhain.

Did you hear that? she mind-sang. *He thinks he can have you killed.*

He may be right, came Draukhain's song, coloured with almost unbearable misery. There was no fight left in the dragon's eyes. The creature stared moodily at Imladrik's corpse, uncaring of the ranks of dawi about him.

Morgrim reached for a casket at his chest. He held it for

a while, lost in thought. 'My warriors wish to kill you, too.'

'Do what you will,' said Liandra dismissively, not looking up at him.

'Will the dragon fly?'

Liandra glanced at Draukhain. He was terribly injured, but she had seen drakes recover from worse. 'He might.'

'Then take the body,' said Morgrim.

Liandra stared at Morgrim for a moment. If anything, her hatred for him intensified. 'Your grudge is settled, is that it?'

'Far from it, but we are not animals.'

Liandra shook her head in disdain. 'Caledor will come after you. All of Ulthuan will come after you.'

Morgrim nodded calmly. 'We will meet them.'

Draukhain coughed a bloody gout of smoke from his jaws. *Let me bear him, feleth-amina*, he sang. *His place is not here.*

Liandra smiled bitterly. She had never been quite sure where Imladrik's place was. Perhaps he hadn't been, either.

'And the asur who remain?' she asked, glaring at Morgrim again.

'They will be held, once the fighting is over. You may go. For the others, I make no promises.'

Liandra glanced at the few soldiers who had made it with her to the courtyard. They deserved better. Surrounded by dwarfs, their blades lowered, they looked resigned to their fate.

'I know their names,' she said. 'If they are not returned, I will hold you accountable.'

Morgrim bowed. 'So be it.'

Liandra rose, shakily, to her feet. Ahead of her, the dragon hauled itself free. Its flanks glistened wetly. Many barbs protruded from its flesh, each one weeping blood. She had never seen Draukhain brought so low, and that alone stabbed at her heart.

'There is a prisoner in the dungeon below,' she said to Morgrim, stooping to carry Imladrik. 'If she has not been killed already, you should do so. She is a witch.' She hoisted Imladrik into her arms, his feet dragging on the stone. He was impossibly heavy in his armour, but no dwarf came to aid her.

'Elgi crimes are not our concern,' said Morgrim.

'They should be,' she said wearily. 'If you had listened to him you would know why. If you care for anything other than bloodshed, kill her. Kill her and cut the heart from her body. And tell her Liandra of House Athinol ordered it.'

In truth, though, she could not bring herself to care overmuch. Drutheira had done her work. If she lived on she was now a ruined thing, destined for nothing but some petty oblivion. The seeds she had planted had grown into dark fruit and would keep growing now whatever else was done.

She dragged herself over to Draukhain. The dragon dipped his shoulder as low as he could. It was hard work getting the body in position. Several times Liandra nearly slipped, crying out with frustration and anger. Eventually, though, Imladrik's corpse settled in the hollow between the dragon's wings. His cloak hung limply over the armoured hide.

Liandra turned before mounting. In front of her stretched the carcass of Oeragor, destroyed by the dawi who now occupied it. They stood in silent ranks, still bristling with sullen anger. She could tell that they did not want to see her leave alive, but none would gainsay Morgrim.

'You will never know how much he held himself back,' Liandra told him. 'He was the best of us, and you have ended him.'

Morgrim nodded again. The dwarf seemed almost numbed by what he had done. 'He will have a place in our annals. *Govandrakken*. He will not be scorned.'

Liandra shook her head. She could take no comfort from the dwarfs' obsession with records and grudges. More than ever it seemed pathetic to her, a dull rehearsal of rituals that signified nothing. If they could not see what tragedy their

Master of Dragons

stubbornness had unleashed then they deserved the war that would cripple them.

She climbed into position, no longer looking at the dwarfs below.

Can you fly? she asked Draukhain, feeling his pain as her own.

The dragon's legs tensed, ready for the pounce that would propel him aloft. His ravaged wings spread, casting a tattered shadow over the stone.

I will bear you to Tor Alessi, he sang, his mind-voice stricken with a dull kind of emptiness. *But fly? Truly fly? Never again.*

CHAPTER TWENTY-SEVEN

Drutheira re-wrapped the linen around her head again, knowing that it would do little good. The sun seemed to beat down between the weave, torturing her already scarred skin further. She wanted to drink again but their supplies were scant enough. Malchior, Ashniel and she each carried a gourd of gritty water and a few hard loaves – all they had managed to scavenge in the wreckage of the city – and she didn't hold out much hope they would last them long enough.

Ahead of her, Malchior still walked with reasonable fluency. Ashniel was weaker, carrying a couple of injuries. One had been sustained when the red mage's dragon had demolished the mountainside she'd been standing on; the other when her disguise had slipped and an Oeragor guard had recognised her. The knife-fight, Drutheira understood, had been vicious.

'We should look for shade,' Drutheira complained.

Malchior halted, and looked around him. The scrubland ran away from them in every direction, flat, hard and open. 'You see any?'

Drutheira pushed her headdress up a little, squinting in

the light. The sun was high in the sky still; it would be hours before the relative cool of dusk. Smoke rose from the northern horizon, now miles away. Oeragor would burn for a long time before they put the fires out. It was fortunate, in a way – slipping out amid all the confusion had been trivial, aided a little by Malchior's subtle arts.

'Walk at night, rest by day,' she said.

Malchior's expression was unreadable; like all of them he'd wound fabric around his face to ward off the worst of the sun.

He reached down for his gourd and took a swig. Ashniel did the same, swaying slightly.

'So how did you find me?' asked Drutheira at last. She'd been putting it off, not wanting to give Malchior the satisfaction, but curiosity got the better of her.

'I could follow you,' said Ashniel quietly.

Drutheira turned to face her, surprised. Ashniel had always been the quiet one.

'I could sense you,' Ashniel repeated. 'Ever since the dragon came. Something in the aethyr.'

Drutheira didn't like the sound of that. If some part of her resonated in there then there were plenty of other things that might be able to track her down.

'It took days to cross the desert,' said Malchior. 'I argued against it.'

'But we needed the dragon,' said Ashniel. 'To get home.'

Drutheira smiled acidly. 'A shame it died, then.'

'It didn't take much art to blend in once we got to Oeragor,' said Malchior, rather pompously. 'Their minds were on other things.'

'By then you knew the dragon had gone,' said Drutheira. 'Why did you still come for me?'

Malchior shrugged. 'We missed your company.'

'We needed you,' said Ashniel, more seriously. 'We know nothing of this land.'

Master of Dragons

'Neither do I,' said Drutheira.

'You must do. You were in Malekith's circle.'

Drutheira winced. 'Don't assume that means very much.'

Malchior exhaled irritably. 'We need to get away from this Khaine-damned place.' He looked at Drutheira reluctantly. 'You studied the maps longest.'

Drutheira enjoyed the admission, wrung from him like sweat from his headdress. 'That, of course, is true.'

Ashniel looked like she was going to collapse. 'Do we have to do this now? And where are we going?'

Malchior's mouth twisted in scorn. 'South,' he said. 'Everywhere else is crawling with dawi.' He glanced at Drutheira. 'You agree?'

Drutheira nodded.

'Nowhere else to go,' she said. As she spoke, she tried to remember the charts she'd seen so long ago. Naggaroth seemed almost like a dream. 'There was a river marked. There must be one, sooner or later. Vitae, was that it? Some arcane language. Malekith knew something about it.'

'How far?' asked Malchior.

'A long way. We can't walk. We'll need to find somewhere to recover, or try to get to the coast. A boat – that would be useful.'

Malchior snorted derisively and turned away. 'I'll keep an eye out.'

Drutheira looked briefly north again, over to where Oeragor smouldered. The evidence of its ruin was like a premonition, a harbinger of what was to come for all Elthin Arvan. Soon there would be nothing in the colonies but fire, a blaze she had helped to start.

Who would know it, though? Would anyone ever whisper her name with reverence in the hallowed courts of Naggaroth? Drutheira, the destroyer of empires. If she couldn't find a way back, then no one would, and that silence would be worse than death.

Malchior started to walk again. Haltingly, Ashniel followed him. Drutheira took a sip of water before falling in behind them, trying to ignore the residual pain in her joints.

But I am alive, she thought to herself, remembering the malice in the eyes of the red mage, the certainty that she had finally run her down. To be breathing still, to be free, that was more than improbable. *Despite it all, my heart still beats.*

She kept walking. The southern horizon stretched away from them, shaking in the heat. The emptiness looked like it went on forever.

Morgrim hobbled through the streets of Oeragor. He could feel blood sloshing in his boots. His ribs were cracked, his shoulder-blade fractured. When he breathed it felt like dry grass was being shoved down his throat.

Everywhere he went, his warriors saluted him. They raised their fists and bowed their heads. Some of the younger ones shouted *Khazuk!* They all knew what had been achieved. His name would go into the records, carved into the stone tablets buried in the vaults of Karaz-a-Karak. Starbreaker would summon him to the throne. The runelords would honour him. The pall of disgrace that had hung over his bloodline since Snorri's death would lift.

It should have made him fiercely proud. Part of him was. He could still see the carnage caused by the drakes. It felt good to have repaid some measure of pain. Morek's rune-artistry had answered at last, and Azdrakghar had tasted blood.

It was, at least, a beginning.

But beyond that he felt removed from all that had transpired. The long marches had battered his body into submission. He knew when he peeled his armour off, all he would see would be calluses, bruises and blisters. His flesh was now a carpet of them, weeping blood and pus under the hard shell of his battle plate.

Master of Dragons

He could cope with the pain. It was the other things he found difficult.

Imladrik had been an obstacle. No other elgi commanded such respect. His removal had been necessary, and not just for the satisfaction of grudgement. Morgrim could not have returned to the Everpeak with the Master of Dragons undefeated and still claimed the title of *elgidum*.

Yet, for all that, his heart remained uneasy. He had tried to speak to Imladrik at the end, though he doubted the elgi had heard him.

'You did not need to fight here,' he had said, almost angrily. 'You did not need to come.'

Then the mage had arrived, bursting into the courtyard with her anger and her witch's fire. The order to release the body had almost been an afterthought. It would certainly not placate any of the asur. In a war that had already seen atrocity unleashed, it would do nothing to restore restraint.

He reached again for the casket at his breast, the one containing Snorri's remains.

All it had been was an exchange. A barter. The dawi understood such things.

'*Tromm*, Morgrim!'

Brynnoth's gruff voice rang out. He was walking towards Morgrim, his armour in terrible shape. An elgi arrow still protruded from his pauldron, the shaft snapped. His grizzled face spread in a wide grin.

'We have broken them!' Brynnoth roared, embracing Morgrim roughly. 'And the dragon! Wings torn to ribbons. That was a mighty feat.'

Morgrim nodded weakly. 'They can be beaten. We know that now.'

'They can, and they will.' Brynnoth's blood was up. He looked ready to march off again that instant.

Morgrim couldn't share his ebullience. 'We should secure the city.'

'Secure it?' Brynnoth laughed. 'From what?'

Morgrim felt like collapsing but kept his feet. He would have to do so for hours. The ale had not even been hauled into the city yet, ready for the hours of ritual drinking and oath-taking to come. 'From ourselves. Let there be no mindless slaughter.'

'Of course not.' Brynnoth looked at him hard. 'Are you all right?'

Morgrim knew he would be. Dawn would come, and he would remember the sacred runes he had sworn over. He would remember his hatred and his pride. He would speak with Brynnoth about the weapons in Barak Varr, and the foundries would soon be ringing with industry. Everything would grind into motion again. They would sweep west, this time knowing what they faced, knowing they could beat it.

In time, all of those things would happen. For now, though, he felt empty, like a clawed-out mineshaft.

'I did not know how victory tasted until today,' Morgrim said, remembering how Imladrik's blood had coursed over his gauntlets. 'It will take some getting used to.'

The three of them sat together in Imladrik's high chamber: Yethanial, Thoriol and Caradryel. The windows were unshuttered and let in the evening light in warm bands of gold.

Caradryel felt awkward. He wasn't sure why he had been summoned. It felt like he was intruding on some private family affair.

'Was he angry?' Yethanial asked, speaking to Thoriol.

The youth shook his head. 'A little. More surprised, I think.'

'He should have been angry.' Yethanial's voice was soft but harsh. 'You have had every advantage. You could have died.'

Thoriol looked resigned. 'So he told me. Look, I see the truth of it, so you do not need to tell me again.'

Caradryel shifted in his seat. Clearly this was something

Master of Dragons

that would be best thrashed out between the two of them.

'My lady, I–' he started.

'Stay where you are,' ordered Yethanial, before turning her severe face back to Thoriol. 'This is not some game we are playing at. None of us gets to choose, not when we are at war. There is *duty*, Thoriol, and that is all.'

She sounded so much like her husband. Thoriol looked chastened, and did not argue.

'I will try again,' he said, lifting his head to return her gaze. 'I can return to the Dragonspine.'

Yethanial looked at him carefully, as if assessing whether he meant it.

'It is not easy,' she said at last. 'Imladrik tells me they wake slowly now, but we need all the riders we can get.'

Thoriol's expression didn't change. Caradryel thought he looked very little like his father; much more akin to the mother.

'And you?' Thoriol asked, his eyes glittering with challenge.

Yethanial bowed her head. 'I should have been here from the start. It was only pride that kept me away.'

Caradryel cleared his throat. 'But a good time to return, if you'll pardon me for saying. Salendor and Aelis are consumed with their own business, and Caledor's gaze remains fixed on Naggaroth. There are opportunities here, lady.'

Yethanial looked at him coolly. 'Opportunities? For what?'

'Power.' Caradryel had never quite got the hang of meeting Yethanial's steely gaze, but worked hard at it. 'Influence. Imladrik destroyed the dwarf host; his prestige has never been higher. We can use it.'

Yethanial looked uncertain. 'I do not follow.'

'The gods' favour is fleeting: one moment all is golden, the next it lies in ruins. You and I both know this war is a disaster, and sooner or later others will realise it. We have armies here, whole legions whose loyalty is now to Imladrik alone. They would do anything he ordered. Anything.'

Thoriol stirred uneasily. 'You mean–'

'Caledor is a fool.' Caradryel said. 'Why apologise for saying it? We need to think to the future. We have what we need here. All that remains is picking the moment.'

A tense silence fell over the chamber.

'This is not why I employed you, Caradryel,' said Yethanial.

'Was it not? I serve the House of Tor Caled, and its destiny is to rule, one way or another. So let me at least point out the possibilities.'

Thoriol shook his head. 'Imladrik will not allow it.'

'Not now, no,' said Caradryel. 'But he knows that no end to this can come while his brother rules. The bloodshed sickens him – he told me so. I think we can persuade him if we need to.'

Yethanial, somewhat to his surprise, did not immediately demur. She thought hard, teasing through the possibilities. Caradryel began to wonder if, of the two of them, she might be the better player of such games.

'The time is not ripe,' she said at last.

'No,' agreed Caradryel.

Yethanial gave him a distasteful look. 'You will need gold?'

'Some. More important is your patronage. Tor Caled is a powerful name; it opens doors.'

Yethanial nodded slowly. 'So you told me before.'

Thoriol looked at both of them uncomprehendingly. 'What are you saying? You talk of duty, and then… this?'

Yethanial shot him a withering glance. 'Have you understood nothing? Your duty is to Ulthuan, to your bloodline.'

Caradryel found himself nodding. 'So she says.'

Thoriol looked like he wished to protest, but his words were cut off by a sudden call of trumpets from the walls. All of them turned to the east-facing window. Caradryel got to his feet, but not as quickly as Yethanial. She hurried over to the sill, leaning out into the dusk air.

A dragon was riding towards the city, its flanks glowing dull blue in the failing light.

Master of Dragons

'He returns!' cried Yethanial.

Caradryel saw the sudden hope in her face. The soft greyness lifted from her features and her eyes sparkled. For a moment, a fleeting moment, he saw unalloyed joy there, a profound delight that banished her severity. It was transformative, and quite unexpected.

'Why does he fly so low?' murmured Thoriol.

Caradryel looked back out of the window. He had seen Imladrik tear through the air many times and this flight looked nothing like that. The dragon seemed to limp along, dipping frequently. Its wings were ragged. As it neared the walls its tail hung low, trailing feebly.

Caradryel stared harder. An awful feeling crept over him.

'My lady, I think–' he began, but she was already moving, running out of the chamber and towards the spiral stairway leading up to the roof.

Thoriol followed her. Cursing, Caradryel did likewise, taking the steps two at a time to keep up. The three of them broke out into the open, on to the same wide platform where Caradryel had last bid farewell to Imladrik.

The dragon swooped down on them, its flight erratic. Droplets of black blood splattered on the stone.

'Isha, not this…' breathed Yethanial, horror written on her face. She looked like she'd suddenly aged. As Draukhain touched down she hurried over, gathering her robes around her.

Thoriol held back, his face white. Caradryel stayed beside him. The dragon's aroma was awful – like rotten meat mingled with old embers.

He saw Liandra dismount. How she came to be riding Imladrik's dragon was a riddle he knew he did not want to solve. She looked as dishevelled as her steed, her face streaked with tear-tracks over grime and blood. She tried to say something to Yethanial but the grey lady barely noticed her.

Yethanial approached Imladrik's corpse hesitantly, carefully, as if he were terribly wounded and might still get up. Caradryel could see the futility of that – his master lay awkwardly, as slack as sackcloth, his armour dark with blood.

Yethanial's grief then was terrible to witness, so powerful and so complete that for a moment none of them could speak. The dragon wheezed sclerotically, its huge eyes weeping black tears. Across the city, the trumpets were stilled as the celebrating heralds realised that something was terribly wrong.

Thoriol stumbled forward to stand by his mother, his feet shuffling unwillingly on the stone. For a moment the two of them just stood there, staring stupidly, emptily, at Imladrik's body. Then Yethanial's tears came at last – huge racking sobs that made her bend double. Thoriol held her up, his body erect, his face like stone. The two of them clung to one another, grasping greedily as if they could somehow insulate themselves against the truth.

Caradryel looked away, unwilling to intrude further. He felt nauseous.

'What happened?' he asked Liandra.

The red mage looked exhausted. 'Dawi,' she said, coldly. 'They got to Oeragor ahead of him.'

'And you? Where were you?'

Liandra glared at him. 'It can wait.' Her gaze travelled to Yethanial. Sympathy was etched on her features. Sympathy, and perhaps a little envy.

Caradryel felt wretched. Just moments ago the future had been mapped out. His decisions had been vindicated, his path clear.

Now, nothing. He remembered the first time he had seen the sapphire dragon, high above the waves, swooping earthwards like a messenger of the gods. It had looked invincible then, something that no force of the earth could ever vanquish.

Master of Dragons

Now it slumped on the stone, bleeding like any mortal, still carrying the body of its dead master. Around it huddled the remnants of the House of Tor Caled, one weeping, one silent with shock.

What now, then? he asked himself weakly.

The wind picked up, cold from the west. The east was darkening quickly, sinking into the deep night that made the forest so forbidding. That dark had always seemed contestable before; now it looked infinite and unbreakable.

Caradryel didn't know where to look.

What now? Who will follow him?

But no answer came.

EPILOGUE

Sevekai had no idea how long he'd been on the cusp of it. He didn't know where he was, nor how far he had travelled since leaving the Arluii behind. In the beginning he had tried to remember. He had vague memories of going south, heading down into the lowlands until the trees blotted the sky. Measuring time, though, no longer seemed like something he should concern himself with. The rhythm of the forest was less exact: languorous, shackled to a lower, more eternal measure.

His crow perched on a branch above him, its black eye glinting. It seldom left him now. The others, the ones that had made their way to the forest as he had done, they all had their companions too: Aismarr had a lean hunting dog, as skinny as bones; Elieth had a hawk; Ophiel had a fox that slunk timorously in the shadows. They came and went, these creatures of the wood, but never departed for long. They were like echoes of thoughts lingering under the eaves.

Sevekai watched the others. They bore the same dreamy expression. They had renounced the old passions. None of them hated or loved any more; it was like being half-asleep.

A few of them, he knew, were kin from Naggaroth; just a couple, skulking amid the briars like thieves. They came into the centre of the circle only slowly, just as he had done at the beginning, unable to entirely forswear the hatreds they had been born into.

The forest worked on them, though, just as it did the others. They gradually lost their pale mien and took on a healthier blush. Their tattoos faded somehow. Their oil-slick hair seemed lighter under the green glow of the canopy.

The rest had the healthy light of Ulthuan in their eyes. He didn't know where they had all come from. Neither did they – the old life drifted out of mind and memory so quickly. Some of them had taken on new names. Sevekai, for the moment, clung to his. It seemed important. He didn't know how long he would feel that way.

He didn't even want to hurt them. That was novel.

None of them had penetrated far into the heart of the wood. They lingered on the edge where the light still shafted down between the branches. They heard creaks and snaps from the deep core, buried in arboreal gloom. They heard night-noises – squeals and rustles, low groans that were almost elf-like, though distorted and alien.

What is this place?

He asked that question less often as time went on. At first he had been consumed by it, desperate to know what was slowly altering his mind. He would look at a leaf in the sunlight, seeing its veins standing dark against the translucence, staring at it in fascination. He would breathe deep of the musty soil aroma. He would hear the brush of the branches as the moons wheeled above him.

He never thought of escape. Where would he go?

The wood called them. All of them heard it. Soon they would have to enter, ducking under the curved and twisted branches and stooping into the shadows. He had dreams of what lay in there, waiting for them, though he never remembered them once the sun was up.

Aismarr smiled at him. She was standing a few yards away, her smock stained green and her cheeks ruddy. Sevekai liked the way her hair fell about her face – tangled, flecked with dirt, half-plaited.

'I dreamed of dragons,' she told him.

Sevekai remembered a dragon, though only vaguely. 'Oh? What did it tell you?'

'Their souls are broken,' Aismarr said, sadly. 'Someone has died, someone they loved.'

Sevekai remembered Drutheira then. Of all of them, she was the one he still remembered. He hadn't ever loved her. There had been passion, of a sort, but that was part of the old pattern. Here things were simpler – more direct, more honest. He wondered where she was.

'Then is it time?' he asked. He knew that something would have to change. Some signal would be given and then the deep wood would beckon.

Aismarr frowned. Her hunting dog slunk around her calves, snagging at her smock.

'No.' She glanced over to her left, to where the path ran down like a river into the heart of the forest.

Sevekai followed her gaze. He didn't think it was time either, not yet.

'This is the start,' he said, not really knowing where the words came from. 'The dragonsoul is gone; others will follow. The world must change.'

Aismarr looked at him with shining eyes.

'And then will we enter?' she asked.

Sevekai couldn't take his eyes off the trees. They called to him, though silently, and with neither malice nor affection.

'When the word is given,' he said.

'And what then?'

Sevekai looked back at her. He no longer saw an asur

standing before him, just a kindred soul. All of them were kindred souls now.

'Rebirth,' he said, smiling.

CHARACTERS

House Tor Caled

Menlaeth, called Caledor II – Phoenix King of Ulthuan
Imladrik – Master of Dragons; Menlaeth's brother
Yethanial – Loremaster; Imladrik's wife
Thoriol, called the Silent – Imladrik and Yethanial's only son

The Council of Five

Liandra of Kor Vanaeth, House Athinol
Salendor of Athel Maraya, House Tor Achare
Aelis of Tor Alessi, House Lamael
Gelthar of Athel Toralien, House Derreth
Caerwal of Athel Numiel, House Ophel

Other Asur

Caradryel – House Reveniol
Kelemar – Regent of Oeragor
Baelian – Archer captain
Loeth – Archer
Taemon – Archer
Florean – Archer
Rovil – Archer

Dawi

Morgrim Bargrum – Thane of Karaz-a-Karak
Morek Furrowbrow – Runelord
Grondil – Thane of Zhufbar
Brynnoth – King of Barak Varr

Druchii

Drutheira – Sorceress
Malchior – Sorcerer
Ashniel – Sorceress
Sevekai – Assassin

⤙ GLOSSARY ⤚

Anurein – River running through the southern reaches of the Great Forest to the sea, later called the Reik

Arluii – Mountain range to the south of Elthin Arvan, later called the Grey Mountains

Asur – The elves of Ulthuan, known to men as High Elves

Athel Maraya – Lord Salendor's lands, located in the heart of Loren Lacoi

Athel Numiel – City in the north-east of Elthin Arvan, destroyed by dwarfs during the early years of the war

Athel Toralien – City on the western shores of Elthin Arvan, ruled for a time by Malekith

Druchii – The elves of Naggaroth, known to men as Dark Elves

Elthin Arvan – The lands east of the Great Ocean settled by the asur, later called the Old World

Ifulvin – 'Bitter-blade'; sword borne by Imladrik

Kor Evril – Imladrik's citadel in the mountains of Caledor

Kor Vanaeth – Settlement east of Tor Alessi founded by Lord Athinol, father of the mage Liandra

Lathrain – 'Wrathbringer'; sword borne by Caledor II, inherited from his father

Loren Faen – Forest south of the Arluii, said to be perilous and enchanted, later known as the Fey Forest or Athel Loren

Loren Lacoi – Forest between the Saraeluii and the coast, bounded on the south by the Arluii and in the north by unsettled wasteland, later known as the Great Forest

Oeragor – Asur city in the far south, chiefly settled by Caledorians of Imladrik's household

Saraeluii – Mountain range to the east of Elthin Arvan, home to the majority of the dwarf holds, later called the Worlds Edge Mountains

Sith Rionnasc – Common name for the port at the head of the River Anurein, later the site of the free city of Marienburg

Tor Alessi – Pre-eminent city of the asur in Elthin Arvan, later the site of the Bretonnian city of L'Anguille

Tor Caled – Home of the House of Tor Caled and the court of Caledor II

Tor Vael – City of loremasters in Cothique; ancestral home of Yethanial

Ulthuan – Homeland of the asur in the Great Ocean

THE HOUSE OF TOR CALED

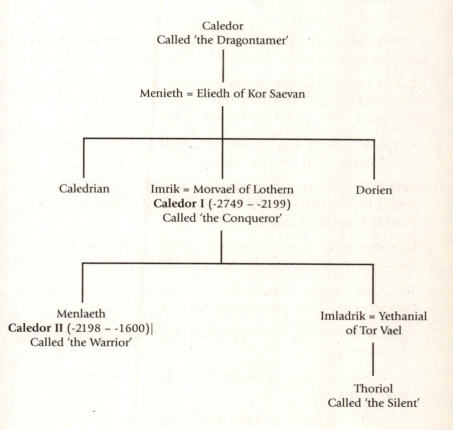

ABOUT THE AUTHOR

Chris Wraight is the author of the Space Wolves novels *Battle of the Fang* and *Blood of Asaheim*. He has also written the Space Marine Battles novel *Wrath of Iron*, along with *Schwarzhelm & Helborg: Swords of the Emperor* and *Luthor Huss* in the Warhammer universe. He's based in a leafy bit of south-west England, and when not struggling to meet deadlines enjoys running through scenic parts of it.

READ IT FIRST

EXCLUSIVE PRODUCTS | EARLY RELEASES | FREE DELIVERY

blacklibrary.com

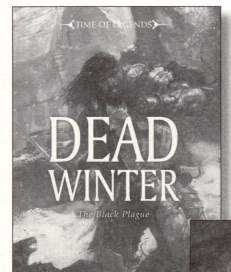